12-13

PRAISE FOR THE NOVELS
OF SUSAN DONOVAN

"Impossible to put down. . . . Susan Donovan is an absolute riot."   —Romance Junkies

"Goofy comedy, white-hot sex, and ticking-bomb pacing."   —*Publishers Weekly*

"Donovan proves that she will have serious star power in the years to come."
     —Romance Reader at Heart

"Donovan's blend of romance and mystery is thrilling."   —*Booklist*

SEA OF LOVE

A Bayberry Island
Novel

Susan Donovan

A SIGNET SELECT BOOK

SIGNET SELECT
Published by the Penguin Group
Penguin Group (USA) LLC, 375 Hudson Street,
New York, New York 10014

USA | Canada | UK | Ireland | Australia | New Zealand | India | South Africa | China
penguin.com
A Penguin Random House Company

First published by Signet Select, an imprint of New American Library,
a division of Penguin Group (USA) LLC

First Printing, December 2013

ISBN 978-0-451-41928-6

Printed in the United States of America
10 9 8 7 6 5 4 3 2 1

OMG!—this book is for you. Thank you for showing
me I could fly with a broken wing.

ACKNOWLEDGMENTS

This book would not exist if it weren't for the long list of those who saved my life, prayed for me, got me strong again, and loved me back to health. My immense gratitude goes to the surgeons, physicians, nurses, technicians, and aids at University of Maryland's Shock Trauma and Meritus Medical Center; my dear friends, family, readers, and neighbors; my agent; my fellow writers and their families; my physical therapists; my prosthetist; my guardian angels; and everyone else who had a hand in my continuing recovery.

Since "thank you" doesn't cut it—and since I'm a romance writer—I'll just say this: I love you all.

Chapter One

"Is it true what they say about the mermaid statue?"

"Yeah, like, can she really hook us up with some hot guys while we're here?"

Rowan Flynn's eyelid began to twitch. She gently closed the cash drawer and smiled at her latest arrivals, grateful they couldn't read her thoughts. But holy hell—this had to be the hundredth mermaid question of the day! At this rate she'd never make it through festival week without completely losing her mind.

"And, like, where's the nearest liquor store?"

But wait . . . what if this were the opportunity she'd been waiting for, the perfect time to knock some sense into the tourists? Maybe these girls—two typical, clueless, party-hungry twentysomethings checking into her family's godforsaken, falling-down bed-and-breakfast—would be better off knowing the awful, horrible truth about the Bayberry Island mermaid legend. And love in general.

The thought made her giddy.

Rowan was prepared for this opportunity. She'd rehearsed her mermaid smackdown a thousand times. The words were locked, loaded, and ready to *zing!* from her mouth and slap these chicks right on their empty, tanned foreheads, perhaps saving them from years of heartache and delusion.

Yo! Wake up! she could say. *Of course there's no truth to the legend. Trust me—the mermaid can't bring you true love. It's a frickin' fountain carved from a lifeless, soulless hunk of bronze, sitting in a town square in the middle of a useless island stuck between Nantucket and Martha's Vineyard, where . . .*

"Uh, like, hell-*oh*-oh?"

The girls stared at Rowan. They waited for her answer with optimistic, wide eyes. She just couldn't do it. What right did she have to stomp all over their fantasies? How could she crush the romantic tendencies nature had hardwired into their feminine souls? How could she jack up their weeklong vacation?

Besides, her mother would kill her if she flipped out in front of paying guests. The Flynns relied on the B and B to keep them afloat—a predicament that was 100 percent Rowan's fault.

So she handed her guests the keys to the Tea Rose Room, put on her happy-hotelier face, and offered up the standard line of crap. "Well, as we locals like to say, there's no limit to the mermaid's magical powers—but only if you *believe*."

"Awesome." The dark-haired woman snatched the keys from Rowan and glanced at her friend. "Because I *believe* we need to get laid this week!"

The girls laughed so hard they practically tripped over themselves getting to the grand staircase. Rowan cocked her head and watched them guffaw their way to the landing, banging their rolling suitcases against the already banged-up oak steps. For about the tenth time that day, she imagined how horrified her loony great-great-grandfather would be at the state of this place. Rutherford Flynn's mansion was once considered an architectural wonder, a symbol of the family patriarch's huge ego, legendary business acumen, enormous wallet, and enduring passion for his wife—a woman he swore was a mermaid.

"Oh! Like, ma'am, we forgot to ask. Where's our room?"

Ma'am? Rowan was only thirty, just a few years older than these girls! Since when was she a damn *ma'am*?

Oh. That's right. She'd become a *ma'am* the day she'd left the real world to become the spinster innkeeper of Bayberry Island.

"Turn right at the top of the stairs." Rowan heard the forced cheerfulness disappear from her voice. "It's the second room on the left. Enjoy your stay, ladies."

"We are so going to try!"

As the giggling and suitcase dragging continued directly overhead, Rowan propped her elbows on the old wood of the front desk and let her face fall into her hands. So she was a ma'am now, a ma'am with three check-ins arriving on the evening ferry. She was a ma'am with one clogged toilet on the third floor, twenty-two guests for breakfast tomorrow, four temporary maids who spoke as many languages, and eight hellish days until the island's annual Mermaid Festival had run its course. Oh, and one more detail: The business was twenty-seven thousand dollars in the hole for the year, losses that absolutely *had* to be made up in the coming week or bankruptcy was a distinct possibility. Which also was this ma'am's fault, thank you very much.

And every second Rowan stayed on the island playing pimp to the mermaid legend was a reminder of the lethal error she'd made while visiting her family exactly three years before. She'd dropped her guard with that fish bitch just long enough to leave her vulnerable to heartbreak, betrayal, and the theft of what little remained of the Flynn family fortune. It was hard to believe, but Rowan had been happy before then. She'd studied organizational psychology and had a career she loved, working as an executive recruiter in the higher-education field. She had a great apartment in Boston and a busy social life. So what if she hadn't found her true love? She'd been in no rush.

But she'd returned for the Mermaid Festival that year and met a B and B guest named Frederick Theissen. He was so charming, handsome, and witty that before she could say, "Hold on a jiff while I check your references," Rowan had fallen insanely in love with a complete stranger determined to whisk her away to New York. Her mother and her cronies insisted it was the legend at work and that Frederick was her destiny.

As it turned out, her charming, handsome, and witty stranger might have loved her, but he also happened to be a Wall Street con man who used her to steal what remained of her family's money. Destiny sucked.

Of course, her mother wasn't entirely to blame for her downfall. Rowan should have known better. But she still had the right to despise anything and everything related to the frickin' mermaid until the day she died.

The familiar *putt-putt* of a car engine caught her attention, and Rowan raised her head to look out the beveled glass of the heavily carved front doors. She watched the VW Bug plastered with iridescent fish scales come to a stop in the semicircle driveway. Since it was festival week, the car was decked out for maximum gawking effect, with its headlights covered in huge plastic seashells and a giant-assed mermaid tail sticking out from the trunk. Her mother got out of the car and strolled through the door.

"Hi, honey! Everything going smoothly? How many more are due on the last ferry?"

Rowan gave Mona the once-over and smiled. Like the car, her mother was in her festival finery, in her case the formal costume of the president of the Bayberry Island Mermaid Society. Mona's flowing blond wig was parted in the center and fell down her back. She wore shells on her boobs, sea glass drop earrings, and a spandex skirt of mother-of-pearl scales that hugged her hips, thighs, and legs. The skirt's hem fanned out into a mermaid flipper that provided just enough ankle room for her to walk around like Morticia Addams. Unlike Morticia, however, Rowan's mother wore a pair of coral-embellished flip-flops.

"Hi, Ma." Rowan checked the B and B reservation list. "Two doubles and a quad—parents and two kids."

"Will you put the family in the Seahorse Suite?"

"No. I've already got a family in there. I'm putting the new arrivals in the Dolphin Suite."

Her mother approached the front desk, leaned in close, and whispered, "What's the status of the commode?"

"I'm hoping it'll get fixed before they check in."

One of Mona's eyebrows arched high, and she tapped a finger on the front desk. "You'd better do more than hope, my dear. The Safe Haven Bed-and-Breakfast has a reputation to uphold."

Rowan held her tongue. Some might argue the establishment's only reputation was that it had seen better days and was owned by the island's first family of cray-cray.

"But why worry?" Mona waved an arm around dramatically, a move that caused one of her shells to shift slightly north of decent. "The evening ferry might not even make it here. Did you hear the forecast?"

This was a rhetorical question, Rowan suspected, but she could tell by the tone of her mother's voice that the news wasn't good. "Last I heard, it was just some rain."

Mona shook her head, her blond tresses swinging. "Ten-foot swells. Wind gusts up to forty-five knots. Lightning. The coast guard's already issued a small-craft advisory. And the island council is meeting with Clancy right now to decide if they should take down the outdoor festival decorations—a public safety concern, you know. We wouldn't want that giant starfish flying around the boardwalk like back in 1995. Nearly killed that poor man from Arkansas."

"Absolutely." Rowan pretended to tidy some papers on the desk as she forced her chuckle into submission. They both knew the real public safety risk was that council members could come to blows deciding whether to undecorate for what might be just a quick-moving summer squall. She didn't pity her older brother Clancy. Tempers were known to flare up during festival week, a make-or-break seven days for anyone trying to eke out a living on this island, which was nearly everyone. And that didn't count the latest twist. A Boston developer's plans to build a swanky marina, golf course, and casino hotel had split the locals into two warring factions. About half of the island's residents preferred to keep Bayberry's quaint New England vibe. The other half wanted increased tourism revenue, even if it meant crowds, traffic, noise, and pollution. And the Flynns were at the center of the dispute, since their land sat smack dab in the middle of the mile-long cove and was essential to the development plans. Much to the dismay of every other property owner on the cove, both Mona and Frasier were listed as owners, and Mona forbade Rowan's father to sell the land. This meant that one little, middle-aged, spandex-clad mermaid was holding a major real estate developer, every other cove landowner, and half the population of the island hostage.

Rowan had come to view the conflict as a kind of civil

war, and like the more historically significant one, the conflict had pitted family member against family member, neighbor against neighbor. The weapon of choice around here wasn't canon or musket, though. It was endless squabbling, ruthless name-calling, and an occasional episode of hair pulling or tire slashing.

Rowan might not be thrilled about running from Manhattan with her life in shambles, but one thing could be said for her place of birth. It wasn't dull.

"Well, Ma, I'm sure Clancy will handle the situation with tact and diplomacy. He always does."

"That is so true." As Mona's gaze wandered off past the French doors and into the parlor, a faint smile settled on her lips. Rowan was well aware that her mother was enamored with her two grown sons—Clancy, a former Boston patrol officer who was now the island's chief of police, and Duncan, a Navy SEAL deployed somewhere in the Middle East. As the baby of the family, Rowan had grown up accepting that her mother was unabashedly proud of her two smart, handsome, and capable boys. Of course Mona had always loved Rowan, too—but *enamored?* Not so much. Exasperated was more like it, especially starting in about fifth grade, when Rowan began talking about how she couldn't wait to escape the island and start her real life.

"This *is* your real life," her mother would say. "Every day you're alive is real. And if you can't be really alive here on Bayberry Island, you'll never be really alive, no matter where you go."

God, how that used to piss Rowan off. It still did.

Mona adjusted her shell bra and returned her attention to her daughter. "I told Clancy to come over here after the meeting and help you with the storm shutters. God knows your father is useless when it comes to that sort of thing, if he cared enough to check on the house in the first place."

Rowan ignored the jab. She'd adopted a hands-off policy when it came to her parents' ongoing power struggles, including their opposing positions on the development plans. "Only a few shutters are in good enough condition to make a difference, and besides, Clancy's got more important things to do right now."

Mona didn't like that response, apparently. Her brow crinkled up. "Who's going to help you, then? Has a handsome and single handyman managed to check in without me noticing?"

"Not possible, Ma."

"It's not possible that such a man would want to visit Bayberry Island?"

"No—it's not possible you wouldn't have noticed."

"True enough." Mona giggled. "It *is* my job, you know."

Rowan's eyes got big, and all she could think was, *Dear God, not this again.* Her mother was the retired principal of the island's only school, but she'd just alluded to her other "job"—that of Mermaid Society president and keeper of all things legend related. It was a wide net that Mona and her posse used to fish around in other people's love lives.

Her mother glanced down at Rowan and put her hands on her scale-covered hips. "You look like you have something facetious to say."

"Nope. Not me, Ma. I'm totally cool with the legend. Love is a many-splendored thing . . . all you need is love . . . back that ass up and all that shit."

Mona gasped. "*Rowan Moira Flynn*!"

Just then, the *tap-tap* of quick footsteps moved through the huge formal dining room and headed toward the foyer, which was enough to divert Mona's attention.

"Imelda!"

The petite older woman clutched her chest in surprise, then cut loose with a long string of Portuguese-laced obscenities. "You're gonna give me a heart attack one day, Mona."

"I was just happy to see you."

Imelda Silva, who had once been the family's private housekeeper and was now the B and B's cook, shook her head and marched through the foyer on her way to the staircase. "I've been working for your family for twenty-five years. You and I both know you're not happy to see me. You just want me to do something for that fruity mermaid group of yours and the answer is still *não*! I'd rather fix the toilet in the Dolphin Suite! And you, Rowan." Imelda pointed an accusatory finger in her direction. "Stay out of the butter pecan ice cream. It's the topping for tomorrow's waffles."

Mona looked hurt as she watched Imelda trudge up the grand staircase. "What is *wrong* with everybody this year?" She sighed loudly. "Everywhere I turn, it's just one bad attitude after another! What happened to the joy and delight of the biggest week of the whole summer season? Why aren't people filled with excitement?"

"We're tired."

"Ha!" Mona narrowed her eyes at Rowan. "We are the people of Bayberry Island, my dear, caretakers of the mermaid, the sea goddess of love. This week is nothing short of sacred to us, to our way of life. We have no time to be tired." She paused for dramatic effect. "Mark my words, honey. If we don't perk the hell up around here, we're completely screwed."

It took some fast-talking, but Ash had managed to bookend his business on Bayberry Island with two weeks of vacation. He'd needed the time to think, untangle the minutiae in his mind. As it turned out, there were quite a few details to sort out once a person decided to rip up his life and start all over. Eight solo days on his boat—

four out and four back—would go a long way toward clearing his head.

Though nobody back at the real estate development firm Jessop-Riley knew it, Ash had already decided that the Mermaid Island deal would be his last. He never considered himself a spiritual man, in fact quite the opposite; but even he couldn't ignore the signs that it was time to move on. For ten years now he'd been a free-lance closer for big developers, and the underhanded bullshit the job required was getting old, leaving him hollow and burned-out inside. Even before his best friend Brian died, he'd known he was done.

And this particular deal—a hotel-casino-golf-marina monstrosity—smelled worse than the usual Jessop-Riley venture. Sure, Ash would go in there and convince the mermaid worshippers to let go of their land for less than top dollar, but then he was done with this part of his life. He wanted out. The only question was how, exactly, he would go about pulling the plug.

No matter how he decided to do it, Ash's life was about to take a decidedly different turn. At the time of Brian's death, he had been chairman of Oceanaire, a nonprofit foundation dedicated to marine conservation and education. In his will he stipulated that Ash would take over as chairman. He couldn't refuse his best friend, but Ash also saw it as an opportunity to kick-start changes in his life. Obviously, saving the oceans was a much nobler cause than the pursuit of wealth. Ash had more than his share of money, anyway. What he didn't have was his lifelong best friend, a meaningful relationship, or anything close to a higher calling. And once he pulled out of his retainer agreements—with J-R and a whole slew of East Coast developers—he could give his full attention to Brian's passion.

Nothing would bring Brian back, of course, but Ash

had come to see that his dearest friend's request that he lead Oceanaire had been his last, great gift to him. If Brian dying in the small-plane crash had taught him anything, it was that life shouldn't be taken for granted and he should stop wasting it on a soulless job that meant nothing to him.

He checked the wind once more and glanced to the northeast. The white jib of the sailboat was pulled taut, luminous against a rolling purple-gray sky. Most of the sun was obscured by the storm clouds now, though at that moment, a pinpoint of light tracked the tiny dot of his sailboat as it cut through the vast sea, and the wonder of it took his breath away. Ash had always thought the foul-weather sea and sky were among the most gorgeous sights Mother Nature had to offer. It was Brian who had long ago pointed out that like many women they'd known, nature could be at her most beautiful when angry.

A sudden gust of wind forced Ash to return at least some of his focus to the wheel and prepare to jibe, though it was a task he could probably accomplish in his sleep. He had complete faith in his skills as a sailor and in this boat. He'd inherited the thirty-two-foot classic cruiser from his grandfather, who had taught him to sail. Over the span of twenty years, Ash and Brian had survived many a hairy Atlantic storm in the *Provenance*. She was big enough to handle rough seas while maneuvering with speed and grace. That's why Ash couldn't help but laugh at what he was about to do—fake a breakdown and send out a distress call for a tow, an embarrassment he hadn't suffered since he and Brian were inexperienced kids.

If Brian were alive, he'd be the only person Ash would confess his devious methods to. Brian would disapprove, as he usually did when hearing about Ash's job, but he would laugh until he cried at this particular story.

As he turned the boat, Ash's own laughter died. It had been six months, but Brian's absence still felt like a knife twisting in his gut. Well-meaning people assured him that time would lessen his sense of loss, but he couldn't see it happening. Because Ash was an only child of parents long dead, Brian had been more family than friend, and now that he was gone, Ash knew how it felt to be truly alone.

It felt like being a tiny speck afloat in a vast foul-weather sea—only without the bright pinpoint of light to keep him company.

Bayberry Island popped up on the horizon about two nautical miles from his position. The winds were picking up right on cue, coming in at thirty-two knots from the northeast. The next big gust should do it, Ash figured—one blast of heavy air hitting directly into the mainsail and his staged breakdown would be under way.

Leaving Martha's Vineyard that morning under engine power, he'd drained most of the oil and then let the engine run until only about ten minutes' worth of gasoline remained in the tank. Then he'd loosened the rigging enough that the doctored chain plate would rip out of the deck, leaving the boat crippled in the water. Yes, whoever came to tow his sorry ass to Bayberry would look at him funny, wondering how a novice idiot who didn't know enough to buy gas and perform basic maintenance could end up with a beauty like the *Provenance*. But he decided it was the best way to pull this thing off. His plan was to arrive on the island as if by accident, oblivious to the fact that it was the eve of the island's blowout party week. He welcomed the worse-than-expected storm, since it added a dash of drama to his predicament. He was going to milk it for all it was worth.

Ash would be the proverbial stranger in the storm, a rich guy with a busted-up sailboat who just happened to wander into the Safe Haven Bed-and-Breakfast looking for shelter, a rich guy willing to pay a boatload of money to an innkeeper barely making ends meet. He figured ten thousand should do it, an amount that was too much to pass up but not enough to balance the B and B's books. From that point on, his objective would be simple: He'd use his proximity to the Flynns to convince them to sell their hilltop property and private cove, because without their centrally located acreage and beach access, the two-hundred-thirty-million-dollar project was dead.

As always, Ash had done his research. He knew the best way to infiltrate the Flynn family was through Rowan, the daughter. She was the one who had the most to gain from selling and was the perfect target for his seductive sales pitch. Ash knew that Rowan had sulked home after a disastrous romance with a man who stole what was left of her family's money, and she now ran the B and B, the family's only remaining business venture. But Ash figured after twelve years of living and working on the mainland, the choice to come home hadn't been one she'd made freely. If he could flirt with the lonely Miss Flynn enough to remind her that life was passing her by, she might guilt her mother into dropping her opposition to selling. Within hours, Ash would have cashier's checks drawn up and delivered. The marina, golf course, hotel, and casino would go forward, making a whole lot of people, including Ash himself, even richer than they already were.

And by the time Rowan Flynn and her family realized they'd been set up, Ash would be long gone.

Chapter Two

"Please take him home, Clancy." Rowan whispered her plea out of politeness, though she needn't have bothered. Her ninety-one-year-old neighbor was deaf as a dinghy. "He's gonna frighten the guests again."

Rowan's brother slowly approached the old man, his palm outstretched as he tromped up the steps and crossed the wide porch. "Come on now, Hubie," Clancy shouted. "There's no need to be waving that sword around. You don't want your daughter bailing you out of jail, do you?"

"*What*?"

Clancy increased his decibel level. "I said, you don't want to go to jail, do you?"

"I'm too old for jail! And anyway, she took all the knives out of the house, so the sword's all I got!"

"I'll walk across the road with you." Clancy spoke directly into the man's ear and pried the decorative antique weapon from his hand.

"How am I supposed to defend myself?"

Clancy supported the old man by the elbow and gently guided him down the steps to the circular drive, where he walked around the police vehicle. "Let's get you home before the storm hits, okay? How about a lemonade?"

"*What*?"

"LEMONADE!"

"Why the hell are you shouting at me? Damn you Flynns!"

Rowan followed along, reaching Clancy as he handed off the sword with the flair of the track star he'd once been. "Be back in a minute," he told her.

"At that speed, it'll be more like an hour." Rowan cleared her throat and called out, "Have a nice evening, Hubie!"

"We'd all be filthy rich by now if it weren't for you!" Hubie tried to wrestle free of Clancy. "I've always hated you Flynns! You think you own the whole island and everyone on it! Always have!"

Poor guy, Rowan thought. Sure, he was a total pain in the ass and even slashed the tires of the family's ancient Subaru last week—which was why his daughter removed the knives—but her heart went out to him. She'd known Hubie since she'd been born, and all he wanted was to live out his remaining days in comfort. This was his once-in-a-lifetime shot at striking it rich, along with everyone else who owned property on or near the cove. Every one of them hated the Flynns at this point, and Rowan couldn't blame them.

Her family was being ridiculous about the whole thing. They owned three hundred prime acres at the island's highest elevation, right in the middle of the cove, plus the entire beach. Clearly, the developer couldn't do a thing without this land, and the interesting dynamic that had existed with her parents for decades had taken center stage in the land battle. To say Mona wore the pants in the marriage was an understatement. She also wore the jockstrap and controlled the checkbook. On more than one occasion in the last year, Rowan had heard her father say that he rued the day he agreed to put Mona on the title to the house and land. And now Mona forbade Rowan's father from even meeting with the developers to discuss selling. Their disagreement got so heated about eight months ago that they'd decided to separate. What a mess.

Her elderly neighbor glared at Rowan over his shoulder, offering up one last smirk as Clancy guided him through the front gate. If it could still be called a gate. There was a time when the twin twenty-foot-high scrolled wrought-iron structures provided the kind of grand entrance this place deserved. These days it was little more than a heap of corroded scrap metal, an irony that didn't escape Rowan. A gate that had once kept out the riffraff now kept Rowan mindful of her own servitude. Hey, at least everything around here was decorated in the same style—shabby-as-shit chic.

Rowan sighed heavily and turned back to the house. Who was she kidding? Even if the B and B broke even this year, there would be no extra money to make repairs. Her family was delusional if they thought keeping things the way they'd always been was the answer, let alone possible. If the decision were hers to make, she would have accepted the developer's offer without giving it a second thought. It sure would have made things easier. No fighting with the neighbors. No endless zoning hearings and council meetings. No money worries—ever again—for every member of the Flynn clan and generations to come. Not to mention she could go back to New York and resume her real life.

The sky began to rumble, and Rowan's eyes followed the storm clouds. She decided to walk around the southeast end of the house, where she could get a look at the open water and sky. Bayberry Islanders didn't put much stock in satellite TV weather reports and Web sites. The mood of the ocean, smell of the wind, and dance of the clouds were always more accurate.

As she rounded the corner, Rowan averted her eyes. She took a wide berth around the screened-in side porch, giving some privacy to the canoodling couple on the old glider sofa, a piece of furniture long dubbed the love magnet by her family. They were the only festival-week honeymooners at the Safe Haven this year, though surely not the only ones on the island. The Mermaid Festival was pretty damn romantic, after all. For those who believed in true love.

On the back lawn, Rowan smiled at the kids from the Seahorse Suite, who were involved in a rules-free version of croquet. It was the same kind of game she'd played with her brothers and her best friend, Annie, when they'd been children. Even the language was familiar.

"You're cheating, you doofus!"

"I am not! You're too stupid to even know the rules!"

"Mom! He's cheating!"

The parents held hands from their Adirondack chairs, tuning out their bickering kids. As Rowan passed them, she smiled politely but kept her distance. One thing she'd long ago learned about the bed-and-breakfast business: If the guests wanted conversation, they'd ask for it.

"Oh, you must absolutely love living here," the mother said, noticing Rowan and grinning up at her. "I don't think I've ever seen a place so charming and quaint. Our friends back home, the Woodwiths from Akron? You might remember them? Well, they recommended this place."

Rowan slowed her pace. "That's very kind of them. We always appreciate recommendations."

The dad chuckled. "Yeah. The place reminds me of camping, only a lot more expensive."

"Roger!" The wife dropped his hand and smacked his forearm before she looked up at Rowan again. "Ignore him. He's just mad because there's nowhere to play golf."

"That's okay," Rowan said. "Maybe at some point there will be. A Boston company wants to buy up this whole cove and build a resort."

"No!" The wife straightened in her chair. "But that would completely ruin this place!"

Her husband snorted. "Little late for that."

"Roger!"

Out of the corner of her eye, Rowan saw the two young women from the Tea Rose Room trying to open the door to the carriage house. It took every bit of patience she had left not to groan and roll her eyes. "Would you excuse me, please?"

"Of course," the wife said. "But we're a little worried about the storm. We checked Weather.com and saw a severe thunderstorm warning."

Rowan had already started to walk across the lawn. She glanced over her shoulder to answer. "Oh, we get summer squalls all the time—just part of life on Bayberry Island."

"Of course," the wife said, sounding unsure.

Her husband lowered his voice. "You can get rained on in a campground for a lot less than two seventy-five a night."

"Roger!"

"I'm just sayin'."

Rowan had already started to jog toward the carriage house, horrified that one chick was giving the other a leg up so she could peer into the first-floor windows. Rowan

wondered which part of the NO ENTRY—PRIVATE RESI-
DENCE sign they didn't understand.

"May I help you?"

"Oh, snap." The blond woman lost her balance. She
landed on her butt in the crushed shells of the walkway
and they both scrambled to regain their composure.

"We were just looking around."

Rowan nodded. "Unfortunately, this is not a public
area."

The brunette put her hands on her hips. "But it's part
of the B and B, right? I mean, it's near the house."

Rowan took a deep breath, hoping the rush of oxygen
would stop her from using her very favorite bad words.
She couldn't wait to tell Annie about these two women.
"At one time, yes, this building was the mansion's carriage house."

"But not now?" The brunette looked puzzled.

"Uh, no." Rowan felt her eye twitching again. "The
residents of Bayberry don't often rely on horse and
buggy for transportation these days. The upstairs was
once the living quarters for the footmen, but since the
1930s, when automobiles became commonplace, it's
served as a private apartment. And right now, it's *my*
private apartment."

"You don't have to get all snarky." The woman's eyes
suddenly flashed, and she pointed in the vicinity of Rowan's left knee. "OMG! She's got a sword!"

"What?" Rowan looked down and realized she was
still carrying around Hubie Krank's weapon. She tried
not to laugh. "Oh, that." She raised it high and bran-
dished it theatrically. "It's just for decoration."

"Like, whatever."

The girls reached for each other and nearly tripped
over themselves racing across the lawn and down the

steps leading to the beach. Rowan was beginning to worry about whether they had some kind of inner-ear disorder that affected their balance.

"I need a drink," she muttered to herself, lowering the sword.

"That bad?" Clancy patted her shoulder.

Rowan hadn't heard him approach, but he'd always been light—and fast—on his feet. She grinned at him. "As a matter of fact, yes. It's that bad. Care to join me?"

"You know I can't. The usual festival-week craziness has begun. I really gotta go."

"Right." Rowan slipped an arm through her brother's and walked with him toward the back of the house, where he'd parked his police Jeep. "Let me guess—frat guys hurling onto the boardwalk, maybe a couple gettin' it on in the grass at Public Square."

Clancy laughed. "If I'm real lucky, that will be on tomorrow's agenda. At the moment, all we've got is a non-payment for an order of fish and chips at Frankie's, another lewd behavior complaint out at the nude beach, and a couple of stranded boats, including some Boston blue-blooded douche who forgot to gas up his damn sailboat. From what I hear, the boat's worth twice as much as my house."

"A lot of stuff is worth twice as much as your house."

"Hey, now."

Rowan laughed, knowing her brother loved his little island shack, though he preferred to refer to it as a cottage. "So, you heard anything from Duncan?"

"Nah." Clancy used his key fob to unlock the Jeep. "If he got leave to come home this year, we would've heard by now."

"Does Ma know?"

He hoisted a dark eyebrow over one of his deep blue eyes and hopped into the driver's seat. Rowan smiled at her lanky, handsome brother. Everybody knew she and Clancy were tight. He was just a year older than her and a lot closer to own her temperament than Duncan. Clancy was a goofball and a good-natured trouble-maker, while their older brother, Duncan, was as intense and serious as they came. Clancy had been forgiving after Rowan convinced her family to invest all their money with Frederick, and he'd helped keep her from drowning in a sea of self-pity. Duncan, on the other hand, had been full of told-you-sos. "What did you expect, Row?" he'd asked her in a Skype call from overseas. "A lot of dudes aren't as advertised. You can't take anything at face value these days. You gotta stop being so damn trusting."

It probably didn't help that Duncan was even more distant geographically than emotionally—the last time anyone had heard from him, he'd been somewhere in Pakistan. But that had been several weeks earlier.

Clancy started up the engine. "Ma suspects he's not coming. She doesn't talk about it, but I think she's pissed. This is the first cookout he's missed since basic training. And she's worried as hell about him."

"I know. We all are. And I'm worried about her, too." Rowan leaned in the Jeep door.

"Her arthritis, you mean?"

"Yeah." Rowan propped her chin in her palm. "I think she's in a lot more pain than she lets on. Her hands seem more locked up than usual."

Clancy nodded. "I know. Her constant stressing out about the damn resort has made it worse, but I've already made plans to take her to her rheumatologist appointment in Boston this fall. She'll be okay, Row."

Just then, the police radio began squawking about an argument between a tourist and one of the island's taxi drivers. "I gotta run."

"Thanks for helping me with Hubie."

"No problem." Clancy turned the wheel and smiled at her, letting his eyes travel to her left hand. "So you got plans for that sword?"

Rowan looked down and chuckled. "Maybe I'll hack some weeds out of the daylilies. Or chase the bimbos around some more. Hey, maybe I'll go after Frederick!"

Clancy shook his head. "Unfortunately, the SEC beat you to it. See ya, sis. Oh, and you might want to get all the guests in from the beach. Gonna be a real bitch of a storm."

Rowan watched the white Jeep with the iridescent blue lettering pass through the gate. Slowly, she raised her hand and stared at the curved blade with the tarnished but ornately carved silver handle. Hubie always said he'd inherited it from an English uncle who'd fought in the Boer Wars, a claim no one could verify. But Rowan did know this much—Frederick Theissen was damn lucky he'd been convicted of sixteen counts of fraud and embezzlement and was doing ten to fifteen in the Otisville, New York, federal prison camp, where bitter ex-girlfriends with swords generally weren't given visitation privileges.

"You picked a hella bad time to break down out here!"

"I know!" Ash stumbled into the protected confines of the tugboat operator's cabin, checking over his shoulder that the *Provenance* was safely bobbing along behind. "I didn't know the storm was going to be this bad!"

The captain glanced over at him with outright contempt, then snorted. "I ain't talking about the storm, mister. I'm talking about festival week. It's crazy busy right now. Not sure when we'll get to the repair."

"What festival? How long do you think it will take?" Ash had to shout over the drone of the tugboat engine.

"Mermaid."

"Did you just say 'mermaid'?"

The captain laughed. "Yup. Every third week of August we got a Mermaid Festival on Bayberry. It's what we're famous for." He quickly glanced at Ash. "Don't sail much, do ya?"

Ash shrugged. "Occasionally. I inherited the boat from my grandfather. I'm still learning."

The captain shook his head, not bothering to say aloud what his body language so clearly conveyed—that Ash was a spoiled rich snob from Boston who didn't deserve such a beautiful boat.

"So how much will a repair like this set me back?" he asked.

The captain shrugged. "Gotta take that up with Sully at the marine yard. He'll let you know what he finds and how much it's gonna cost to fix it. But you did a real good job bustin' up your chain plate. Didn't notice it was corroded, eh?"

"No! I have a guy who does my maintenance."

Ash watched the captain squeeze his eyes shut. There was nothing more ridiculous than a sailor who lacked the time or knowledge to care for his own boat.

"And the engine?" There was an edge of sarcasm in the captain's voice. "Any idea why it didn't start after I gassed it up? Did you make sure there was oil?"

"Not sure what happened." Which was a lie, since the engine had seized only because he'd planned it that way. He was prepared for bad news from this Sully character. Either the engine would have to be taken apart and put back together, with uncertain results, or the whole thing would have to be replaced. Either way, he'd write it off as a business expense—all part of the job.

"Boy, the wind has really picked up," Ash said, craning his neck to look out the Plexiglas windows to the sky. "Will this Sully character let me sleep on board while he works on the boat? Or is there a place I can stay near the marine yard?" Of course Ash knew the answer to this question.

The captain shook his head. "Look, mister. Bayberry Island rooms book a year or more in advance for festival week. I don't know what to tell you. My job is to tow your ass into the yard. Where you go after that is up to you."

About forty-five minutes later, Ash was giving his cell phone and credit card numbers to Sully, a man he hoped to God was better with boats than people. Then he locked down his belongings in the *Provenance's* cabin and was on his own. He wandered through the marine yard, making sure as many people as possible noticed him looking lost and confused. Eventually he found his way toward the center of town and decided to stop at the tourist information kiosk on the public dock.

"Can you recommend a place to stay?"

The girl looked at him and blinked. "You don't have a reservation on island?"

"Unfortunately not. My sailboat broke down and I got it towed to the marine yard. I don't know how long it will take to fix."

The young woman shook her head. "I'm sorry, sir, but if you don't have a reservation, I'm not sure what I can do. There are no vacancies at the moment."

Ash sighed dramatically. "Yeah, I heard there was some kind of festival going on. Mermaids, right?"

The girl looked shocked. "Seriously?" She laughed. "You don't know about the festival?"

"Not really. The tugboat captain mentioned it. Do you have a brochure?"

Still laughing, she reached underneath her stool and pulled out a stack several inches thick. "If I were you, I'd head over to Frankie's, just off the dock. You might want to get inside somewhere before the storm hits." She hitched her thumb over her shoulder. "It's the best sea-food around, and since it's not peak hours and the storm's got a lot of tourists taking cover in their hotel rooms, you might not have to wait. If you've got a cell, you can start making calls from Frankie's. All of the motels, hotels, and B and Bs are listed in this brochure, and one might have a last-minute cancellation." She tapped a finger on the top one. "It would be a miracle if you found anything, though."

Ash briefly flipped the pages. "All these places look really tiny."

"Well, yeah. We're a tiny island. At peak season, we have only about three hundred rooms, and that's including the locals who rent out their houses for the week and go stay with relatives on the mainland. Most of our festival-week visitors stay on Nantucket or the Vineyard and take the ferry."

"Hmm. So there's no resort here or anything?"

"God, no! But some jerk wants to build one."

Ash flashed her a pleasant smile, and he noticed her blush. "Sounds like a resort might actually be good for the island. Anyway, I do appreciate your help."

Ash pulled the mermaid legend brochure out from the stack and opened it, grinning. "Wow. This is really something."

The girl shrugged.

"Huh." Ash shook his head as if this were his introduction to the legend. "So this Rutherford Flynn guy is out on a fishing boat in a nor'easter and a mermaid rescues him and his crew? And when he gets married, he tells everyone his wife and the mermaid are one and the same?"

"Yeah." The girl gazed up at him.

"Whoa. And then this Flynn guy becomes a multimillionaire?"

"Yeah. That huge building over there?" She pointed over Ash's shoulder. "That used to be Flynn Fisheries. It was in operation until the late 1980s, when overfishing led to the collapse of the whole industry. Now it's our museum. You should really go check it out. That's where the theater troupe puts on the reenactment on the fourth day of the festival."

Ash nodded, looking off toward the nineteenth-century redbrick building surrounded by tidy landscaping. "Sounds interesting." He returned his attention to the brochure. "So this Flynn guy commissions a fountain in the mermaid's image and people think it has magic powers? Really? What's the statue supposed to do, anyway?"

She flipped her hair coyly. "If you go to the mermaid with an open heart and no set idea about who your perfect match might be, and you kiss her hand and ask her to help you, she'll lead you to your one true love."

Ash chuckled. "Do you believe in the legend?"

She shrugged. "I don't know. Not really, I guess." She leaned forward out the window of the kiosk. "But I'm not supposed to say that to the tourists."

Ash winked at her. "It'll stay our little secret."

Just then, the sound of a large group of kids made Ash direct his attention toward Main Street. He saw about thirty screaming and laughing children under the age of twelve running toward the dock. He laughed with them. "What's this all about?"

The girl stood up and craned her head out of the information booth, then immediately sat down again. "Looks like the grab has started."

Ash didn't even have to feign ignorance on this one—he had no idea what she was talking about, and he thought he'd researched everything about this place and its nut-job festival. "What's the grab?"

The voices became louder. Then Ash felt the rumble of the kids running on the dock.

"Uh." The young woman glanced around nervously. "It's kind of the unofficial start of festival week. Kids run from the mermaid fountain in the square and search for a single male tourist to grab. They drag him back to the fountain, where he has to ask the mermaid to find him his true love, right there in front of everybody."

Ash laughed. "You're joking. Poor bastard."

She shook her head quickly, then bit down on her lower lip. "Um, sir? I hate to tell you this, but—"

Ash's left elbow was jerked so hard he almost toppled over. Suddenly, he was surrounded by kids pushing him across the dock and toward the Main Street boardwalk. Hundreds of tourists milling around began to clap and cheer, though their enthusiasm was cut short by the low roar of thunder.

"Are you married, mister?" The biggest kid of the bunch was pushing into Ash's back and yelling into his ear.

"What?"

"Married? Are you married?"

"Uh, no."

The kid began barking orders to the others. "Hurry up! My mom's gonna make me go inside in a minute! We need to hurry!"

A flash of lightning cut the sky in half, and the wind picked up. Ash bent his knees and tried to dig his heels into the asphalt of Main Street, but his boat shoes offered little traction. Tourists began to run for cover, but not before some of them took out their smartphones and snapped photos of Ash and his insistent Lilliputians.

He could barely believe his eyes when he saw what appeared to be a professional film crew running along at his side.

"Good luck, fella!" An older man in plaid shorts gave him the thumbs-up sign. "If the mermaid grants your wish, you're sure as hell gonna need it!"

Ash decided he'd had enough. This wasn't at all how he'd planned to make his arrival known on Bayberry Island. It was one thing to wander around the marine yard looking like a complete loser, but it was another to be the center of attention, someone's potential Facebook post, or worse yet, a human interest story on *Good Morning America.* Something like that would blow his cover. "All right, everyone. Stop, now. Cut it out. I'm not your man."

"Keep going, mister. We're almost there."

"You need to pick someone else. I have no interest in—"

"Here he is!"

Ash gasped in surprise. When the kids corralled him past a stand of trees and into what was clearly fountain square, he was met by a row of human-mermaid hybrids.

"Come along," said one of them. He realized he was standing before members of the Mermaid Society he'd read about, possibly even Mona Flynn herself, though he couldn't be sure. How was he supposed to tell with the wig and the costume? "All right, children! You can let him go!"

The kids fell away and Ash staggered for a moment. The mermaid lady touched his arm and led him toward the fountain, whispering in his ear, "We're going to have to hurry this along, I'm sorry to say. The rain is going to start any moment now."

"But I really don't want—"

"What's your name? Just your first name is fine." She looked up at him sweetly, blinking as she waited for him to answer.

"You've got the wrong guy."

Her mouth tightened. "First name," she said, the sweetness now absent from her voice. *"Now."*

"Ashton."

"Lovely." She grabbed his right forearm and pulled him to the edge of the fountain. The crowd was in motion, some people putting up umbrellas, some backing away and jogging down the street in search of cover, others taking their abandoned spots. The mermaid cleared her throat. "Gather 'round, ye 'maids and ye visitors! We've found our lucky winner in this year's Man Grab!"

Applause, whistles, and cheers exploded all around. Ash felt a big, fat raindrop fall on his forehead.

"Give me your hand, Ashton," she said with the flair of a master of ceremonies. All Ash could think was that the woman was Vanna White with a flipper. "Now take the mermaid's hand in yours."

Ash felt his hand being thrust onto the cold and damp fingers of the bronze fountain. He dared to look up through the plumes of water to the impressive creature towering over them. Waves of thick hair covered only the business ends of her ample breasts. Her beautiful face serenely gazed off toward the sea. A faint smile tickled her lips. Ash let his eyes travel downward to her rounded hips, the delicate indentation of a belly button, and the flirty flip of her tail.

Up close like this, he decided she was quite impressive. Powerful looking. She seemed a lot more human than the pictures and videos he'd studied. And really quite beautiful.

For a statue.

"Ashton, you may kiss her hand."

The crowd broke into giggles.

"Kiss it!" a female voice yelled out.

Ash's head began to spin. His arms and legs tingled. "Hold up," he said, looking into the upturned face of the real woman in the fake mermaid outfit. He leaned down close to her ear. "You've got to cut me some slack, lady. I'm not here for love. Seriously. My sailboat broke down and I only wanted—"

She smacked him in the arm. "Oh, Ashton, you are such a funny young man!" The mermaid woman glanced over her shoulder and rolled her eyes at the crowd. "Someone remind him this is a G-rated event!"

"Oh, for the love of God," he mumbled.

"You may kiss her hand," the woman repeated. Something about the steely, no-bullshit gaze made him think this was, in fact, Mona Flynn. Sure, she was in costume and it was difficult to tell with certainty, but it would fit. The school principal had single-handedly brought the Mermaid Island Resort to a halt with her stubborn refusal to negotiate.

Fine. Whatever. He'd kiss the hand. What could it hurt? Maybe doing so would earn a few points with Mona, and later, when he casually brought up the subject of the resort, she might even listen.

Ash lifted his mouth to the wet, slick coolness of the bronze. He pursed his lips. It was a short peck, but there was definitely some lip-to-statue contact, enough that for a split second, Ash wondered if maybe he'd been electrocuted. Because his lips were on fire.

He straightened. "Happy now?" he whispered.

The woman smiled at him, then continued on with her three-ring-circus voice. "Repeat these words after me!"

Another drop of rain. Another. And another.

"I, Ashton, come to the mermaid in search of my heart-mate."

He complied, though the words *I come to the mermaid because I've been abducted by a bunch of unruly brats* would have been more accurate.

"I understand that true love is like the sea . . ."

He repeated those words, too.

"It is beautiful, deep, and life-giving . . ."

Those, too.

"Yet it can be unpredictable, powerful, and even dangerous."

Done.

"I set out on my journey with a heart that is pure and true . . ."

More rain. Harder. He repeated her words, noting that the crowd had begun to disperse, though the professional camera crew was still there, tarps now draped over their equipment.

"I am prepared to be tossed by waves of passion."

Whatever.

"I am willing to drown in love's undertow."

God, when would this end?

"I, Ashton, pledge to go wherever love may lead."

He said it. "Can I go now?"

"Of course! Enjoy your stay on Bayberry Island. You're eligible to ride on the island council's parade float tomorrow, if you wish."

"I'll get back to you on that."

Ash started to run. The rain was coming down so hard that he could barely see his feet hit the grass, the boardwalk, and eventually Main Street itself. He knew if he ran about a half mile down Shoreline Road, he'd find the gates that opened to the Safe Haven B and B. He was going to be soaked to the bone by the time he got there.

It was strange, really, but as he ran, an image he'd seen only in photos or videos began to waft across his mind. He saw Rowan Flynn's face. She really was a very pretty woman, and oddly enough, he looked forward to meeting her. He wondered what she'd be wearing. What she'd smell like. Whether her voice would be softer in person than how she'd sounded in the news footage from her boyfriend's embezzlement trial.

Ash was nearly out of breath by the time he ran through the falling-down gates. He looked up and stopped dead. There it was, shrouded in rain and set against the rough sea. The three-story wood shingle and stone Victorian mansion was something to behold, with dozens of windows of varying styles and sizes, an arcaded stone front porch, and a complex roof system with dormers on all sides. Ash knew the history of this place and was aware that all of it—including its famous architect—had been shipped in from the mainland. Yet the structure somehow managed to look like it belonged here, like it had grown from the sandy soil beneath it.

He blinked the rain from his eyes. He admired how the mansion stood steady and dignified in the howling wind, hardly taking notice of what was just the latest in a hundred and thirty years of island storms.

Ash marched toward the huge front porch, climbed the steps, and reached for the brass doorknob on a pair of beautifully carved double doors.

It was almost a shame the place would have to be leveled. But this was just business.

Chapter Three

R owan heard the front doors open, dropped her handful of silverware onto the tablecloth, and cocked
her ear in the direction of the foyer. She wasn't expecting guests until later that evening—if the ferry made it
through—and all her checked-in guests were accounted
for. The canoodling honeymooners were still on the
side porch. Six older guests were enjoying tea in the
sunroom, which was anything but sunny at the moment.
The unbalanced girls from the Tea Rose Room were
loudly enjoying their liquor store booty in the upstairs
library. And everyone else was either riding out the
storm in their rooms or in the parlor watching movies
or reading.

She heard the doors close. Footsteps. A heavy sigh,
definitely male. Rowan thought maybe her dad had
stopped by to see if she had everything under control.

"Dad? Is that you? I'm in the dining room."

No answer. Rowan draped the old linen kitchen towel
on the back of a chair and headed toward the foyer.
Though it was only five o'clock, inside the house it was
dark as midnight, and the antique banker's lamp on the
front desk didn't provide much illumination.

He was quite tall. Quite wet. He was looking down at

his shoes and remained still as he dripped all over the front door rug.

Suddenly, Rowan's feet felt like concrete bricks. Her heart pounded hard and fast. For an instant, she had to concentrate on finding her breath. There was something mesmerizing about the set of his broad shoulders, the way his wet hair held its curl. Then the man raised his head, his eyes met hers, and for a long, long moment, they remained locked in this way, silent and unblinking.

Hot damn! Rowan's hand flew to her mouth, as if she were afraid the words might come tumbling out.

"I didn't mean to startle you."

She shook her head rapidly, trying to regain her balance. When a white flash of lightning revealed the lines of his extremely handsome face, Rowan felt a sudden heat rush from her chest all the way to her belly. A clap of thunder shook the house. She took an awkward step back and squeezed her thighs together. Honestly, Rowan had no idea what all this mouth-covering and thigh-clenching was about, and it bothered the hell out of her that she'd react this way to some guy off the street.

"Is there something I can do for you?"

"I hope so." The man raked his hand through his hair and glanced at his feet in dismay. "I apologize for dripping on your rug."

Rowan laughed nervously, crossing her arms under her breasts. "Yeah, and that's one of the newer rugs around here—only about a hundred years old."

A small smile tugged at his lips. Rowan couldn't help but stare. The guy was gorgeous, with what looked like dark blond hair, maybe dark blue or green eyes, taller than Clancy, who was plenty tall at six one. True, she had no idea what he was doing standing in her foyer, but that seemed like a minor detail at the moment.

"I . . . uh, I need a place to stay."

Rowan let her arms fall to her sides. She tipped her head and stared at him. The man might have been soaking wet, but she could tell that his clothes, though casual, were expensive and well made. He was obviously from New England money. Why he'd be wandering around lost in the storm made no sense. "You mean you need a room?"

"You're booked up, aren't you?"

"Well, yes. Since last October, actually."

The man nodded, then took a moment to glance around the front hall, his eyes traveling up the formidable oak banister, to the mahogany paneled walls, the decorative tin ceiling, the stained-glass window at the landing. It almost seemed like he was sizing up the joint.

He sighed again and smiled at her—this time showing off a set of ridiculously perfect teeth. "I figured as much. Well, thanks anyway. I appreciate your time."

Rowan stepped forward, as if he'd just tugged her closer to him. "If you don't mind me asking, are you here for festival week?"

He chuckled, deep and soft. "Not really. I've got nothing against mermaids, but I sure didn't plan to be here. My sailboat broke down near the island and it's at the marine yard. They don't want me sleeping on board because they need cabin access to repair the engine. I don't have anywhere to stay."

Rowan frowned, thinking back to her conversation with Clancy and figuring she must be face-to-face with the Boston douche bag who forgot to gas up his boat. "That's rough," she said.

"It is."

"I'm sorry I can't help you. Honestly, every room is booked. If I didn't have part-time maids in all the old servants' quarters on the third floor, I'd offer you one of those rooms."

"Well, it was a nice thought."

She smiled politely. They looked at each other again, their gazes lingering longer than appropriate for strangers. He wasn't making a move toward the door. She wasn't in a hurry to usher him out.

"I suppose I could offer you a cup of tea."

"I'll give you ten thousand dollars for the week, and I prefer coffee."

Rowan felt her knees buckle. She put a hand on the front desk for support. "Say what?"

"All I need is a bed and access to a shower. I'll pay you ten thousand up front, and even if repairs to my boat are finished before the week is out, you can keep it all. I've got no other option."

She nearly choked. "You're kidding me, right? Even our nicest suite would be worth a small fraction of that. We aren't exactly a five-star resort."

He produced a genuine smile, big enough that she could see the indentation of dimples in the dim light. "If you could find a way to put me up, you would rate five stars in my book."

Rowan touched her fingers to her forehead and looked away, thinking, *Ten thousand, ten thousand, ten thousand.* That was insane! She'd be crazy not to take this man's money! Rowan plopped down in the desk chair and looked up at him. "Perhaps we could work something out, Mr. . . . ?"

The man reached into the sopping-wet front pocket of his khaki trousers and pulled out a wallet. As he approached the front desk, his shoes squished. He gently placed a black credit card on the polished wood and Rowan picked it up, turning it toward the light.

"Ashton Louis Wallace the third?"

"Yes, but it's pronounced Loo-*wee* Wallace."

"Of course." Rowan scanned his card, thinking that Ashton *Loaded* Wallace III would be more like it. Frederick had a black card like this once, and she knew it was nothing less than the mack daddy of credit cards. No limit. No questions. No way anybody wouldn't give you whatever the hell you wanted. So Rowan promptly opened up the booking program on the computer and created a new account for her handsome and stupid-rich guest, overriding the standard room options and typing in the words *carriage house*.

"Here you are, Mr. Louis Wallace."

"Please call me Ash."

"I will, thank you. My name is Rowan Flynn, and I'm the big cheese around here." She stood, entertained by her own sarcasm. "All right, then. Let me take you back to the sunroom and we'll get you set up with some coffee while I prepare your room."

"Wonderful." He followed her down the center hallway to the back of the house.

"How do you take it?"

"Cream and sugar, please."

"Of course." Rowan could feel him close at her heels, and she swore she felt his eyes on her butt. Clearly, this Ash guy wasn't gay, but she hadn't picked up on anything overtly sexual on his part either, so the idea that he'd be so bold as to ogle her ass within five minutes of meeting her was a bit surprising. She intentionally added a bit of a roll to her stroll.

He cleared his throat. "This is a charming place. Unusual architecture. I bet there's an interesting history to go along with it."

"You could say that. It's been in my family since it was built in 1886, and my family is plenty interesting."

She heard him chuckle again. Rowan decided she liked the sound of it, mellow and sly. They had almost reached the sunroom, and six sets of senior-citizen eyes were now focused on Rowan and her wet friend.

"If you don't mind me asking, Miss Flynn, where will I be sleeping?"

Rowan turned to face him, looked up, and smiled. "My bed," she whispered. "It just so happens I'm running a special."

Imelda continued dicing up onions, peppers, and mushrooms for the morning omelets, slowly shaking her head. "You're getting as crazy as your mama," she told Rowan. "Nobody's cleaned that room since Prohibition."

"It's just for a week. I'll survive. I just need a place to crash while he's in my apartment."

Imelda shrugged, obviously not approving of Rowan's plan to stay in the tiny third-floor storage room under the eaves. "And you're stubborn, too. Has anyone ever told you that?"

Rowan popped a piece of bell pepper into her mouth. "Yeah, well, that's not exactly news to you, is it, Mellie?" She leaned across the butcher block and kissed her on the cheek.

"Hardly." Imelda smiled. "I'll tell Zophie to sweep, dust, and damp mop. She can push the cleaning supplies to the back wall so you have room to turn around. I'll get you some clean bedding, although we're running low on the decent linens. I don't know why you don't just stay with me in my apartment."

"Oh, you are such a sweetheart, but I don't want to impose." She began making coffee, thinking that as much as she adored Mellie, the tiny efficiency off the kitchen was too small for two women to share. Rowan decided she might as well fill the industrial-sized coffee machine with fresh water, since Mr. Wallace wouldn't be the only guest looking for a cup. On stormy days like this one, guests could suck the stuff down faster than she could keep the dispenser filled. "What's in the oven, Mellie?"

"Just some cranberry and blueberry scones, plus some shortbread."

"God, you're so awesome." Rowan retrieved a cut-glass sugar and creamer set and began to fill both.

"And what about your place? You need a hand getting it presentable?" She glanced up at Rowan with a sly smile on her lips. "I know you're not exactly the tidiest person on earth."

"What?" Rowan turned from the coffeemaker and clutched at her chest with mock offense. "Are you implying I'm crazy, stubborn, *and* a hoarder?"

Imelda laughed hard, which brought a rosy flush to her cheeks and a sparkle to her eyes. She was the prettiest seventy-year-old woman Rowan had ever known, with her thick black hair, dark eyes, and delicate bone structure. Sometimes Rowan swore she hadn't changed at all in twenty-five years, since the day she arrived on the island looking for work and a place to stay for herself and Lena, her young daughter. That was back when the fishery was still in operation and the Safe Haven was the Flynns' private residence. Since they'd recently lost their help, Mona hired Imelda as the family's housekeeper and cook on the spot, announcing that the single mother had "excellent energy." From that day forward, Imelda and Adelena Silva were like part of the family, and it became clear that Imelda's skills stretched far beyond cooking and cleaning. She was a master gardener. She was a wicked good seamstress. And she had a high, clear singing voice that echoed through the house, signaling all was right with the world.

When Rowan's father shut down Flynn Fisheries twenty years ago and converted the house to a B and B to make ends meet, Imelda had stayed on as the cook.

These days, she was slowing down. Her daughter was making a ton of money as an artist and Imelda was well past retirement age, yet she refused to leave the job. "Safe Haven is my home," is all she'd say when anyone broached the subject, and anyone who knew her well knew better than to question her again.

"You're not a hoarder, dear girl," Imelda said once her laughter subsided. "Maybe just a little on the free-spirited side. And I'd be more than happy to help you after I'm done with the breakfast prep."

"Thanks, but I'm good." Rowan pulled a large bag of roasted coffee beans from the pantry and kicked the door shut with her foot. "Our guest knows not to expect the Ritz. I'll vacuum, run the dishwasher, change the sheets, and clean the bathroom, but he'll have to put up with the clutter."

Imelda put the knife down and wiped her hands on her apron, frowning. "But what about your privacy? Aren't you worried he'll snoop around in your stuff?"

It was Rowan's turn to laugh. "Jeez, Mellie. What do you think I do up there? 'Cause I can tell you—I do *nothing* up there but sleep and read." Rowan buried her nose in the freshly ground coffee beans and inhaled. "But yeah, I'll bring my laptop here with me. There's nothing else I'm worried about. The guy's filthy rich, so I don't think there's anything of mine he'd want anyway."

"If you say so."

"Besides, he's paying me so much that it's worth whatever inconvenience I have to deal with."

Imelda tucked in her chin toward her chest and scowled. "How much?"

"Ten thousand."

"Ten thousand dollars?" She smacked her palms onto the butcher block. *"Oh meu Deus!"*

Rowan held her index finger to her lips. "Keep it down. He's right there in the sunroom."

Imelda's mouth hung open and she blinked several

times. "But . . ." She shook her head as if to throw off the disbelief. "That's enough to get the central air fixed! Or you could refinish some of the floors or even get new storm shutters!"

"I know. What did I tell you? It's totally worth a little inconvenience, right?"

Rowan added the coffee and turned on the machine. Almost instantly, the big kitchen began filling with the heavenly scent of rich, dark coffee. She turned around to find Imelda back to her chopping, her head bent, eyes down. The silence pouring off of her small body was plenty loud, however.

"Uh-oh." Rowan returned to the butcher block and placed a hand on Imelda's shoulder. "What?"

She shook her head but didn't say anything.

"Mellie, what? Seriously. I can tell you're upset."

Imelda's knife stilled and she gazed up at Rowan, her expression shadowed with worry. "I don't know, honey. It just seems too good to be true that a man appears out of nowhere and gives you all that money. And he's not even from Publisher's Clearing House!"

Rowan giggled, then gave Imelda another kiss on the cheek. "Maybe it's karma. Aren't we overdue for some good luck?"

Ash nodded courteously to his fellow sunroom occupants and took a seat in a retro rattan chair set apart from the others. It was beginning to look quite ugly outside, and the oak, pine, and beech trees that lined the edges of the lawn were taking a beating. It was no wonder the trees here grew short and squat—anything tall and slender would be reduced to splinters in this kind of wind.

He appreciated that the other guests didn't expect him to chitchat and angled his chair so that it faced directly toward the wall of windows. Truth be told, he needed a few minutes to settle his nerves. He felt off balance, and though he couldn't put his finger on what his problem was, he knew it had to do with his bizarre reaction to Rowan Flynn.

She'd surprised the hell out of him. She was much prettier in person than in the photos or videos he'd been studying for the last month. Her eyes seemed to be a mysterious green-gray in the dim light. Her hair was fashionably cut to shoulder length, straight, and a shiny, soft brown color, details he hadn't noticed in his research. Her mouth was adorable, too, all pink and full and kissable.

Plus she was sweeter than he'd anticipated. Ash hadn't assumed Rowan Flynn would be a screaming harpy, but she'd sounded plenty bitter in interviews after the trial and at sentencing. For good reason, he supposed. Rowan had been screwed by Frederick Theissen. That put her in good company, since Theissen had screwed eighty-seven people out of millions of dollars. The difference was that he'd asked Rowan to marry him before he'd stolen from her and her family. The guy was a real prince. Yet only a year after his sentencing, here Rowan was—sweet, friendly, and trusting.

She was a whole lot sexier than he'd expected, too. Sure, it hadn't escaped Ash that she was easy on the eyes and looked great in a pencil skirt standing on the courtroom steps, but on Bayberry Island her demeanor was different. She seemed looser than in Manhattan, more suited to her surroundings. When she'd marched into the foyer, her perfectly lovely body looked at ease in a pair of worn jeans, a simple V-necked T-shirt, and Teva sandals.

She happened to be funny, as well. And charming. Polite. And Ash hadn't expected to find that she was any of those things, let alone all of them, and it bothered him. He hadn't come to Bayberry to be smitten by the Flynns' only daughter. He'd come there to seduce her, twist her mind, and get her to do what he needed her to do, which was convince her family to sell. And though an argument could be made that it was more enjoyable for a man to seduce a lovely and charming woman than a homely and annoying one, Ash wasn't there to find a date. He was there to make Jessop-Riley, and himself, a boatload of money. This was just business.

Looking out at the choppy sea and menacing sky, he made a promise to himself that he wouldn't lose sight of that this week—no matter how much Rowan Flynn appealed to him.

After a blessed ten minutes of silence, an older woman to Ash's right cleared her throat, and he knew that was his signal to speak. He turned in his chair. "Good afternoon," he said. "I hope I didn't intrude."

All six of the senior citizens answered him, assuring him that he had not, and then stared him down with quizzical expressions. He glanced at himself and laughed, deciding to angle the chair into the room again in order not to appear rude. "I had to run all the way here from town square. Unfortunately, I don't have anything to change into at the moment."

The eyebrows of all three older women rose in unison. Ash realized too late that he'd probably wandered into TMI territory.

Or perhaps not.

"Absolutely nothing?" The woman who asked this sat frozen in her chair, teacup stopped midway between her saucer and her mouth.

"Well, no. My belongings are locked away in my sailboat, which is at the marine yard getting repaired. I'll need to get my things once the storm passes."

"Did you kiss the mermaid's hand and ask that she grant you true love?"

Ash laughed. "I wasn't given much of a choice. I was kidnapped." He watched the group exchange knowing glances.

"You're this year's Man Grab?"

He smiled at the woman who'd asked. "So I've been told." There was another round of knowing glances.

"You're a guest here?"

"I am," he answered the man. The group seemed inordinately curious about him, and he was about to learn why.

"The six of us have been coming here for festival week since 1974, and we've stayed here at Safe Haven since it opened twenty-some years ago. We've never seen you before."

"This is my first visit to the island."

"What room are you staying in?"

"I don't know. I haven't been checked in yet."

"Do you have dinner plans?"

"Uh, not at the moment."

"Are you here alone?"

"Well . . ."

"We're nudists."

Ash had been looking forward to enjoying a hot cup of coffee since Miss Flynn had so kindly offered, but it was a good thing he hadn't yet received it—because the coffee would have just been spewed across the sunroom.

"There's a nude beach here, you know."

He knew, but he seemed to have lost his ability to speak.

"The textiles aren't the only ones who have fun around here during festival week, let me assure you."

Ash felt his hands grip the rattan armrests. He must have looked lost, because the third woman laughed and waved her hand around languidly.

"Oh, that's what we call people who wear clothes all

the time," she explained. "You know, textiles are fabrics, and clothes are made of fabric, so the people who wear clothes are textiles."

Ash cracked his neck and tried to keep that polite smile in place because, really, this was some wicked funny shit. These people had to be in their sixties at the very least, still running around naked in their retirement years! It was times like these that he missed Brian the most. He would have loved this.

"You seem shocked," one of the men said.

He shook his head.

The laughing woman waved her hand around again. "Then you should join us at the beach tomorrow. We're having our own version of the parade, just without the costumes."

Ash swallowed hard.

At that exact moment, Rowan Flynn arrived with a coffee tray and placed it on the small wicker side table next to Ash. He had never been so glad to see anyone in his life.

"Here you go, Mr. Wallace. Sorry it took so long. I made a fresh pot."

The lights suddenly flickered, then went out completely, leaving them in the dark for several seconds. When the power came back on, Ash gazed up at Rowan as if mesmerized by her face. She was absolutely *adorable*. That's the only word that came to mind.

"Sorry about that. The wiring in this place is pretty old." She looked at him quizzically. "Everything all right?"

When she tipped her pretty head to the side and blinked, Ash felt something stir in him. It was a need, a longing he couldn't name, and it spread from his chest up to his head and then down through his whole body, ending in the soaked leather of his Sperry Docksiders.

Oddly enough, the sensation wasn't as much about getting something from her as giving something to her. Where had *that* come from?

"Mr. Wallace?"

He snapped to. "Yes. Yes, everything is fine. Thank you so much for the coffee." Ash gladly turned his attention to the tray, noting that she'd provided both cream and sugar for him. She'd remembered.

Rowan turned her attention to the others, asking if they wanted more tea, and Ash took advantage of the opportunity to really check her out, leaning just a bit forward in his seat. She was on the short side, maybe about five four, and her curves were on full display in those jeans. She had a perfectly beautiful booty and graceful arms that had been kissed by the sun. And she held herself with elegance. Her feet appeared delicate, even in sport sandals.

"We've got everything we need," answered one of the women.

"All right then, if there's nothing else?"

Rowan turned toward Ash again, and he nearly fell off his chair. When had he scooted so close to the edge like that? "While we've still got power, let me go prepare your room, Mr. Wallace. If you need anything, Imelda is in the kitchen."

Ash purposefully stared at his shoes so that he didn't stare at Rowan's backside as she left the room. Then he poured himself a cup of coffee, added sugar and cream, and took his first sip. The taste was nothing less than blissful. He couldn't help but let go with a sigh of satisfaction as he sat back in his chair.

His new friends shared yet another round of knowing glances between them. When they turned and smiled at him in unison, Ash felt uncomfortable. It was almost as if they knew something he didn't.

*   *   *

"Have we heard anything from Wallace?"

Though Kathryn Hilsom was team lead on the Mermaid Island project, she decided to let someone else answer Jessop's question. She didn't want to appear to take pleasure in how Wallace had dropped the ball, even though she most certainly did.

"Nothing. But the day's not over. Plus there's a wicked storm headed that way."

Kathryn gazed out the row of tall windows surrounding the luxurious Jessop-Riley conference room and tried not to smirk. Brenda Paulson was probably the most impressionable member of the J-R acquisitions team, and she'd had a crush on Wallace for years. So of course she'd cover for him. It was embarrassing, really. Every time they hired Wallace to slither in under the radar and close a property deal by whatever means necessary, Brenda fawned all over him. It was like she worshipped him. Her behavior was a sloppy, career-busting weakness.

"Also, it's Friday afternoon." Brenda smiled and shrugged. "Ash is probably preparing an update for us first thing Monday morning."

Oh, dear God. Kathryn looked down at her precise manicure, annoyed that there was already a tiny chip on the nail of her right pinkie finger. That was exactly why she always chose a barely tinted natural polish color instead of something loud and bright. One tiny chip or crack in a bright color and even the best-dressed woman suddenly looked messy, unkempt, and even a little sluttish. Kathryn couldn't afford a misstep like that.

Jerrod Jessop took a loud sip from the straw of his customary extra-large 7-Eleven cherry Slurpee, then leaned back in his chair at the head of the conference table. "Yeah, well, he'll come through for us. He's bagged every deal he's ever been hired to close." In his usual

ADD style, Jessop suddenly launched himself forward again and rested his elbows on the table. "I'd hoped to hear from him by now, but Wallace has his methods, and frankly, I don't give a damn how he does it, as long as he does it."

It was difficult, but Kathryn managed to hold her tongue. She knew she was just as capable of closing this deal as Wallace, but her boss couldn't see that. So what did Jessop do instead of allowing her to close the deal in-house? He offered Wallace nearly a quarter million to wrap it up as a consultant. Jessop even approved Ash's ridiculous scheme to mosey out there by sailboat. All of it was nothing but a colossal waste of time and money, in her opinion. Kathryn knew she could have been there in a matter of hours—a short trip on the company's private plane to Martha's Vineyard, a quick helicopter connection, a few choice words with the locals, and bam! Done. It wasn't quantum physics, for God's sake. She had the same killer instinct for negotiation as Ash Wallace. She had the same brains and the same cunning . . .

She began to seethe in silence. Damn Jerrod Jessop. Damn this company. Damn this job that was beneath her talents.

But most of all, damn Ash Wallace for not taking her on as a partner when she'd offered three months ago. Not only would working with Wallace have gotten her out from under Jessop's twitchy thumb; it would have been the perfect fit for her skill set. There would have been no limit to what they could have accomplished together. So who did he think he was turning her down the way he had, with that arrogant look, that insipid response? "No. I work alone."

God, she hated that man.

"Anything you'd like to add, Kathryn?"

She set her face in a pleasantly bland expression. "We are paralyzed without the thumbs-up from Mr. Wallace. Our legal team is on standby, and the bank is simply waiting for the numbers. But despite our detailed vision of what would arguably be New England's premier seaside multiuse resort, we can't make another move until we own the land. Bayberry Island is by far the best location, but unless Wallace succeeds, we will have to rethink the entire project."

Jessop began rocking back and forth in his chair, his agitation kicking into high gear. "You don't sound particularly confident in our boy."

"Oh, that's not my point at all," she said, keeping her voice calm and even. "You asked if there was anything to add, and there isn't. But we have eighty million in outside capital and fifty million of our own on the line, and if we don't get that land, we'll have to settle for a less than ideal location. And we all know that nothing comes close to the charm of Mermaid Island. That is a fact."

Jessop scrunched up his nose, sniffed repeatedly, and drummed his fingers on the conference table. Kathryn had been dealing with her boss's infamous "manic genius" for seven years now. It was a mystery to her why he didn't just get medicated like everyone else. "All right, people." Jessop stood up. "I guess that does it for now."

Kathryn shut her compact laptop and tucked it away in her bag. She smiled and chatted with her team as they wandered into the central hallway of the J-R corporate suite. She broke away from the others and was heading toward her office when Brenda Paulson pulled up alongside, matching her stride.

"Why are you so hateful toward Ash?" She pretended not to be having a conversation with Kathryn and kept her gaze focused in front. "You know his friend Brian died in a private-plane crash not too long ago. Cut him some slack."

"I am not hateful toward anyone, but my job does not include making excuses for overpaid consultants." Kathryn increased her speed.

"What did he ever do to you?"

"The real question is why you have a puppy-dog fixation on that man. You aren't doing yourself or your career any favors."

"You're just jealous. Ash doesn't like you."

Kathryn laughed. "I have actual work to do, Brenda, and no interest in helping you through your unresolved self-esteem issues. But do yourself a favor and face reality—he doesn't even know you exist."

"That's not true!" Brenda caught herself before her voice rose above a frantic whisper, and both women smiled at their coworkers as they approached Kathryn's office door. Brenda waited until they were out of earshot of other employees to continue. "He's nice to me when he comes here. He always stops by my office and asks about my daughter. He gave me Red Sox tickets earlier this summer. They were box seats, too!"

Though it would have been far more satisfying to rip poor Brenda Paulson to shreds, Kathryn decided the kinder approach would be to feel sorry for her. After all, she'd been knocked up out of wedlock and was forced to attend night school instead of real college. She was at least fifteen pounds overweight, and her skin looked like it could use a good exfoliation. Her wardrobe choices weren't the wisest selections possible, even within a limited budget.

Kathryn stopped before they reached her door. "I hate to break this to you, but Ashton Louis Wallace the third gives Red Sox tickets to everyone. He's a consultant. He uses tickets to schmooze his clients and then writes them off as a business expense. It has nothing to do with him liking you, or thinking you're cute, or wanting to take you to prom. Do you hear what I'm saying?"

Brenda's face blanched. She looked like she might cry. Or throw up. "You are such a *bitch*." With that, she spun around and ran off like she'd had her feelings hurt in gym class.

Kathryn entered her private sanctuary and gently shut the door. She removed her suit jacket and hung it on her solid cherry suit valet. She approached the three potted plants on her credenza and spritzed them with equal amounts of distilled water.

Then she balled her hands into fists and bit her bottom lip until she tasted blood.

Ash had never stopped by her office. Not *once*. He barely spoke to her. It was if he didn't even *see* her. She'd had no idea that his best friend had died, or even that his name had been Brian.

And she'd certainly never received Red Sox tickets, not once in the four years J-R had been sending Ash out to do their dirty work.

So that was that, then. Kathryn knew what had to be done.

Ash Wallace had to fail to close the Mermaid Island deal, and his failure had to be so spectacular that Jerrod would turn to Kathryn to pick up the pieces. And afterward, not only would she finally get the recognition she deserved, but no one in New England would want to do business with Ashton Louis Wallace III again.

Served him right.

Chapter Four

"I'm telling you—he's beautiful. I mean a Greek god, otherworldly kind of beautiful."

"Uh-huh." Annie didn't sound overly enthusiastic. "So how many of those cranberry-vodka thingies have you had?"

"This is only my second." Rowan propped her bare feet on a kitchen chair and crossed her ankles. "Besides, this has nothing to do with cocktails and everything to do with raw, potent sexual attraction. I'm telling you, when I showed him around the carriage house, I almost had an orgasm just saying, 'and here's the bedroom.'"

"I still have power at the house and the shop. How about you? Do you still have power up there?"

"You're trying to change the subject on me."

Annie laughed. "You bet your ass I'm trying to change the subject! The last thing you need is to fall in lust with a rich and handsome Safe Haven guest during festival week. Ring any bells?"

"This guy is nothing like Frederick."

"Okay, so does the Greek god have a name?"

"Don't laugh."

"Why would I laugh? Unless his name is Zeus or Poseidon or something, and in that case, it would be against the law not to laugh."

Rowan took a sip of her drink for courage. "His name is Ashton Lou-*wee* Wallace the third."

Annie guffawed so hard that Rowan had to hold her cell phone a good ten inches from her ear. Since the laughter showed no sign of slowing, she placed the phone on the butcher block, dropped her feet to the floor, and went to get some fresh ice. While she was there, she added another splash of cranberry juice. Which meant she needed to add another splash of vodka, if only to preserve the cocktail's integrity. When Rowan retrieved her phone, got back to her chair, and propped her feet again, Annie was still chortling. "You said you wouldn't laugh."

"Okay, okay. Sorry, Row." She took a deep breath. "I'm done."

Rowan and Annabeth Parker had been best friends since preschool, and in those twenty-five-plus years, they had come to know each other quite well. That's how Rowan knew Annie was, in fact, not done laughing. She sipped her drink and waited patiently while her friend laughed some more.

"Whew! God!" Annie paused to collect herself. "Okay. I'm serious this time, sweetie. I'm done. I apologize."

"See, here's why you shouldn't laugh at me, Annie. You've got a man. He's a wonderful man. Nat is sweet and fun and is so in love with you that he can't see straight. He moved across the continent to be with you. He proposed to you in front of the mermaid fountain and half the population of the island."

Her friend sighed with contentment. "I know. I'm the luckiest woman on earth."

"Yes, you are. So don't gloat. Let's look at what I have by comparison, shall we? Nothing. I have no man. No money. No SoHo condo. No career. No sex! Not since the feds showed up and dragged Frederick out of our bed, which was almost two years ago. In fact, I don't even have the bed anymore."

Annie remained uncharacteristically quiet. Eventually she said, "Rowan, we all love you. Your mom and dad, Clancy, Duncan, Mellie, me, Nat. I know it's been a rough year since the trial and I know you're frustrated with where you are in life right now. But things will turn around."

"They'd better."

"The point is, festival week isn't the time to try to start a relationship with someone. It's too crazy. There's no time for you to really get to know each other. I just don't want you to get hurt again."

Rowan chuckled. "I don't want to have his children, Annie. I just want to get naked and roll around with him for a few hours."

"Well, if you can handle that."

"Of course I can. I'm only interested in sex."

"Well, good, because if you ever became Mrs. Thurston Howell the third, I'm not sure we could be friends anymore."

"That's not his name, but whatever." Rowan took another sip of her drink, thinking she could use another dash of lime juice. She reached across the butcher block and cut a wedge, squeezing it into the ice-cold pink liquid. Really, cranberry and vodka was a very pretty drink.

"You're absolutely right," Annie said. "Who cares what his name is? All that matters is the type of person he is, that he's a good man, that he'll leave you panting and happy and then go home."

"Amen." Rowan swished the lime juice around, held

her glass up to the light, and chuckled. Within seconds the chuckle escalated into a full-out guffaw. "But, seriously, is that the most stick-up-the-ass name you've ever heard, or what?"

"God, yes. So what's Thurston do for a living?"

Rowan gazed up at the punched-tin ceiling of the kitchen, still holding her glass high. "You know, I have no idea what he does. Maybe nothing. Looks like a T-fer to me."

"A trust funder? Nice."

Rowan heard her best friend whisper, then put her hand over the receiver. It didn't prevent Rowan from hearing muffled whispers of affection and a squeal or two. It was obvious what was going on over at Annie's place. It was depressing.

"I'm sorry, Row. I'm back."

"Tell Nat I said 'hi.'"

"Nat says 'hi' to you, too."

"Were they filming today?" Annie's fiancé, Nathaniel Ravelle, was a documentary filmmaker shooting a movie about Bayberry's mermaid legend. That's how he and Annie met—Nat traveled from Los Angeles to the island just before Christmas last year to do advance scouting for the reality show he was working on at the time. He fell on the ice in front of Annie's tourist tchotchke shop, and by the time she'd nursed him back to health, they'd fallen in love. Nat had since quit his job in LA, and he and his crew had been filming all of August in preparation for the blowout party atmosphere of festival week.

Rowan would have liked Nat under any circumstance— he was funny, smart, and kind—but she absolutely loved him for making Annie happier than Rowan had ever seen her.

"The crew was out all day, even in the rain," Annie

said. "They had to drape the equipment with tarps in order to get footage of the Man Grab."

"Who was this year's sucker?"

"No idea, but Nat said the guy wasn't at all happy about it. Had no sense of humor, apparently."

"Sounds like a real douche." Rowan sighed. "Seriously, why bother coming for the festival if you aren't willing to let loose a little and—" The lights in the kitchen flickered, then went out completely. Rowan reached for the flashlight she'd propped on the butcher block and flicked it on. "Well, thar she blows. We just lost power."

"We did, too. Better go. I hope Poseidon knows how to operate a flashlight. Talk later, sweetie."

As Rowan clicked off her cell phone, it hit her. She'd forgotten to give Mr. Wallace a flashlight in case the island lost power. This meant that he was alone in her apartment—in the dark. Just before she'd called Annie, Rowan had personally handed over one flashlight— along with extra batteries—to each of the twelve guest rooms. Then she'd trudged up to the third floor and handed one to each of the maids. Imelda had her own stash. That left Rowan with the only remaining flashlight in the whole house, the flimsy little thing about the size of a tampon that she now held in her hand. Of course, she really didn't need it, since she knew every odd angle and protruding fireplace mantel in the house. But how could she have forgotten Mr. Wallace?

Rowan jumped up and headed toward the pantry. "Ow!" She rubbed her toes, shaking her head at her own clumsiness. Apparently, she'd forgotten to factor in the location of all the kitchen stools. She held the flashlight between her teeth and climbed on a chair to reach the top pantry shelf, where she knew she'd stored some utility candles for just this kind of emergency. Rowan grabbed two, hopped down—carefully—then rooted around in the junk drawer for a lighter. She tossed everything into a plastic freezer Baggie, shoved the Baggie into the waistband of her jeans, and raced out the kitchen door. Almost immediately, she regretted that she'd been too rushed to grab a foul-weather slicker.

The rain was flying almost horizontal to the lawn, stinging her face. She tucked her head down and ran as fast as she could, her bare feet splashing in the saturated grass. An ear-piercingly loud crack of thunder startled her so much, she screamed. Rowan dared a glance toward the beach and saw nature's laser light show taking place not so far out at sea, jagged streaks of lightning piercing the black sky and lighting up the waves, one flash right after the next. It was a jaw-dropping display of destructive beauty and power, and if Rowan hadn't been afraid of being burned like a matchstick, she might have paused to watch.

Instead she ran on, slipping on the gentle slope of lawn leading toward the carriage house. She pushed herself to a stand and continued. When she reached the stone and shingle building seconds later, she found the door to her apartment wide open and banging in the wind.

A slice of fear went through her. Had something happened to Mr. Wallace? Had he run toward the main house while she'd been running out to him? Had he been struck by lightning?

"Hello?"

Rowan heard her shout die in the wind. She braced her bare heels on the slate walkway and grabbed the edge of the door. "Mr. Wallace?" She backed into the entrance to the stairway, then used all her strength to yank the door shut. Instantly, she was wrapped in silence, protected by the thick fortresslike walls her great-grandfather had insisted upon. Even for his staff. Even for his horses.

It was black in the narrow, windowless stairwell. She fished the tampon flashlight out of her jeans pocket and toggled the switch several times. Nothing. It must have gotten wet. "Perfect." Rowan shoved the useless thing back into her pocket and pushed away the wet hair that was plastered to her face. She slowly climbed the stairs. Since there were no railings, she dragged her hand along the wall for reassurance.

As she very well knew, there was no door to the apartment. That meant that once she reached the top of the stairs, she would be in the living room, which would be a clear invasion of her guest's privacy. But this was an emergency. If Mr. Wallace was still up here, he was in the dark and quite possibly concerned for his safety.

Rowan reached the last step, curled her fingers around the corner of the wall, and stepped into the living room.

"Mr. Wallace? It's Rowan Flynn. Are you all right?"

Just then, a flash of lightning illuminated the room just enough to show her it was empty. He'd gone back to the main house, then. All this running and falling had been for nothing. With a sigh, Rowan reached into the front of her jeans and pulled out the Baggie, leaving the candles and lighter on the dinette table for when he returned. She turned to go, but the loud *thunk* coming from the bedroom made her jump in surprise.

"Go*dam*mit!"

He was here. "Mr. Wallace?" Rowan suspected he hadn't heard her because a rumble of thunder had drowned out her shout. She hated to surprise him, but what if he were hurt? What if every wasted second could mean the difference between life and death? She rushed toward the bedroom door with her hands outstretched. "Are you all right?"

Whump. It felt like she'd hit a wall—a full-frontal wall of wet, hard, bare flesh. A hand grabbed her elbow. She screamed in surprise.

"Rowan?"

She tugged her arm free and started jogging backward, her mind racing. This had been a mistake. It was dark. From what she could tell, he was naked. She'd had two cranberry vodkas—well, technically, two and a half. And she hadn't had sex in nearly two years.

Severely undersexed and half in the bag had never been a good combination for her.

"Oh!" The back of Rowan's heel hit something, and she began to fall backward, not sure exactly where she was or where she'd land. Was she in the hallway? The living room? The dining area? What had she just tripped over?

His hand grabbed her arm again, but both of them were wet and slick so she slipped from his grasp. That's when his hand clutched at the bottom of her T-shirt and tried to pull her to a stand. The shirt ripped. Rowan fell on her ass. Ash fell on top of her, catching most—but not all—of his weight on his hands. She'd been flattened onto her back.

Oh God! He smelled delicious! He smelled like *sex*! He must have been in the shower when the electricity went off, because his own mysterious scent had mixed in with Rowan's familiar soap and shampoo. The result was the exotic elixir now flowing through her nostrils and penetrating the exact part of her brain that didn't want her to stay a sex-starved spinster, *"ma'am"* innkeeper for another minute!

He panted. She panted. He hovered close. She felt his warm, big body pressing into hers from thighs to chest, his bare skin against her own. She gasped. If she felt skin-on-skin, it meant her shirt had ripped from hem to neck, leaving her whole front exposed. A Greek god had just ripped off her clothes!

What a difference a day could make.

A brief flash of lightning illuminated his face, not an inch above hers, beautifully masculine and serious. Another flare revealed his hair was wet. Another showed his lips were parted. Thunder rumbled low and angry, vibrating across the sea and through their bodies. She felt his breath on her face. It would be so easy just to grab his head, force his lips onto hers, and kiss him until he begged for mercy. No one would ever know. But the window for that kind of outrageous act was rapidly closing. Another few seconds and one—or both—of them would come to their senses, apologize, and shove each other away. Rowan knew that if she didn't make her move now . . .

"Oh, fuck it," he whispered.

"God, yes!"

Ash lowered his mouth onto hers. He shoved his fingers into her wet hair, angled her face exactly how he wanted, then kissed her with such perfection that her mind went blank. Rowan felt everything suddenly stop—her blood, her breath, her rational thought, her awareness of anything but *him*. His kiss was tender but without a trace of hesitation. This was a man who knew what he was doing, knew what he wanted. And it was clear that Ashton Louis Wallace III wanted her.

Rowan raised her hands to touch him. He felt so damn good beneath her fingers. His back, upper arms, and shoulders were built from hard muscle and smooth skin. His neck was strong. She figured it was her turn to be bold, so she yanked on his hair and took the kiss where she needed it to go.

Total pleasure. Her entire being was nothing but a nerve ending designed to receive pleasure. She felt out of control, wrapping a leg around his and then slipping her hands down his muscular back to his ass. This was already so outrageous that Rowan figured it didn't matter what she did next—so she grabbed his booty, pulled him tighter to her, and arched her back.

Two thoughts penetrated the lustful fog in her brain. The first was that this was prime man beneath her hands and on top of her body. The second was that her dry spell was about to end, and probably with a lot more than a trickle.

"Are you sure?" He asked this question in between her increasingly demanding kisses.

"I'm sure." Rowan pushed up into him again, feeling his long and hard arousal poke against her sweet spot. At least it used to be her sweet spot. For too long it had been just another spot.

Thunder pounded. Lightning cracked and flashed. Rowan groaned with disappointment when Ash removed his lips from hers, but sighed with relief when he ripped what remained of her sopping-wet shirt from her body, then unhooked the front closure of her bra faster than she ever could. Immediately, his hands were on her breasts, teasing her nipples, pulling and flicking at them until she cried out. The way he handled her was so . . . *carnal*.

Ash stopped. He raised his face just as another strobe of light filled the apartment. That's when she saw the single-minded glint in his eyes. Ash was a man on a mission. He lowered his mouth to her nipples, left then the right, back and forth he went, tugging and sucking until Rowan began squirming beneath him.

"Too much?" he asked, his voice husky in the darkness.

Lightning illuminated the room again, and Rowan shook her head. She had to shout over the thunder. "Take my pants off! Please!"

He pushed up to his knees, and Rowan lifted her hips off the floor to assist him. It was then that a series of lightning hits created several seconds of on-again-off-again illumination, allowing Rowan to get her first good look at Ash's naked body as he threw her soaking-wet jeans across the room.

Damn. Pure male perfection. Big across the chest and shoulders, defined arms, flat and hard abs rippling as he moved, and . . . She stopped breathing. Her eyes went big. Rowan slammed her palms onto the old wood floor and tossed her head back, thanking the storm gods for washing this truly gifted man upon the shores of Bayberry Island.

Pants gone. Arms wrapped tight around her back. Ash's mouth went back where it belonged, on hers, as he lifted her off the floor.

"Spread your legs."

That would work for her.

"Wider. Open your legs wider."

Rowan flipped her legs up and over Ash's thighs as he sat back on his heels. He pulled her to his chest. Mouth rough on hers. Hands on her ass, then moving across her hips, along her back. Oh God. She could feel his big cock pressing into her belly. All she had to do was lift up and forward just the tiniest bit and they'd be in business.

She heard herself whimper. Rowan clutched at his wet skin, slapped her hands onto his back, and opened her mouth so that he could have her. In that moment, she knew she would give Ash anything and everything he wanted.

She was drowning in the lust, lost in it, and so incredibly hungry for relief. "Please," she whispered as he kissed her. "God, please."

Ash slid one hand from her hip to inside her open legs. A vague sensation of embarrassment went through her. It had been so long since she cared about how her body would look and feel to a man. Had she shaved her legs that morning? Her underarms? The tip of his finger brushed against her swollen clitoris and her brain exploded.

"Please. Please." She knew she sounded like a desperate woman, but she didn't give a damn what she sounded like. The same went for the shaving. Who cared? His finger slid down into the opening of her sex, and she cried out from the shock of it.

"Rowan. God. You're so wet. So incredibly beautiful." Ash spread her open with his fingers, teasing and pushing and teasing some more. He dragged his lips from hers and began kissing her cheeks, hair, and throat. "Are you sure? We can stop. Tell me what to do."

His words sounded as desperate as her own, which surprised her. This was a huge deal for Rowan. Maybe it was for him, too. Of course, she had no way of knowing because Ashton Louis Wallace III was a stranger. She knew almost nothing about him, except that he possessed a gorgeous face, perfect body, and black credit card.

Stupid. Stupid. Stupid. She shouldn't be doing this. She *knew* this wasn't a smart move. On every level. First, she didn't have a condom. Of course she didn't! This wasn't exactly planned.

And what about afterward? How ridiculous would she feel? True, she was sex starved, but she'd been sex starved before and it had never left her lost to herself like this, helpless, feeling as if she were being swept up and *claimed*. But that was exactly how she felt at that moment.

Lightning split the air. Thunder rolled through them. Rowan knew it was far too late to stop, even if she wanted to. Whatever this was, it would have to be. It had a weight to it. A force. It felt like fate.

Ash's fingers suddenly stilled, and Rowan realized she'd gotten so absorbed in her own internal battle that she hadn't noticed that he'd produced a condom as if from thin air. She also realized she hadn't answered his question.

"Don't you dare stop," she said. "Take me. Make love to me. *Do* it."

Ash didn't need to be asked twice. He resumed the beautiful torment with his fingers, and Rowan could hear the extent of her own arousal. He hadn't been joking—she was as soaking wet as her clothes had been. He found her nipples again with his mouth, and Rowan felt it building—rushing, driving, hot—so intense it was almost painful. Ash gently closed his teeth on a nipple and the lid blew off of Rowan's being.

She heard the strangest sound, something so raw and fierce that it didn't even occur to her that she was responsible. Orgasmic waves hit her over and over, leaving her fingers numb, her breath ragged. Lightning ripped the darkness apart and Ash looked up at her. Their eyes remained locked as more lightning flashed, and Rowan's gaze was glued to Ash's as he lifted her and slowly, so slowly, guided her limp body onto his rock-hard cock.

It was too much. Too much pleasure and release. Rowan felt the tears roll down her cheeks as she called out again, squeezing and pulling on him as he moved her up and down.

Ash might have been speaking to her. She couldn't tell for sure. The thunder was too loud. She was washed away in a sea of sensation. But her eyes held his in the on-and-off light, and she saw the tension drain from his expression. She wasn't sure if it was a trick of the light, but she swore a shadow of emotion fell over his face.

She had no time to dwell on it. Ash somehow rolled off his knees, laid her on her back, and put them right back to where the whole thing began—Rowan trapped beneath him, Ash's hands in her hair, both of them on the edge of doing something they could never take back.

But this time, Ash was buried deep inside her, controlling the movement of both their bodies with his physical strength and the force of his will.

Rowan closed her eyes. Nothing existed but the fierce heat of their need. She allowed him to carry her away and pull her under.

Mona Flynn blew out the match and dropped it, half incinerated and still smoking, into the Mother's Day clamshell ashtray Rowan had made for her in second grade. Yet another clap of lightning was followed by yet another growl of thunder. The flash momentarily illuminated the faces of the eight Mermaid Society members assembled in her small living room.

"This is a pretty bad one," said Abigail Foster, stating the obvious, as usual.

Izzy McCracken put her flip-flopped feet up on the center coffee table. "Good thing the council decided to take down the giant starfish. With all this wind, we could have had another decapitation."

Polly Estherhausen groaned. "You aren't talking about that man from Arkansas, are you? Because *he wasn't decapitated.* We've been over this a hundred times."

"Well, he did have to have several stitches."

"A couple stitches do not a severed head make."

Abigail Foster pulled off her wet wig and threw it to the center of the table with a flourish. It landed with the thud of a lifeless animal and smelled almost as musty. "Can we stop arguing about whether or not that tourist's head was cut off? It was twenty years ago, people! It's time to move on."

"I could not agree more." Izzy crossed her arms under her shells and pouted like a grumpy toddler.

"Pass the merlot," Polly said.

"Let's move along, shall we?" Mona was just as wet and irritable as everyone else in the room, yet she couldn't let it show. As president, it was her responsibility to keep them on point. The official festival kickoff was now a little more than twelve hours away, and the Mermaid Society had actual business to attend to. She grabbed her indexed three-ring binder and placed it with a solid thud on top of her knees.

"Day one—the parade. We must be at the judging stand by one p.m. and not a minute later. I've received confirmation that all the floats were garaged before the storm, so the order is as we originally planned."

"Thank God." Abigail rolled her eyes. "It was like pulling teeth trying to get even two dozen entries this year. Enthusiasm is way down."

"It's all this resort bullshit." Layla O'Brien's eyes widened and she slapped a hand over her mouth, but the words were already out. She stared at Mona.

"Oh Jesus." Polly poured herself a giant glass of wine.

"I only meant—"

"It's all right." Mona closed the binder with a sigh, taking a moment to gather her patience. She couldn't blame people for thinking her position was nothing but stubborn folly. For more than a year now she'd been called a control freak. A bitch. An idiot. And because she'd only married into the Flynn family and wasn't born and raised on island, some of the people she'd counted as friends for nearly forty years had taken to calling her an interloper, an outsider, and a party crasher. Or worse.

Mona took it in stride. She knew that by refusing to negotiate with the developers, she had become the defender of all that was good and honorable. It wasn't always fun and games standing by one's principles. Which was all right by her. Not everyone had the distinction of being born a leader.

Take Frasier, her beaten-down and passionless estranged husband, for example. He was proof that just because a man happened to be mayor didn't mean he possessed the gift of discernment, or a backbone. Simply put, the smell of money had made him lose his mind. It poisoned their thirty-eight-year marriage in the process, leading to their separation. So the mayor of Bayberry Island now hid out in a studio apartment over the boogie board shop on Main Street, while Mona took up residence in the rental home they owned on Idlewilde Lane. Love wasn't the issue. Mona most certainly still loved her husband. But, oh, how he'd disappointed her.

She didn't blame him for being tempted. Two decades of financial struggle had been hard on Frasier—closing the fishery after more than a hundred years of continuous operation, turning the family home into a bed-and-breakfast to make ends meet, and then watching Rowan lose what little was left of the once-impressive Flynn fortune.

But she believed money wasn't all that mattered, and losing money was no excuse for losing your moral footing. What about a sense of history? Family tradition? Loyalty to one's roots? Mona knew that if it weren't for her, Frasier would have sold the land out from under them without a second thought. And then what?

She'd always been more of a visionary than her husband, and Mona had no doubt that in his old age, Frasier would regret that decision with every fiber of his being. It would have made him heartsick to see his island destroyed.

So that's how Mona had become the only landowner on the cove to tell Jessop-Riley and their league of gluttonous jackals to go screw themselves.

This had made her rather unpopular.

"I ask only that we get through festival week as a co-hesive unit," Mona told her group. "These seven days are about the power of love, not the lure of cash. Can we aspire to live as our higher selves for just this one week? That still leaves us fifty-one weeks of the year to wallow around in our greed and fight like schoolchildren."

Polly raised her hand. "I've pretty much drained the merlot. Is there any more of that chardonnay in the fridge?"

Abigail cleared her throat, which meant she wanted to say something she feared would receive a less than stellar approval rating. "I was thinking about that very issue this morning, in fact."

"The chardonnay?"

She narrowed her eyes. "Only you think of wine over your morning coffee, Polly. I'm referring to the lack of enthusiasm this year. All this infighting has left us exhausted—jaded even."

"No shit," Polly said.

Abigail ignored her. "So I was thinking that what this island needs is something to believe in, something big. We need to be reminded of what is special about this place and what connects us, not what divides us."

"You're right," Layla said. Her comment was met with nods and murmurs of agreement around the circle.

Mona had to concur. "We have Annabeth Parker and Nathaniel Ravelle's wedding this fall."

"Bigger," Abigail said, spreading her arms wide to demonstrate. "It needs to be huge and it needs to hap-pen in public during festival week, while the world has its eye on us."

"The world?" Polly drained her glass. "Let's not go completely apeshit, here."

Mona smiled. "I know we'd all love to see the mermaid bring two people together in a made-for-TV moment, but as we know all too well, the magic never happens on cue."

Suddenly a small, soft voice jolted everyone to attention. Darinda Darswell, who had barely made a peep since she left the fairies and joined the mermaids five years before, had just spoken.

"Sometimes magic needs a little push to get started."

Everyone looked with stunned expressions toward the tiny woman in the long black wig whose eyes burned in the candlelight like two dark marbles.

"Please go on, Darinda." Mona reached her way and patted a knee of blue iridescent spandex scales. "We'd absolutely love to hear what you have to say."

"Well, the Man Grab . . ." Darinda's focus darted around the room. "He was very handsome, wasn't he? A kind of elegance to him, I thought. And I know this is going to sound silly, but I swear I saw something in his eyes when he looked up at the Great Mermaid. He seemed, well, I don't know . . . *in awe of her.*"

Every woman in the living room had stopped breathing. "We're listening," Mona said.

"I think something happened when he touched her hand."

A collective gasp escaped from the group.

"And I'm talking about something *real.*"

Mona placed the heavy Mermaid Society planning binder on the coffee table and leaned even closer to Darinda. "What do you mean by real?"

"I . . ." She stopped. "You must think I'm nuts."

"No!"

Darinda pressed into the sofa back as if the group's answer had startled her. Maybe it was just the decibel level.

"Tell us," Mona said.

"I've been carefully watching the Man Grab for five

years now, and I've never seen someone react the way he did. He was special."

"I thought he was kind of a dick, really."

"Polly!" Abigail shook her head and looked up at the ceiling in exasperation.

"Well, I'm sorry, but he acted pissed off. Bored. Like he couldn't wait for it to be over."

Izzy grunted. "At least he wasn't drunk and laughing and making obscene comments like last year's Man Grab."

"True enough," Layla said.

"Polly does have a point." Mona thought back to the man the kids had brought to the fountain just hours before. He hadn't been enjoying himself; that much was beyond debate. She'd had to basically threaten him to get him to join in on the fun. She turned toward Darinda. "But what does he have to do with our made-for-TV moment?"

"Ah." Darinda smiled. "I think we should keep an eye on this guy, just in case the Great Mermaid has something special planned for him this week."

"But we don't even know who he is!" Izzy was obviously distressed. "We don't know where he's staying!"

"Oh, dear God." Polly held the bottle of merlot perpendicular to her wineglass and shook it, dramatically forcing out the last few dribbles. "The island is the size of a bar coaster. He can't exactly hide from us."

"His name was Ashton."

Mona looked at Darinda, curious about why the usually silent Mermaid Society member had chosen that particular moment to become Chatty Cathy. "Go on, Darinda."

"All right. I guess what I sensed about him was that he was empty, completely alone, an island unto himself. And extremely sad. But by the time the ceremony ended, he was filled with a new sense of purpose." She bit her lip shyly. "As I watched him run off through the rain, I had the feeling I was watching a man running headlong into his destiny."

She tasted like cranberries and lime. She smelled like rain and summer grass. She felt slippery like satin against his skin. She was the finest vise of velvet around his cock.

How had this happened? Why had he let a legitimate accident turn into this, something that had already messed with his head and twisted his heart into some unknown shape? Who *was* this woman, and what was she doing to him?

At the moment, she was coming all over him again for about the fourth time in the last half hour, which just spurred him on to make sure that this orgasm would not be her last. Ash was aware that Rowan Flynn hadn't been dating since her scumbag fiancé destroyed her, but the sheer power of her sexual hunger astounded him.

He'd never been with a woman quite like her.

In the back of his mind, he was aware that this was the exact wrong thing to do. His plan was to slowly earn her trust, seduce her with such subtlety that she wouldn't even notice she was being seduced, and carefully win his way into the Flynn family's good graces.

What they were doing on the floor of her carriage house apartment wasn't slow or subtle and it sure as hell wasn't careful.

It was outright recklessness. It was wild. It would complicate *everything*. Probably destroy it.

Ash clutched her perfect round ass in his hands and continued to give her every inch he had, keeping her in the position he liked best, her legs bent back by the weight of his body. He kept his mouth on hers, because the thunder and lightning had subsided and nature was no longer providing cover for her screams of pleasure.

He felt her fingers on his back. By now he had become accustomed to her touch. Even at its most gentle, it delivered a kind of hot electricity that penetrated into his muscle and bone.

Ash felt her tighten around him yet again, and he felt her lips move under his.

"Ash," she whispered.

It was the first time he'd heard her say his name. He was sure of it. Despite his request at check-in, she'd continued to refer to him as "Mr. Wallace" even when she came to check on him in the storm. No, she hadn't referred to him that way in the clutches of passion, but she hadn't said his name, either. The sound of it now, in her hoarse whisper, made him ripple with delight.

Rowan freed her mouth from his. "You are incredible, Ash," she whispered, her voice catching as she threw her head back. "So good. I—"

"Shhh."

"No. You don't know. You just don't know." When he touched the side of her face, he felt tears traveling from the corners of her eyes into her hair. "Thank you, Ash."

Oh God, it was too much. Her sweetness, her tears, her beauty, the force of her desire. And the way she said his name. Ash put his mouth over hers once more, tasted her passion, then exploded into her.

That's when the lights came on.

Both of them froze. Ash kept his face buried in her fragrant shoulder, trying desperately to regain his senses, his breath. He felt her body stiffen beneath him, and not in a good way.

Oh shit.

Slowly, he opened one eye. In the light, he saw golden

brown hair. The sharp glint of a small silver earring—one of those dangly things women seemed to like. He saw the barest glimpse of a soft, pink cheek.

What the hell had he just done?

"I should be going," she whispered.

Ash felt her withdraw. It had been a sudden transition—as soon as the lights came on, the hot, open, and ravenous woman in his arms turned off.

"Rowan." He angled his face toward her and left a gentle kiss on the side of her neck. He inhaled—suddenly overcome with sadness and dread. He'd just had the best sex of his whole life and the whole thing was wrong. Totally *messed up*. It would likely be the first and last time she'd ever be this close to him, and the thought of that was painful.

"Please. Let me up. I need to get back."

Ash pushed on his arms, rose over her, and withdrew from her body. He made a point of meeting her gaze, but she glanced away. He felt like a guest who'd overstayed his welcome.

He rolled over, landing on his back on the hallway rug, still gasping for breath. Just then, he realized he had no idea where they'd crash-landed. All his attention had been on the woman, not the surroundings.

She popped up with such speed and determination that Ash half expected to see her do a series of back handsprings across the living room floor. He groaned and threw an arm over his eyes.

Ash remained silent as he heard her open and slam drawers, racing around the small apartment in bare feet, no doubt doing whatever had to be done so she could make her escape. He decided to push himself to a sitting position just in time to see Rowan standing like a crane, with one leg inside her jeans and the other bent in preparation to slide down into place. She wore an un-ripped T-shirt and a tiny pair of black bikini panties. Despite everything, the sight of her made his dick twitch.

He was a complete dog.

Rowan's eyes flashed toward him. She looked angry. Disheveled. Well fucked. Embarrassed. And she couldn't zip her jeans fast enough. She walked right past his naked, slumped form on her way to the steps.

"Please say something to me." Ash didn't turn around. He figured it might be easier for her if he wasn't making eye contact. She stopped walking, but was silent. Ash swiveled around and saw her back. She was breathing hard and had a hand propped against the stairwell wall. She looked so fragile that his heart contracted.

This was nuts. They were both adults. It wasn't like he'd attacked her. He'd asked at every turn whether this was really what she wanted. Not to mention that she'd been as demanding as he'd been!

He saw her shoulders tremble as she took a deep breath. It sliced him open to think he'd hurt her.

"Rowan, please. Talk to me. Say something."

"Sure." Her voice was mechanical. "Breakfast is served tomorrow from seven to ten." She clomped down the steps. "Let us know if there's anything we can do to make your stay more comfortable."

Wham! The carriage house door slammed shut.

Ash suddenly felt as if his body weighed eight hundred pounds, four hundred of which were made of utter confusion and the other four hundred, something he didn't have the word for. *Lovesick* seemed close. But that couldn't possibly be right.

Chapter Five

"What in heaven's name is wrong with you this morning?"

Rowan stared at the shattered coffee cup at her feet, Imelda's question barely registering. She'd already begun strategizing the best way to deal with the complete mess she'd just made. First she'd need the broom and dustpan to get the sharp, broken pieces of china off the kitchen floor and safely in the trash. Next she'd need paper towels to sop up the puddle of liquid.

The other mess—the one she'd made with the guest now eating blueberry scones at table six—that was going to be a little more complicated.

Imelda stood over Rowan as she squatted down with the dustpan. "Are you ill? Did you catch cold running out to the carriage house yesterday?"

Rowan's head snapped up. She blinked in surprise. Imelda had *seen* her? Oh crap. "I forgot to give Mr. Wallace a flashlight before the storm. I had to get some candles to him."

"I figured as much."

Rowan's heart pounded in her chest. She finished her task in record speed, nearly running to the trash can. Then she threw the broom in the pantry and snagged a handful of paper towels, immediately returning to finish the job. Rowan had already decided to never speak a word to anyone about what had happened with Ash. Maybe not even Annie. But if Imelda were even the slightest bit suspicious, it would be a matter of seconds before her mother was informed.

There weren't many things in Rowan's life that were absolutes, except this: Mona and her mermaid mofos would never again get to mess with her love life. One matchmaking cluster-fuck per lifetime was all she could spare, thank you very much.

"All done!" Rowan stood up and smiled cheerfully, noting Imelda's rather odd expression. "What?"

"Are you sure you're all right?"

Rowan laughed. "Uh, no. I'm not all right. I've got twenty-six guests in this place—no, twenty-seven—and, thanks to the storm, the yard is full of downed branches and there's a new leak in the roof. And the parade starts in a couple hours."

Imelda nodded. "I suppose your mother insists you wear your mermaid costume?"

"Of course." It was at that moment Rowan realized her head was pounding. It was difficult to pick only one cause for this, since there were so many possibilities to choose from. Was it the vodka? How about the out-of-body and out-of-her-head sex-a-palooza with a total stranger—on the floor, no less? Or was it the knowledge that soon she'd be shoved into a tight spandex mermaid skirt and a pair of shells and forced to wave and smile from her perch atop the Safe Haven Bed-and-Breakfast parade float?

"I need another cup of coffee," was the only thing Rowan could think to say.

Just then the swinging door to the kitchen opened and Zophie came bounding through, a huge tray of dirty dishes balanced on one palm. She seemed flushed and out of breath. Rowan was almost afraid to ask if there was a problem, since she spoke no Czech. Of course, she didn't speak Russian or Polish and very little French, so it had been difficult to build relationships with her temporary summer help, all of whom spoke limited English.

"You okay?"

Zophie was a cute and hardworking nineteen-year-old who'd arrived on Bayberry in May looking for a job. Like thousands of foreign students on J-1 visas, she'd picked a sand-and-sea summer vacation spot to try to find work. Rowan had liked her immediately. Her smile was infectious and her laugh was genuine. But at that moment, Zophie looked like she was about to cry.

Imelda threw up her hands. "Is it a full moon? Is everyone on the same female cycle?" The oven timer buzzed, and she marched off to remove the latest batch of scones.

Rowan slowly approached Zophie, placing a hand on her shoulder. She felt the girl's breath coming hard. Suddenly, Rowan got a very bad feeling about this. Had one of the guests done something? One of the male guests? Her blood chilled in her veins.

"Zophie." She turned her employee around, to see that her mouth was trembling and tears were in her eyes. Rowan used her finger to push the girl's chin up so she could make eye contact. "Hurt?" She checked her arms and hands.

Zophie shook her head.

It was moments like these that Rowan wished she knew the Czech words for *Did some asshole give you a hard time?* She sighed and began gesturing for her employee to tell her what had happened.

Zophie shook her head again, then wiped the tears from her face. She dug into the front pocket of her apron and pulled out a wrinkled and water-damaged hundred-dollar bill. She held it up with trembling fingers. "Teep," she said.

Rowan laughed. This was so much better than what she'd feared. "A guest gave you a hundred-dollar tip?"

Zophie nodded, a huge smile breaking across her face. Rowan hugged her. "That's so cool! Who was it? Show me!"

Her employee grabbed her hand and took Rowan to the swinging door to the guest dining room. She pushed the door open a crack so Rowan could peer out.

"Him," Zophie said. "Good, nice man." She pointed to Ash.

Rowan felt herself go stiff as a mast. She forced herself to smile as she retreated from the door. "That was generous of him."

Zophie picked up on Rowan's discomfort and frowned. "I take? Mine? Okay?"

"Of course!" Rowan patted her shoulder.

Zophie thanked her and went back to the sink, where she began to rinse off the dishes, humming sweetly as she worked. Rowan stared at her a moment, unable to move, trying to identify why this development bothered her so much.

Ash was filthy rich. A hundred bucks was a penny to him. So it was nothing to leave a huge tip for a pretty, young girl who barely spoke English but had a smile so bright it could guide ships to shore. What was the big deal about that? Men were mesmerized by the beauty of young women every hour of every day at every corner of the globe.

Then it hit her. She'd seen plenty of rich men come through here over the years, including all the summers she'd done the job Zophie did now—and none of them had been as generous as Ash. It was a private act of kindness, too, not done for show. It would have been easy for Rowan to never learn of his bighearted gesture.

She realized this was what bothered her. Rowan would have preferred to think of Ashton Louis Wallace III as a prick. It would have made it easier to dismiss what had happened with them as a horrible, awful mistake. Knowing he had a decent streak only complicated things.

"Take this into the dining room, please?" Imelda stood next to Rowan, holding out a silver serving tray lined with a decorative white paper doily and stacked high with warm scones. This batch looked like cranberry.

"Rowan?"

"Sure. Absolutely." She grabbed the tray and slammed into the swinging door with her butt, determined not to look at him sitting alone at a table for two by the south window. Rowan approached the sideboard, then paid attention to the tasks at hand, the way any innkeeper would. She checked the coffee dispensers. The cream, sugar, and half-and-half. She made sure there was enough cereal, cream cheese, fresh fruit, and jams and jellies. Even the chafing dishes of scrambled eggs and sausage were filled, small cans of cooking fuel burning at just the right level. Her staff had done a wonderful job this morning.

Out of the corner of her eye, she saw him stand. She froze.

"Rowan?"

The tiny hairs on her forearms pricked to attention at the sound of that voice. She swore she felt the heat of his breath on her skin. Tingling energy surged up from her toes all the way to her scalp. Before Rowan turned to answer him, she did a quick sweep of the dining room. Seven tables were still occupied, including the annual group of nudists and the unbalanced girls from the Tea Rose Room.

For some reason, everyone was staring intently in her direction, which made her worry that something was showing. Her bra strap? Her nervousness? The brain-numbing lust she possessed for the guest standing at her elbow?

Telling herself she could get through this, she looked up at Ash and smiled politely. "How was your breakfast, Mr. Wallace? Would you care for more coffee?"

The barest frown appeared between his eyes. Those eyes . . . The only time she'd seen them had been in the dim light of the reception hall and then during lightning flashes. When the power came on, she'd done everything she could not to look at him. But now there was no escaping the fact that his eyes were staggeringly beautiful, the deepest, darkest of blues, wide-set and framed in dark blond lashes and brows. But it was the intangible quality in those eyes that knocked the breath from her. Desire. Pain. Confusion. Wonder. Sweeping her face like a lighthouse beam.

"Everything was delicious. Thank you." His voice was soft and hoarse.

"Wonderful. And was your room comfortable?" Rowan hoped she didn't sound artificially chipper. After all, this conversation was designed for the guests still staring in her direction. If she had her way, she'd never speak to this man again.

Because talking to him was too unnerving. Too baffling. It brought up too many feelings.

Rowan started to sweat.

"Extremely comfortable," he answered, the barest smile now twitching at the corner of his mouth. Oh God. That mouth. That wet, searching, skilled, hot mouth of his . . .

"In fact, it was probably the most enjoyable room I've ever stayed in."

Boing! His words made her head snap up. Had he said what she thought he said?

His smile expanded just the smallest bit, and though she figured she had about fifteen seconds of small talk left in her before she did something incredibly stupid — like hurl herself into his arms — she used a few of those seconds to examine his face. He was a fine, fine-looking man. His forehead was smooth. His cheeks were broad but not cartoonishly masculine. His jaw was just a bit on the square side, and two deep grooves framed his lips when he smiled — which he was doing now. It was a full-on smile that showed his white, straight teeth and pushed his cheeks up into the dusky blue of his eyes. A dark blond curl cupped one of his ears, and Rowan desperately wanted to kiss him there.

All she could think was . . . *Fucking Frederick.* This was so much like what had happened three years ago. She'd met him in the dining room at breakfast, and he'd had the balls to just sit himself down at her table. And that was it — she'd fallen under his spell and she'd stayed hypnotized while he played her for a fool and her family for everything it was worth.

So, no. Never, ever again. And, yes, she'd made a terrible mistake yesterday, but it was done. It wasn't too late to pull up the plane.

"Good to hear. Enjoy your day, Mr. Wallace." Rowan turned toward the kitchen, still feeling the eyes of everyone boring into her back.

"Does the festival start today?"

Rowan stopped. Was he toying with her? Torturing her? She spun around to face him and realized that wasn't it at all — he seemed to be unwilling to let her go. She couldn't mistake the look in his eyes; he was grasping for an excuse to keep her close to him.

She gulped. "Yes, it does. The parade is followed by

the opening ceremony at the fountain. Please feel free to take one of the brochures from the display rack near the front desk. There's a list of events for the week—the community clambake, the children's play, the reenactment at the public dock, the Mermaid Ball—there's always something going on. Let me know if there's anything else you might need."

Again, she turned to go. Again, he stopped her.

"I do need a few extra towels."

"I'll have Zophie bring you some."

"Thank you."

Rowan couldn't wait to escape to the protection of the kitchen. She burst through the door and immediately went to the butcher block in the center of the large room, where she placed her palms on the wood, closed her eyes, and rested. She needed a minute to shove down all the wildly inappropriate emotions that threatened to strangle her.

If she didn't need the money so badly, she'd tell Ash to get his hot ass out of her B and B.

Imelda not so subtly banged some pans around until she got Rowan's attention.

She slowly twisted her head in Imelda's direction. "Yes?"

"Maybe this is none of my business—"

"Maybe it isn't." Rowan regretted her rudeness as soon as she spat out the words. It wasn't like her to snap at Imelda that way. She loved her, relied on her, and would be lost without her. She shook her head, ashamed of herself. "Mellie, I'm so sorry. Forgive me."

She shrugged. "I don't mean to intrude. I'm only worried about your well-being."

"I'm not sick."

"That's not what I mean."

"Oh." Rowan straightened up. "You mean my mental

health? Yeah, okay. I'm going bat-shit crazy this week, but that's to be expected, right? And it's temporary." She stopped. "I hope so, anyway."

Imelda shook her head. "Not that, either."

"Then what?"

She smiled sadly. "Your heart, honey girl. It's your heart I worry about."

After breakfast, Ash walked the half mile or so to the marine yard to retrieve his belongings from the cabin of the *Provenance*. He decided to take his sweet time on the half-mile walk, since reaching his destination wasn't his primary goal. More important was examining the baffling and powerful attraction he felt for Rowan Flynn and figuring out a way to put an end to it.

His behavior the day before had been inexcusable. Period. Ash shouldn't have taken advantage of the situation. Just because a beautiful woman happens to slam into your naked body in the dark doesn't mean it has to escalate into an episode of hot, out-of-control sex on the floor. But that's what happened, and it made no sense to Ash. He wasn't a horny high schooler. He was a grown man with principles, responsibilities—and a free will, for God's sake—and he couldn't remember the last time he'd lost his head like that.

True, most men would have found it difficult to resist temptation in the form of Rowan Flynn, but he could have at least tried.

Rowan was beautiful. Soft. Giving. Uninhibited. Wild. And *maddening*. She'd practically ignored him this morning! Of course she needed to behave professionally in front of her guests, but she'd completely closed herself off to him. How does a woman go from scorching hot to ice cold in a span of twelve hours?

He produced a groan of exasperation loud enough to

scatter birds from the bushes. He watched them fly up from the roadside as if the flames of hell were nipping at their tail feathers.

Ash shoved his hands deep in the front pockets of his khakis and walked. He breathed in the salty air. He listened to the tap of his feet on the pavement and the screech of the seagulls. He felt the morning sun and fair-weather breeze on his face. And, of course, since the Flynns owned the best views to be found on Bayberry Island, he took the time to enjoy the stunning seascape. The main road may have been several hundred feet back from the south-facing bluff, but the blue-green ocean looked close enough to touch. It was no wonder Jessop-Riley wanted this particular piece of land to build what they hoped would be the finest destination resort in New England.

He'd viewed the architectural models often enough, but standing there in the salty breeze, he could really see the finished product—the sprawling cedar-shingle hotel and casino with sparkling white trim, huge decks and porches, a pool, a full-service beach area, and a first-class marina. West of the hotel would be the golf course. Jessop-Riley was in preliminary talks with pro golfer Greg Norman's company, their dream design team for a one-hundred-sixty-three-acre, eighteen-hole beauty. And once construction began, the firm would fund improvements to the tiny Bayberry airport, making it feasible for small private jets to land on the island.

How satisfying it would be to come back here in two years and see a glittering first-class resort where the rotting and rickety disaster of the Safe Haven B and B once stood.

But only if he could make it happen. And if he wasn't careful, everything could fall apart.

Ash had taken this job because he'd figured out a perfectly doable approach to closing the deal. But what was doable yesterday had become a tangled mess of confusion overnight. What was wrong with him? Why the hell had he felt powerless to fight his hunger for Rowan? She was supposed to be a pawn in a land deal, not the object of his lust and longing.

He'd really fucked this up. And he had to find a way to fix it—fast. Ash had exactly seven days and six nights to win her trust and get access to her mother, father, and the one brother who still lived on the island. But instead of seducing her from a level playing field, he now had to dig himself out of a mile-deep hole before making any progress. Ash knew that if the frosty glare she'd given him this morning was any indication, he was in for a serious challenge.

Just then, it dawned on him: Brian would have loved Rowan and definitely would have been pissed that Ash was using her.

He stopped walking.

Where had *that* come from?

Ash shook his head and continued on. He'd never enjoyed playing with people's feelings. It didn't give him any kind of twisted thrill. But it was sometimes the only way to get the job done. At least the Mermaid Island deal would be his last foray into this kind of sneaky shit, and he sure wasn't going to miss it.

He soon reached the center of town, and it was rocking with activity. Everywhere he looked, he saw people preparing for the parade and kickoff ceremony. A swarm of volunteers was cleaning up tree branches, leaves, and windblown trash from the streets. A jazz quartet was setting up in the makeshift band shell in fountain square. Shopkeepers were hanging mermaid flags, streamers and bunting, and street vendors were claiming spots along the parade route. The rustic century-old seaside town appeared to have been scrubbed clean by the storm, and was putting on its Sunday best for the celebration. Ash looked out across the wide Atlantic, past the sailboat masts, and into the late-morning sky, now a canopy of perfect blue clarity.

He couldn't help but smile.

On his way to the marine yard, he saw the ferry unloading—hundreds of adults and children spilling out onto the public dock, many in costume. For a fleeting moment, he wished he were the kind of guy who'd be comfortable walking around in public dressed like an idiot. But that was never his thing. He'd always been the kid too cool to wear anything but jeans and sneakers to the Halloween party.

Ash found the *Provenance* exactly where he'd left her, rocking gently against the temporary slip's fore and aft bumpers, the sound of her halyards ringing like dainty bells in the breeze. Ash opened the combination lock and climbed down the companionway into the cabin. He grabbed a duffel bag from a narrow closet and crammed in a few days' worth of clean clothes, an extra pair of shoes, his iPad, and some toiletries.

With a twinge of dread, he picked up his cell phone, which he'd left charging on the galley countertop yesterday afternoon. Five voice mails? How could that be? He couldn't even name five living souls who had this number, especially since his attorney was on vacation for the whole month of August. However, he was on the clock for another week or so, so he figured he should at least check.

Ash's eyes went wide. Jerrod Jessop had called him, which was a first. He decided to listen to the message.

"Wallace. It's close of business on Friday. I'm assuming you're alive. If not, let me know."

Ash laughed.

Four more calls were from the Oceanaire offices, probably in regard to next month's board of directors meeting in Boston. Brian's death had halted plans for the foundation's proposed research and education institute and offices, but the board was ready once again to pursue Brian's dream, and they expected Ash to guide them. He'd get back to them Monday.

Ash tossed the phone into his duffel bag, then retraced his way up the steps, locked the cabin, and hopped onto the walkway. He hadn't gotten twenty feet before he ran into Sully, the mechanic.

"Mr. Wallace." Sully wasn't much for eye contact. "Got a minute?"

"Of course." Ash threw the duffel strap over his shoulder. "Have you had a chance to look at my boat?"

Sully shook his head, then changed his mind and nodded. "Uh, briefly—enough to know that you're going to need a whole new engine. You really messed her up good."

Ash produced the appropriate expression of shame. "I feel like an idiot."

Sully let that assessment slide. "Uh, I can order one from a guy I know in Hyannis—runs the best shop on the Cape. But only if that's okay with you. If it's not okay . . ." He looked away.

Ash realized he wasn't going to finish the sentence. "That'll be fine."

"But, uh, it's gonna cost about four thousand . . ."

"All right."

"You're lucky it's gas, though, since diesel would've been five times as much."

Ash sighed with exaggerated relief. "Well, that's good. Would you like me to get my checkbook?"

"Got your credit card on file."

Ash nodded. "So we're good?"

"Uh, got another problem."

Despite Sully's halting conversation style, Ash knew exactly where this was headed: He was about to be the victim of supply and demand. "Yes?"

"Slips are at a premium this week."

"Of course. How much?"

Sully glanced away again. "It's peak season. I know you can't overnight on your boat, but . . ."

"Name your—"

"Five hundred a night."

Ash pursed his lips, trying not to laugh at the outrageous number Sully had just pulled out of his ass. Not that he was surprised. In his years of negotiating, Ash had seen that even the most hesitant and insecure people could make themselves perfectly clear when cash was involved. "Go ahead and run the card for the slip rental and use it to buy whatever you need for the boat. Will that work?"

"Absolutely, Mr. Wallace." With that, Sully turned and headed back toward his tumbledown shack of an office.

"Nice doing business with you." Ash got no response. He made his way back through town and headed to the B and B, noting that the streets were filling up with locals and tourists alike. The storm had added a dash of anxiety to the goings-on, which meant the stressed-out folks running around trying to get things done were Bayberry locals. Otherwise, it wasn't clear who was a visitor and who was a resident, because a majority of the people Ash saw were oddly dressed, to put it politely. In one of the many articles he'd read in his research, a travel writer had called Bayberry the Key West of New England. Ash was beginning to see how accurate that description had been.

First off, there were mermaids. *Everywhere.* The mermaids were tall and slender, short and chunky, dark-skinned and pale, and everything in between. They ranged in age from crying babies to frail old women being pushed around in wheelchairs.

The mermaid costumes ran the gamut from off-the-rack Walmart purchases to elaborate, custom-designed works of performance art. One woman glided down the boardwalk wearing a Statue-of-Liberty-slash-mermaid ensemble, complete with the torch, crown, and red, white, and blue scales on her fish tail. Ash decided he hadn't seen this many long wigs and bikini tops since he watched part of a Beyoncé special on cable TV the year before.

A close second to the mermaids was the number of sea captains and sailors of varying descriptions. There was also a staggering number of hippies, neo-hippies, hippy-hipsters, and quasi-Rastafarians from preteen to postprime ages. Then there were the pirates, fishermen, King Tritons, and even a few mermen. The undersea characters from the cartoon *SpongeBob SquarePants* were well represented, as were costumes that defied easy classification.

Just then, Ash blinked in an effort to clear his vision. The six-foot-tall "mermaid" sashaying down the middle of Main Street sported thick chest hair, big biceps, and a pronounced Adam's apple. Ash barely had time to regroup when he spied the gaggle of fairies walking toward the public dock. He had to stop and watch.

He'd read about them. Apparently, there had been a mutiny within the Mermaid Society back in the late nineties, and several members founded a rival all-female club called the Bayberry Fairy Brigade. As the name implied, these ladies decided to pledge their loyalty to mythical forest creatures instead of mythical sea creatures. And despite what Ash was looking at now—the gossamer wings, frilly skirts, and overall delicate appearance—he knew these fairies were anything but wusses. He'd read about how their act of defiance had never been forgiven, and there had been several fairy-mermaid melees to which the police had responded. He hoped he would witness a skirmish while on the island, but wondered if such a treat might be too much to ask for.

Stuck in the middle of all this weirdness were normal-looking families, salt-of-the-earth locals, and a whole bunch of retirees who seemed to be having a ball.

Ash chuckled as he walked in the direction of the B and B. He'd traveled all over the world—Asia, Africa, Europe, South America. He'd been to Mardi Gras in New Orleans, Chinese New Year in Hong Kong, and *Carnaval de Buenos Aires*. And he could safely say that the tiny Bayberry Island Mermaid Festival packed more per-capita spectacle than any of them.

Back at the carriage house, Ash enjoyed a leisurely hot shower. At some point he realized his thoughts had once more gravitated toward Rowan. Her body, to be exact. He raised his face into the steaming water, remembering how greedy she'd been for his touch, how she'd arched up against him and pushed her breast into his mouth, how she'd bared her neck to him and clutched at his back like she would die without him.

He groaned at the memory of Rowan's kisses. They were everything from fierce to demure. Her hair smelled like a summer storm. And when he was buried deep inside her—oh God, he didn't think he'd ever felt anything as true and as right in his life.

He shut off the now-cold water with a shake of his head, amazed that he was once more fighting the direction taken by his own thoughts. And his dick. He'd always seen himself as a disciplined man, not one prone to daydreaming and sentimentality. In fact, every woman he'd ever had a relationship with claimed that was his primary defect. He'd been called closed off, shut down, and just plain cold. So to find himself off balance like this was way beyond odd. It was fuckin' nuts.

Ash put on a pair of cargo shorts and a T-shirt, then set off toward town again. He hoped he'd get there in time to catch the beginning of the parade.

And if he were lucky, he'd get a glimpse of Rowan. He needed to know what she looked like when she was happy and laughing. He decided if he were allowed only one more guilty pleasure during his time on Bayberry Island—Rowan's laugh or mermaid-fairy fisticuffs—he'd choose Rowan in a heartbeat. He bet the sound of her laughter was lovely beyond words.

Chapter Six

"Shoot me now."

Rowan groused to herself as she settled into the giant-assed half-shell throne atop the Safe Haven B and B parade entry. How had this happened? It was all a blur. How had she allowed her mother to talk her into doing this? Why the hell had she agreed to be the B and B's so-called Mermaid Queen? For very good reasons, she'd refused to ride on the family's float since high school.

Then she remembered. *Guilt*. She was doing this out of a profound sense of guilt. Rowan felt a dead weight settle onto her bare shoulders as it hit her—when, exactly, could she expect this guilt to go away? How long would it be until she felt, in her heart, that she'd made amends to her family? How long would she have to carry the weight of the Safe Haven in her strong and healthy hands because her frail mother couldn't? Five years? Ten years? The rest of her freaking *life*? Yes, Rowan knew it was selfish to even think this way, but she wished Mona would just agree to sell the Safe Haven and set her free.

"Lookin' real good." Clancy stood at the side of the float, smiling up at Rowan, his shoulders shaking. "Lovely flipper."

"Bite me."

He laughed loudly, bending forward at the waist and leaning into the flatbed's crepe paper fringe trim. At any other time, Rowan would have laughed right along with him. She'd never been able to resist the contagious nature of her brother's full-throttle guffaw. But there was nothing funny about this particular situation.

"Don't you have some kind of emergency to handle?"

Clancy shook his head and gestured at the float. "None more important than this violation of everything holy."

"Whatever."

She looked away, trying not to give him the satisfaction of her chuckle. After all, he was right. The float was a joke. Mona and her buddies had pulled out all the stops this year. Liberace himself would consider this thing a little too flamboyant. The sides had been trimmed in corrugated cardboard waves, each two-foot-high peak embellished with an ornate swirl of a glittery whitecap. There were decorative displays of real seaweed, sand, and shells, along with strategically placed bouquets of sea grass. But it was the sturdy papier-mâché shell cupping Rowan's butt that was the most over-the-top element of all. It was blinged from its base to its scalloped edges with so much glitter, rhinestones, and sequins that Rowan feared innocent bystanders could be blinded should the sun hit it just right.

She sighed, knowing she wouldn't be the only one to notice the irony; the glammed-out Safe Haven B and B parade float had no resemblance whatsoever to the worn-out B and B itself.

Just then, all four of the seasonal maids clambered aboard, obviously enjoying this new and unusual experience. They waved and greeted Rowan before taking their places around the shell throne, and she had to admit they looked adorable in their costumes. Mona had come through with the outfits, as always, but where her mother managed to store all her spare mermaid gear in the off-season was anybody's guess.

The float began to move, inching its way out of the parking lot of the old Flynn Fisheries warehouse, now the island's museum. Clancy walked alongside. He tipped his police chief ball cap to the giggling maids.

"Have fun, lovely ladies." When he produced a chivalrous bow, the girls blushed and giggled louder. Rowan supposed the language of flirting was universal.

She narrowed her eyes at him. "Dude. Step away from the help." Clancy knew the rules—temporary summer employees were strictly off-limits. "Is Dad riding up front with the council?"

"Yep."

"Is Ma riding with him?" Rowan already knew the answer to that and supposed asking was a form of wishful thinking. She'd been holding out hope that festival week would give her parents a reason to stand within five feet of each other and possibly even speak in pleasant tones to one another. But there would be no truce until the resort issue was resolved, and even then they might not be able to reconcile. A lot of ugly things had been said since the developers came to Bayberry, and Rowan knew her parents. It wasn't easy for either of them to forgive and forget.

But it hadn't always been like this. When she was young her parents had loved each other. Rowan still remembered how the house echoed with their laughter. Sometimes at night they'd put old records on the stereo and dance in the main dining room, and all three kids would hide behind the stair banister to watch as their father twirled their mother in his arms. When the fishery closed, the laughing and the dancing became less frequent, and the bickering more commonplace.

"Ma and Dad together on a float? Are you kidding?" Clancy frowned and shook his head at Rowan's suggestion, then switched gears. "Do us proud, now!" He smiled at the girls and waved as the float lurched onto the public dock service road. With the first bump, Rowan grabbed her bikini top, unhappy that her C cups were shoved into what were clearly B-sized plastic shells. She felt ridiculous riding around half-naked like this. Her mother had instructed her to look regal while the employees threw bubble gum to the kids. Rowan could already tell that was going to be a serious challenge.

The Safe Haven float had been assigned midparade placement, right behind the mainland's Falmouth High School marching band, a perennial fan favorite. Rowan appreciated John Phillip Sousa as much as the next person, but the thud of the drum line had already given her a wicked headache. She waved and smiled despite the pounding behind her eyeballs.

The first ten minutes went by without mishap, and Rowan felt her headache dissipate in the sea air and bright sunshine. Her shoulders began to loosen and her waves became broader. She began to smile. Fine. It would take a complete jerk not to enjoy at least a portion of this. It was one of those postcard seaside days, the sky and the ocean on their best blue behavior, a friendly breeze causing decorative banners and flags on the gaslights to dance. And, whether she liked it or not—putting the guilt aside for a moment—this island was home. This was her history. And if the festival did anything, it gave people a reason to cut loose and be ridiculous for a few days, locals and tourists alike.

True, she hated the mermaid, and she hated all the work that went into this week. But people came from all over to be a part of this, to party on the beach, to laugh and drink and maybe, if they were lucky, fall in love.

Rowan stiffened, suddenly sensing something was different. She gasped. She felt *him*. Oh God! Rowan couldn't see him, but he was there, no question. Ash's eyes were on her, and it took every bit of courage she had not to flip her flipper to the side, jump off this bitch, and take cover in the nearest shop.

"Mermaid! Mermaid!" A little girl in a too-big costume ran along, waving and calling out to Rowan. "You are so pretty! Are you real?"

Something in the child's upturned face made Rowan want to cry. She was pure innocence. The kid was too young to know that there was no such thing as mermaids, or magic, or happily-ever-afters. Then Rowan noticed how her housemaids were enjoying themselves almost as much as the children in the crowd, giggling and smiling with that same innocence on their faces. Maybe all women held on to a small piece of that little-girl wonder. The chicks in the Tea Rose Room. Members of the Mermaid Society. Rowan wondered if, somewhere deep down and despite all evidence to the contrary, she might, too.

She grinned at the girl. "Yes, sweetie. I'm a real mermaid. You look pretty, too! Are you real?"

"I am!"

"Miss Flynn! Over here!" It was the family from the Seahorse Suite. The kids stood on the boardwalk with their mouths hanging open, and the mother jumped up and down in an effort to get her attention. Rowan returned the wave, laughing as she noticed how even the sourpuss dad was smiling ear to ear.

Maybe there was magic here after all. If so, it wasn't the paranormal kind. It was the type of magic found in a perfect island summer day, while on vacation, making memories with the people you loved.

Rowan's eyes scanned the parade route. She didn't

see him. Not that she wanted him—wanted to see him, that was.

The marching band suddenly switched gears and was now belting out what Rowan swore was a Kanye West medley, and her headache returned.

But she kept waving. And she kept looking.

Ash knew exactly where he would stand to watch the festivities and headed for a tourist trap a couple blocks from the public dock. He hadn't chosen the spot for its view of the parade route, though it would give him a good vantage point as the floats crawled from the old fishery and headed down Main Street. He'd chosen the location for its name—A Little Tail—and the words stenciled upon the shop window: MERMAID-THEMED SOUVENIRS, MERMAID/SEA CAPTAIN EROTIC NOVELS, ADULTS-ONLY CAKES AND CHOCOLATES, X-RATED SEA SHANTIES.

This was the shop owned by Rowan's best friend, Annabeth Parker, a chick who wrote mermaid porno in the off-season and sold it online. He'd purchased a few of her e-books, for research purposes only, of course, and had tried his best to read them. It was safe to say that whatever the stories lacked by way of plot development was more than made up for with sex—the kind of sex that could be had between sea captains and mermaids, which, as far as Ash had been able to deduce, was possible only because of how the mermaid's anatomy morphed once she hit dry air.

Common to all of Annie Parker's books was the variety of scenes dedicated to sex on the beach. Also, there was a good bit of sex in the captain's quarters. And on deck. And under the stars, in front of the hearth, and in rented rooms at the inn. Ash's takeaway from all this research was the knowledge that sea captains and mermaids were randier than a pack of wild bonobos.

Since he still had a good half hour before the parade began, Ash decided to go inside. A little bell tinkled to announce his arrival, not that anyone could hear it over the din of conversation, screaming kids, cajoling parents, and cell phone ringtones.

Ash began to weave in and out of the tourists, shelves, and display racks until he spotted Annie behind a small antique counter. She was prettier, and taller, than she'd looked in her pictures. As she chatted up customers and rang up sales, it was obvious that this was a truly happy woman. Her face was lit up with pleasure. She laughed freely. Her lightly tanned cheeks were permanently pushed up by her smile. Ash figured she either really loved her job or that fiancé of hers knew what he was doing. Ash scanned the shop but didn't see the man who'd been prominently featured on Annie's Facebook page.

So, pretending to be in the market for tacky New England mermaid souvenirs made in China, Ash took his time looking around. Crammed onto shelves were license plate frames, key chains, bumper stickers, coffee cups, ashtrays, photo frames, holiday ornaments, and temporary mermaid tattoo kits. Beach cover-ups, shorts, T-shirts, and sweatshirts of every description lined the walls. There were smartphone covers, children's storybooks, shot glasses, and stuffed animals. Suddenly, Ash saw something that truly spoke to him: a hoodie sweatshirt featuring a vintage-inspired pinup mermaid tagged with the caption SLIPPERY WHEN WET. He found a men's size large and tossed it over his arm, then headed toward the main attraction at the back of the shop. He figured any door with a sign that read ADULTS ONLY BEYOND THIS POINT was a door worth opening.

He stuck his head inside. The room was packed with so many people he could barely squeeze in. He was almost overwhelmed by the scent of sunscreen and stale clove cigarettes. Obviously, this was the place to be if you were curious about any facet of mermaid sensuality.

Since the crowd seemed to be flowing clockwise, Ash began with the chocolate display to his left. He couldn't help but chuckle. Despite his Boston blue-blooded origins, he was no prude, a point well illustrated with Rowan Flynn the night before. But Ash had never seen the likes of what lurked behind the glass display windows in this room. Most of the white, milk, and dark chocolate candies were standard-issue body parts. Some, however, featured human-human or human-mermaid encounters so complicated that Ash had to tilt his head to decipher the physics involved.

"I love, love, love this!" A young woman pulled her boyfriend to the glass and pointed to one of the more graphic depictions. "Will you get it for me?"

The guy's grin indicated he loved, loved, loved anything she did. "We'll take one of those," he said to the shop assistant behind the counter.

"Hit me up as well," Ash said, feeling swept away in the moment.

The cakes and cupcakes were next and, except for the proportions, most items were garden-variety sexual equipment. But Ash burst out laughing when he saw Annie Parker's creative use of jujubes on all of her bare-breasted mermaids.

Annie's novels were displayed under a banner that read, ALL *SEA OF LUST* BOOKS ON SALE HERE! Ash kept walking, past familiar titles like *Desire at High Tide* and *Ship of Surrender*, because he needed some air. He already knew how they ended, anyway.

A few minutes later, Ash stood at the cash register. Annie smiled at him as she totaled his purchases and reached for a small paper gift shop bag. "This sweatshirt design is my favorite. Totally retro."

"It is." Ash smiled at her in return and handed her two twenties.

"Enjoy your candy." Annie had a twinkle in her eye as she gave him his change.

"I will."

"Do I know you from somewhere?" Annie looked puzzled. "Have you been to the shop before?"

"Nope. First time on the island, as a matter of fact."

She shrugged. "Huh. Well, enjoy your day. Try not to miss any of the parade."

"Not a chance. I'm looking forward to it."

By the time he reached the boardwalk out front, a ragtag band approached, its lines staggered and the music's time signature undetectable. Ash leaned his back against the shop's weathered shingles, stuck his bag between his feet, and crossed his arms over his chest. Parade viewing was one of the few times that being six foot three was convenient, so although people were piled four deep in front of him, he could see everything and hear everything just fine. Maybe too fine. The local school's rendition of "When the Saints Go Marching In" was the most pitiful thing he'd ever witnessed, but that didn't stop the crowd from going wild in appreciation. Two small kids struggled to carry the official parade banner but grinned like it was the best day of their lives.

Immediately following was the official Bayberry Island float, featuring elected and appointed officials. They gathered behind a cardboard version of the village as seen from sea, every church steeple and building made to scale. Ash had to admit it was well done, complete with tall sailboat masts and fishing boats and the random sizes, elevations, and hues of the island's old buildings. Included among them was an unmistakable landmark — Rutherford P. Flynn's mansion, the Safe Haven.

A cheerful, big man stood on a raised platform toward the center of the float, holding on to a rail built to mimic that of the bow of a ship. A recorded version of the movie sound track from *Titanic* blared out from a set of large speakers. Ash glanced around. No one else seemed to think the island council could have chosen a more optimistic theme song.

Mayor Frasier Flynn looked just like his photos, Ash decided. In fact, he looked like all the Flynn men who had come before him. He had a wide, ruddy face, an oversized smile, and an impressive physique for a man in his sixties. He waved like a true veteran of politics and parades, his arm making wide sweeps over his head and then to either side. He was dressed in an old-fashioned pin-striped cutaway suit, a top hat, and spats with large black buttons up the outside. And just then, the mayor seemed to look directly at Ash as he grinned and waved.

Frasier Flynn's daughter had the same widely set and intelligent sea-green eyes.

A shock went through Ash, and he stood as if his feet had frozen to the boardwalk. For an instant he thought it was a reaction to seeing Rowan in the face of her father, but as he turned and looked toward the public dock, he knew better. Off in the distance, four or five parade entries away, was the most beautiful mermaid of all, and she looked an awful lot like the woman he'd recently held in his arms.

"Excuse me!"

Ash didn't bother hiding his annoyance, because he'd just gotten a look at Rowan and here was some ass bothering him and maybe even about to block his view. He pressed further into the wall of the shop but didn't acknowledge the man who'd just yelled at him over the parade noise.

"Excuse me. Sir?"

Ash turned, looking right into the lens of a camera. It was the last thing he'd expected—or wanted—and his head snapped back. "What the—? Get that thing out of my face."

"I'm sorry to bother you, but my name is Nathaniel Ravelle and I'm a documentary filmmaker working on a short about the island. Would you mind very much signing a release form?"

Ash's eyes went to the clipboard. He saw a legal release with a blank where he was to print his name and then sign and date. That's when it hit him—this was Annie Parker's fiancé. This was the man from her Facebook page. How had this slipped past him in his research? He had no idea the dude was a filmmaker. "I think I'll pass, thanks."

Nat didn't budge. In fact, he lifted the clipboard a bit higher. "We've already got some wonderful footage of you, and we'd appreciate you allowing us to use it."

Ash looked over Nat's shoulder to see Rowan coming closer. He felt his mouth fall open. He could do nothing but stare. And maybe swallow.

She looked *incredible.* She was surrounded by glittering twinkles of light that made her exposed skin appear otherworldly. She posed with her tail tucked demurely to her side and her long brunette wig curling over one shoulder. Those perfect breasts he'd cupped in his hands and tasted with his mouth had been stuffed into a couple clamshells kept in place with either flat-out magic or dental floss, he couldn't tell which. She was beautiful. Elegant. She was sex on the half shell. His chest hurt. His belly clenched. And if he didn't do something fast, he would be tenting his cargo shorts in front of a documentary film crew.

"Fine." Without taking his eyes from Rowan, he scrawled his name, signed, and dated.

"We really appreciate it. The footage we got of you yesterday with the kids was perfect—so funny and sweet."

"Uh-huh." Ash craned his neck to look around the film crew.

"Have a great day."

Finally, they were gone. And just in time, because Rowan slowly glanced over her right shoulder and her eyes met his. She seemed to be unable to look away. He didn't want her to. And even as the parade float passed by, she didn't avert her gaze until she would have had to sit backward in her shell to maintain eye contact.

Having no other option, Ash stared at the smooth skin of her back, the way her delicate spine curved seductively at the base, the way the skintight scales cupped her ass, the tender way her hand waved to the crowd. He stared until she was too far away to see.

It took a moment for his breath to return to normal. He absently looked down at the bag between his shoes, confused. Why was there a bag? Had he bought something? Oh yes, the sweatshirt. The chocolate. Of course.

Then suddenly, the words finally registered, and Ash raised his head and let it fall back against the side of the building. *Yesterday . . . footage with the kids . . . funny . . . sweet . . .*

"Fuck!"

"You should be ashamed!" A mother forced her way in front of Ash, her eyes angry as she pressed her hands over her kid's ears.

She was right, of course. He should be ashamed at what a ridiculous fuckup he'd become, how he'd allowed all the thinking to be done by only one of his heads, and it wasn't the one with neurons and synapses.

"My sincere apologies." Ash reached down into the bag between his feet. "Here. Have some chocolate."

*   *   *

Clancy turned off the chain saw, set the safety latch, and placed the tool on the grass. "Is that it?" He tossed another branch onto the pile, then pushed the protective glasses up on his forehead.

"That's everything in the yard, but do you have time to look at the roof?"

"Let me check." Clancy pulled his cell phone from his pocket and scrolled through messages.

Rowan would understand if he couldn't stay. Her brother was responsible for public safety at a time when thousands of extra people had descended on the island. She'd had a lot of nerve asking him to help with storm cleanup in the first place.

"If you need to go, that's cool," she said, as if she'd been reading his thoughts.

He shrugged. "I've got a little more time. The opening ceremony's still going on, and the boys have everything under control—at least for the moment."

Rowan smiled at her brother. The "boys" consisted of his assistant chief—who was also the island's only other full-time officer—and six of Clancy's buddies from the Boston Police Department who took vacation every festival week to freelance.

"I really appreciate this."

"No problem."

Rowan tried to lift up on the wheelbarrow handles but stopped. Now loaded up with thick pine branches and smaller twigs, it was too heavy to move. She noticed a strange look on Clancy's face and assumed he was about to poke fun at her. "I know. I'm a wimp."

"Allow me help you with that."

Rowan spun around, every nerve in her body on alert. There he stood, Ashton Louis Wallace III. His hands were shoved into the pockets of his cargo shorts. He wore a big smile and one of Annie's tacky tourist sweatshirts. His hair was windblown and he looked relaxed and happy. He was so disarmingly attractive that Rowan could do nothing but stare at him.

"Clancy Flynn." Her brother stepped forward to introduce himself, breaking Rowan's temporary trance.

"Ash Wallace. Very nice to meet you."

Clancy removed his work gloves and the two men shook hands. Rowan noticed how they sized each other up in a matter of seconds, judging each other's height, strength, and the firmness of the handshake. They seemed to give each other a silent nod of approval.

Men.

"I'm Rowan's brother," Clancy said, throwing her an admonishing glare. Obviously, Rowan wasn't doing her job as B and B proprietress.

"Sorry." She cleared her throat and gestured toward Clancy. "My brother is the island police chief." She motioned toward Ash. "Mr. Wallace is sleeping in my apartment this week."

That hadn't come out right. But Clancy was as cool as they came, and the only reaction he had was a barely detectable rise in his right eyebrow.

"I mean he's renting my apartment. He's staying there as a guest. We were booked up and he needed a place to stay. He had an emergency with his sailboat."

"Gotcha."

Clancy's entire demeanor changed. He'd gone from approval to dismissal in a flash, and Rowan didn't know why. There was now a smirk on his face where there had been genuine friendliness before.

"You were towed in yesterday, right?"

Oh. Now she understood. Only yesterday Clancy had referred to Ash as the Boston blue-blooded douche with a sailboat twice as valuable as his house.

Ash didn't flinch at the change in attitude. He didn't

seem embarrassed. He made no apologies. "Yep. Ran out of gas."

"Chain plate broke, too, right?"

Oh please. Rowan couldn't stand the male posturing anymore. "Can you look at the roof, Clancy?"

He turned his attention to Rowan and she swore she saw reprimand in his eyes. Could he know what happened during the storm? Had Imelda said something? Did the entire island know she was a festival-week floozy?

Ash spoke up. "Your family's been generous letting me stay here. If the roof's damaged, I'd be happy to help you with it. I know a little something about roofing."

Clancy shrugged and looked up toward the ancient slate roof four stories above them. "It's pretty steep."

"No problem."

Clancy laughed, and Rowan couldn't tell if he was laughing at Ash or at her, because he'd just glared her way again. "You current on liability insurance, sis?"

She rolled her eyes. "Yes."

"Let's do it, then." Clancy motioned for Ash to follow him. "We'll go up into the attic for tools and we'll be climbing out the cupola. Hope you're not afraid of heights."

"Not at all."

Rowan rested her fists on her hips and watched the two men head toward the kitchen door, a vague discomfort hitting her. If Clancy didn't already know, would Ash let it slip? She had no way of knowing if he was discreet, just as she had no way of knowing anything else about him—because he was a *complete stranger*. It felt like she needed to keep reminding herself of this fact.

"Hold up a second, please." Ash suddenly turned away from Clancy and headed toward Rowan. He had purpose in his stride. His eyes were locked onto hers.

Flashes of memory sliced through her—his kiss, his touch, how he'd coaxed so much pleasure from her body, over and over again. Was he going to kiss her? It looked like he was going to just come up to her, grab her, and kiss the hell out of her.

Rowan's legs weren't going to hold.

"Where to?" Ash lifted the wheelbarrow and waited for her instruction.

"Huh?"

"Where do you need this to go?"

Oh God. Her heart was running itself ragged inside her chest. She was disappointed that there would be no kissing, but was thrilled by his thoughtful follow-through. Rowan pulled herself together enough to point.

"Past the carriage house, down the slope. There's a woodpile behind the old tractor shed. Just dump it anywhere near the pile."

"Will do."

She watched him walk away, taking pleasure in the strain of his defined calf muscles, the set of his broad shoulders under the sweatshirt.

"What the hell?"

Rowan jumped. Clancy had come up behind her. She looked at him over her shoulder. "Is there a problem?"

"You're apartment? Seriously?"

Rowan turned to face her brother. "There's a very good reason."

"Oh, I can only imagine."

"He's paying us ten thousand for the week."

Clancy pursed his lips. After a long moment, he nodded. "Yep. That's a pretty good reason." But then he narrowed his eyes and scanned Rowan's face. "So it's just business, right?"

She produced what she thought was a convincing laugh. "God, Clancy! Of course it's just business."

"Because—"

She held her open palm in front of his face. "Don't even say it."

"It's just that . . ."

"Give me a break, wouldya?" Rowan was sick of being reminded of Frederick. Her family seemed to have forgotten that they'd liked him just fine at the time. They were happy for her. Clancy and everyone else had congratulated her when she'd fallen in love with Frederick. They'd been thrilled when he proposed three months after she moved into his Manhattan condo. Nobody had been concerned about how fast it was going. Nobody expressed any doubts about Frederick's motives.

And now? Now everybody had something to say about how blind she'd been, how stupid and gullible.

Rowan turned to watch Ash disappear down the slope with the wheelbarrow, a twinge of longing and confusion gripping her chest. So far, her unexpected guest had been nothing but kind and generous—not to mention the most incredible nearly anonymous lover a girl could ask for. But Rowan couldn't help wondering if the whole Frederick thing had been nothing but a warm-up for the blind, stupid, and gullible moments she was about to have with Ash Wallace. Maybe she really couldn't trust herself at all.

Something about the dude didn't make sense.

For the past forty minutes, Clancy had kept a close watch on Asheville or Ashley or whatever his ridiculous upper-crusty first name was and decided something definitely was off. Not only did he know his way around a toolbox; he knew his way around a one-hundred-twenty-five-year-old Vermont slate roof. It made no sense at all.

Clancy just watched him remove a damaged tile with a slate ripper, then search for a serviceable replacement from a box of extras. The guy gently tapped the tile with the rubber handle of the slate hammer, listening for the crisp ring that would indicate it was still sound.

"This one's still got a lot of life left in it." After making that call, he flawlessly nailed it in and went about examining the flashing.

In his ten years as a cop, Clancy had learned to value his gut feelings as much as hard evidence. Sometimes even more. And right then, his gut was telling him that a man with this kind of knowledge and skill would never, ever mistreat and neglect the classic 1965 Pearson Vanguard sailboat that was towed to Sully's the day before. Something was not right.

The two men worked together to repair the flashing and a decayed fastener. "Good thing you've got copper nails," he told Clancy. "They last forever. And with the proper maintenance, a roof like this could survive another hundred years, even in storms like the one we got yesterday."

Well, that did it. Clancy couldn't hold his tongue any longer. He sat back on his heels. "So, what's your story?"

The guy smiled. "I'm not even sure I have one."

"Do you go by your full first name?"

"My friends call me Ash."

"What kind of work do you do? Are you in construction?"

Ash chuckled. "No. But I worked for my grandfather when I was in high school and college. He was in architectural preservation."

Well, that made sense. "And now? What kind of work do you do now?"

"I run a nonprofit. And I've owned my own management consultant business for about six years, though I'm thinking of closing up shop."

Somehow, Clancy managed not to laugh his ass off.

This guy was about his age. Must be nice to "retire" from a lucrative consulting business and move into the world of philanthropy all before you hit thirty-five. "Are you based in Boston?"

"Yes."

"Interesting." Clancy stood, gathering the damaged tiles, noting how bare-bones his answers had been. Ash hadn't given anything that wasn't asked for, which was never a good sign. "So that's a beautiful boat you got there. Saw it yesterday down at the yard."

"Thank you. It was my grandfather's. I inherited it when he died." Ash gathered tools and a few stray nails. He stood, too. "Do you sail?"

"Of course."

Clancy gestured for Ash to go ahead along the roof toward the cupola window. He wanted to make sure he got safely inside with the toolbox before he handed him the box of tiles. He climbed in behind Ash.

"I can't remember a time when I didn't know how to sail," Clancy said. "My boat is a seventy-seven Catalina 27. I started restoring her when I came back to the island six years ago."

"Sounds like a lot of work."

Clancy was fishing and Ash wasn't biting. He wasn't sure if that was because the guy wasn't a big talker or because he didn't know enough about boats to have this conversation. They made their way down the back staircase that would eventually end on the main floor between the kitchen and Imelda's apartment, Clancy walking ahead. "So how about you, Ash? Do you sail a lot?"

He laughed. "I sail as often as I can, which isn't as often as I'd like. I've still got a lot to learn, I'm afraid. My grandfather would roll around in his grave if he knew I had to call for a tow yesterday."

Clancy had to admit that Ash's answers sounded solid enough, but it wouldn't hurt to do some snooping around when he had a few extra minutes. He wasn't completely sold on the big spender's story. Some of it seemed a little too convenient. He shows up out of the blue and offers that kind of money to his sister? An offer too good to refuse at a time when it had never been more desperately needed? And what about the sailboat? The chain plate rusting could happen to anyone, he supposed. But not knowing enough to check the gas and oil? That took a special kind of cluelessness, the kind this Ash guy didn't seem to have. Clancy didn't know what this guy was up to, but he was up to something.

Besides, it was obvious that Rowan was attracted to Ash. And that, more than anything, unnerved the hell out of him.

Chapter Seven

"Is this seat taken?"

Rowan glanced over the back of her beach chair and saw her best friend Annie smiling as she walked down the beach toward the water's edge, kicking up sand as she went. With the last of the sun setting behind her, Annie looked like a glowing, statuesque angel, an angel with long blond hair, an angel who'd kick her ass from here to Sunday if she learned about Ash from anyone but Rowan herself.

Annie plopped down into the beach chair next to Rowan's. "So where's Poseidon?"

Rowan thought it interesting that she brought up the topic immediately. Did she already know? It wouldn't be beyond the realm of possibility, since both Imelda and Clancy had kindly reminded Rowan of her festival-week track record of hooking up with dickhead strangers. Clearly, they suspected she was about to repeat—or already had repeated—the mistake with Ash. And they might have already shared their concern with Annie.

"I have no idea where he is." She tried to sound nonchalant.

"Huh," Annie said. "I thought for sure you'd be keeping tabs on him."

"Why would you say that?"

Annie laughed. "Well, because you claimed you nearly had an orgasm showing him around your apartment. I figured you'd be up there showing him how to use the electric can opener or something."

Rowan laughed, too, relaxing a little. Despite her plan to never mention the incident to another soul, she knew in her heart that she had to tell Annie. Of course she did. In all the years they'd been friends, they'd never kept secrets, no matter how embarrassing the details might be. Annie had confided in Rowan the moment she realized she was in love with Nat—even though she'd known him for only a few hours. Rowan had walked her through it, offering loving support and commonsense advice, with a little good-natured ribbing thrown in for the hell of it. It's what they'd been doing for each other since preschool. Rowan knew she'd have to take a deep breath and say what had to be said.

But Annie spoke before she had a chance.

"Thanks for dragging my ass out here this evening." She dug her toes into the wet sand and sighed with relief as the low tide rolled up to her ankles. "It's been completely insane today. I had so many customers that my head was buzzing. I really needed to get out of the store."

"It's been insane for me, too."

"I heard you did the Safe Haven proud out there today, rockin' your wicked-sexy mermaid outfit. Sorry I didn't get a chance to see you float by."

"Psshhh. Nothing you haven't seen a hundred times."

Annie rested her head against the high back of the beach chair and lazily looked Rowan's way. It took her about a half second to see that something was wrong. Annie's eyes widened and she sat straight up. "What is it?"

Rowan didn't know how to begin, so she just shook her head.

"What's wrong? Oh my God—did something happen to Duncan?"

"No!" She felt ashamed of herself. She hadn't meant to look that distraught. Poor Annie assumed it was a life-or-death situation when it was just another man mishap. Rowan needed to pull herself together. "Duncan's fine, as far as we know, though we haven't heard from him in weeks."

"Is he coming home for the cookout?"

"Doesn't look like it."

"Yikes. Mona must be flipping out." Annie settled back into her chair once more, though her eyes remained wide. "So what is it, Row?"

"It's about Ash."

She looked confused. "Ash? What ash?"

"Poseidon."

"*Oooh.* That's right—Thurston Howell the third." Annie rubbed the soles of her feet into the sand. "Let me guess. You discovered he's married, so the whole rolling around naked thing is off the table."

Rowan almost choked. Oh God! Could he be *married*? Just then it occurred to her that she didn't *know* if he was married! In fact, it hadn't even occurred to her that he *might* be married! She hadn't seen a ring, but that didn't mean anything, right? *Stupid, blind, gullible— with a side of reprehensible sauce!*

"Uh-oh." Annie's mouth parted. She gripped the worn wooden arms of the beach chair and stared at Rowan.

"I know. I know. I'm stupid, blind, gullible, and reprehensible."

Annie pursed her lips. "Well, let's not get carried away, here. At least you haven't . . ." Their eyes locked. Annie jumped to her feet. "You've *slept* with him already?"

"Sssshhh!" Rowan pulled her down again, frantic that

anyone walking along the beach could have heard the outburst. Luckily, the party girls from the Tea Rose Room were the only guests within view, and they were too far away to eavesdrop. She thanked God for the ever-present rumble of the ocean.

Annie collapsed into the chair again, out of breath. "When did this happen?"

"Uh, you remember how we were on the phone yesterday when the power went out?"

Annie nodded.

"I realized I hadn't given him a flashlight. So I took some candles over there, but it was pitch-black. He was standing in the hall but I couldn't see him, so I ran into him and he was naked and—"

"He was already naked?"

"Ssshhh! Yes. He must have been in the shower when the lights went out. He was naked and wet."

Annie put her hand over her heart. "I can't believe this."

"Neither can I! And now . . . well, I can't seem to stop thinking about him. I know better than this! I must be completely crazy. What am I going to do?"

Her friend's hand remained on her heart. To a random passerby it might look like she was in the middle of the Pledge of Allegiance.

"Well?"

"Hold on a minute, please. I'm still stuck on the naked, wet, and in the dark part."

"Annie!"

"Okay. Okay." She turned in her chair and leaned in toward Rowan, patting her knee. "You have the standard two choices."

"Yeah?"

"Yeah. You can forgive yourself for having a weak moment and put it behind you. Or, if it was incredible and special and he seems worth the effort, you step back and find a way to get to know him, make it more than a random hookup. You know, a do over."

"How the hell would I do that?"

"Talk to the man. Just sit down somewhere and talk."

Rowan bit the inside of her cheek and stared out at the sea. It was impossible to decipher what the little voice in the back of her head was saying, because it was all but drowned out by the ruckus of conflicting emotions crashing around like bumper cars in her brain. Should she chalk this up as a mistake and move on? Or should she put herself out there and try to get to know Ash as a person, despite the wildly improper way they started? Rowan couldn't help but wonder if a woman was allowed only one "heart-over-head" pass in life. If so, she'd wasted hers on Frederick.

"What are you thinking, Row?"

She shrugged, wiggling her toes in the cool sand. "I'm thinking it would have been better if it had never happened in the first place."

"That bad, huh?"

Rowan raised her eyes to her best friend. She didn't have to say a thing.

"Oh. That *good*, huh?"

She nodded. "Absolutely uh-mazing."

"Nice."

"But here's the kicker. The sex was great, but *he* seems just as great. He gave Zophie a hundred-dollar tip at breakfast this morning, but not when I was around to see him do it, so it wasn't just for show."

"Damn."

"Plus he took the wheelbarrow to the woodpile for me without being asked and then volunteered to help Clancy patch the roof after the storm. He seems to be a genuinely decent guy."

Annie lowered her chin and raised her eyebrows at the same time. "But isn't that what you said you wanted—a roll in the hay with a gorgeous, decent man who was only passing through?"

Rowan laughed. "I did say that, didn't I?"

"So why are you upset?"

"I'm not upset, exactly. I'm totally freaking out!"

Annie tipped her head and frowned. "Let me see if I've got this. He's a Greek god, a good-hearted guy with tons of money, and you had a fabulous no-strings time with him."

"I did."

"You said you could handle that."

"I guess I was wrong." Rowan bit down on her lip to keep from blubbering.

"Oh, sweetie." Annie leaned closer and grabbed both of Rowan's hands. "I know you're thinking about when you met Frederick. It's understandable that you're freaking out a little. But this Ash guy isn't Freder-*dick*. He isn't setting you up to steal from you and your family. He's not asking you to run off with him, and you're not falling hopelessly in love with him. This is not déjà vu, Row. This is a completely different situation, and you aren't some kind of powerless sitting duck. You can protect yourself and your heart."

Rowan couldn't hold her tears another minute. She'd been fighting the desire to cry since the lights came on and she was lying on the floor of her apartment in a stranger's arms, her heart as naked as her body. Maybe Annie had just identified the real problem here. It wasn't only that Rowan had acted impulsively and had sex with a stranger. It was the fact that she was unable to separate the sex from emotion, and she swore that the moment she laid eyes on Ash standing in the Safe Haven's foyer, she began to have feelings for him, and the sex made those feelings more intense. And so here she was, her heart already attached to a man who was nothing more than a one-night stand.

"Oh, sweetie. I'm sorry."

Rowan nodded. When she tasted the saltiness of her own tears, she realized the crying had begun.

"Row, tell me what's going on in that brain of yours. Do the best you can."

"I don't know exactly." Rowan's voice came out in a whisper. "It's so strange, Annie. I knew there was something extraordinary about him the second I met him, and when I smacked into him in the dark it was like I was being pulled in, like a magnet, like I couldn't have saved myself even if I wanted to, which I didn't."

"Oh boy." Annie squeezed Rowan's hands tight.

"I know that you fell in love with Nat immediately. I'm not saying that's what's going on with me. I don't know what I feel, and after everything I've been through with Frederick, I'm not even sure I know what love is. But I can't stop thinking about Ash. I keep hoping he's standing there when I round the corner or come out to the yard. There's a thousand questions I want to ask him about his family and what he likes to eat and what kind of music he listens to and what the most important things are to him. I changed my clothes three times today after the parade, thinking about how I would look to him. But that's not even the weirdest part."

Annie smiled encouragingly. "I'm listening."

Rowan looked into her best friend's eyes, asking for forgiveness in advance for the ridiculous, bizarre, crazy shit that was about to come out of her mouth. "He feels it, too. I see how he looks at me, and I think he's just as blown away by this as I am. It's like . . ." Rowan sighed, giving herself one last opportunity to stop before she said aloud what she'd been thinking silently all day.

"Go on." Annie squeezed her hands tighter.

"I really hate to use these exact words, for obvious reasons, but it's like common sense is no match for whatever I feel. It's like I'm drowning and there's nothing I can do to save myself."

* * *

Soon after the mermaid fountain was unveiled to the people of Bayberry Island, stories began to circulate about her special powers. Lovesick girls swore the mermaid could reveal to them their true loves, if only they would ask with a pure heart. Young men claimed to fall under a magical spell in the mermaid's presence, saying they became consumed with a passion beyond reason for one particular girl they envisioned in their mind's eye—often one they had never met and had no name for! Islanders agreed it had to be magic!

"Or puberty." Ash rolled his eyes, snatching the still-cold bottle of Sam Adams from the nightstand and taking a long draw. He didn't usually drink beer, but it seemed like the right choice for this warm summer night as he lay in bed, alone by the open window, listening to the sea, reading tourist brochures, and trying to keep his mind off the woman who usually slept in these sheets, on these pillows, in this room, atop this carriage house.

And really, that would have been plenty difficult to handle, but he also had the painting to deal with. Even at that moment, he felt the original oil portrait staring at him from the wall. Ash risked a quick glance at the horizontal canvas. Still there. Still about four feet long and at least a couple feet high, Rowan's reclining likeness morphed into mermaid form, her hair and skin alive in rich swirls of color against a blue-black night sky, moon glow dancing in her eyes and upon her bare upper body, iridescent scales, and the water lapping up around her. He looked away.

It made sense for Rowan to have an original Adelena Silva in her apartment. Adelena was Imelda's daughter, and she and Rowan had grown up together. And of course the famous artist would give Rowan the complete mermaid makeover in the fantastical style she was known for.

But Ash hadn't anticipated something this beautiful, so shockingly sensual—the painting or the woman. Maybe there were some things a man simply couldn't prepare for. He returned the beer to the nightstand and resumed reading.

> As the years went by, the legend evolved into its expanded, modern-day form. It goes like this:
>
> True love is like the sea—beautiful, deep, and life-giving but unpredictable, powerful, and even dangerous. To succeed at love, you must set out on your journey with a true heart and be prepared to be tossed by waves of passion or drown in love's undertow.
>
> The legend claims that anyone who comes to the mermaid, kisses her hand, and pledges to go wherever love leads, will find happiness. But beware—those who come to the mermaid with preconceived notions about the "how, who, when, and wheres" of true love will find heartache instead!

Having reached his maximum load for mermaid drivel—and exclamation points—Ash picked up a brochure on the history of the Flynn family and their fishing empire. He'd already read everything on record about the clan and Flynn Fisheries, from far more objective source material, but he found the brochure entertaining, if only for the way it skipped over the more colorful tidbits of the family's history. There was no mention of the legendary drunken brawls between Rutherford's four sons or the generations of grudges, nepotism, and monopoly ownership of the island's businesses, much less the Prohibition speakeasy that had once operated in the Safe Haven's basement.

Though the brochure did summarize the connection between the Flynns and the mermaid legend, it glossed over the crux of the matter: Rutherford Flynn was a nut job.

Ash read on.

> Rutherford Flynn was just twenty-four when he started Flynn Fisheries with two of his brothers in 1879. That was only a year after they'd boarded the *City of Chester* in Queenstown, County Cork, and set sail for Ellis Island. The brothers lived with distant relatives in Boston for about six months before they signed on with a fishing boat out of Cape Cod and decided to remain on Bayberry Island.
>
> Rutherford, or Ruthie as he was called as a young lad, rented a fishing boat and started making money almost immediately from the bounty of Atlantic haddock, cod, halibut, and salmon, plus a variety of shellfish, such as bay scallops, muscles, oysters, and shrimp—all commodities in demand by big-city restaurants and shops on the mainland.

Ash took another swig of beer. The ocean breeze blew through the window and over his bare chest, sending a ripple of pleasure through his body. He thought of the silky heat of Rowan's skin in his hands, how she'd undulated on his lap, the way she'd clutched his body against hers as he entered her. The variety of sounds she made when . . .

"Aauugh! This is insane!" Ash set the beer on the bedside table and breathed deep, pushing Rowan from his mind and continuing with his reading. Anything to stop torturing himself like this.

> By 1880, there were three boats in the Flynn Fisheries fleet and the company employed more than two hundred men, nearly all the able-bodied adult male population of Bayberry Island. By then, one of the original Flynn brothers had passed away in an accident at sea and another had moved to Nantucket to join a whaling operation, a lucrative industry Rutherford refused to engage in.

"Now, that's something I didn't know." Ash bent a leg and propped the brochure against his knee, making a mental note to look into the man's no-whaling philosophy.

> On the evening of March 14, 1881, when an epic nor'easter hit the fishing fleet, Captain Rutherford Flynn was at the helm of the lead boat, the *Safe Haven*. As huge waves and gale-force winds battered the boats, Ruthie knew it was his duty to save the seventy crew members from almost certain death.

Ash reached for another sip of beer, then switched to the mermaid brochure again, preferring to relive the details of that fateful night in a more melodramatic story-telling style.

> He fought valiantly to lead the boats to shore, but all seemed lost! Then suddenly, the captain spotted something at the side of the boat! He stared in disbelief as a mermaid became visible, strangely illuminated in the dark, swirling water. Her raven hair fanned out around her. Her beautiful, dark eyes locked on his as she smiled reassuringly. He couldn't believe his eyes!

Ash laughed loudly, shaking his head. "Wonder what ol' Ruthie was packin' in that hip flask."

> Captain Flynn watched in amazement as the mermaid pulled his boat to the cove and the other boats mysteriously followed. He was so overcome with emotion that the instant his ship was secured, he dove into the frigid Atlantic in search of the divine creature who had saved them, attempting to pledge his undying love and devotion to her!
> He nearly drowned, but his men managed to pull him from the crashing ice-cold sea and dragged him to the island's only inn, where he slipped into a fevered illness for days. When he awoke, his eyes landed on Serena, the beautiful innkeeper's daughter, who had been nursing him back to health. And what did he see? The same shiny raven black hair and dark, beautiful eyes! Despite the girl's protests, Captain Flynn swore she was the mermaid, and he rolled off his sickbed to one knee

and pledged to cherish her and love her until
the end of time!

Ash picked up his beer, dismayed to see it was nearly
empty. He skimmed down toward the end of the story.

Serena and Rutherford Flynn began their
happy, long life together. As his business
boomed and his family grew, the captain built
a mansion for his wife on the island's highest
point of elevation, naming it the Safe Haven,
in honor of his first fishing boat. Not long after,
he commissioned Philadelphia sculptor Henry
Manger to create a bronze mermaid fountain
in Serena's likeness. The fifteen-foot-high,
neo-classical statue was unveiled in a public
ceremony on June 5, 1888. Being that it was
Victorian-era New England, the fountain was
considered immodest, even for a work of art.
Islanders and distinguished visitors gasped
when the drape was removed. The mermaid
wore nothing but a tail and a smile!

Ash chuckled. "Nothing but a tail and a smile."
Sounded like Rowan's parade attire. "Ugghh!"
He pushed himself up from the queen-sized four-
poster bed and headed into the kitchen. Ash swung open
the 1950s-era refrigerator and grabbed another beer.
Looking around, he had to admit he liked the apartment's
pitched roof and dormer windows, rough-hewn pine
floors, and original stable doors used for privacy in the
bathroom and bedroom. Its simplicity was in stark con-
trast to the opulence of the main house, with its chande-
liers, brass light fixtures, decorative tin ceilings, and acres
of rich wood wainscoting, friezes, and crown moldings.

He'd seen a hundred houses like the Safe Haven while working for his grandfather, and every one of them had been built by a man like Rutherford Flynn, a guy who used his home to proclaim his own magnificence. Even as a kid, Ash had appreciated the beauty and historical value of these old mansions, but was confused by one thing—if a man was so great, why did he have to have a big, fancy house to prove it? Ash was about thirteen when he asked his grandfather about this, and never one to miss an opportunity to hit Ash over the head with preachy mumbo jumbo, he'd answered in typical Louis Wallace fashion. "Without solid framing, a house will fall. Without humility, a man will fall. And make no mistake about it—most of these men eventually fell."

Upon his grandfather's death, Ash discovered Louis Wallace had walked his talk. Grandfather often told Ash stories about how he got his first job at age sixteen during the post–World War II building boom, paid his way through college, and earned a degree in architecture. He told Ash that he'd become one of the East Coast's most trusted restoration contractors because he worked hard, lived honestly, and never stopped learning. Of course, his grandfather lived comfortably, enjoying his travel, good food, and restoring and sailing the *Provenance,* but he certainly didn't live like a rock star.

So Ash had been stunned when Grandfather Louis died and left him fifteen million dollars.

Ash popped the cap of the beer bottle, tossed it onto the kitchen counter, and wandered into Rowan's small living room, doing his best to let the memory of his grandfather waft out of his thoughts. He'd loved Louis Wallace. There was no question about that. But he'd never loved the feel of his grandfather's virtuous foot on the small of his back or the pressure he felt to live up to some sort of impossible ideal. After all, today's business world was nothing like it had been in his grandfather's day. As Brian once pointed out, Ash might have chosen a career with questionable ethics as a way to stick it to his dear old deceased granddad. As usual, Brian had a point.

Ash walked through the living room. He'd tried his best not to use his guest status to spy on Rowan any more than he already had. Truthfully, he'd been relieved last night to find the desk locked and the more intimate contents of her bedroom and bathroom drawers emptied. But he couldn't resist breathing her in while he was in her home, surrounded by her things. He smelled her in every room, on every piece of furniture. Her scent took up residence in his mind.

He found himself moving toward the fireplace mantel and the built-in bookcases on either side, heavy with family photos, mementos, seashells, and odd items he knew meant something only to her. Yes, Rowan had appeared tough during Frederick Theissen's trial. She'd testified against him and given a statement at his sentencing. She'd faced the TV cameras stoically, with her chin set and her shoulders back, every word measured and rehearsed for optimum effect. She never let anyone see her sadness or the burden of betrayal she carried.

He knew her better now. He'd seen the loneliness and injury in her expression. He noticed how she'd tenderly arranged the living room toss pillows and set an old milk bottle of dried wildflowers inside the dormant fireplace. He knew she preferred sheets with little yellow polka dots and occasionally read paperback romance novels. He saw how she'd proudly framed her diplomas and a certificate of recognition for her master's degree honors thesis in organizational psychology.

Not to mention that he'd tasted her skin, smelled her

hair, and felt her heat. Somehow, the two of them had turned an unplanned encounter into a chance to *make love.* It was the truth. Ash had made love to Rowan and she'd made love to him. Yesterday his life was simple and clean. Today he didn't know where his heart ended and his head began. He hardly knew which end was up.

Ash's eyes once again wandered to the framed photos on Rowan's mantel. He especially liked the family photo from when she was about six, the age Ash had been when his mother and father died. Rowan was a skinny, freckled wild child who'd obviously been forced into a dress for the occasion and wasn't happy about it. Ash looked closer to see that her smile was accentuated by a stubborn squint of her eyes. Both her knees were scraped and one of her fancy shoes was unbuckled. It made him laugh.

Frasier was the proud father in the portrait, one arm around his wife and a hand resting on Clancy's shoulder. Mona was quite lovely and she knew it, presenting a sly grin to the camera. Clancy looked like a smaller version of himself now, minus the uniform, and it was clear that his father's hand was on his shoulder to keep him from squirming. But it was Duncan who fascinated Ash the most. He looked sickly and withdrawn, leaning a bit into his mother's leg as if he weren't sure he could stand on his own. His face was turned slightly away from the camera.

Ash's attention moved to the photo of Duncan's Naval Academy graduation portrait. He had to shake his head in disbelief. The difference was startling. How did a pale and shy weakling turn into this formidable, steely-eyed officer in his dress whites? As he took a seat on Rowan's sofa, Ash made a mental note to learn a little more about the Flynns' eldest child.

He sighed, dangling the beer bottle between his fingers. Tomorrow was Sunday, the second day of the Mermaid Festival. Ash had been on the island for two days and had little to show for it. Nothing he could report to Jessop-Riley, at any rate. He promised himself that in the morning, he'd really get down to business.

Chapter Eight

"Everything is better when you're naked."

Rowan placed the tray of breakfast pastries on the dining room sideboard and did her best not to laugh. The nudists had insisted that Ash and the party girls join them at their table and were giving them the hard sell on why their version of Mermaid Festival events was the better choice.

"Okay, so you're saying that *everyone's* naked?" One of the Tea Rose Room girls seemed incredulous. "There isn't, like, a bouncer to make sure only the hot people get in? Like at the club?"

"No, dear. Our lifestyle isn't about physical perfection. It's about the freedom to be in the world as nature intended. Our events are invitation only, of course, but body type never determines who gets invited."

The girl looked as if she'd just caught wind of a dead skunk. "Ew. Thanks, but we're busy!" The girls jumped up from the table and said their good-byes, but not before giving coy little head swivels in Ash's direction.

Rowan froze. She'd just witnessed those two bimbos give Ash the universal sign for "let's get together." And— *Oh, no, she didn't!* The dark-haired girl just whispered their room number to Ash before the two of them giggled and stumbled their way out of the dining room.

Rowan turned away, leaned her fists on the sideboard, and glared out the windows. She felt her face get hot with jealousy. Wait. She was jealous? She'd never been the jealous type, even with men she was actually dating. And she wasn't dating Ash. Yet here she was, so jealous she could scratch out the eyes of a couple of ditzy girls who'd flirted with him.

She shook her head at her own ridiculousness. Enough. After festival week, she was going to schedule an appointment with the doctor on Nantucket. She'd get some blood tests. Or ask that her hormone levels be checked. Maybe get a CAT scan or an MRI. *Something.* Because this emotional free fall had to end.

She heard Ash stand from his chair, scoot it in, and excuse himself from the table. "Have a great day, everyone," he said with his usual politeness.

Rowan didn't move. She began to rearrange sugar packets in an effort to appear busy. Her ears strained to hear his footsteps leave the dining room and enter the foyer. Instead she heard footsteps come closer, then stop behind her.

Her shoulders tightened. He was about to talk to her! But this was what she wanted, right? This is what she and Annie had talked about. It was why she'd ironed a cute and somewhat low-cut cotton blouse to wear that day instead of a T-shirt. It's why she'd added a dab of perfume at her throat, shaved her legs, and worn a surfer-girl skirt. So if she wanted him to speak to her, why was she terrified?

"Rowan."

It was a whisper, deep and husky. And close. She clenched her thighs together. She seemed to do that in his presence a lot, as if she'd never been near a decent-

looking man before. Surely she could pull herself together to answer him.

Slowly, Rowan turned, but kept her hands gripping
the edge of the antique sideboard. "Good morning, Mr.
Wallace. Did you enjoy your omelet?"

"It was very tasty."

She was panting like she'd just run a 10K, 9K of which
had been uphill. Nope. *He* laid claim to all the tasty
around here. His tousled short curls ran the spectrum
from sun-streaked light blond to medium brown. The
stubble on his chin, cheeks, and above his upper lip was
more brown than blond. His lashes and brows were
darker still. And she felt that if she weren't allowed to
touch him in all those blond and brown places, she'd curl
up in a ball and turn to dust. Honestly, she was *starving*
to touch him.

Rowan came to her senses enough to peek around
Ash's shoulder. Her nudist regulars were observing
them with great interest, maybe even picturing one or
both of them naked. The thought was enough for Rowan
to snap out of it.

"Is there something I can do for you?" She watched a
sultry, slow smirk appear on his lips. Perhaps that had
been a bad choice of words. She regrouped. "Do you
have plans for today?"

"Maybe." His voice was teasing. Rowan could have
sworn he let his gaze drop to her low-cut neckline. "Do
you have plans today, Miss Flynn?"

For a split second, Rowan saw the two of them in her
bed, without a stitch of clothing between them. *Everything is better when you're naked.*

"Are you going to Island Day?"

"Huh?" Rowan licked her lips. "I'm sorry. What?"

"Today's Island Day, right? Will you be there?"

"Yeah. Yes. Of course. Sunday of festival week is al-

ways Island Day. It's fun. You'll like it. I'll get you a brochure."

Ash laughed. Rowan's hands slipped off the edge of
the sideboard, and when he reached out to assist her, his
fingers brushed the side of her left breast.

"Oh God."

"Are you all right?" He still gripped her gently by the
upper arms. Rowan thought she'd melt.

"Fine. No problem." *No, I'm not all right!* She'd just
heard his laugh, and it sounded like a masculine wind
chime, soothing and cheerful at the same time. She
wanted more. And he was still touching her . . .

Ash dropped his hands and shoved them in the front
pockets of his cargo shorts. He looked almost embarrassed.

"Let me get you an Island Day brochure."

He shook his head. "I have one already. In fact, I
think I have every brochure available at any kiosk anywhere on the island."

"Oh." Rowan heard herself make a sound that was
part sigh and part laugh. "Well, then, enjoy your day, Mr.
Wallace."

"You agreed to call me Ash."

"Of course." She glanced at the nudists again. All six
of them had settled back into their dining room chairs
with their coffees, thoroughly amused by the awkward
exchange between hotelier and guest. If Rowan weren't
more careful, Annie, Imelda, and Clancy wouldn't be the
only ones who knew she had a thing for the man staying
in the carriage house. Everyone on the island would. At
this rate, she might as well go down to Annie's shop and
have her whip up a custom T-shirt that read: ASHTON
LOUIS WALLACE III DID ME ON MY APARTMENT FLOOR.

Rowan smiled at him. "Thank you, Ash." Truly, she
was doing the best she could, but he unnerved her. "To

answer your question, yes, I'll be at Island Day, but I'm working for most of it. The Safe Haven has a booth."

Ash nodded. "Handing out brochures?"

She giggled. "Yes. And we have giveaways for half-priced weekend packages, free breakfasts, and we always raffle off two tickets to the clambake down on the beach, the best night of festival week."

"Wow." He seemed impressed.

"The clambake is our most popular over-eighteen event, but our liquor license limits us to four hundred people on the beach at one time. That's why tickets are hard to come by. We always sell out the year before."

"That's too bad." Ash smiled at Rowan, and this time it was a full, genuine smile that almost knocked the wind out of her. "It sounds like it would have been a lot of fun."

"Excuse me!" One of the nudists stood from his chair. "We have a clambake, too, and we're not sold out!"

"I'll keep that in mind. Thanks." Ash nodded politely in their direction, then grinned at Rowan again. "So I'll see you in town today?"

Rowan tipped her head to the side, completely aware that he was flirting with her. She couldn't say she minded one bit. "Anything is possible."

He chuckled. "Good. Then you'll let me take you to dinner. I think we need to start over. What do you think?"

Rowan had never known how to look more cool than she felt, and now was no exception—the delight was spreading across her cheeks like a bad case of heat rash. He wanted a do over! Oh, thank God! She'd been right—he felt the way she did! "I would happily accept your invitation, but all our restaurants are closed on Island Day. Everyone's busy operating their food tents."

"All right." Ash didn't seem deterred. "Then I'll take

you to the finest food tent on Bayberry Island, and we'll get started on starting over."

"It's a date."

"I look forward to it." Ash leaned down and left a very quick, infinitely sweet kiss on her cheek. "See you soon."

Rowan watched him walk from the dining room, tall, back straight, shoulders solid, engaging in a last bit of friendly—but not too friendly—banter with the nudists. Then he disappeared into the main entry hall and headed toward the front door. She heard the heavy iron latch close behind him.

She had no idea how long she stood there, motionless, her fingers pressed to the place on her cheek where he'd kissed her. However long it had been, it had been too long.

Not only were the nudists staring at her, but Zophie was, too, along with every guest still lingering in the dining room.

"Gather 'round, ye 'maids. Get your coffee and let's do this." Mona gestured for the group to choose a seat on her sectional sofa or the dining room chairs scattered throughout the living room. She opened her three-ring binder to their Island Day schedule.

Once everyone was settled, Mona didn't waste any time. "Darinda has offered to help me with the 'Save Our Island' campaign today, so I expect everyone else to chip in with Mermaid Society work."

When she didn't receive any response, she glanced around, immediately alarmed by the energy in the room—or lack thereof. "How is everyone this morning?" She heard nothing but a few grunts and grumbles in response. "This doesn't bode well for our busy day ahead, does it?"

"Did you know that the word 'bode' is from Old English and is considered an archaic verb form?" Izzy McCracken sipped daintily from her coffee mug before she continued. "It's almost as outdated as 'presage' and 'augur.'"

No one said anything for a good ten seconds. Not surprisingly, Polly Estherhausen took it upon herself to break the silence. "Oh, my flippin' God," she said.

Abigail Foster was next. "Look, I'm already exhausted and we've got five more days of this. The sun was so hot yesterday, I thought the acrylic in my wig was going to melt."

Mona sighed deeply. She loved these women, no matter how annoying they could be. They had known each other forever. And that was the problem.

"I fear for the future of the Bayberry Island Mermaid Society." There. Mona had said it. It was what everyone was thinking anyway.

Silence.

She looked around the room at the faces of her friends. Most everyone was on the downhill side of forty and some, like Mona herself, were past sixty. All of them had faces that had been lived in and bodies that had served them well on land and in the water. Only a few still had teenagers at home. About half of them had lost husbands to death or divorce. They'd been through everything together over the years—bankruptcy, illness, hurricanes, children who ran away or got pregnant or mixed up in drugs, career crises, menopause, brief and unhappy relocations to the mainland, and defections to the Fairy Brigade. Mona couldn't blame her friends for being worn out. They were entitled. There was only one problem . . .

No one was waiting to fill their fins.

None of Bayberry's younger women had the slightest

interest in carrying on the sacred rituals that had been passed down through generations of island women since 1888. Up until now, it had been an unbroken thread of oral tradition and shared understanding. And Mona knew that unless something drastic happened, their circle of female power and magic would cease to exist as soon as they did.

As sad as it was to admit, that grumbling Mona just heard was likely the Mermaid Society's death rattle.

"Maybe we should just get our assignments for today," Layla O'Brien said. "It's already after nine, so whoever has the first shift at the booth has less than an hour to get in costume and get all the materials in order."

"I'll volunteer for the first shift," Abby said.

"Thank you. I'll put you with Polly." Mona began writing names in the two-hour time slots for the booth. "Remember our recruiting efforts, ladies. Who knows when a tourist might decide to permanently relocate. One of them might eventually qualify to join our sisterhood. New blood, ladies. Keep your eyes peeled for new blood."

"Where do things stand with Rowan? Has she shown any sign that she might change her mind one day?"

Mona's head snapped up at Polly's question. She blinked, feeling the intense stares of every society member. As she always did when this subject came up, Mona needed to be careful not to reveal the depth of her disappointment show. She wasn't angry with Rowan for turning her back on the legend. Not at all. But Mona couldn't let the true depth of her sorrow and confusion show.

The group had messed up, simple as that. They had agreed that the Great Mermaid brought Frederick to Rowan, that he was her true heart-mate. Boy, had they had been wrong. And that could mean only one of two things: Either the Great Mermaid had erred or the humans had. After a great deal of debate, their verdict was they must have lacked a piece of information necessary for an accurate interpretation, and they misread the signs. The fault was theirs alone.

Mona reached for her coffee, knowing in her heart that as the Society's leader—and Rowan's mother—she was to blame. She'd wanted Rowan's happiness so badly that it had blinded her, and Mona would have to live with that mistake the rest of her life. "She's not going to change her mind. Not ever. Please don't ask her to."

"It's understandable. Of course it is." Layla looked down at her tennis shoes, then raised her head, suddenly hopeful. "How about Lena Silva? She's a kindred spirit. Do you think she'll be ready soon?"

"Hell, no." Polly rolled her eyes toward the ceiling. "The girl's a mouse. She never leaves her fortress, just hides in her studio all day every day. Her paintings are as close to the mermaid legend as she's ever going to get."

"There's always Annie." Izzy tried to sound cheerful. "Now that she has Nat, she might be willing to drop some of her skepticism."

"Or not." Polly laughed. "Annie has dissed the mermaid her whole life. You think when we tell her what really happened that night, she'll believe us? Let's say we reveal that we performed a winter solstice intervention on her behalf just hours before Nat fell in front of her door. Will she take the leap, or will she brush it off as coincidence?"

"She'll think it was coincidence." Abby scowled. "It's such a cop-out, too. Why do so many people nowadays refuse to see magic when it's right in front of them? It must be such a dry way to go through life—no mystery, no wonder, nothing more miraculous and powerful than your own tiny, little, small-minded preconceived notions."

"That was redundant."

Abby pursed her lips at Izzy. "What in God's name are you talking about?"

"'Tiny, little, and small-minded'—those adjectives all mean the same thing."

"I gotta get my costume on." Polly stood. "Are we done here?"

"I just wonder . . ." That was Darinda Darswell. She'd now spoken at two meetings in a row, which was incredible, since she'd said almost nothing in all the meetings that came before.

"Yes?"

She smiled at Mona, but her eyes were filled with concern. "I wonder if your daughter will ever forgive us."

"Well, Jesus, Darinda." Polly shook her head. "It's not like we set out to hurt her! We adore Rowan. We just wanted her to be happy. We still do."

The group's quietest member seemed unwilling to allow Polly to bully her, which delighted Mona. "Go on, Darinda," she told her.

"Thank you." She squared her shoulders. "My worry is that Rowan's been hurt so badly that she won't open her heart to love again, even when it's standing right in front of her."

That was Mona's worry, too. In fact, every night before she fell asleep, several concerns tortured her enough to keep rest at bay. First, was Duncan safe? Was he even still alive? Where was he? Her worry for her eldest child was a constant, nagging discomfort during the day, but at night it could explode into cold, sharp fear.

Next Mona would worry about whether Clancy would ever find a good woman to share his life with. That boy deserved it. There was a tender heart under his tough exterior.

After that, she would obsess about how long she

could muster the courage and energy needed to hold off the Mermaid Island development.

And always, Mona worried about her daughter.

After Rowan's life fell apart in New York, she graciously had volunteered to run the Safe Haven. Mona had accepted the offer because she believed being close to family would help Rowan heal. Yet lately, she'd noticed how restless Rowan had become. She was often sarcastic and irritable, maybe even downright unhappy. Unfortunately, they were at an impasse.

There was no one else to do the job. Mona's worsening rheumatoid arthritis meant she could no longer manage the Safe Haven by herself. Frasier was so humiliated by the worn condition of the house that he wanted nothing to do with it. More than once he'd told Mona that he saw the mansion's decay as a symbol of his family's precipitous fall. Of course, Clancy had chosen law enforcement as his career, and it was what he was born to do. Duncan was off saving the world, putting as many miles as possible between himself and his home. That meant if Rowan didn't stay on to run the B and B, they might as well board it up and let it crumble—or sell it to the highest bidder.

For all practical purposes, Rowan was the end of the line. Mona knew that without her daughter's help, there would be no Safe Haven and no reason to fight the good fight. Unless she stood up to the developers, Bayberry Island would become just another seaside amusement park, an overcrowded, loud, and dirty tourist attraction stripped of everything that made the island magical in the first place. Eventually, the Great Mermaid would be dethroned. She would fade into the background, overshadowed by golfers, yacht owners, and gamblers.

She could not let that happen.

*   *   *

In the short time Ash had been on Bayberry Island, he'd noticed that each day seemed to have its own unique flavor. Friday had been dramatic and thrilling; Saturday sparkled with anticipation; and today, Island Day, looked like it was an excuse to have a blowout block party.

Main Street was cordoned off and jammed with two opposing lines of open-air tents, their blue, white, and green canvas awnings poking up into the bright sky. Many tents displayed arts-and-crafts stuff like jewelry, clothing, paintings, sculpture, and woodcrafts. There were tents devoted to nothing but cutesy boating accessories, or blown-glass wind chimes, or hand-painted house numbers. The food vendors were too numerous to sort out, but the air was filled with smoke from barbecue pits and fish fries, and Ash could smell everything from funnel cakes to fried clams in the breeze. He'd spied the banner for the chili cook-off already in progress and told himself he'd head over there after he'd located Rowan. The grand-prize winner would be chosen by none other than Mayor Frasier Flynn himself.

Though plenty of revelers had come in costume today, many more had not. The crowd seemed more conservative than on parade day and was made up predominantly of families. Ash guessed that at least some of the more colorful tourists were still sleeping it off after a hard night of partying.

He made his way down the center of the street, doing his best to dodge unsupervised kids with dripping ice-cream cones, teenagers on skateboards, and a few off-leash dogs. He scanned the throng looking for the Safe Haven B and B booth but came to a sudden halt. Right in front of him was a huge red banner in the shape of a stop sign, and in big white letters it said: SAVE OUR IS-LAND! STOP GREEDY DEVELOPERS!

"And here we go." Ash took a deep breath and wandered over. He wasn't surprised to see Mona Flynn at the helm, but what did surprise him was how attractive she looked in her street clothes. He hadn't paid much attention to her appearance Friday, probably because he couldn't see through the downpour and he was in shock from being snatched from the public dock in the Man Grab. Today provided a far more relaxed opportunity to study her. She wore a simple pair of cotton slacks and a crisp blouse of narrow blue stripes. Her hair was cut in a bob and was that striking silver color some older women were lucky to have. Her eyes were pale blue and intense. Rowan had the same heart-shaped chin and pretty mouth.

But Mona was all business that morning, working the crowd like a pro. She forced save our island buttons onto anyone within arm's reach, chatted up the passersby, and shoved a clipboard at anyone who showed the slightest curiosity about her cause. "If you value your authentic experience here on Bayberry Island, please sign this petition," she told them. "Don't forget to put down your e-mail. Thank you so much!"

Ash thought he recognized Mona's accomplice as one of the mermaids he'd seen gathered around the fountain, but it was impossible to be sure, since she, too, was not in her mermaid outfit. He meandered up to the folding table and tried to look only vaguely interested in the cheaply produced brochures (more brochures!) spread over its surface.

"Thank you for stopping by our tent."

Ash glanced up. Yes, he'd been correct. He recognized this woman's dark eyes and pixie face from Friday's public humiliation. She must have recognized him, too. Her hand flew to her mouth and her eyes widened.

"Hello," Ash said, grabbing a brochure. "What's all this?"

When he didn't get an answer, he raised his eyes again. Both Mona and her friend stared at him in surprise. The force of their attention made him vaguely uncomfortable.

"Ashton." Mona remembered his name. "How nice to see you enjoying yourself today."

Ash laughed. "Oh, right. You're the bossy mermaid lady from the other day."

His comment made Mona's friend giggle.

"I suppose I deserve that." She held out her hand. "My name is Mona Flynn, and this is Darinda Darswell. We're both members of the Bayberry Island Mermaid Society, but today we're here as citizens defending the authenticity of our home."

He shook her hand and smiled. "A pleasure, ladies."

"This is nothing short of the most important issue to face Bayberry Island since the collapse of the fishing industry." She smacked a button into his palm. "We would appreciate your support."

"Hmm." Ash pocketed the button and produced a thoughtful expression but refused to accept the petition Mona now pressed to his chest. "I'll need to do my own research on the subject before I sign anything. Forgive me, but politics aren't really my thing."

Mona snapped her head in surprise. "This isn't politics. It's basic decency. It's taking pride in our island's history and choosing reality over some theme-park representation of reality. This is about drawing a line in the sand."

Ash nodded. *Damn, this lady is a ballbuster.*

"We've collected more than ten thousand signatures from locals and tourists since the project was announced last spring."

Ash crossed his arms over his chest. "That's impressive."

"It's war."

Ash had been here before. He knew how it would end. This was such a classic David and Goliath matchup it almost made him feel guilty. Obviously, Mona Flynn was a smart woman and she was plenty fired up—for good reason, he supposed—but Ash knew she'd already lost the war she believed she waged.

He produced a smile and said, "Sounds like you're making a lot of progress." He skimmed over the brochure as if it were his introduction to the Mermaid Island plans. "So you're trying to stop a golf course?"

Mona laughed. "If only that was the extent of it! The company wants to build a huge casino hotel and a marina in addition to the golf course. Their environmental impact assessment was a joke—in fact, it was fixed. So not only would this ruin the island culturally, it would be an environmental disaster as well."

Ash didn't need to pretend that her accusation bothered him. He'd glanced at the environmental impact summary Jessop-Riley provided, and he hadn't seen anything amiss. That said, he knew environmental impact results were subjective and sometimes controversial. But flat-out fixed? He asked himself if Jessop-Riley would go that far, and the answer was—probably. If they could get away with it.

Suddenly, he had a very bad taste in his mouth.

"Did you know that just to the northeast of Bayberry is a unique underwater mountain range called Friendship Ledge?" Mona raised one of her eyebrows as if to challenge him. "Its ridges and basins and mix of currents have created an ideal environment for marine life—all kinds of species congregate there, including endangered North Atlantic right whales and wolffish. It's also home to one of the largest and deepest cold-water kelp forests on the Eastern Seaboard."

"Don't forget the gray seals," Darinda added. "And the wetlands."

"Of course." Mona nodded, continuing on. "And let me assure you, if somehow the developers get away with this bullshit environmental impact study, we plan to fight it. If necessary, we are prepared to testify before the general court in Boston, and we've requested a meeting with the governor."

Ash smiled politely. Mona and her supporters didn't realize that if they made it that far, they would face a team of pit bull Boston lawyers and Washington lobbyists, people with nearly unlimited resources and deep ties to decision makers at every level. They would rip Mona and her group to shreds before they even got started. Though he admired Mona's tenacity, he felt sorry for her, too. He was tempted to sit her down, pat her hand, and advise her to give up. It would save her a lot of grief.

Darinda Darswell smiled sheepishly. "I think we're overwhelming him, Mona."

Ash shook his head. "Not at all, ladies." He tucked the brochure into the side pocket of his shorts, next to the button. "It's always wonderful to meet people who are passionate about a cause that's important to them."

Darinda smiled again. "Are you having a nice time on the island?"

"I am, thank you."

"And where are you staying?"

"Well, I—" Ash felt a sharp pain in his lower back, and when he spun around he got a fairy wing in his eye.

"Give me some room here."

Ash took a step back.

"Really, Sally?" Mona put her fists on her hips, and a look of disgust appeared on her face. "You're going to pick a fight with me on Island Day? Seriously?"

"You lied to me, Mona." The fairy jabbed an index finger into Mona's chest. "You said you weren't renting space on Island Day, so that's why the HCLC didn't get a tent. But this is just more of your underhanded, sleazy game, isn't it? You Flynns will stop at nothing!"

"Is there a problem here?" Ash attempted to step between the women.

The daintily attired fairy turned toward Ash. She assumed a Clint Eastwood–like stance and looked him up and down at least twice before she said, "Mind your own damn business, punk."

"That's it. I'm calling Clancy." Mona reached for her cell phone.

"Sure! Go ahead!" Sally's voice was so loud many people stopped to watch the altercation. "It's nothing but a monopoly on this island, anyway. Always has been. If you dare cross Mona Flynn, she'll go crying to her son, the big, bad policeman!"

Ash put his hand on the shiny fabric of the fairy's shoulder. "How about we—"

"I said, back the hell *off*!"

"I'm so sorry," Darinda said, looking at Ash with embarrassment. "It's kind of a long story. The Haven Cove Landowners Coalition is in favor of the development."

Ash nodded. "I only want to prevent anyone from getting hurt."

"Oh yeah?" The fairy looked up at Ash, tears of rage in her eyes. "It's a little late for that, I'm afraid, tourist guy!" She pointed at Mona. "This lady is holding everyone hostage. The only reason why we're all still scrounging and scraping for every dollar on this lonely rock is because Mona Flynn thinks she knows what's best for all of us, like we're imbeciles who can't make decisions for ourselves. In the meantime, people's lives are falling apart!"

Ash saw two uniformed police officers jog up toward the tent, hands on their billy clubs. Sure, he'd thought it might be fun to witness a fairy-versus-mermaid event, but he hadn't pictured it being quite this gritty. Once Ash was sure the police had the situation in hand, he stepped away and disappeared into the crowd.

It took him a moment to get his bearings. The whole concept of the Mermaid Island Resort now made him slightly nauseated. And though Ash had intended to find Rowan, what he needed now was open air and relative peace so he could sort out his uneasiness. He began to walk, realizing after the fact that he'd veered from the noise of Main Street and was headed to the docks. Instinct was sending him to the *Provenance*, because what he really needed was to be far out at sea, salt spray and wind on his face, slicing through the water with uncomplicated precision. He laughed at the irony of his situation—because he'd intentionally crippled his boat, that was the one thing he couldn't do.

Chapter Nine

"I appreciate your help, Zophie."

"Yez, yez!"

Rowan had to admit that the two of them had managed to communicate rather well in their three hours inside the Safe Haven booth. Liberal use of pointing, facial expressions, and basic charades had done the trick. So far, they'd sold about a hundred and fifty clambake raffle tickets, which would definitely help with costs. The B and B sponsored the event every year, and despite the steep cost of one hundred dollars per ticket, it had never been much of a moneymaker. It was never meant to be. Long before Rowan was born, the Flynns started the tradition as a way to welcome visitors to the Mermaid Festival. Over the years it became more elaborate—and costly—but her parents insisted on keeping up the custom. With a single ticket good for an all-you-can-eat seafood buffet with all the trimmings and up to four beers, there wasn't much room for profit, especially once all the other costs were factored in—liability insurance, the disc jockey, lighting, and the rental of tables and chairs.

Rowan once made the mistake of pointing out to her mother that if they endorsed this contrived, behemoth of an island "clambake," they might as well endorse the development deal. Mona nearly bit her head off. "This is tradition! It's one night during festival week—not every day and night of the tourist season!"

She sighed. Like everything else about festival week, Rowan tried her best to stay focused on the task at hand while her brain simply longed for the clambake to be over. In fact, her carrot-on-the-stick was the idea that at the stroke of noon on Friday, the closing ceremony would end the festival and the whole damn thing would be behind her.

"Prrehteh." Zophie touched the hem of Rowan's sleeveless blouse and smiled. "Many clohz today?"

It took a moment, but Rowan realized Zophie had noticed she'd changed clothes twice since breakfast. She laughed and nodded, a little embarrassed.

"Nize. For Mr. Vahllahz? Zo much hot, yez?"

Rowan noticed someone glance toward the booth and, in order to avoid Zophie's question, she waved her arms around to catch his attention. Never in her life had she been so happy to sell four raffle tickets. Once he'd gone, Rowan decided to keep Zophie occupied, hoping she'd forget the subject of Ash. So she told her to deliver the cash deposit bag across the street to Annie's shop, where the receipts would be locked away in the safe until day's end. Then Zophie could take her break.

Rowan pulled her cell from her skirt pocket and called Annie to give her the heads-up.

"Yep, she's coming in the door now. I'm waving her over to the cash register."

Rowan could tell her friend was frantically busy. "I appreciate it. Talk tonight, maybe."

"Wait! What did you decide with Poseidon?"

Rowan chuckled. Annie had the ability to wring every last drop out of even the lamest joke. "I think we're doin' the do over."

"Ohmigod! Wait. Hold on. Hold on." Rowan heard Annie speaking to Zophie for a moment before she resumed her squealing. "That's great! Wow! So when do we get to meet him? I'm dying!"

"Well, I'm thinking of inviting him to be my date to the clambake tomorrow. He asked me to dinner tonight, but I told him the restaurants were closed."

"He asked you to dinner? That's awesome!"

"Yeah. So what do you think of the clambake idea? Too much? Too soon?"

"It's perfect, Row. Seriously. Just relax and enjoy. Gotta go."

"Bye."

With a sigh, Rowan propped her butt on the high wooden stool and took a moment to relax. She should be pleased to see so many people crammed onto Main Street for Island Day, because she knew each body translated into income for the B and B, either directly or indirectly. She'd been schooled in the dynamics of microeconomics from early on. Once the fishery closed its doors, she'd watched her family and all Bayberry residents struggle to survive on tourism-related income alone, and there was an obvious lesson—if anyone here was going to make it, everyone had to work together. Islanders pitched in to paint the outside of a new restaurant because who knew? Maybe if it got off to a good start, a few more day-trippers would decide to get off the ferry and give it a try. While they were at it, they might pick up a Mermaid Festival brochure, wander into Annie's shop, and stop in the museum. They might even be interested enough to walk down the road a half mile until they came upon Rutherford Flynn's Safe Haven and its spectacular views of sea and sky.

Though the tourist season lasted only from May to September, every day of every year was spent in pursuit of the tourist dollar. Sure, the Internet and social media had put a technological spin on the marketing approach, but it didn't change the fact that the island's economy was about one thing: attracting visitors and convincing them to return.

Rowan knew that's why Mona didn't have many friends left on the island. Her mother's rabid opposition to the resort appeared at odds with that shared goal. Most seemed to agree that more money would make life easier for everyone involved, but Rowan wasn't entirely convinced it would make life better. Maybe her mother knew something she didn't.

Rowan wished she were wiser. She wished she knew the answer. For the time being, anyway, all she could do was give her best to the B and B, and by doing that, give her best to her family. She'd never been very good at having faith, but at this point she knew she had no other option—she was just going to have to believe things would work out the way they were supposed to.

"May I buy a raffle ticket?"

Rowan pasted a smile on her face and absently reached under the counter for the roll of printed tickets. She looked up and gasped.

Ash.

She'd blown it. Her plan had been to keep an eye out for him, fluff her hair, appear to be busy, then act pleasantly surprised when he arrived at her booth. Instead, she'd been daydreaming and had then become dorkishly alarmed to see him standing there. "Hi."

"Hi, Rowan. Are you busy?"

"No. Yes."

Ash placed his hands on the booth and leaned in. His sparkling eyes narrowed and he scrunched up his lips as he studied her, the way he might examine one of the taxidermy yellowfin tunas on display at the museum.

"You're a fascinating woman."

"Thank you. I think."

"Oh, it was definitely a compliment." She watched as his shoulders relaxed and his expression softened. "Look, before another minute goes by, I want to apologize for what happened in the carriage house the other night."

Because Ash kept his voice low, Rowan had to lean forward to hear him. At that close proximity, she could smell his skin—clean and hot in the summer air. But why was he apologizing?

"I don't know what I was thinking. It was completely wrong of me to take advantage of you like that, and I hope you can forgive me."

Wrong. Right. But what Rowan needed to clear up was why, exactly, he thought it wrong. Did he think it was inappropriate to jump into sex the way they had, when all she knew about him was his AmEx expiration date and all he knew about her was that she could be bribed? Or did he just regret it, period? Or . . . She felt her eyes go wide as the worst-case scenario dawned on her.

"You're married, aren't you?"

Ash pulled away, a look of surprise on his face. "Uh—"

"Oh my God!" Rowan cupped a hand over her mouth.

"No. No. Hold up. I am not married. Never have been."

Relief rushed through her, and she felt her hand fall away from her mouth. She thought she heard a whispered obscenity escape her lips, but then again, it might have been Ash's whispered obscenity. Regardless, she still needed to press the point further. "You're not involved with someone back home in Boston?"

"No, I'm not. Not for over a year."

Rowan didn't know what to say next, so she just sat

there like a doofus, her fingers still clutching a clambake raffle ticket.

"Why do you ask?" He let one corner of his mouth quirk up. "Are you forbidden to sell raffle tickets to men who aren't single? Is this a singles-only clambake?"

Rowan blinked and pulled herself together, giggling slightly. "No, I'm allowed to sell raffle tickets to anyone who's gullible enough to buy one. It's just that I'm not supposed to . . . you know . . ." She glanced around to be sure no one was eavesdropping. "I'm not supposed to *sleep* with the ones who are already spoken for. I'm kind of a stickler like that."

"Ahh." He leaned even closer. His lips were right next to her ear and his breath tickled her. "Technically, sweetheart, neither of us did any sleeping."

She turned to him so she could whisper her response. "It's all coming back to me now."

He breathed out the barest, softest laugh, so deep and sexual that Rowan did that gripping thing with her thighs again.

"So you'll sell me a raffle ticket?"

Rowan wasn't imagining things—Ash just gently bit down on her earlobe when he spoke. So she returned the favor, leaving a delicate kiss right behind his ear. "I won't sell you one."

"Why not?" He briefly flicked his tongue where he'd just bit her.

"Because you don't need one."

"Why is that?"

Rowan realized that she was squeezing her thighs so tightly she was in danger of cutting off the circulation to her lower extremities. "Because I'd like you to be my date to the clambake."

"Are you asking me out?"

"I am."

Ash began to pull back, and as he did so, he turned just enough that his lips got dangerously close to hers. She knew she was in trouble. If anyone were to see the notoriously imprudent tourist-loving Rowan Flynn kissing a festival-week visitor in the middle of Island Day, there might be some complications.

But Ash seemed to know better than to go too far, and he continued to draw back, smiling at her. He raised an eyebrow devilishly. "Run away with me, Rowan."

She nearly fell off the stool. *Run away with me, Rowan?* Of all the flirtatious and fun sentences he could have chosen from the English language—and there had to be thousands of those, right?—he chose the one that had nearly ruined her life! She stiffened. Then trembled. It was all she could do not to smack him. Or burst into tears.

Ash's eyes widened with alarm. "Oh my God." He swallowed hard. "I am so sorry for saying that."

She shook her head, still reeling, unable to reply. Besides, something bothered her about this whole exchange, tempting her to resurrect her wall of caution. But she couldn't put her finger on what it was . . .

Ash straightened, his expression serious. "What I meant was, well, obviously, I just said something I shouldn't have. I don't know what I've done to upset you, but I'm sorry."

"It's okay." Rowan took a deep breath and tried to smile. She'd overreacted. This was her issue, not his. He couldn't know how much his words hurt or why, so she couldn't be angry with him.

Still, something troubled her . . .

"I only wanted to ask if you'd like to get something to eat. Can you get away for a little bit?"

Rowan sensed her muscles relax. She felt bad for freaking out on him like that, for being paranoid. And now Ash looked so guilt-ridden that she was tempted to apologize to *him*. "I'd like that. As soon as Zophie gets back, I can take a break. Can you stop back in about a half hour?"

"Of course. See you then." Ash gave her a quick smile, shoved his hands in his pockets, and turned to go. Though he got swallowed by the crowd, his blond head bobbed along above most everyone else, making her smile.

The smile didn't last.

Damn you, Frederick. Rowan shook her head, as if that would get rid of the sour taste of fear on her tongue. She could not let that jerk hold her back, make her afraid of life. It was time to send him packing—once and for all. Silently, she told him how it was going to be.

You're not allowed to crush my happiness, got it? You don't get to decide what I feel or who I trust. I won't let you.

"Don't go anywhere! We'll announce our winner as soon as the judges calculate their scores!"

Ash hung back on the edge of the chili cook-off crowd, arms crossed over his chest, watching Frasier Flynn in action. The mayor obviously preferred double-grip handshakes. He seemed to enjoy patting people on the back, too. But Frasier doled out bear hugs and hearty laughter to a select group, people he seemed genuinely thrilled to see. From what Ash had been able to gather, the residents of Bayberry Island held their regular visitors close in their collective heart. The island's gregarious mayor was no exception.

The concept fascinated Ash, really. He wondered what it would be like to live in one place your entire life, a place with an unchanging seasonal rhythm, where tourists flowed in and out like the tides. He supposed it would allow you to share a history with people from all walks of life, people you would never meet otherwise. Just watching Frasier, Ash could tell he shared memories that stretched over decades with these tourists-turned-friends. He likely remembered what they looked like in their prime. He probably knew their struggles, their children and grandchildren, their achievements and disappointments.

Ash looked up to the summer sky and saw a solo cloud passing overhead, the only brushstroke on an endless blue canvas. Suddenly, the truth hit him. He hadn't seen it coming, but it stung and then spread hot and sad through his whole body—his life couldn't have been more different from the ones lived on Bayberry Island.

He smiled wistfully, trying his best to reach back and find even the smallest detail from his first few years, the ones he'd spent with his parents. Was there ever a flicker of the kind of belonging the Flynns took for granted, a belonging of place and people? It pained him that he couldn't remember, but he did know this—when he'd lost his parents, his world had shrunk. Ash's life became the surface friendships he made at boarding school, his grandfather, and the kindness of Brian Martin and his family. The Martins often took Ash along on trips, opened their home to him on holidays, and came to consider him one of their own. It was probably the greatest stroke of luck Ash ever got, because when he was just nineteen and a sophomore in college, Grandfather Louis passed away. Brian and his family became Ash's only anchor to the world. But that hadn't lasted, either.

Now Brian's brother, James, was the only one who remained. He was friendly enough and a competent chief executive officer, but the only time Ash saw him was at Oceanaire board meetings. James was ten years older than Brian and had his own wife and kids to focus on.

So where did that leave him? Ash knew his only

thread of connection was cut when Brian died. There was no one alive now who shared a history with him, knew his secrets, his weaknesses, his potential. There was no one he could turn to in times of trouble, no questions asked.

"Don't try number two, whatever you do. Dad said it nearly blew a hole through his esophagus."

Ash was startled, but he laughed at the familiar voice. He glanced over to see that Clancy now stood at his shoulder, watching Frasier glad-hand the crowd. The police chief kept his eyes focused ahead, nodding as he gave Ash the insider's guide to the Mermaid Festival Annual Chili Cook-off. "Number nine's got some kind of unidentifiable mushroom in it, and the judges are only pretending to taste it. Dad plans to pull it before the public gets samples."

Ash was surprised by this news. "You think they're poisonous?"

"Ah, hell no. But two years ago some bozo put magical mystery mushrooms in his entry, and half the judges were sure they saw dolphins on roller skates by the end of the day." Clancy winked. "But you can't go wrong with number one. It's been the winner for three years running."

"I see. Sounds like the fix is in."

Clancy chuckled. "Nah. That's not how we roll." Apparently, their short conversation had loosened up Clancy enough that he made eye contact with Ash. He smiled. "How's your boat?"

"I'm waiting for a new engine. Sully said he ordered it from a guy he knows on the Cape."

Clancy nodded in approval. "Probably old Clay Harwell in Hyannis. He'll set you up. So, you finding your way around all right?"

"I am, thanks."

"Anybody giving you a personal tour around the island?"

Now we're getting somewhere. Ash grinned at the lanky, dark-haired cop, thinking he was glad for another chance to chum it up. He genuinely liked Clancy, and of course, having his approval would make his job easier. Clancy could clear the way to getting closer to Rowan, and even Mona. "Are you asking me if I'm spending time with your sister?"

Clancy gave his gun holster a tug. Ash didn't miss the message. "Are you?"

As much as Ash enjoyed this banter, he knew he needed to stay as close to the truth as possible with Clancy. Anything less would set off alarms. He might be a small-town cop now, but Ash knew he'd spent eight years as a patrol officer on the Boston police force and surely knew bullshit when he heard it. "I'd like to spend time with Rowan, but she's been pretty busy. She told me I could take her around to grab a bite to eat in a little bit. Any suggestions?"

A frown appeared between Clancy's brows. "Suggestions for what?"

"What she might like to eat. Hey, if I hadn't run into you, I might have served her up a big bowl of number two."

Clancy laughed loudly, and it sounded a lot like his dad's guffaw. He then patted Ash on the back, which made him decide that the Flynn DNA was mighty strong stuff.

"You're all right, Wallace."

"Thanks."

"Ice cream."

Ash turned his full attention toward Clancy. "You mean to tell me that with all this food to choose from, she's going to want ice cream?"

Clancy raised his chin. "Trust me on this one."

That made Ash laugh. "Right. Let me guess—she's allergic. Or lactose intolerant."

Clancy shook his head. "No lie, man. I'm giving you a break here. If you fix Rowan up with some ice cream, she'll be happy. If you buy her a butter pecan hot fudge sundae, she'll start picking out your china pattern."

Ash nearly choked on his own spit, and Frasier was upon them before he could collect himself. Clancy had done that on purpose.

"Dad, this is Ashley Wallace the fourth."

"Ashton. The third."

Frasier clasped Ash's hand between his two beefy palms. "Nice to meet you, son. I hear you know a thing or two about old slate roofs. I'm impressed."

"Nice to meet you, Mayor."

Frasier slapped his back—a little too hard. Ash had the distinct impression he was being fucked with, by no fewer than two Flynn men at once.

The mayor dropped Ash's hand and sighed. He lowered his voice by a wide margin and spoke to both him and Clancy, his eyes scanning the crowd for eavesdroppers. "Jesus H., boys. These are the worst entries I ever tasted. I need a cold one to wash away the taste of what I swear is shark piss."

"So Ashley here wants to take Rowan on a date."

Frasier's head snapped around. He lowered his chin and locked his laser-sharp green eyes on Ash's. He was sure the mayor was going to tell him to watch his back, but Frasier just laughed. "You got any set plans?"

"Well—"

"Get her ice cream."

Clancy held his hands out. "See? Did I tell you I was giving it to you straight, or what?"

"Oh, it's true." Frasier's eyes crinkled up with his

smile. "The girl can go through a pint of Ben & Jerry's like nobody's business. Now, with that said . . ."

Frasier clamped a big hand on Ash's shoulder, the same kind of warning grip he'd placed on Clancy for the family photo on Rowan's mantel.

"My daughter's been through a lot lately, so you treat her right and you'll have no quarrel with me."

Ash glanced toward Clancy and noted that his smile looked a little too gleeful.

"Well, sir, then I should be going. I promised Rowan I'd meet her at the booth about now."

Frasier nodded and shook his hand again. "Ice cream. Don't forget the ice cream."

Clancy wagged his eyebrows. "Butter pecan sundae, man. I'm telling you straight up."

"See you soon, gentlemen. It's been a pleasure, Frasier."

Ash probably should have been pissed at the display of territorial testosterone he'd just been subjected to. Under any other circumstance, he'd have met the two of them jab for jab. But he wasn't some schmo looking for approval from a girl's father and brother. Ash had a job to do: worm his way into the Flynns' good graces and get them to sell. That was the whole reason he was here. And so far, the events of the day had brought him a lot closer to his goal. He decided to review the checklist of accomplishments in his head.

Had he made contact with Mona again and started a dialogue about the resort? Yes, he had.

Had he met Frasier and managed to get Clancy to relax a bit? Yes, and yes.

Was he about to woo Rowan with ice cream and, as a bonus, had she invited him to join her at the clambake? Oh yes.

Ash shoved his hands into his pockets and strolled into the middle of Main Street again, wondering why—if everything was going so great—he felt as if he were on the verge of disaster.

"You've got more hot fudge on your chin, Miss Flynn." Ash leaned in and used the tip of his hot and silky tongue to scoop it up, then smacked his lips dramatically. When he laughed, Rowan realized she must be looking at him with giant, bugged-out eyes.

Her plastic spoon hovered in midair. It hung there a few seconds too many, and a blob of butter pecan, fudge, and whipped cream melted enough to fall onto her left thigh. From there it skidded down the inside of her leg to the weathered boards of the dock where she and Ash were perched.

"Now you've got some between your legs."

"I've got a napkin."

"And I've got a—"

"I know exactly what you've got."

Ash tipped his head back and laughed, laughed, and laughed some more.

Rowan bit the inside of her cheek to keep from joining in, then set her cup of melting ice cream on the dock. Ash had been a lot of fun on this little outing. Incredibly sweet and flirty. Ballsy, really. He seemed to have no shortage of confidence. Rowan wouldn't lie to herself—she found the combination of wit, playfulness, and bravado completely intoxicating. After only twenty minutes in his company, she felt drunk on it. Of course, the sugar hadn't hurt, either.

"You're wrong, you know."

Rowan crumpled up the sticky napkin and shoved it into the ice-cream cup. "About what?"

"You don't know the extent of what I've got."

She shook her head and chuckled. "Does this routine work on most women?"

Ash gave her a crooked grin but didn't reply, and Rowan realized just how stupid her question was—of course it worked. This man was so gorgeous that even if he were a complete tool he could have most any woman he wanted.

"I wouldn't know." His smiled faded and his voice went soft. "I've never tried it before."

It was her turn to burst out laughing. "Yeah, right."

"No. I'm serious." Ash reached over and grabbed her sticky hand, lacing his fingers with hers. "I've never been in this situation, to tell you the truth. I've never done things so totally ass-backward and been forced to retrace my steps and dig myself out of a hole."

"You're in a hole?"

"I'm in deep."

"Hmm." Rowan glanced down at their entwined hands. The skin on his forearm, wrist, and back of his hand was tanned, covered in a dusting of sun-bleached hair. He had long, elegant fingers, and she could feel the hint of calluses on his palm. "So how are you going to get yourself out? I mean, in addition to the ice-cream sundae, which was a stroke of genius."

He chuckled. "Well, we've already taken the most important step—we're talking. The way you stormed out of your apartment, I thought you'd never speak to me again. In fact, it seems like I'm getting to chat it up with the whole Flynn family today."

Rowan unlaced her fingers from Ash's and tried to keep her frown at bay. "You are?"

"Yes. I ran into Clancy at the chili cook-off and he introduced me to your father. And right before that, I spent some time with your mother. She's very determined to fight those resort plans, isn't she?"

Rowan leaned away. Ash seemed pleasant enough, but she suspected his encounter with Mona had been a lot more intense than he was letting on. "Did she molest you with facts and figures? Browbeat you into signing petitions? Make you want to run away screaming?"

"Pretty much."

Rowan laughed then sighed, looking out past the marina to the ocean. "She's obsessed with the resort. It drives all of us crazy. I know she doesn't want to sell the Safe Haven, but lately she's been totally focused on the environmental impact study, claiming it was fixed or something. Honestly, if the developer would just do another one, it might take some of the fight out of her. Sometimes . . ." She let her voice trail off. She heard herself sigh again. "Sometimes I wish she'd just give up. Agree to sell. It would make everyone's life so much easier and . . . oh. I think I just ruined the moment. I'm sorry about that."

Ash slipped his arm around Rowan's waist, pulling close enough that their hips touched. She slowly raised her eyes to his, and *bam*! It was thigh-squeezing time. She let out a little whimper.

"Is this okay? Am I being too forward?"

Rowan laughed. "You're being backward, remember? Digging yourself out of a hole? I told my friend Annie about you, and she recommended I do the same, just start from scratch with you. She called it a 'do over.'"

Ash frowned a little. "You don't have anything to do over, Rowan. It was my fault."

"It was no one's fault." Rowan put a little more room between them and looked up into Ash's face. "We're both grown-ups, you know. I'm thirty years old and you're . . . ?"

"Thirty-four."

"The point is I should know better." She sighed. "Look, it was probably a combination of things. My last relationship ended about two years ago, and it ended badly. I haven't been with a man since."

"That's a long time."

"*Yep.* So when you were there all naked and wet and slammed into me in the dark and everything, I didn't have my defenses up."

Ash nodded. "I wasn't exactly expecting company."

"I yelled for you, but you didn't answer."

"I couldn't hear anything but the storm, but that's no excuse."

"I should have jumped up and got out of there."

"And I should have let you. No, I should have *insisted* that you do that."

"So why didn't that happen, Ash? Why didn't I try to leave and why didn't you make sure I left?"

He shook his head. "Honestly, I don't know. I was on autopilot, and I'm not just talking about the normal way men are on autopilot, either. It was almost like I had no choice but to completely ravish you."

"Yeah." Rowan looked away and stared at the lapping water of the marina slip, where, just feet away, Ash's beautiful sailboat was tied up and rocking gently. "I guess we ravished each other. That would make it a mutually inappropriate ravishing. We're both to blame."

"Rowan." Ash reached across his body and used his fingertips to tilt her chin. He looked down into her eyes. "There's no blame, okay? It just *happened*. You are a very special woman . . ."

She straightened. "Is there a 'but' coming?"

Ash shook his head. "No 'but' except that it's really a miracle that we ever met at all. We probably never would have crossed paths if it weren't for the storm."

"Probably not." When Ash stroked the side of her

face, Rowan leaned into his touch. If she were a cat, she'd be purring.

"But I got lucky. I've been given the opportunity to know you, and I plan to take advantage of it. I want to learn who you are and how you got so smart and beautiful and funny." Ash tugged on her chin and locked his eyes with hers once more. "Will you let me?"

Rowan blinked. Oh God, she knew exactly what was happening here—she was being seduced. And why not? Ash was right—she was smart and funny, and maybe even beautiful, though it had been so long since a man had said as much that she couldn't be sure. Of course she'd never needed a man in order to survive, and she didn't now, but it certainly felt good to hear someone tell her she was wonderful.

She'd been starving for it.

"So? Are you going to let me?"

Rowan came out of her private revelry. "Of course, Ash. As long as you let me get to know you, too."

The tiniest flash of something changed in Ash's expression. Rowan thought it might have been alarm, but then she thought, *That can't be right,* and he bent down and placed his lips on hers and every thought vanished from her head.

His lips were soft, tender, and seeking as they slid over hers. This kiss was nothing like the ones they'd shared in the dark, on the floor of the carriage house. Those kisses had been shouts. This kiss was a whisper. The carriage house kisses had been exclamation points. This kiss was a question mark. Those were off the chain. This was pure tenderness.

This kiss was the bomb.

Because Ash was kissing *her* this time, not some anonymous woman in a storm. He wanted to know

Rowan Flynn. He thought she was beautiful, funny, and smart.

Rowan turned her body to his, slipped her arms around his neck, and offered herself up to the seduction.

Ash wasn't Frederick. He deserved a fair chance. Besides, what was the worst that could happen?

"What the hell did I just do?"

Ash tossed his smartphone to the table and glanced around Rowan's apartment, the dread ripping through him. He was disgusted with himself. He'd just left a message on Jerrod Jessop's voice mail, telling him that Mona Flynn might cave if he'd simply arrange for another environmental assessment. And with that, he'd officially betrayed Rowan and her family.

So now what?

Ash squeezed his eyes shut and raked his hands through his hair. He couldn't continue with this charade. He had intended for the Mermaid Island project to be his last assignment as a closer. But on the walk back to the Safe Haven, Ash realized he'd misjudged both his appetite for this particular job and this kind of work in general. And after making that call to Jessop, he knew he couldn't do it. He'd barely started this job and he was done. He would resign immediately, before he could do any more harm to the Flynns. The last thing he wanted to do was explain himself to Jessop over the phone, however. This was business and his lawyer would take care of returning his retainer and canceling his contract. That's what lawyers were for.

During the ten-minute walk back from town, it started to occur to him what had been bothering him all day. It was the Flynns. It was this island. It was the realization that what he was hired to do to this family and this place was wrong. More than anything, it was Rowan. Just moments ago on the dock, when she'd wrapped her delicate arms around his neck and he felt her melt against him, he wondered if he could live with himself if he continued to mislead her. Frasier had said she'd been through a lot. Of course she didn't deserve this. She didn't deserve another betrayal.

How had he not seen this? How was it that he'd spent weeks researching the Flynns and Bayberry Island in order to make a tactical strike and never *once* had he seen the human beings involved? They'd been stick figures to him, weaknesses to exploit. Not real people.

What the hell was *wrong* with him?

Ash went into the bedroom, glanced nervously at the mermaid painting of Rowan, then grabbed the iPad from his duffel. He fell into the bed and began to compose a message that would serve as his letter of resignation.

It took only a few minutes, and after he sent the e-mail to Jerrod Jessop, he clasped his hands behind his head and fell back into Rowan's comfortable pillows. He gave himself permission to study the painting, really taking his time to analyze the bend of her elbow, the heart shape of her face, and the way the left corner of her mouth quirked up when she smiled. He noted the shallow dimple of her belly button, the smooth curve of her hip, the way her breasts spilled out from their shells.

Even as he smiled, a knot of sadness formed in his chest.

Rowan Flynn was so much more than the video clips and the newspaper articles revealed. The truth was, she smelled like sugar and fresh air. She made him laugh and touched his heart. She was flat-out adorable, with that faint splash of freckles across her nose, shiny hair, and those gorgeous sea-green eyes.

She wore her heart on her sleeve. Her kisses were re-markable—a perfect combination of heat and silky sweetness.

And she trusted him.

Ash stared up at the slow whir of the bedroom ceiling fan. He knew he had no other choice. He needed to leave Bayberry Island the second the *Provenance* was repaired. He had no idea what he was capable of in a relationship, because he'd never been in love enough to want to find out. But he did know this: Rowan deserved better. She was a beautiful and sweet woman who'd had her heart ripped out by a lying scumbag. The last thing she needed in her life was a man who had been less than up front with her from the start, a man who had no idea if he could stick around long enough to learn how to love her.

He'd already gone too far. His careless words had hurt her, and he couldn't live with that. *Run away with me, Rowan?* Had he really been that insensitive? Of course he knew that had been Frederick Theissen's game. But he hadn't been thinking of Frederick when he said those words—he hadn't been thinking at all, just *feeling*. He would do well to remind himself that he hadn't come to Bayberry to feel anything. He'd come to close a business deal.

It wouldn't take long for Rowan to forget him, and though she might be pissed off or temporarily sad, she'd get over it. And she'd never know the deadly bullet she'd dodged.

It was the kindest thing Ash could do for her.

Chapter Ten

His hands gripped Rowan's flesh. She couldn't get close enough to his naked body, and Ash couldn't get deep enough into hers. She heard herself moan and cry out and she was lost, drowning, falling . . . And the thunder! It pounded the earth over and over and over, keeping time with the way Ash took her . . . *ravished* her.

Thudding. Pounding. Throbbing.

"Rowan! Wake *up*!"

She jolted to a sitting position, blinking, not having the faintest idea where she was. What kind of room was this? Cardboard boxes? A steeply pitched ceiling? Were those toilet paper rolls she saw stacked against the wall? Why wasn't she in her own bed?

"Rowan!"

"Oh hell!" She threw the sheet off, jumped from the cot, and pulled on a pair of shorts. She started apologizing even before she got to the door. "Sorry, Mellie! I overslept!"

Imelda stood in the narrow third-floor hallway, her lips pursed tightly. She seemed in no mood for excuses.

"What time is it?" Rowan rubbed her itchy nose and ran her fingers through her hair.

"It's exactly an hour before twenty-seven hungry people begin showing up for breakfast."

Rowan gasped. "It's six o'clock? Oh my God! My cell phone alarm didn't go off!"

"I worry about you." Imelda shook her head.

"I'm fine. Just let me get my shoes on."

She raised an eyebrow. "You might want to wear a shirt and a bra, too, unless you plan on scandalizing yourself."

Little late on that one.

Rowan looked down at herself and saw the stretched-out camisole she'd worn to bed last night. Then a flash of the NC-17 dream she'd been having raced through her brain, and she gasped again.

"Are you all right?"

"Of course." Rowan smiled reassuringly. "I think I was having a strange dream."

Imelda turned on her heel and marched toward the back staircase. "Breakfast service is going to be a strange nightmare if you don't get down there soon."

"Coming!"

Five minutes later, Rowan entered the kitchen via the door near the butler's pantry. Imelda was at the stove, her back to Rowan. So she tiptoed toward the coffeepot, hoping to at least get one good gulp before Imelda started in on her again. Rowan reached into the tall glass-front cabinet without making a sound, gently picked up a mug, and added a splash of cream. Just another couple of seconds and the coffee would be flowing past her lips.

"How much have you learned about him?"

Rowan lunged forward so the coffee dribbling down her chin wouldn't stain her shirt. She grabbed a paper towel and wiped her face.

"Him who?"

"Our handsome guest. Mr. Wallace. The one who's got you acting so out of sorts."

"I'm not out of sorts."

Imelda made a clucking sound.

Rowan tied an apron around her waist and started setting out the chafing dishes, serving utensils, and heating elements for the buffet. "Anyway, I've just started to get to know him a little bit. We're talking. Enjoying each other's company. It's nothing."

Imelda remained quiet.

"But so far he seems very nice." Rowan reached into the industrial-sized refrigerator and grabbed the five-pound package of bacon, quickly slapping the strips onto two large baking sheets. She popped them into the double ovens Imelda had already preheated, washed her hands in hot, soapy water, then pulled out the commercial mixer. "Waffles, right?"

"It's Monday, Rowan. We serve pancakes on Monday. We've been serving pancakes on Mondays for the last twenty-five years."

"Jeesh, it's Monday already? I've lost track."

"Uh-huh."

"I'm stressed out, Mellie. This is only the second festival week I've been responsible for. There's a lot on my mind."

"I can see that." Imelda glanced over her shoulder and Rowan was relieved to see she looked more amused than disapproving. "You're doing a great job, honey girl. You're handling the business end of things, which I know isn't easy. You've been great with the summer help. And you've been an angel to help me out in the kitchen. Everyone's very proud of you. But I see you every day, and I see what's going on. I only want you to be careful."

"Don't worry. Really."

Just then, the maids filed through the swinging door, and Rowan was relieved she didn't have to continue with Imelda's preferred topic of discussion. After everyone shared their morning greetings with Rowan, they set about gathering flatware, glassware, and tablecloths, or filling juice and milk pitchers, cereal containers, or baskets of baked goods.

While she prepared the pancake batter, Rowan observed her staff. She was impressed with how the four seasonal employees worked together seamlessly, their breakfast shift running like a fine-tuned assembly line. Despite the language issues everyone had faced that summer, each girl had grown sure of her responsibilities, the order in which things needed to be accomplished, and how long each task would take. It always seemed to go this way—as soon as everyone had perfected their jobs, the tourist season drew to a close and it was time to let them go. Rowan wished there was a way she could justify keeping them on a little longer, at least so they could earn income until their visas were up. But that wasn't an option.

The first guests wandered in at seven on the dot, and the table turnover seemed slower than usual, which meant the dining room was packed to the rafters by nine o'clock. Since friendships had been formed among guests by now—both the regulars and the first timers—many decided to linger over coffee and chat about their lives back home and their plans for the day. Of course Rowan was pleased to see everyone enjoying themselves and couldn't shoo them out, so when Ash arrived about nine fifteen, there was nowhere for him to sit.

She was refilling the fresh fruit when he appeared in the doorway to the front hall. She looked up and couldn't help herself—she smiled so hard she thought she might sprain her cheeks. He smiled back with the same enthusiasm.

In movies and books, Rowan had often heard fictional characters say that falling in love made them feel like a kid again, the way they'd felt in high school. She'd never been able to identify with that. There had been thirty-two kids in her senior class, eleven of whom were boys. Of those, only three were even remotely cute, and only two of those liked girls. And even then, she'd known those boys since before kindergarten. It wasn't exactly a breeding ground for romance.

That phase of Rowan's life didn't start until she showed up as a freshman at Tufts. She went on to date several guys before graduation and there had been several more since, but it was safe to say that in all her dating experience, she'd never had the kind of reaction she was having right then, with Ash.

As she saw him standing in the doorway, head tilted slightly and hands shoved into the pockets of his preppy shorts, she felt a little thrill course through her. Nervous knots began to form in her belly, and a lifting, buoyant feeling filled her chest. She wanted to laugh and dance and throw herself into his arms.

Fortunately, the huge bowl of honeydew melon slices balanced in her hands kept her from public humiliation.

Ash walked toward her. "Good morning, Miss Flynn." His voice came across as friendly—but not overly so. To anyone overhearing his greeting, it would seem he and Rowan were courteous strangers. Oh, but she knew better.

They had parted ways late yesterday afternoon, agreeing they'd had a wonderful time hanging out and eating ice cream. Their last kiss was one Rowan wouldn't be forgetting anytime soon. While standing next to his boat, Ash had wrapped his arms around her and lifted her feet off the dock. He managed to hold her up with one arm while he shoved his hand into her hair and kissed the living hell out of her. When the kiss ended, Rowan felt goofy-happy. She staggered back to the Safe Haven booth drunk on endorphins.

Was it any wonder she'd fallen victim to a sex dream last night?

"Should I come back a little later?"

Rowan shook her head slowly. "Of course not. In fact . . ." She lowered her voice to a whisper. "Why don't you make yourself a plate and I'll escort you to our VIP dining room."

Ash looked surprised. "You have one of those?"

"We do now."

A few moments later, Rowan sat at the small table on the side porch, smiling as she watched Ash finish his second helping of pancakes and bacon. Seeing him enjoy her cooking sparked some kind of bizarre sense of pride in her, which was a first. When she'd lived with Frederick in Manhattan, she'd never cooked. They ate out or ordered in almost every night. Only now did Rowan realize how empty that had felt to her. Maybe one day, after festival week was over, she'd prepare a romantic dinner for the two of them. Or a picnic they could take to the beach.

"What are you thinking over there?" Ash leaned back in the small porch chair, one arm draped over the back. He looked happy and full.

Rowan shrugged, a little embarrassed that she'd been fantasizing about a future with Ash that extended beyond this week, or even beyond this breakfast. After all, he would be leaving as soon as his boat was repaired. "Oh, nothing much. I was just wondering what you like to eat and whether it was in my culinary repertoire."

He grinned. "I never would've pegged you for a woman with a repertoire."

"Ha. That shows how little you know me." Those words were intended to sound like witty chitchat, but Rowan realized they had weight to them. The truth was, he didn't know her all that much, and she didn't know him. In fact, maybe Imelda had hit on something that morning when she'd asked how much Rowan had learned about their handsome guest.

"What would you like me to know about you, Rowan?"

"You mean in addition to the fact that I'm smart, funny, and beautiful?"

"I've got that part memorized." Ash tapped the side of his head, which made Rowan laugh. He stood then and reached out for her hand. "Can you sit and talk for a minute?"

"Sure."

She smiled as Ash led her to the love magnet, then put his arm on the back of the glider. He immediately set it in motion, a slow and soothing back-and-forth—with an annoying squeak. "This is a real classic," he said, patting the smooth metal of the armrest. "My grandfather had one of these at his house."

"In Boston?" Rowan snuggled up against him and let her head rest against his arm. She knew Imelda was probably wondering where she'd disappeared to, maybe even cussing under her breath in Portuguese. Rowan decided to allow herself fifteen minutes before she went back to work.

"Yes, Boston." The tone of Ash's voice had changed. He'd gone from loose and comfortable to wary, so Rowan glanced up at him. His face was tight.

She sat up. "We don't have to talk about your family if you'd rather not. Let's start with me. What have you been dying to know about me?"

Ash smiled at her, aware she'd changed the subject for his benefit. He seemed appreciative. "How about we compromise? You tell me something about you and then I tell you something about me."

"Deal." Rowan folded one foot under her and took a breath. "My last relationship ended two years ago. His name was Frederick, and I met him here when I came home to help out during festival week. He was quite charming, and he charmed me into moving in with him in New York. It went downhill from there."

"I'm sorry to hear that." He nodded gravely. "My last relationship ended a year ago. Nanette and I had been together for three years when she moved to San Francisco for work. The relationship wasn't what either of us hoped for, so it ended amicably."

"What had you hoped for?"

Ash shrugged and lowered his eyes. His dark blond lashes hid his expression. "I wanted the love of a gorgeous, brilliant woman with impeccable taste."

That made Rowan laugh. "Who doesn't? So it turned out she wasn't those things?"

He looked up. "She was every one of those things—except she didn't love me and I didn't love her. Unfortunately, I was so blinded by *what* she was that it took me far too long to see *who* she was."

She let that information sink in for a moment. Of course a man like Ash would want a woman like Nanette. And it was impossible to ignore the obvious; Rowan wasn't the Nanette type. She knew she needed to keep this conversation moving so she didn't appear insecure. Nanette probably wasn't insecure.

"Well, I'm the youngest of three kids. My brother Clancy, you met, and my other brother, Duncan, is a Navy SEAL on active duty. My mom is a retired school principal, and my dad has been mayor of the island since the fishery closed."

"I know all those things."

"You do?"

"Of course. I'm staying in your apartment. I've seen the photos. Plus I spoke to both your mother and father on Island Day."

Rowan snorted. "Then I don't have to tell you how, uh, *eccentric* everyone is. If you can believe it, we're not half as nuts as the Flynns of a few generations ago."

"I know about that, too."

Rowan leaned back in surprise. "Have you been investigating us or something? Are you with the IRS?"

Ash laughed and shook his head. "I got one word for you, sweetheart."

She frowned. "Ookay."

"Brochures."

Rowan giggled. "Hey, don't hate. Brochures really are a time-saver, you know. It gets old answering the same questions all day every day, and it's easier just to point to the display rack of brochures."

Ash's eyes crinkled up as she talked. He seemed to be enjoying their time on the love magnet. "I've read all about Ruthie and his mermaid wife, too," he added.

"Great."

He touched the side of her face with his fingertips and let his gaze drop to her lips. "Do you believe in the mermaid legend?"

It was an innocent enough question. After all, they were getting to know each other, and if she were Ash, she'd want to know if the woman on the glider with him was tragically insane. "No. I do not." She decided to keep things moving. "Did you get a chance to read my mother's brochure?"

Ash's body stiffened at the question. His reaction had been barely noticeable, but Rowan had learned to read him.

"Not yet, but I will the first opportunity I get." Ash was always so diplomatic.

Rowan glanced down at her hands. "You've probably heard about my family by now, that we're the only holdout, and everyone else who owns land on the cove is plenty angry."

Ash nodded, listening.

"Wait. That's not technically accurate—it's just my *mother* who's the holdout, along with a few of her brow-beaten friends. Honestly, if it were up to me, I'd sell to the developers right now. My dad wants to sell, too, and my parents fought so much over it that they ended up separated. Clancy is on the fence—he sees things through a law-enforcement perspective and worries about the gambling element. And Duncan doesn't care. He's doesn't give a damn about the island."

Rowan noticed that one of Ash's eyebrows had arched high. She must have said too much. "Sorry for rambling."

He reached for her hand and held it with both his. The feel of his warmth and strength was soothing to her, and she took a deep breath.

"I know firsthand that money—the lure of it—can do a lot of damage." Ash seemed pensive. "I've spent all of my adult life chasing money, telling myself that it was never enough. But I've recently learned that money is just money. It's not what really matters. It isn't real."

Rowan snorted. "I'd *love* to learn that lesson. I'm up close and personal with so much 'real' shit—broken ce-dar shingles, crumbling tuck-pointing, a bum roof, ineffi-cient windows, iffy air-conditioning, peeling paint, splintering wood—"

Rowan stopped herself. She closed her eyes in em-barrassment. "Wow. I'm really sorry. Let's talk about something else." She pasted on a pleasant smile. "So. I got my bachelor's in education and a master's in psy-chology from Tufts."

"I know that, too—the diplomas on your wall."

"Oh jeesh. Okay. Clearly I'm at a disadvantage here, since I'm not living in *your* apartment. So how about you? Tell me about your consulting business. Your family."

Ash shifted his weight in the glider and blew air from his lips, like his answer was going to be complicated.

"If you want," Rowan added.

He leaned in and kissed her cheek, as if to reassure her. "I'm happy to. I grew up in Boston and attended boarding school, then went to Harvard and Harvard business school. Both my parents were Harvard graduates." He stopped there, self-conscious.

Rowan decided to make it easier on him. "That's not much of a shocker, Ash. I figured you for a blue-blooded T-fer the minute you whipped out your black credit card."

Ash looked stunned, then burst out laughing. "So much for going incognito, huh?" He kissed her again, this time on the lips. It was a peck, but a sweet peck. "So, anyway, I worked in the banking industry for a few years and then started my own consulting business. I—" Ash stopped. "It's pretty boring stuff. I act as a middleman between large corporations and investments they might be interested in—real estate, mostly. But I've recently started working for a nonprofit foundation called Ocean-aire. Our focus is marine conservation and education."

"That sounds wonderful."

"I'm enjoying it. So what did you do before you moved here from New York?"

"I worked for a headhunter in Boston for many years, in the secondary education market—you know, deans and provosts and stuff. Then when I moved to New York with Frederick, I joined the same kind of company there." She shrugged.

Ash seemed to be waiting for more details, which wasn't something Rowan wanted to give. She didn't want to waste another second talking about Frederick. So she changed the subject.

"Okay, so, my best friend is Annie Parker—I told you about her. She owns a tourist shop on the Main Street boardwalk."

"I think I was in her place the other day. I bought a sweatshirt and some of her, you know, special chocolate."

Rowan laughed. "Seriously? Well, she'll be here for the clambake tonight with her fiancé, Nat, so you'll get to meet them. I mean"—maybe Rowan was being presumptuous—"if we're still on for tonight."

His eyes widened. "Of course. I look forward to it. I meant to ask you—do I have to wear a costume?"

"A costume?"

Ash frowned. "Yes. Look, I'll just come right out and say this—I'm not a costume guy. I've noticed that everybody wears costumes to everything around here, so . . ."

Rowan couldn't help but laugh. "I guess you have a point, but no. The clambake is a costume-free zone."

"I'm relieved. I thought I was going to have to wear a set of waterproof coveralls and an eye patch or something."

"As much as I'd like to see you in the eye patch, what you've got on right now would be fine. Just bring a sweater. It can get cool on the beach at night." She smiled at him. "Have I told you that you make me laugh?"

"That's a good thing?"

"A very good thing." It was her turn to kiss him, and she stretched up until her lips found his. Her kiss was also in the peck category, but she stayed a second or two longer than necessary. God, did she love his kisses.

Rowan had a silly grin on her face when it was over, but she saw no reason to hide it. "So how about you? Who's your best friend?"

The glider stopped. They'd been so wrapped up in their conversation that Rowan hadn't even realized they were still moving. He didn't answer her question. Obviously, he was willing to discuss some things, but not everything. The ex-girlfriend had been fair game, as was school and work, but anything related to his family—and now his best friend—seemed to be off-limits. Rowan figured he'd had enough getting-to-know-you time.

"It's okay, Ash. I should probably get back to work."

"Stay." He grabbed her hand tighter. "It's . . . well, my family isn't—it *wasn't*—like yours. I had a very different experience."

Rowan tucked her chin toward her chest and looked up at him. "Is this a polite way of saying you don't come from a long line of Mermaid-worshipping head cases?"

Ash laughed, pulling her close again. "That's not at all what I'm saying. Since I've been here on Bayberry, I've been thinking about how my life seems . . . I don't know . . . *dry* compared to yours, I guess."

"Dry?"

"Well, yes. You have two parents and two brothers and a lifelong best friend. You have history here on the island, a place where you will always belong, no matter what. I've always been more of a . . . I suppose you could call me a loner."

Rowan decided to stay where she was, snuggled into the side of his body, and let him talk. It took a moment for him to continue.

"I was an only child, and my parents died when I was six. I went to live with my grandfather, who raised me."

Rowan's body went still. She had no idea how to respond to that, so she opted to stay silent.

"They were young, in their late thirties, and they'd traveled to Kenya for a safari to celebrate their tenth anniversary. There was a flash flood and they were washed away. Their bodies and the body of their driver weren't found for weeks."

Rowan closed her eyes. She continued to hear the rhythm of the sea, birdsong, and the beat of her own heart, so that's how she knew the world was still intact. But it might have skipped a breath in sympathy—such loss at that age was impossible to imagine. The pain and confusion must have been crushing for him. "Ash, I'm so very sorry."

"It was a long time ago." The glider began its back-and-forth movement again, and he pulled her even tighter to his side. "Grandfather Louis was a wonderful man, very principled, a typical stoic New Englander. He was all about work and honor. I wasn't always easy to deal with when I got to my teenage years. No, let me rephrase that." He chuckled slightly. "I was a complete *ass*. And we butted heads a lot. He died when I was nineteen, a sophomore at Harvard."

"That's so sad, Ash."

"It was. But my saving grace was my best friend, Brian Martin, and his family. They kind of took me under their wing and made me an honorary member of the family. I met Brian in boarding school, and we went to Harvard together."

Rowan's heart lifted—Ash had a best friend! She knew how crucial that was when life got rough.

Ash laughed uncomfortably. "You know, this all sounds so tragic when I say it out loud, but Brian died six months ago. He was in a private plane doing research for Oceanaire when it went down off the coast of Nova Scotia. It's been . . . it's hard for me."

Rowan's limbs felt lifeless and heavy. Her cheeks went hot. She pushed herself up to look in Ash's face, but he stared blankly out toward the grounds. Since she didn't have any words that would possibly make a difference, she laced her fingers in his.

"Thank you," Ash said.

They sat like that in silence, rocking back and forth, the squeak of the love magnet moving in time with the breathing of the sea. All Rowan could think was that she had no idea how one person could absorb so much loss. It seemed like Ash's entire life had been about loss. No wonder he felt like a loner.

"Ah, there you are."

Rowan bolted up from the old glider so fast it slammed against the side of the house with a *crack*! Ash stood seconds later.

"Good morning." Imelda looked Ash up and down, frowning.

Rowan regrouped quickly. There was nothing for her to be embarrassed about, after all. They'd just been talking.

"Ash, this is Imelda Silva, the only member of the family you haven't met. She's the boss around here." Rowan grabbed Imelda's hand and coaxed her out from the doorway. "Mellie, meet Ash Wallace."

"A pleasure, Ms. Silva." Ash extended his hand gallantly, no hint of solemnness in his expression. It was startling how quickly he'd switched gears. Being a female, Mellie couldn't stay grumpy for long in his presence.

"Hello, Mr. Wallace. Are you enjoying your stay?"

"I am, thank you." He gave her one of his heart-melting grins. "If those blueberry and cranberry scones are your creation, I should be bowing at your feet."

"*Meu Deus*." Imelda's cheeks flushed, but she collected herself. "I do need your help, Rowan."

"Of course. I'll be right there."

Imelda headed back into the house, but smiled over her shoulder at Ash.

Rowan turned toward him. She took both his hands in hers and looked up into his eyes. He offered her a sad smile but held tight to his emotions. Rowan was stunned. She didn't know how a person could carry all that sadness and still be standing, let alone functioning in the world.

"You deserve happiness." Rowan thought her words must sound puny and obvious in the face of everything he'd just shared, but that was all that kept going through her brain—it was time for him to be happy.

He leaned down and kissed Rowan gently, resting his forehead against hers as he stroked her hair. "You deserve to be happy, too, sweet Rowan." Then Ash pulled away and smiled. "You'd better get back to work. I don't want to be on Imelda's bad side."

"Okay." Rowan's knees felt wobbly as she turned to go, as if she'd taken on some of the weight of Ash's sadness. Suddenly, her own tribulations seemed minor. "See you about six. On the beach, okay?"

"I wouldn't miss it for anything."

Chapter Eleven

To: Jerrod Jessop
From: Ashton Louis Wallace III
Subject: Mermaid Island

Jerrod,

I am writing to inform you that I can no longer offer my services to Jessop-Riley and am resigning from the Mermaid Island job immediately. My reasons are of a personal nature. I understand this is sudden, and I will be happy to refund my retainer as well as any expenses your firm may have incurred on my behalf to this point. When my attorney returns from vacation, I will ask him to contact you regarding the terms of our contract and any punitive damages you may seek. I regret any inconvenience my withdrawal from the project may cause you.

I wish you the best in all your endeavors. Please note that I will be ending all my consulting work, effective immediately, and closing my office. Feel free to contact my attorney if you have any further questions, as I will not be available to speak on the phone.

Best regards,
Ash

Kathryn Hilsom sat back in her desk chair and read the e-mail again, just to be sure she hadn't been hallucinating first thing on this Monday morning. When she was certain she'd read correctly, she giggled like a girl.

This was a godsend. It was true that she'd spent the last three months hating Ash Wallace with every breath she took, but right now she wished she could kiss the man. He was just . . . gone! Out of the picture! She didn't have to do a thing! She wished she could thank him for his impeccable timing—he'd burned out just as she was ready to shine.

Kathryn jumped from her desk, checked her reflection in the mirror behind her office door, and grabbed her suit jacket from the stand. As she smoothed the fabric over her hips, she took a moment to give herself a little pep talk.

This was it. This was her moment. She would finally get an opportunity to use all the untapped people skills and business acumen in her professional arsenal. She would go to Bayberry Island and do what Ash Wallace could not, and a whole world would open for her. A huge bonus? Probably. A promotion to vice president for acquisitions? It was quite possible. But maybe she wanted something better for herself; maybe she was thinking too small. Maybe this was the time to blow out of this corporate box and set up her own consulting firm, filling the market void Ash Wallace had handed to her all tied up in a bow.

Kathryn shivered with pleasure and smiled at herself in the mirror. Closing the Mermaid Island deal would make anything and everything possible. It would mean that her new life was about to begin.

She rushed across the J-R office suite, then knocked on Jerrod's door energetically.

A muffled voice came from within. "I'm busy."

"It's Kathryn, Jerrod."

"And I'm still busy."

She refused to let his nasty mood affect her. She gently opened his door a crack. Her boss was seated behind his desk with his head in his hands.

"I just need a minute of your time, Jerrod."

He jerked his head up and glared at her, but didn't tell her to leave, which Kathryn took as an invitation.

"I can handle Mermaid Island," she said, stepping inside and approaching his desk. "I can close the deal. I know I can. I can salvage this, Jerrod."

Her boss laughed and shook his head. He reached for his usual Slurpee and began to suck on the straw like he was trying to extract a golf ball instead of a bit of frothy corn syrup and artificial coloring. He leaned back in his chair when he was done. "I just forwarded that e-mail to you. You sure didn't waste much time."

"We have no time to waste."

"I'll think about it." He frowned at Kathryn. "Ash did leave me a voice mail before he resigned. He said Mona Flynn would be more willing to negotiate if we'd get another environmental assessment."

"That's fabulous!"

"I wouldn't go that far. We'll have to find another firm who'll tell us what we want to hear, and that will cost money."

"We should move on this right away."

"I said I'll think about it." He took another loud slurp. "I'm busy. I'm busy breaking out in a rash—a fucking two-hundred-and-thirty-million-dollar rash."

Kathryn tried her best not to show how disgusted she was. Jerrod Jessop was a self-absorbed, hyperactive, spoiled little boy. She'd hated every day of the seven years she'd worked for him. His behavior certainly was making her decision easy, though. In a week or so, when she'd closed the Mermaid Island deal, she would gladly accept the bonus. Then she'd tell Jerrod to stick his vice presidency offer all the way up his Slurpee straw.

She smiled pleasantly. "We cannot look at this as a problem, Jerrod. It's a real *opportunity* for us. We need to seize it."

"Close the door on your way out."

"Of course."

Idiot.

There was no way around it—Ash had to get out of the clambake. He had to get off the island. He had to extricate himself from Rowan Flynn before it was too late.

As he walked to town, he felt the anger and bewilderment pull at him like a wicked undertow. Never before in his life had he felt ensnared like this. A woman— worse yet, a woman he'd just met—had a pull on him that was too strong to resist. Too intangible. Too unexpected. How was he supposed to fight something he couldn't name and had no reference for? It was driving him nuts.

He'd felt the pull the instant he'd laid eyes on her, standing in the front hall of the B and B in her T-shirt and jeans, greeting him with wary politeness. And just moments ago, sitting with Rowan in the old porch glider, he couldn't avoid the truth—with every moment he spent in her company, the pull grew stronger. How had he allowed this to happen? How had he let her charm him, kiss him, intoxicate him, make him laugh, and seduce him into chaos?

Most of all, how had she coaxed the truth from him like that? He didn't share his sob story with people. It had taken him two years to tell Nanette about how his parents died. In the six months since Brian's death, he'd barely spoken his name aloud.

And why the hell had he agreed to be her date—*her actual date*—to the clambake? If he were still Ash Wallace, the closer, he would have accepted her invitation as a strategic move. It would give him a way to gain her trust and get access to her family. But the damn job was an afterthought at this point. It wasn't about the job anymore. He'd quit the fucking job. And he'd already met the Flynns and he'd already earned Rowan's trust.

So why would he accept her invitation to the clambake? There was only one answer to that question. If he showed up, he would show up as a man who was interested in the woman who had invited him.

Ash looked up at the flawless blue sky. His footfalls became heavy on the pavement as his thoughts went to Nanette—he'd actually talked to Rowan about Nanette! He never opened up like that to a woman. Brian had been his one and only sounding board for anything personal.

Ash laughed out loud, thinking that "closed off" had been only one of the many labels women had given him over the years, along with stoic, distant, cold, shut down, and—his personal favorite—*an imitation human being*. That had been Nanette's parting shot, a wound she tried to inflict when she told him she planned to relocate to San Francisco and his reaction wasn't what she'd hoped to hear.

"Do whatever you think is best," he'd told her.

She'd stared at him for a moment, her mouth hanging open. Then she blew up. "After three years together, that's all you can say? Are you kidding me? Are you really that empty inside?"

So that was the real mind-bending mystery here. Why now? Why was Ash suddenly feeling things he'd never felt before? Was it something about Rowan? Was it something about the tiny island she called home?

Whatever it was, he hadn't asked for it and he sure as hell didn't have faith in it.

Ash reached the marine yard just after eleven. He poked his head into the shack that served as Sully's office and was immediately assaulted with the smell of low tide mixed with diesel fuel, dirty oil, and how he imagined a bologna sandwich might smell after a month in the summer sun.

"Sully?"

A clanging sound rang out from behind a door marked PRIVATE. It opened, and Sully poked his head out, then looked down at his feet. "Oh, it's you."

Once again, Ash was struck by the small businessman's lack of small business skills. "I came by to check on the engine. Are you done installing it?"

Sully raised his eyes. "You in a hurry?"

"You could say that."

He shrugged. "Well, I ordered it Friday afternoon and then we had the weekend come along, you know, so I'm sure it will be here soon."

Ash laughed. "Are you serious? It takes several days to get a part from Hyannis? In that time, I could've swum there and back with the engine anchored to my neck."

Sully scowled, wiping his hands on a paper towel. Ash realized he must have interrupted his lunch. "Good thing you like swimming, Mr. Wallace, because that boat of yours ain't going anywhere till it's fixed."

Ash was growing tired of this conversation. "I need the repairs done today."

Sully nodded, but said nothing.

"I'll be back this evening."

Sully closed one eye and looked at him quizzically. "You want to leave this evening?"

"Well, I'd like to leave right now, but since that obviously isn't an option, I'll wait until tonight."

Sully studied the wad of paper towel in his hand like it was the most fascinating thing he'd ever seen. He looked up again. "I mean no disrespect, Mr. Wallace, but even if I could get the engine mounted by tonight, which I can't, are you sure you'd want to attempt a night sail?"

He laughed. "I've been sailing at night since—" Ash stopped himself. He was supposed to be a novice sailor. God, but he was so sick of all this *lying*. "Maybe you're right. I'll leave in the morning."

Sully shook his head. "Well, I got a couple more jobs ahead of you. I can't make any promises."

Ash laughed again. "So it seems. I'll be back tomorrow." He heard the condescending tone in his voice but wasn't overly concerned about it. After all, he was being royally screwed by this slow-moving yahoo. He left the shack and headed down the dock toward the *Provenance,* giving it a quick inspection. Right at that moment, he realized how he longed for his solitude, his only company the wind and water. How had he let Rowan get under his skin the way she had? How had he allowed himself to like this silly island as much as he did? This was a job, not a vacation. These people weren't his friends, and this place wasn't some kind of home away from home. Ash couldn't get off this island fast enough.

Feeling restless and needing to kill time, Ash wandered into town. He found an unoccupied bench on the public dock, stretched an arm out over the back and crossed his legs. From his perch he did some more people-watching, studying another wave of families and couples as they disembarked from the ferry. He saw couples with their arms draped casually across each other's shoulders and over hips. He saw parents gripping their kids' little hands. Ash stared out over the sea, suddenly overwhelmed with uncertainty. Why was it that he longed so for his solitude? Was it because he truly wanted to be alone, or was it because he wanted to hide in what was familiar and safe?

"Hello, sir."

Ash dragged his eyes from the ocean to find a little girl in a mermaid costume standing by the bench. She held out a flyer. "The children's play starts in ten minutes in the museum parking lot. It only costs five dollars."

He accepted the piece of copy paper and smiled at the kid. "Thanks. Five dollars sounds like a bargain. I'll try to make it."

She grinned. "Really? You're not just saying that?"

Something about the girl's face made his chest tighten. It occurred to him that she looked a bit like Rowan, with her straight light brown hair and freckles. "I'll try."

"Come on, then!" She grabbed his hand and tried to tug him to a stand. "I'm going there now, so I can show you where it is. I'm in it. I play a mermaid. There's hot dogs and popcorn balls for sale, too."

Ash looked at where her small hand grasped his and found himself smiling. Here he was again—getting kidnapped by a kid. Just then it dawned on him that he'd been kidnapped many times since he set foot on Bayberry Island—by children, by Rowan, by the unconventional rhythm of life around here.

"You coming?"

"Sure," he said, standing. "Lead the way."

Why not? It wasn't like he had anything else to do.

Plus it had been at least twenty years since he'd had a decent popcorn ball.

Not long after, Ash stood at the outer fringes of the parking lot, the midday sun beating down on him. A horde of proud parents held up every kind of recording device imaginable—smartphones, digital cameras, video recorders—as the drama unfolded on the raised platform against the old brick of the museum wall.

"Oh no!" The first mate gestured wildly as he looked over the railing of the fishing vessel. "We shall perish! All is lost!"

An audio recording of wind and thunder was cranked up high, and whoever was operating the spotlight added a bright flash for added suspense. Just then, a double layer of corrugated cardboard waves at the stage edge began to move back and forth in opposing directions, depicting the rough seas, and about a dozen cardboard mermaid tails popped up and disappeared again in unison. It occurred to Ash that he'd seen some of the stage set before, at the parade. The fishing boat was a stripped-down version of the vessel from Frasier Flynn's float, and the waves were from Rowan's. He had a feeling it wouldn't be the last time he saw recycled festival-week decorations.

"Trim the sails!" one of the junior fishermen cried out.

"We're taking on water!" called another.

Someone from offstage tossed a single bucketful of water onto the fishing boat, which prompted a ripple of laughter to move through the crowd. The special effect must have been Captain Rutherford Flynn's cue to make his appearance, and a chubby boy bounded up onstage. With his fake beard askew, Ash thought he looked like a cross between C. Everett Koop and the cartoon fisherman from a package of Gorton's Fish Sticks. Then he realized it was none other than his friend from the first day he arrived on the island, the boy who'd given orders to have Ash abducted from the dock and dragged to the mermaid fountain. Whoever this kid was, he sure enjoyed being in the public eye.

"Do not despair!" The junior-sized Captain Flynn pointed over the railing and into the water. "Look!"

"But I don't see anything, Captain."

"Look again. Right there. Don't you see her?"

A mermaid girl in a long black wig appeared from the shoulders up, rising above the cardboard waves. She beckoned to the captain before she disappeared again. Seconds later, a dozen mermaids began to swim alongside the fishing boat in unison, as more thunder, wind, and lightning came from offstage. A second bucket of water was hurled toward the actors, missing the stage entirely this time.

Ash laughed out loud.

"Hello, Ashton."

He jerked his head in surprise and encountered the smiling face of the nice lady from Mona Flynn's tent. She was sporting a SAVE OUR ISLAND button.

"Oh." Ash didn't manage to hide his surprise.

"I don't mean to disturb you." Her voice was so soft that he could barely hear her. "They're getting ready to change the set and take the drama to the inn, where Captain Flynn meets Serena, his heart-mate and one true love."

"No, no. It's fine." Ash smiled. "Besides I think I know how the story ends."

She laughed, holding out her hand. "You probably don't remember my name, but I'm Darinda Darswell. I really apologize about the hubbub yesterday. You got caught in the crossfire, unfortunately."

Ash shook her hand. "Ashton Wallace, and there's no need to apologize, though it was the first time I've been poked in the eye by a fairy."

Darinda laughed again, and Ash decided there was something sweet and earnest about this lady.

"Are you busy? Are you here with anyone?" Darinda examined him from shoes to hair. It didn't feel like she was hitting on him, but she sure was curious. "Would you like to get a cup of coffee or something?"

"I'm not busy at all, and I'm here alone. I'd enjoy that."

A few minutes later, the two of them were seated at a small café table under an umbrella. Ash had ordered an iced coffee and Darinda was sipping a frozen mocha latte. His initial impression of the woman had held true. She was gentle and kind, but he couldn't shake the feeling that this little excursion wasn't as innocent—or random—as he'd first assumed. Darinda had just asked him about his line of work and how he came to visit the island, and he repeated his cover story. This time, however, his voice was so halting, he knew she didn't believe him. He didn't blame her. Once again, he knew he needed to get off this island before things got too tangled, too messy. He couldn't wait to stop lying.

Darinda sipped from her straw and frowned. "Hmm. So you don't plan to stay for the rest of the week?"

"No. As soon as my boat is fixed, I'm heading out."

She cleared her throat and looked around the busy boardwalk, as if she were worried about eavesdropping. "Well, if your boat is with Deacon Sully, he'll do a great job—that's for sure."

Ash had never wondered if the mechanic had a first name, but "Deacon" seemed an odd choice for one. "He's a strange bird."

Darinda laughed at that assessment. "We've got more than our fair share of strange birds around here, or haven't you noticed?"

"Oh, I've noticed." Ash smiled.

"So what did you think of the Man Grab?"

He rolled his eyes and casually draped an arm over the back of the small café chair. "I'd have to say it was one of the more excruciating experiences of my life."

A smile trembled at Darinda's mouth. "We mean well. It's all part of our tradition. So." She folded her hands on the table and looked serious. "Out of curiosity, did you feel differently after you kissed the Great Mermaid's hand?"

He nearly spat out a mouthful of iced coffee. "Uh. No."

"Sorry." Darinda waved her hand as if to dismiss that question. "Anyway, so what did you do right after the Man Grab?"

Ash thought that was a peculiar question. He shrugged. "I had to find somewhere to stay."

"Oh."

"I read a brochure for a bed-and-breakfast at the dock and decided to go find it."

Darinda's body stiffened. "Really? Which one?"

"The Safe Haven. I understand it belongs to Mona's family."

Darinda's eyebrows rose and her eyes got as big as hockey pucks. "You're staying at the Safe Haven? But they're always booked in advance."

"They were, but the owner . . . I guess she's Mona's daughter, right?"

Darinda nodded, her eyes even bigger.

"She rented me her apartment until my boat gets fixed. It was very generous of her."

The small woman looked down at her hands for a moment, as if she were pulling herself together. She looked up again. "So you've gotten to know Rowan?"

Uh-oh. Wait a minute. What was this woman getting at? So far her questions had focused on him, Rowan, and the mermaid. *What the fuck?*

"Some," he said.

"I see. Well, I've enjoyed this, but I need to go. I'm helping Mona with the clambake tonight and I have a lot to do." She stood and held out her hand again, more stiffly this time. "It was a pleasure to see you again. Enjoy the rest of your time on the island."

Ash watched her scurry off like a woman with a mission. He shook his head, took another sip of his iced coffee, and decided it would be a relief to get back to Boston, where the crazy-to-sane ratio of the population seemed far more manageable.

Since Kathryn had decided that Jerrod Jessop could go to hell, she dialed the familiar number and waited. After five rings, Mona Flynn picked up, and Kathryn launched her well-rehearsed spiel. "Mrs. Flynn, this is Kathryn Hilsom from Jessop-Riley in Boston. Please don't hang up. I am not calling to pressure you into anything."

Silence.

Kathryn continued. "I hope you and your family are doing well and made it through the storm okay. I heard there were damaging winds and high waves."

More silence.

"Mrs. Flynn?"

Mona blew out a long breath of air, then said, "You've got a lot of nerve, young lady. I've told you a hundred times that I will never give in to your company's evil plot to destroy Bayberry Island."

Kathryn rolled her eyes. "Well, now, that's a little melodramatic, don't you think? Everyone here at Jessop-Riley understands where you're coming from, and we know your priority is your family's happiness and financial security. And that's what this is really about, Mrs. Flynn—we want Bayberry to experience an economic and cultural renaissance to carry it through the next hundred years, and we know the Mermaid Island Resort can be the lynchpin for such a rebirth."

There was another moment of quiet; then Mona burst out laughing. Her laughter was so loud that Kathryn had to lower the volume on her speakerphone.

"Cultural? You people are unbelievable!" Mona laughed again. "Obviously, you think we're nothing but a bunch of chowderheads out here, too dumb to figure out what you're up to."

"That is not true. We here at Jessop-Riley—"

"You there at Jessop-Riley can keep your slimy hands off our historic island! You are nothing but corporate criminals! Your project would destroy the fabric of life around here forever. And the only way you'll get your hands on this land is if I'm dead and gone. Are we clear?"

Kathryn was stunned. She'd expected some resistance, but Mona Flynn sounded like a crazy woman. "We're willing to do another environmental assessment. You can even be involved in the process if you'd like to ensure that it's done fairly and impartially." Mona Flynn was silent.

"Mrs. Flynn?"

Mona slammed the phone in her ear.

Kathryn slowly rose from her chair and began to spritz the plants lined up on her windowsill, a ritual that always seemed to clear her head a bit. As she did so, a thought occurred to her.

Maybe she shouldn't have jumped the gun with Mona Flynn. Maybe she should've waited for Jerrod to give the go-ahead to close. What if he somehow found out and was angry that she'd walked right out of his office and ignored his decision? What if she'd just ruined her chance at a bonus? A vice presidency? Or her chance to make the big close that would launch her solo career?

She spritzed some more, staring out at the Back Bay Boston skyline. Kathryn told herself that this was no time to begin doubting herself. She would stay the course.

"Gather 'round, ye 'maids. Thank you for making time for this emergency meeting."

Mona shoved the stacks of papers and magazines to the edge of her coffee table and collapsed into her regular spot on the semicircular sofa. Her heart hadn't stopped pounding since Darinda showed up with the blockbuster news a half hour before.

"This had better be good. I was taking a bath." Polly sighed as she took her usual seat, too.

"Is it about the clambake, Mona? Because you've already given us our assignments for tonight." Abby Foster stared with annoyance at the three-ring binder by Mona's side. "And, by the way, this is the third year in a row that you've got me manning the steam pots, and you know how my hair frizzes in humidity."

Mona would have preferred to ignore their complaining, since it was completely off topic, but knew she couldn't. "All of you are aware that the clambake won't be a success without your help. Our family can still afford some of the costs of this event, but we rely on volunteers to make the whole thing work. As always, I've tried to spread the jobs around, so that everyone will have time to work and time to play."

That seemed to calm them down, but several society members continued chatting by the front door. "Hurry up, everyone!" When they failed to move, Mona realized she had no patience left in her—the phone call from Boston had grated on her nerves. "This is serious shit, girls! Now sit the hell *down*."

Everyone scurried into place.

"All right now." Mona took a deep breath, putting the resort worries aside in order to concentrate on more important things. "Darinda has some startling news, and we need to act immediately. Darinda?" Mona gestured for her to speak.

She looked a bit skittish.

"It's okay. Just tell everyone what happened."

"All right. Well, I saw our Man Grab at the children's play just a little while ago."

"Oh Jesus. You dragged me out of the tub for this?"

"Polly!" Mona slapped her open palm on the table. No one dared move. "Go on," Mona said to Darinda.

"Uh. Okay. Well, we chatted and I invited him for a cup of coffee."

"You went on a *date* with him?" Izzy McCracken clutched at her chest. "Since when are you a cougar?"

"Oh, my flippin' God," Polly muttered.

Mona could not believe these women. Sandpipers had longer attention spans. "All right, that's it! The next person to interrupt Darinda will get after-hours cleanup duty at the clambake."

"Please go on, Darinda," Izzy said demurely.

"All right, so Ashton Wallace is his name and he is a business consultant in Boston and his sailboat broke down Friday and that's how he ended up on the dock and became this year's Man Grab." Darinda paused. Everyone was too scared to make a peep, so she went on. "Do you remember how I said that I sensed something special about him? That I thought when he left that he was headed toward his destiny?"

"Hey, Mona. Are we allowed to answer her?" Polly bobbled her head back and forth in challenge.

"Yes."

"Then yeah, I remember."

Everyone else agreed.

"Well, guess where he went right after he kissed the mermaid's hand. Guess who he met immediately following the ceremony. And guess where he's staying right now."

Everyone looked to Polly, who shook her head. "I'm not even going there."

Mona was growing impatient. "The Safe Haven! Rowan! He's been staying in Rowan's apartment!"

Pandemonium broke out. Mona had to yell for everyone to settle down. "Be quiet! There's more! Darinda?"

Clearly, the usually reserved Darinda was caught up in the excitement. Her voice had risen to a squeak. "When I asked him if he felt differently after he kissed the Great Mermaid's hand, he said 'no.' But I think he wasn't telling the truth. And when I asked if he'd gotten to know Rowan, he said 'some,' but that wasn't true either."

Mona scooted to the edge of the sofa. "I made some calls. I ran this up the flagpole with Annie, Clancy, Imelda, Zophie the maid, and even the nudists."

"'Zophie and the Nudists.' Sounds like the name of a punk-rock band."

Mona pointed in Polly's direction.

"Oh, for God's sake. I'm just adding some levity."

"Levity?" Mona laughed. "Let me assure you, this is quite serious. Ashton Wallace and my daughter are *falling in love*."

The sentence fell with a thud upon the room. No one moved or breathed or even whispered.

"Here's what I found out." Mona whipped out a single sheet of paper from her three-ring binder. It would help her keep her facts straight. She was too wound up to rely on her memory.

"Fact number one: He basically bribed Rowan into letting him stay there. Fact two: Soon after they lost power on the cove, Imelda saw Rowan run out to the carriage house but didn't see her return until the power came back on and that was more than an hour later, and the next morning Rowan seemed preoccupied and was dropping things."

Mona scanned the room and nodded at the shocked expressions. "But wait. There's more. Fact three: The nudists said they met Ashton immediately after the Man Grab and that he couldn't take his eyes off Rowan. They said the poor boy reminded them of a stunned bird after it ran headfirst into a plate-glass window. Fact four:

Clancy and . . ." Mona couldn't bring herself to say Frasier's name aloud. She started over. "Ashton spoke to Clancy and his *father* during Island Day, saying he planned on taking Rowan out for ice cream. Fact five: One of the summer workers at the marine yard told Zophie that he saw Rowan and Ashton kissing by his boat and—"

"Hold up." Polly raised her hand. "If this goes on much longer, I'm definitely going to need a glass of merlot."

Mona ignored her. "Fact six: Imelda caught them canoodling on the love magnet this morning after breakfast. And fact seven is the best one of all. I spoke to Annie just a few minutes ago. I asked her if she knew anything about Rowan and the man staying in her apartment and she *hung up on me*!"

"Imagine that," Abby said.

"So what does this mean?" Izzy looked puzzled. "Did the mermaid send him to the Safe Haven? To Rowan?"

"He said it was a brochure." Darinda looked embarrassed to share that detail.

"But the Great Mermaid sent him to Rowan, right?" Layla O'Brien was breathless.

Mona shook her head very slowly. "That is what we must decide. We need to investigate further. Observe the two of them. Eventually we'll need to speak to Rowan."

"Oh boy." Polly ran a hand over her whole face.

"But that's not our most pressing concern. Our first job is to stop Ashton from leaving the island. He told Darinda that he planned to leave as soon as his boat was repaired."

"Wait a second." Izzy waved her arms around. "If he's in love, why is he planning to leave?"

Mona expected this would come up. "That's something else we'll have to investigate further. Our first job is to make sure that isn't even an option for him."

"I'm going to talk to Deacon Sully." Darinda smiled devilishly. "I'm going to tell him to work real slow."

"Shouldn't be a problem," Polly said.

"Listen up, ladies." Mona clapped her hands together. "Zophie says that Ashton is Rowan's date for the clambake. No matter what your duties are tonight, keep an eye on them. Listen in if you can. We need to get a handle on this situation."

"Uh, Mona?" Abby looked worried.

"I know what you're going to say."

"But, Mona. We messed up so badly last time. Are you sure it's a good idea to interfere with Rowan's love life again?"

Mona was prepared for this. "We're going to go about things differently this time. If the Great Mermaid has made this love possible—and if it's a real, right, and true love—Rowan will reach that conclusion on her own." She smiled. "We will be close by to help her along, but on an as-needed basis, of course."

"Great." Polly stood up. "My ass is needing that merlot right about now."

Chapter Twelve

"She did *what*?"

"About a half hour ago." Annie clearly hated to be the bearer of bad news. "She knows about Poseidon. She was asking about the man in your apartment and whether you'd been spending time with him. I knew I had to call you right away."

Rowan tipped her head back and stared at the pressed-tin ceiling of the kitchen. This wasn't completely unexpected news, but she'd deluded herself into thinking she had another day or two of undisturbed bliss before her mother stomped all over her life.

"I hung up on her."

She managed to laugh. "Thanks. I guess." Rowan knew that a dial tone would be nothing more than the *ding, ding, ding, ding!* of victory for her mother. "Tonight's gonna be real interesting."

"Maybe you should talk to her in advance of the clambake."

Rowan shook her head. "No. I'm just going to steer clear. Maybe, if I'm really lucky, she'll be cool."

"Hmm," Annie hummed.

"Okay. Forget that."

"So what are you wearing?"

Rowan appreciated Annie trying to cheer her up with a change of subject. "I don't think I've worn it since I left New York, but I have this retro halter sundress, you know, kind of a fifties va-va-voom vibe. It's got a low-cut sweetheart neckline."

"Perfect. What color is it?"

"White."

"Sounds gorge."

"How about you?"

"Probably some pale blue crop pants and a matching tank."

"That will look beautiful with your eyes."

"Thanks."

"I'm *so* freaking pissed off right now."

Annie sighed. "I know you are. You have every right to be. Listen, want me to run interference with her?"

Rowan shook her head and shut her eyes. "No. Obviously, if Mona knows about me and Ash, everyone knows, and you can't very well go around slapping duct tape over everyone's mouth, especially since they paid a hundred dollars for an all-you-can-eat buffet."

"Sounds kind of cathartic, actually."

Rowan chuckled. "I do need to give Ash some kind of heads-up, but I'm not sure how much to say. You know how whacked my mother and her crazies are. I don't want Ash to think the whole island expects us to love each other until the day we both drop dead."

"Yeah." Annie paused. "Not a lot of men respond positively to shit like that. Tends to make them run screaming."

Rowan laughed. "No kidding, especially since we've known each other only a few days. So what do I tell him?"

"I'm drawing a blank here."

Rowan checked the kitchen clock. It was four p.m. She had about an hour before she had to start getting ready, and she still needed to get her dress out of her apartment closet. "I'll come up with something."

"I have complete faith in you."

Ash lolled his head around as the hot water cascaded down his neck, shoulders, back, and arms. He hummed along to the tunes playing on his smartphone, which he'd propped up on the sink. This particular music dredged up a lot of memories—all good. During day sails on the *Provenance,* these songs by folk rocker Ray LaMontagne would pour from the cabin. He and Brian would drink beer, laugh, and work together to harness the power found in the wind and water as the music played.

But those days are long gone. Now he leaned a palm against the tile wall of the shower and let his head fall forward, water spilling over his face. The weight of the guilt was unbearable. A few feet away, on Rowan's bed, was his duffel. It was packed with the few items he'd brought from the boat to the carriage house, ready once more to toss over his shoulder. He'd head to the boat as soon as he was dressed. He'd sleep in the cabin tonight, or on the deck under the stars if the weather held. He'd get out of Sully's way if there was more work to be done, but he knew he couldn't stay here another night.

He felt surrounded by Rowan. It felt like every minute he spent in her bed, in her apartment, in her world, further infused him with her essence. That wasn't good. It wasn't right. Because he was just an imposter, and he'd let too much time go by without telling her the truth. Even if he ran to her right this minute, sat her down, and spilled everything, it wouldn't fix the fact that he'd already deceived her. Nothing could undo what he'd already done.

Rowan would forever see him as a fraud. She'd see another Frederick Theissen.

He turned off the water, wiped his body down with a towel, and quickly wrapped it around his hips. He stepped out into the hallway just in time to see Rowan coming up the stairs.

Ash froze. The instant she cleared the stairwell, she stopped moving. Her mouth fell open and her gaze widened, then slid down his body.

This wasn't your basic dose of déjà vu, the kind that tickled your curiosity and teased your memory. This felt like he'd just been shot down by the déjà vu death star.

"I . . . Oh God, I'm so sorry. I called for you but—"

"It's okay." Ash laughed uncomfortably. "But you do seem to have reliable timing."

Rowan shook her head and covered her face in her hands. "I didn't think you were here. I just needed to get something out of my closet. I know this isn't ideal. . . . You don't have a lot of privacy—"

"Rowan, it's okay. Really."

She slowly let her hands fall away from her face. She smiled back at him tentatively, her sea-green eyes asking him a thousand questions of the heart.

He wished he was the man who could answer them, but he knew he wasn't.

Rowan came to him, wrapped her small hand around his forearm, and popped up on her toes so that she could kiss him. She tasted like honey and sunshine, and Ash felt the ballast of guilt move to the pit of his stomach. He needed the kiss to go on and on but was relieved she ended it, returned her heels to the floor, and grinned at him.

"Mind if I get something out of my closet real quick?"

"Of course not."

He knew the duffel bag was on the bed, his clothes set out to wear on the boat. Of course she would notice.

Rowan walked right past the incriminating evidence to the walk-in closet, and Ash tried to block her view of the bed by standing in the closet doorway.

Rowan began riffling through hangers, looking for something specific.

"That's beautiful music. I think I recognize his voice—who is it?"

"Ray LaMontagne."

"Oh, that's right! I saw him at a club in New York a couple years ago. What a wonderful show."

Ash couldn't hide the fact that he was surprised she knew his music. Ray LaMontagne wasn't exactly a superstar.

"You might want to wear something a little less casual," Rowan said, still focused on the contents of her closet. "It's not dressy by any means, but just something a little nicer than that."

"You mean I can't wear my towel?"

Rowan found what she was looking for. She tugged a white dress from a hanger and draped it over her arm, her smile teasing. "Don't get me wrong. I love the towel. You could wear a towel around me any day. But I was referring to the swim trunks and T-shirt I saw laid out on the bed."

"Ah."

"So I'll see you on the beach at six?" Her gaze moved from his face to his chest. She placed her warm palm on his breastbone.

It was such an innocent question. This beautiful and sweet woman had no idea what a bastard he was and how the heart hidden below that breastbone was cracking from sorrow.

He kissed her forehead, then tapped her on her perfect bottom. "I look forward to seeing you in that dress."

She wiggled her eyebrows at him and left a tender kiss on his chest. "See ya around, Ashton Louis Wallace the third."

Ash watched Rowan bound down the stairs, knowing that would be the last time he'd ever see her. The kiss she'd pressed to his damp skin would be the last time he felt the touch of her lips.

The bottom fell out of his heart.

Ash was late. Which was not a huge deal, since there was no drop-dead start time to the clambake and people straggled in throughout the night. What bothered her was that he'd promised to meet her at six. It was now six twenty. And that meant he hadn't kept his promise.

Rowan fiddled with the full skirt of her dress, trying to ignore the tide of dread now rising up from her belly, into her throat, threatening to choke her.

"Hey, hey, pretty lady." Rowan felt a man's kiss on her cheek and turned to see Nat Ravelle, Annie's fiancé. He was debonair in a pair of ivory linen trousers and a white linen shirt. Annie was at his side, and she looked so beautiful that Rowan gasped. Of course, Annie had never been anything but lovely, with all that long blond hair, expressive blue eyes, and a killer body, but lately she'd looked like she was lit up from the inside. Love had made her nothing less than *magnificent*.

"So? Where's Poseidon?"

Rowan shrugged, doing her best imitation of laid-back. "Running a little late."

It was lightning fast, but Rowan saw the worry flash in Annie's eyes.

"Would you ladies like me to get you something to drink?" Nat was either psychic or a hopeless gentleman. Rowan suspected it was both.

"That would be great. Thanks."

He wandered off toward the beer tent, and Annie took Rowan by the hand.

"Okay. First off, you look incredible. I love your hair pulled up like that."

Rowan managed a smile. "Thanks."

"And second off, where the hell is he? Did you go to the carriage house to look for him?"

She shook her head.

"Oh hell."

Rowan would not cry. She *would not cry*.

"That's it. Be right back. Gotta go kick some Greek god ass."

She grabbed Annie's arm. "Don't be ridiculous. I'm sure there's a good reason he's running late. Maybe he got a call or something."

Her friend didn't seem convinced.

"I just saw him an hour ago and everything was fine. He'll be here, Annie. I know it. I trust him."

Exactly why he stood in front of a fifteen-foot-high half-naked bronze mermaid was a mystery to him. It was like he'd arrived here on autopilot. Ash remembered leaving the carriage house and walking up the lawn and out the Safe Haven gates. He remembered walking the half mile down Shoreline Road. Though he'd had no intention of stopping in town square on his way to the *Provenance*, his subconscious apparently had other ideas.

He watched, mesmerized, as plumes of water danced along the fountain's circular base. They created a playful, see-through curtain that seemed to lift the mermaid toward the sky. Ash looked up and up . . .

This really was one very saucy female.

He remembered reading an article a few years back that analyzed the body measurements of a Barbie doll. Scientists determined that if good old Barb were human, the size of her breasts would make her freakishly top-heavy, her skinny waist would be unable to accommodate ribs or internal organs, and her toothpick legs would be incapable of holding her upright. At the time, Ash thought the judgment was pretty harsh. But looking at this bronze spectacle of the female form towering over him, he understood the point those researchers were trying to make. The Bayberry Island mermaid was all woman—well, except for the fish tail, of course. She was round and soft in all the right places, with a set of real hips and some spectacular cleavage. She held herself with purpose. Her lips were full and sensual, with just a hint of attitude, like maybe she knew something her observer didn't. The flowing hair, the graceful turn of her neck, and the regal set of her shoulders led Ash to imagine that this mermaid was fully aware of how hot she was. Surprisingly, it was immaterial to her. Her strength didn't come from her outer beauty. In fact, it was the opposite—her beauty came from her inner strength.

Ash adjusted the duffel on his shoulder and laughed at himself. If he were having a mind meld with a bronze mermaid, it was time to head out. He would remember this little detour onto Mermaid Island forever, but it wasn't his home. He didn't belong here.

He didn't belong anywhere.

Ash reached up, held the mermaid's graceful hand in his own, and kissed it. "It's been real."

He turned away. He took three steps. On the fourth, his foot crossed over the circle of inlaid stone around the fountain. And that's when Ash heard it.

You belong with her.

He didn't dare breathe. Where had that voice come from? Ever so carefully, he pulled his foot back inside the circle, returned it to the ground, and swiveled his head around, searching for the person who'd just spoken to him.

He saw a group of teenagers with skateboards by the hedges, smoking and trying to look cool. There were a few families with ice-cream cones. He saw some Chinese tourists taking photos at the fountain. But nowhere did Ash see the source of that voice.

Turn back.

His spine stiffened. This was nuts. He was hearing things. He was suddenly dizzy. Trying his best not to attract any attention to himself, Ash staggered toward an unoccupied concrete bench at the edge of town square. By the time he sat down, his legs felt as useless as Barbie's.

Ash let his head fall into his hands as a series of scenes began to unfold in his mind's eye, out of order and heading in no particular direction. Rowan naked and wet underneath him, tears streaming down her face; the laser of sunlight that tracked him in the storm; his mother's loving face; a slate roof; the sight of Haven Cove framed by the sea; the sound of Brian's laughter; "an imitation human being."

"Shit."

Ash stood. He pulled his smartphone from the pocket of his shorts, seeing that it was almost six thirty and that the Oceanaire offices had called him again. Shit. Again. He'd forgotten to call them back. Where had his head been lately?

He began to run. He ran to the edge of town, to Shoreline Road, and up the hill until he saw the broken and rusted gates leading to the Safe Haven. He encountered a frail old man in the circular drive of the B and B, shuffling his way toward the lawn. He wore a summer fedora that was frayed at the brim. For some reason, he clutched a butter knife in his hand.

"Are you all right, sir?"

"What?"

Ash yelled, "Can I help you?"

"Yes, goddammit! You can get Mona Flynn to shut her trap and hand over my money!"

Okay. That definitely wasn't what Ash expected to hear. He yelled again. "Where are you going?"

"Stop shouting at me! Jesus! I'm going to the damn clambake, of course!"

"If you can wait a few minutes, I'll walk you to the beach."

The old man either didn't hear him or didn't feel like dealing with him anymore, and continued his slow shuffle toward the lawn, butter knife drawn for battle.

Ash headed for the carriage house. He was so late. Rowan was down there on the beach thinking he'd stood her up—which he had—and the truth of that twisted at his guts. In fact, his belly was in knots for more than that reason alone. Now that he'd decided not to leave, how the hell was he going to explain the whole story to Rowan? How horrible would it be for her to learn that he came to Bayberry and bribed her to stay at the Safe Haven under false pretenses? How angry and hurt would she be when she learned she'd been seduced by a man who wasn't as he appeared? That he'd seduced her in order to get her family to sell their land?

It would break her heart. After what Rowan had been through with that idiot Theissen, hearing how he'd deceived her would rip her up. Ash prayed he would find the right time and the right words to ease her through the truth. He hoped she would sit still long enough to hear him out, let him walk her through to the happy ending—he was falling in love with her.

In record time, he ran up the carriage house apartment steps, threw everything out of his duffel and found the khaki trousers and button-down shirt he'd worn the day he arrived on Bayberry Island. His clothes were a little wrinkled. Under normal circumstances, he wouldn't tolerate looking so disheveled, but these weren't normal circumstances. Tonight, his outer imperfections would just have to reflect his inner ones.

When he returned to the lawn, Ash found the old man had made precious little headway. Though it would make him even later than he already was, he couldn't just leave him there, hobbling along. Ash offered his arm, but the old man slapped it away. He sighed, deciding he could do nothing but walk along with him.

"My name is Ash Wallace."

"What?"

"Never mind."

It was nearly seven by the time they made it to the wooden steps. Fortunately for his companion, they provided the safest and most level access to the beach anywhere along the cove. Ash stood on the landing at the top, scanning the crowd below. In typical Bayberry Island fashion, the beach was heavy with delicious smells and the air was filled with music. This time it was a reggae band complete with steel drums. He tried to spot her. Rowan would be wearing that white dress she'd wrangled from her closet, but he soon realized that knowledge wouldn't help him find her. Half the people on the beach were in summer whites.

"Well?" The old man glared up at him. "Aren't you going to help me down the goddam steps?"

Ash laughed loudly and looped the man's frail arm with his, then held him snug against his side.

The pace was excruciatingly slow. It took five minutes to ease down as many steps. Ash was so focused on keeping his bird-boned companion upright that when he glanced up to check on their progress, he noticed Rowan chatting and laughing with a group of people not far from the steps. Suddenly, she turned her head and looked up, and her eyes locked with his. He couldn't make out the nuances of her expression, but she didn't look overly pissed off. Slowly, she began to smile. She turned her body to face him, standing with her pretty bare feet close together and her hands clasped at her front.

They made it down another step.

Ash couldn't take his eyes off her. Her hair was loosely pulled up and to the side, clipped behind her ear with a delicate white flower, little tendrils falling around her face. Rowan's white dress was incredible. The top was an old-fashioned halter, tied behind her neck, and it was cut into a low vee in the front. The dress cinched in her waist and flared out over her hips, falling in soft waves of fabric to just above her cute knees. Once again, the first word that came to his mind while looking at Rowan Flynn was *adorable*. Unlike most other times, however, a whole string of descriptive words and phrases followed. Some of them were not suited for a general audience. He took another step.

She was *juicy*.

So fucking hot.

Radiant.

Another step. Ash wondered if it would be considered disrespectful to flip this old man over his shoulder and carry him down the rest of the way, because he was going crazy. He had to touch her.

Silky.

Luscious.

Soft, welcoming, sexual.

He wanted to lick her across the top of her breasts and drag his tongue down the front of her body.

He wanted to reach up under that full skirt.

He wanted to hold her in his arms.

He wanted to tell her everything and beg for her forgiveness.

Another step.

"Hey, you! Clark Kent! I'm talking to you!"

Ash shook some sense into himself, realizing the old man had been trying to get his attention. "I'm sorry. What did you say?"

"You must be stone *deaf*!" The old man looked up to the sky and rolled his eyes. "I asked you if you had a girlfriend."

"Oh." Ash didn't know how to answer that. He couldn't call Rowan his girlfriend. There were a few things standing in the way of that. For example, they'd only just met. Then there was the fact that he'd been lying to her since the moment they laid eyes on each other. But the idea appealed to him. "Not technically."

"Well, you'd better watch out. That Flynn girl is looking at you like she wants to dip you in drawn butter and suck the meat off your bones."

Another step.

Rowan smiled at him.

He smiled at her.

That's what he would do, the first opportunity he got. He would lay her down, spread her legs, and put his lips on that perfect pink, wet pussy of hers and suck her until she couldn't breathe.

Another step.

Her little tongue licked at her lips.

Ash thought his fingers would ignite in flames if he couldn't touch her. *Now*. The wait was agonizing. Only two steps to go. The people Rowan had been chatting with had wandered off, and she stood alone watching the two of them hobble down the steps. Just then, Ash heard someone cough behind him. He looked over his shoulder to see about a dozen people waiting to get to the party. He glanced to his right to see one impatient couple sliding down a steep dune to the beach.

It would be only another minute or two. Ash and his new friend were almost there.

That's when he managed to drag his eyes from Rowan. *Oh.* She was with a posse—police chief Clancy, mayor dad, mermaid mom, BFF Annie, and the man who was obviously Annie's fiancé. Rowan was the only one of the bunch who looked pleased to see him.

The instant they reached the sand, a middle-aged woman ran up and took the old man from Ash's control. "Thank you! I hope he wasn't too much trouble."

"Not at all."

The woman gasped. "Give me the knife, Daddy!"

"No!"

"Come on, now."

"How will I protect myself?" As his daughter wrestled the blunt piece of silverware from his hand, he glared at Mona Flynn. "Nothing but sharks on the beach tonight!"

And then there they were. He and Rowan were barely a foot apart. All Ash had to do was reach out and touch her. He was nothing but a living, breathing force of desire. Need. Hunger. He raised his nose into the breeze and realized he could smell the intoxicating scent of her skin.

You belong with her.

"Hi, Ash. Glad you could make it."

He needed to stay focused. "I'm truly sorry I'm so late. Please accept my apologies."

She tilted her chin toward her chest. Ash could tell she didn't want to forgive him right away but was having trouble sticking to her principles. He knew that if he, himself, had any principles, he'd be similarly challenged.

Damn! He felt helpless around her. The only thing he was sure of was that he needed her and would do anything to win her.

"It's okay." She grabbed his hand. Ash felt a hot bolt of energy travel up his arm into his chest, and he knew that wherever she led, he would follow. "You know my mother, father, and Clancy, of course."

Ash nodded pleasantly at everyone. "Great to see you all again. It's a beautiful night for a beach party."

Clancy and Frasier scowled. Mona looked extremely worried. Obviously, they'd assumed Ash had stood Rowan up.

"And I want you to meet some very special people." Rowan nodded toward her best friend. "This is Annie Parker. You said you were in her shop."

Ash smiled. "I was. Very nice to formally meet you."

Annie smiled, but the smile didn't reach her eyes. *Uh-oh.*

"And this is Annie's fiancé, Nat Ravelle."

"We've met." The snappy dresser held out his hand and Ash shook it.

"Of course. The documentary filmmaker. Very nice to see you again."

For about ten seconds, time seemed to freeze. Ash felt something began to boil just below the surface of the group dynamic. It was a feeling of anticipation, hesitation, and just plain discomfort. Ash had no idea who was thinking what and who would say something to crack the frozen ice of their social intercourse, but he did know this: *He* was the problem here.

Could they possibly know?

"So." It was Nat. He gave a casual shrug and took a sip from his plastic beer cup. "Been doing anything interesting since the Man Grab?"

Ash watched Rowan's face blanch white. Her eyes

widened, and she began to slowly shake her head side to side. "What?" Her voice was so soft, it was almost a whisper. "No." She looked around at her family and friends, then at Ash once more. "Please tell me this is a joke. Please tell me you're not the Man Grab. *Please*."

"Uh, well, I guess I am. Not that I had much say in the matter." Ash smiled, but his smile was lost on Rowan. Her usually cheerful face had fallen flat. "What is it? What's wrong?"

Rowan spun around in the sand and walked away, leaving Ash perplexed. He went after her, and her family and friends went after him. So a convoy of people began to follow Rowan as she stomped off past the buffet setup and down the beach.

"Rowan! Wait! I don't understand why you're upset!"

She straightened her shoulders and ignored him. He caught up with her and touched her arm. "Please talk to me."

Rowan pulled her arm away. "I need some space. Give me room."

He attempted to lean down so he could see her face, but she turned away. He even thought she might be crying. "Sweetheart, please talk to me."

"Talk to him!"

Both Ash and Rowan turned toward the peanut gallery. Mona had clasped a hand over her mouth and muttered, "I'm sorry."

"My God." Rowan shook her head. "Am I not allowed to be alone for five minutes? Would all of you just back off?"

"Yes. That would be appreciated," Ash said, assuming he wasn't included in her group dismissal.

"That means you, too! I don't want to be around you right now." She spun away and headed down the beach, her shoulders becoming more rigid as her steps quickened.

Ash turned to search out Annie. Rowan's best friend was holding Nat's hand, sadness in her eyes. For some reason, Nat looked guilty. Ash had no idea what was going on.

"Annie, why is she so upset? What is this all about? Somebody help me out here."

She shook her head. "Only Rowan can explain why she feels the way she does. Give her some time."

Chapter Thirteen

Rowan held her ground. Annie had been relentless in her attempts to get her to "talk about it," but Rowan didn't want to *talk about it*. She'd managed to fulfill her duties at the buffet—dishing out massive quantities of coleslaw and potato salad—but she really didn't want to discuss any of this crap. She'd fallen in love with this year's Man Grab? It couldn't get any worse.

"More slaw, please." Annie attempted to look pathetic as she held out her Chinet dinner plate.

"No more slaw for you."

"But isn't it supposed to be all you can eat?"

"I told you I can't deal with this right now."

Just then, Rowan felt her mother's hand on her bare shoulder. "Please take a break, sweetheart," she whispered into her ear. "Go on and have fun with Ash. Maybe dance a little bit. I want you to be happy."

Rowan tossed the serving ladle into the stainless-steel catering pan, and the loud *clang!* made quite a few people stop talking and look her way. She turned around to face Mona. "Mother, do you really think that another round of your 'help' is what I need right now?"

Though Mona jerked back like she'd been slapped, Rowan couldn't stop. She knew it was wrong to unload

on her mother like this, but she couldn't stop herself—
the anger and hurt were exploding inside her chest. "I
am completely, utterly miserable, Mother. Don't you get
it? I hate the Safe Haven. I hate my life here on this
stupid island. I know it's my punishment for losing all
the money, and I get that, but you know better than anyone that this isn't what I wanted for myself!"

That stung. Rowan saw the pain in her mother's eyes.
But to her credit, she said nothing.

"And my love life? Ma, are you freakin' kidding me?
Your last attempt to guide me in love was a complete
disaster, remember? But let's not even go there. You're
the last person in the world who should be giving anyone advice because your own love life is a joke. You and
Daddy still love each other but you're both acting like
children—stubborn, selfish, angry little children. It's
painful to watch."

Mona's face had turned to stone. Rowan watched
her mother take several deep breaths before she spoke.
"Take a break, Rowan. I think you've done enough tonight."

Annie had wound her way through the buffet crowd
and now joined Mona behind the line of serving tables.
She stared at Rowan like she was a wounded bird, or a
patient in a mental hospital.

"I'm outa here." Rowan untied the apron from her
waist and whipped it off over her head.

Annie touched her arm. "Wait. Listen to me. I did see
some of Nat's footage, but I swear I didn't realize Poseidon and the Man Grab were one and the same. If I'd
known, I would have told you, Row. You know I would
have."

Mona nodded, her face still tight. "And I would have
told you as well, had I known he was staying here and
you were falling for him."

"I am *not* falling for him! What the hell?"

Mona and Annie shared a quick glance in each other's direction.

"I'm going for a walk." Rowan turned in the sand, already shaking her head. "And no, I do not want company."

She got away from the crowd and the food tent, steam pots, and beer wagon as fast as possible. Once her feet reached the hard-packed sand near the water's edge, she knew she could put some serious distance between herself and the party. That's what Rowan needed—distance. She wanted out. She wanted out of this life, this job, and she wanted off this island. It felt like she was positively *cursed* by it.

If she'd hated that fish bitch before, Rowan *really* hated her now. The ridiculous superstitions that ruled the island did nothing but mess with people's heads and set them up for misery. And who gave Mona and her friends the right to run around proclaiming deeper meaning where there was none? It was no different from someone who alerts the media because they've seen the face of Jesus on a potato chip!

Enough. She'd had enough of this bullshit. The mermaid legend wasn't harmless and it wasn't just a cutesy tourist attraction, and she'd be happy if she were never again forced to utter the syllables *mer* or *maid* as long as she lived.

Rowan walked, her heels thudding on the hard sand. It was total darkness now, but it didn't matter. She'd been walking this beach from the day she learned to put one foot in front of the other. She knew every rock, ever wayward tree trunk, every eddy in the sand. She could safely stroll blindfolded all three miles of the cove, all the way to the privacy fence at the edge of Lena's property.

By now Rowan was far enough from the clambake

that she could go entire minutes without encountering a rogue fire pit, the faint whiff of pot in the wind, or a couple making out in the shadows—including one of the Tea Rose Room bimbos. Ha! At least someone was getting lucky around here!

It wasn't fair. For two hours now, ever since Nat had announced that Ash had put the "man" in this year's Man Grab, she'd been battling back the rush of adrenaline from the shock of it. She'd also been battling back the tears. All of it had exhausted her.

Rowan shut her eyes and groaned out loud. Then she shouted her frustration into the roar of the surf. "Unfucking-believable! The Man Grab! Please, God—give me a break!"

Rowan knew what she had to do. It was painfully obvious. If Ash was the Man Grab, then in the eyes of her mother's psycho sect, the tourists, and about half of the island's year-round residents, he was ground zero for the mermaid's magic. And Rowan wanted no part of it.

There was no effin' way she'd slow dance with the Man Grab at the clambake, putting herself on display again like that. Never again would she snuggle with him on the love magnet or go out with him for ice cream or kiss him on the dock. Because Ash had a big-assed bull's-eye on his back, and Rowan had suffered enough public humiliation for several lifetimes.

And it wasn't like she could just up and leave the island and follow Ash to where none of this Bayberry Island drama mattered. Because she was stuck here. She had made a commitment to run her family's B and B. Unless her mother changed her mind about the resort, Rowan would be trapped here for the foreseeable future. The irony was so blatant, it made her dizzy—her mistake with Frederick had ruined her chances with Ash.

She felt her chin tremble. She *would . . . not . . . cry . . . .*

It was a warm night. The breeze was light. Rowan realized she'd begun to perspire and wiped her face, but found tears instead of sweat. It pissed her off. She decided to run, telling herself the exertion would take her mind off Ash.

But she wouldn't lie to herself. It would take a lot more than a jog to rip him from her heart.

A couple hundred feet down the beach, she saw a form coming toward her, and she found comfort in the fact that another lost soul had wandered far from civilization that night. It was sometimes awkward to cross paths in the darkness like this, but Rowan was a master at beach etiquette. She knew that on the off chance the person coming near was a Safe Haven guest, she should be prepared to at least nod in their direction.

Rowan slowed to a walk again, wiped the tears from her face, and felt gratitude for the privacy night provided. The form came nearer, and Rowan could tell it was a man. A rather big man. And just then, the moon decided to peek out from behind a cloud, and she turned her head to see the first ray of light play upon the black water.

When she refocused her gaze straight ahead, she saw Ash.

"Rowan."

She stopped. Ash's shoes dangled from his hand. His shoulders—those straight and strong shoulders she loved to touch—had become rounded. She noticed that his face was shadowed in sorrow, but it might have been a trick of the moonlight.

She shook her head. "You need to keep walking, Ash."

"You need to talk to me."

Standing near him in the increasingly bright light, Rowan knew she needed more than just a couple hours of space. "Please let it go, Ash. It's for the best." She felt her heart thud too fast and too hard under her ribs. Her knees shook and her throat tightened. It was like her body was telling her to stop talking and continue walking.

Ash tipped his head to the side, studying her. He really was a gorgeous man, but that wasn't the point. Rowan needed someone who'd never set foot on this scraggy rock—better yet, a man who had never even heard of Bayberry Island or its legend. She needed to meet a guy the normal way—if there was such a thing these days—and steer clear of any type of mermaid-man connection. She might not believe in the mermaid's powers, but she knew she needed to keep her love life as far away as possible from the legend and its associated flakiness and drama. She'd learned the hard way that they didn't mix.

Ash straightened his shoulders, leading Rowan to suspect that he'd been as caught off guard by this meeting as she had. He sighed. "There's a lot we need to discuss."

"There's no point. Sully will have your boat fixed soon and you can leave. No regrets."

He chuckled sarcastically. "So that would work for you? You want me to sail off not having the faintest idea what happened with us? What *could* have happened with us?"

She shook her head sadly. "There is no 'us,' okay? Let's just leave it at that."

Ash's body stilled. He stared at her intently for a moment, rubbed his chin thoughtfully, then said three simple words: "I will not."

Rowan burst out with a startled laugh. "What did you just say?"

"I said I'm not going anywhere, which is kind of funny, since I'd almost convinced myself that I'm not the

right man for you—not loving enough, decent enough—
and that leaving would be the nicest thing I could do for
you. But I've changed my mind."

Rowan's body felt numb and the inside of her head
sounded like the roar of the sea. When she finally spoke,
her voice came out small and soft. "Why?"

Ash shook his head. "No more words, Miss Flynn. I'd
rather show you than tell you." Ash walked toward her,
moving slowly and confidently, a slight smile twisting his
lips. Ash had just refused to play by her rules. Clearly, he
had his own agenda.

He reached her, stopping so close he almost brushed up
against the front of her body. His blue eyes appeared black,
intensely locked with hers as he looked down into her up-
turned face. Rowan heard the sound of his shoes dropping
to the sand. That's when he grabbed the back of her neck,
pulled her to him, and took her mouth with his.

Oh hell. How could she argue with *this*?

His lips—hot and demanding and without words—
laid out the rules that would apply here, on the beach,
under the moonlight, between the two of them.

Rowan went limp. Why didn't she have the strength
to push him away? How did he have this power over her
and why did she let him? As her mouth yielded to him
and she grabbed onto his upper arms, Rowan's brain was
flooded with dire warnings. *You will regret this; he is the
Man Grab; your mother will ruin this; the whole thing is
pointless because his life is in Boston; you must stay smart
and in control.*

But none of the warnings took hold.

And then the strangest thing happened—suddenly,
Rowan didn't even care. The warnings dissolved into
harmless background noise. All Rowan wanted was this
man who was kissing her, claiming her, making her forget that her heart had ever been broken.

Ash's kiss mellowed, but he was just changing it up. While his lips never left hers, he angled her head the way he wanted, slipped his tongue into her mouth, and cupped her head in his hands with tenderness. Rowan felt as if she were floating, falling, giving herself over to him in a way that she'd never done with Frederick, or with any man. She felt the bindings break. This wasn't about predicting the future or reliving the past. Ash was here with her, right at that moment, and it was perfection.

That had to count for something, right?

He ended the kiss slowly and gently, then brushed the side of her face with his fingertips, his gaze traveling from her mouth to her hair, then back to her eyes.

"You are so pretty, Rowan. I really like your hair up like this."

She felt her cheeks go hot. "Thanks, but it's probably a little messed up."

"It's lovely. You're lovely."

Rowan looked out over the water, smiling to herself, then refocused on Ash. "You've known a lot of lovely women, I'm sure. I bet Nanette was one of them."

He laughed. "Only on the outside. But I'm not talking about Nanette or anyone else. I'm talking about you." Ash traced her bottom lip with his thumb. "You know what struck me about you right away?"

She shook her head.

"You're so *alive*, Rowan. You sparkle. Your skin, hair, eyes—everything about you shines. When you smile, I forget my own name."

She froze, not wanting to say anything that might ruin the moment.

"I just wish we could start all over."

"No kidding." She laughed. "I wish we'd met at a bar in Iowa. Or a baseball game in, I don't know, Alaska, or something. Anything, anywhere but here."

He smiled. "Baseball in Alaska?"

"You know what I mean. Somewhere very far away."

Ash placed his hand on her shoulder and caressed her, then stroked her back with long, gentle passes of his palm. It felt so incredibly good. "I kind of like it here on the island, Rowan. I only wish I'd gone about things differently from the beginning."

"How?"

"Well, for starters, I wish I hadn't let those kids drag me to town square and into your mother's clutches."

Rowan winced and sucked in air through her teeth. "Yeah . . . about that."

"Will you tell me why you got so upset?"

"Ehh." Rowan dug her toes into the sand, trying to decide how to answer his question without sounding as crazy as her mother. "Well, remember how I told you that my last relationship didn't end well?"

Ash nodded.

"That's glossing over a few of the more pertinent details." She took a deep breath to steady herself. "I met Frederick three years ago, during festival week, right here at the Safe Haven. He was staying there as a guest, just like you. And . . . well, he was the Man Grab that year, just like you. I fell for him really hard, the way I'm falling for you."

Ash nodded slowly, his face showing nothing but patience. Rowan figured he was giving her room to say what needed to be said, and she appreciated it.

"He played me perfectly. I followed him to New York, where he headed an investment company, to his apartment, and to his bed. He proposed to me." Rowan stopped, checking Ash's reaction. She saw concern in his eyes and decided to keep going. "I do think he loved me, at least at first. I don't think his intentions were a hundred percent awful from the start. But the truth is, once he'd hooked me, he went fishing for my family's money. He convinced all of us that he could take what remained of the Flynn fortune—which wasn't a lot, let me assure you—and earn us enough to restore the Safe Haven and never have money worries again."

Ash's mouth pulled tight.

"Yeah. I know. He's serving time in prison for stealing from a lot of people, not just us. But my parents lost their retirement and my brothers and I lost every dime we'd inherited from our grandparents. It was all very tragic, and it was all my fault—because I was gullible and stupid and I let a man seduce me."

"Rowan, sweetheart." Ash placed a fingertip under her chin and lifted her face. "It wasn't your fault. Truly. The man was a criminal and you and your family were victims of a crime. But I don't think I fully understand . . ." Ash frowned.

"Right. The Man Grab." She groaned. "I told you I don't believe in the mermaid legend, right?"

He nodded.

"It's deeper than that. I *hate* the legend."

"Okay."

She sighed again. "Right after I met Frederick, my mother kept telling me to go to the mermaid and ask for my true love. I did it—not because I believed in that crap but because I was sick of her riding me. I fell crazy in love with him, and, of course, her goofy group went off and had some secret ritual on my behalf and came back with the big news. The Great Mermaid had sanctioned my romance with Frederick and that I could be sure it was true love. He was my destiny. And she made a big, public deal of it."

Ash's eyes went huge.

"I know. It's complete idiocy, but I was already so in love with him that I let it slide. Unfortunately, when everything fell apart with Frederick and I came slinking home, my screwup was just as big a public event as my romance had been. The whole thing has made me pretty skittish. So tonight, when I found out you were the freakin' Man Grab . . ."

"Oh."

". . . the man who's supposed to find his heart-mate as soon as he finishes the ritual, I lost my damn mind! If people see me with you . . ."

"I understand," he said, his voice so soft she barely heard his words over the rhythmic waves of the ocean, now lapping at their feet. As if Ash knew what she needed, he opened his arms and brought her to his chest. He just held her like that for many long moments, occasionally kissing her hair or holding his hand to the back of her neck. "Rowan?"

She nodded, her cheek rubbing against the cotton of his shirt. Good God, he smelled so good! She closed her eyes tight.

"I don't think any of that matters—not what your mother says or which fairy tales people believe or don't believe. If you and I decide we want to enjoy each other, get to know each other, and maybe fall in love, it's nobody's business but ours. And the only magic at work is the magic the two of us create together."

Slowly, Rowan peeled herself from Ash's body, smiling. Honestly, that was the most romantic thing she'd ever heard a man say.

He continued. "So if we're confident in that, if we know where we stand and why, then all the weird shit swirling around us is just noise."

Rowan raised her fingers to Ash's cheek. "But you're aware that Bayberry's weird shit is weirder than most weird shit, right?"

Ash laughed. Rowan enjoyed the loose and comfortable sound of it and knew she'd never heard him laugh with such abandon before, without inhibitions. But even as she enjoyed his laughter, she couldn't stop staring at his face. Then it dawned on her—he looked different.

Lines that had been there just that morning were gone, and it definitely wasn't the moonlight playing tricks on her. The set of his mouth was kinder. His forehead was smoother.

"What are you looking at?" Ash grinned.

"You. You seem more relaxed tonight. Like a weight's been lifted from you."

"Ah." Ash released his hold of her, took her hand in his, and directed her down the beach toward the Safe Haven. "You might be right. Walk back with me?"

"Of course." Rowan leaned in to Ash and felt immense pleasure as he slipped his arm around her waist. They fell into a matching rhythm, Ash slowing his stride to accommodate her shorter legs. "I have a confession to make."

Rowan's head snapped up so she could see him. "About what?"

"Why I was late tonight."

She groaned. "I'm really sorry about Hubie. He's old and grumpy and he hates Mona with a passion. You know that knife he was carrying?"

Ash nodded. "Yeah. What was up with that?"

Rowan figured since Ash had already met Hubie Krank, he would know that he posed no real threat. "About a week ago he took a steak knife to all the tires on my family's old Subaru. His daughter wrote us a check, marched over there, and removed everything sharp from his house—scissors, nail files, hedge trimmers, even the blades to his food processor—cleaned the place out."

"She was thorough."

"But not quite thorough enough. Hubie showed up a couple hours before you did Friday, waving around an old antique sword he'd found in the attic or someplace, saying he had to protect himself from the Flynns."

Ash stopped walking. "Is all this about the resort plans? Does Hubie live on the cove?"

Rowan nodded. "Directly across Shoreline Road."

"Huh." He started up again, and they walked together in comfortable silence for a moment. "Well, swashbuckling Hubie wasn't the reason I was late, Rowan. He just made me a little later than I already was."

"Okay. Why were you so late, then?"

He glanced sideways at her. "Remember how I said I had almost convinced myself that I wasn't the right man for you? Well, I made up my mind not to come tonight. I packed up and headed to the boat, deciding I'd sleep on the dock if I had to. I made it to town before I turned around and came back. I guess it took a little time to sort out how I felt."

Determined not to make a face or say something snarky, Rowan kept strolling. She couldn't blame Ash for having doubts—she'd been plenty conflicted herself that evening. They were both grown-ups with baggage, and things were moving fast between them. And what was happening wasn't something either of them had been looking for. "So what made you come back?"

Ash sighed, pulling her tighter to his side as he slowed the pace. "This may sound crazy, but I heard my own voice in my head telling me what to do. Have you ever suddenly known what path to take, the right choice coming to you almost out of nowhere?" He looked down at her, moonlight sparkling in his eyes. "I mean, really *known*. From here." He gently poked her belly with a finger.

Ash was about to pull it away, but changed his mind,

spreading his fingers over the bodice of her dress, flattening his palm and holding it there. Rowan felt his heat penetrate the thin dotted Swiss cotton, and it spread through her stomach and down between her legs. If it were possible to press her thighs together while walking, she would have done it.

"I think I know what you mean."

"When was the last time it happened to you?"

Rowan laughed. "Um." She draped her hand over his hip. "About fifteen minutes ago, when you told me to stop talking and kissed the bejesus out of me. I heard a little voice tell me to let it happen, that it would be all right."

Ash kissed the top of her head, then slowed to a halt. "Rowan Flynn, may I have this dance?"

She giggled, looking around the deserted moonlit beach. "The dance floor's pretty crowded."

"True, but this is my favorite song."

"All I hear is the ocean."

"Exactly."

Ash gently turned Rowan until she faced him, slipped an arm around her back, then laced his fingers with hers. Rowan gazed up into his eyes and knew, without a doubt, that finally—at the age of thirty—she was having one of those impossibly romantic moments that seemed to happen only to other women. She'd always imagined that if this sort of thing ever happened to her, it would take place in Paris, or Rome, or even Boston. Not here on the Bayberry Island beach, the most unromantic place on earth.

Until tonight. Until Ashton Louis Wallace III had made it romance central.

He leaned down and gently kissed the side of her neck left exposed by her hairstyle. He nuzzled her as he swayed back and forth, bringing her even tighter to his body. He handled her like she was precious to him, like he didn't want to let her go. Unbelievably, he began to sing to her, his voice tender and sweet. She recognized it—some of Ray LaMontagne's most haunting music and lyrics, where a man assures his woman that she'll forever be his lover and friend.

Her entire body took a deep breath and held it. Wouldn't that be just wonderful?

Ash would start to set things right in the morning, but for tonight, he simply wanted to keep dancing with Rowan under the twinkling lights of the clambake's dance floor, allow himself to marinate in the strange sensations that had somehow penetrated his defenses. He didn't think much of pop psychology, but even he admitted that all the loss he'd experienced in his life had left its mark. It had settled around his heart like layers of silt, the shell growing harder and thicker with each blow. But on this magical night, that shell had cracked open enough that an entire world had forced its way inside.

Rowan was in his arms, and she felt perfect against him as they swayed in the warm glow of tiki torches and the thousands of tiny white lights strung overhead. The musical stylings of the clambake DJ seemed a little schizophrenic to Ash, veering from hip-hop to country without warning, but the beer-lubricated crowd enjoying this pleasant seaside night didn't seem to mind. Annie and Nat were dancing right next to them, and Annie had just said something that made Rowan toss her head back and laugh.

Ash stared at her in wonder. He wasn't the only one taking a risk. This resilient, funny, and beautiful woman had been willing to open up to him, and the stakes had been just as high for her. He knew when he told her his whole story it would take every one of his persuasive sales techniques to get her to sit still and hear him out. But Ash had faith in himself, and in Rowan, and in their willingness. He knew they would get through this.

The music ended and Ravelle gestured for Ash. "Want a beer?"

"Sure." Ash kissed Rowan quickly. "Be right back."

In the last hour or so, Ash had decided Nat Ravelle was a great guy, despite the Los Angeles–isms that occasionally slipped from his mouth. His view of the world was just slightly askew, a by-product of his years working as a producer for a paranormal reality series, no doubt. But he had a wicked, dry sense of humor that Ash enjoyed. It was a relief to Ash that he genuinely liked the man who would soon be Annie's husband. Anything less could have caused some problems.

"Tell me more about your foundation," Ravelle said, pulling the keg lever and filling another plastic cup.

"Thanks." Ash accepted the beer and took a sip. "Oceanaire is an educational nonprofit focused on marine ecology and preservation. We fund a lot of research, provide scholarships, and sponsor marine biology camps for younger kids."

Ravelle nodded, his brow arching. "Nice. So is marine biology your background?"

Ash chuckled. It was obvious that Annie had sent her fiancé out to do a little man-to-man fact finding. He didn't mind, and even appreciated Annie's concern for Rowan.

"My background is mostly sales and business consulting. My best friend was the marine biologist, and the foundation was his family's undertaking. When he died, his will specified that I should take his place as chairman of the board."

Ravelle shook his head. "Sorry to hear about your friend, man."

"Thanks." Ash took another sip of beer.

"So what does a chairman of the board do, actually?" Ravelle started walking back to the dance floor, but at a leisurely pace. Ash suspected he couldn't return to Annie unless he had something substantial to report.

"Your guess is as good as mine," he said, laughing. "I've been at it only a few months. Right now the board is trying to find a place to locate a research and education institute, along with its headquarters. I'm supposed to be looking around for them, since I've had some site acquisition experience."

"Really?" Nat's beer cup hung in midair. "Bayberry Island could use something like that. Shit, it sounds a whole lot better than a big casino hotel and golf resort — that's for sure."

Ash stared. He thought his head might explode. Knowing he needed to stay cool, he looked down at his bare feet moving through the sand, but Ravelle was too quick.

"Oh man. I'm sorry for poking around like that. You're here looking for a site for your nonprofit, aren't you? Is it a hush-hush sort of thing?"

Ash knew that how he responded to this question would impact his relationship with Rowan, her family, and everyone who called the island their home. He knew that he couldn't show the rush of excitement, ideas, and to-dos that now flooded his brain.

"No." He looked at Ravelle and shook his head. "It hadn't even occurred to me, to tell you the truth. My sailboat broke down and I had to be towed in. Oceanaire was the last thing on my mind when I set foot on Bayberry."

"Oh." Ravelle shrugged, looking disappointed. "Hey, it was a thought. It's none of my business, really."

The men returned to the dance floor and decided to switch partners for the last dance. As Ash spun Annie around, his mind short-circuited with a thousand questions and ideas about how he could bring Oceanaire's institute to Bayberry Island. Nat was right—it just might be a perfect fit. The foundation needed a new home, room to grow. And the island needed something to revive the economy. No, an education and research facility wouldn't bring in anywhere near the revenue of a huge resort, but it also wouldn't destroy the quaint and quirky nature of the island. And, most important, the landowners along the cove would still get the payday they needed. Ash would see to it that they received fair market compensation for their valuable property.

"You seem out to sea, Ash," Annie said over the sound system.

He snapped to attention. "I'm sorry."

Annie tipped her head and looked up at him. "You really like her, don't you?"

"I really do." Ash twirled Annie around playfully, thinking how he wished he could run to Rowan and tell her all about the brilliant idea of bringing Oceanaire to Bayberry Island. But he knew he couldn't. That decision wasn't his to make alone. It required a vote from the board of directors and James's approval. Besides, he didn't want to get Rowan's hopes up only to let her down. Another disappointment was the last thing she needed.

As he completed the series of twirls, Annie began laughing. "You're quite the dancer, Mr. Wallace."

"It's easy when you have a lovely and accomplished partner," he said, grinning at her. Ash was glad he had a chance to get to know Annie. He wanted Rowan's best friend's seal of approval, and for no other reason than Annie was important to Rowan and Rowan was important to him. It felt wonderful to have no ulterior motives. But Annie was easy to get along with—he had to admit that the queen of mermaid porn was a lot of fun.

As soon as the song ended, the two couples walked together up the beach steps and through the sprawling lawn of the bed-and-breakfast. They said good night near the circular drive with a round of hugs and handshakes.

Ash stood at Rowan's side, her hand in his. It was nearly midnight. He didn't want to presume anything. He had no idea how tired she was, what she was thinking, or how slow she wanted to take this. He knew only that he'd been picturing her naked in that nice bed of hers for hours and he would be one poor excuse of a man if he didn't give it a shot.

As their friends passed through the fallen gates, Ash squeezed Rowan's hand tighter. "So."

"So." She squeezed his.

"I hope you don't find me forward, Miss Flynn."

"That would be unfortunate."

"But I must admit something."

"Please do."

He looked down into her face. "I hope to have such a wild night with you that I shall require fresh bed linens in the morning."

She giggled. "Anything to make your stay a pleasant one, Mr. Wallace."

Mona remained perfectly still long after the young couples left the beach. She'd been sitting at that same table at the edges of the clambake for hours now. Clancy stopped by to check on her several times before he had to leave. Frasier had given her a half dozen scalding looks, which she surely appreciated. And since Rowan's little outburst hadn't exactly gone unnoticed, Izzy, Abby, Darinda, and Polly had joined her for a beer, trying to cheer her up. But now the beach crowd was thinning out and the caterers were packing up. The moon, done with its arc over the beach, was in hiding beyond the bluff and beginning its journey across the mainland.

Mona looked at her fingers laced together on the tabletop. She was getting to be an old lady. Her knuckles were swollen with arthritis, more painful than ever these days. Her nails were brittle, and her skin was crinkly. Her life had gone by too fast, faster than the moon's sweep across the beach on an August night. And now the light was fading.

The day she gave birth to Rowan was one of the happiest of her life. Mona recalled in great detail the delight she felt bringing a pretty little bundle of femininity back home to the island. How she'd enjoyed watching Rowan grow into the spirited, smart girl who butted heads with her at every opportunity. The day she graduated from Tufts, Mona had been filled to the brim with pride and happiness for her daughter.

By that time, Duncan had long since found his stride in the world, leaving his tough early years far behind. And Clancy, in typical easygoing fashion, was well on his way to pursuing his dream, too. So for Mona to see her daughter blossom into an accomplished and hardworking young woman was a profound honor; it was the crowning glory of the years she'd spent as a mother.

And who was Mona now? Not a wife. Not a mother. Not a grandmother. Not an innkeeper. And certainly not a beloved neighbor. Mona's sole purpose was to corral an unruly group of "ladies of a certain age" and keep them on point in their service to the legend of the Great Mermaid.

It was a thankless job. She knew many people, including her own children, saw her work as pure lunacy.

Mona couldn't drag her gaze away from the torch-lined beach steps. That was where she'd seen the last little snippet of Rowan, so lovely in her summer dress, tucked arm in arm with the handsome and kindhearted Ashton. She shook her head, feeling as if her heart would tear apart with the irony of it.

All she'd ever wanted was for her girl to be happy, and Mona had never seen Rowan happier than she'd been tonight, dancing, safe in Ashton's arms and mesmerized by his adoring gaze. She'd laughed joyously with her friends. She'd looked so pretty, flowing and peaceful just being herself, a young woman falling in love. But all that happiness wasn't due to her mother's intervention—it was *in spite* of it.

No wonder Rowan resented her so.

Mona let her head fall into her hands. She was haunted by what had happened with Frederick Theissen. Mona had steered her own beautiful girl into the clutches of a charming monster, and when the charm fell away and the monster emerged, Mona never really took responsibility for her own spectacular lack of judgment. Instead, she accepted Rowan's guilt-ridden offer to manage the Safe Haven, a job Mona could no longer do because of her arthritis. Mona allowed the B and B to become just another burden on her daughter's already burdened shoulders. How could she have done that to her?

Mona knew that everything Rowan had said in anger earlier that night had been correct. She had no right to advise anyone else about romance when her own story was so twisted and confusing. And tonight, watching Rowan on the dance floor with Ash, Mona had been flooded with a memory.

Many years ago, she'd had a night much like it. It was the festival-week clambake, an event made magic by moonlight and new love. A twenty-five-year-old girl had been sheltered in Frasier Flynn's strong arms that night, and she'd been swept up in his humor, his beautiful green eyes, and the way his body felt against hers. Mona's own mother hadn't been thrilled at her daughter's decision to leave New Hampshire and move to Bayberry Island to be with Frasier, but she'd done it anyway. Mona had followed her heart. At the time, she'd maintained that she was a grown woman entitled to chart her own course. All these years later, despite everything, she didn't regret that decision. She had three wonderful children, and underneath it all, she still loved that man who'd danced with her on a moonlit night so long ago.

Maybe it wasn't too late to rebuild the marriage they'd allowed to fall into disrepair.

Mona blinked back tears. Her daughter was now a grown woman entitled to chart her own course. She had a right to live her life, wherever she pleased, in whatever way she wished, and with whomever she wanted. Just as Mona had done so long ago, Rowan had a right to make her own decisions about career and love, and no one, especially her mother, should stand in her way.

It still crushed her heart to think she'd misread the situation with Frederick so terribly. In her eagerness for her daughter's happiness, Mona had sent Rowan to the mermaid after she'd already met Frederick, forgetting the most important part of the legend. "Those who come to the mermaid with preconceived notions about the 'how, who, when, and wheres' of true love will find heartache instead!"

Mona raised her head. It was quite late, and she needed to make her way down the four blocks to her little house on Idlewilde Lane. It was time to take stock of her life. She had wanted nothing more than to improve life for her family and friends, but it was now clear to her she'd caused discord instead. Maybe her blind devotion to the Safe Haven and its grand past wasn't about others after all. Maybe it was simply her own ego at work, the stubbornness of an old woman holding on to a time and way of life that was no longer practical.

She pushed herself to a stand and grabbed her shoes from the sand, her hands aching from the simple effort. There was much that would have to be sorted out in the weeks and months to come, but if she was going to set things right, there were two things she knew must happen—immediately.

First, Mona would stop meddling in Rowan's love life, *no matter what*. Rowan and her new beau were adults. They could figure it out for themselves. That meant Mona had to find a way to keep the legend and her daughter separate.

Second, Mona would contact that pushy woman from Jessop-Riley in the morning and tell her she was done fighting. They could have the land.

With that, Mona would set her daughter and the rest of her family free. They would no longer be slaves to a dilapidated old mansion and too much land to take care of, and they would have the money to live however they pleased. It was the greatest gift she could give them.

Mona's face was wet with tears and her knees ached as she climbed the beach steps, but her heart already felt lighter. The time had come for the Flynns to start their real lives.

Chapter Fourteen

The nearer they got to the top of the carriage house stairs, the slower they seemed to move. Rowan suspected it was because there was weight to this decision. Once she and Ash entered the apartment, fully intending to make love, there would be no way to brush it aside as a fluke.

The first night she and Ash were here together, there were no lights. They didn't know the first thing about each other. And they had no context for what was about to happen between them. Tonight was different. The lights were on. They had decided there was potential for a relationship. And they'd already had a taste of each other.

No wonder she had butterflies in her stomach.

Rowan was first to step into the living room, and she looked over her shoulder to give Ash a shy glance. For some reason, she'd started to feel embarrassed.

"Come here, my lovely Rowan." Ash reached out for both her hands and drew her toward him, his intense blue eyes filled with tenderness. Then he pressed her close and simply held her, not asking for a thing, and Rowan felt the steady cadence of his heart against her cheek. There was much she still had to learn about this man, but one thing she was sure of: He'd been through a lot and he had managed to hang on to his kindness. That was the type of man she had always wanted. And here he was—in her apartment and in her life. Very soon now, he'd be in her bed.

There was a lot at stake here, but she decided she would be brave tonight. She would explore the possibilities with the man the universe had been kind enough to send to her door.

"I've been looking forward to being alone with you all night, from the first second I saw you standing at the bottom of the beach steps in this dress." Ash's hands roamed over her back and up her sides as he whispered into her ear. "You looked like an angel."

"I was going for something a little less chaste."

Rowan felt Ash's body shake with laughter, and she smiled against his chest.

"Then I guess you can handle the whole truth, Miss Flynn."

"Oh yeah?"

Ash grasped her bare arms and set her apart from him. The smile he gave her was seductive. "I took one look at you in that smokin'-hot sexy thing you've got on and all I wanted to do was get it off. I pictured you naked and spread out on your bed, trembling because I was about to bury myself deep inside you."

Rowan's breath hitched. "Oh." That was all she could manage.

"So?"

She blinked. "Yes?"

"That's a yes?" Ash chuckled.

"Yes. Please."

Without warning, Ash grabbed her behind her knees, lifted her from the floor, and carried her across the living room, down the hall, and into her bedroom. In the dim light of her bedside lamp, she could see that the place looked as if it had been ransacked by burglars.

"Sorry. I forgot I made such a mess."

Ash set her gently on the edge of the bed and started picking up clothes, shoving everything back into his duffel. Rowan wondered why his toiletry bag was zipped and packed, but she didn't have time to dwell on it. Ash was dropping to his knees in front of her, wedging his big body between her legs and spreading them wide. He reached up and carefully removed the flower and pins from her hair, placing everything on the floor. Then he raked his fingers along Rowan's scalp, sending a shiver of pleasure through her as her hair fell around her bare shoulders.

Ash looked up, a wistful expression on his face. He slid a fingertip up the inside of her exposed thigh, leaving an electric tingle on her skin as he went. He managed to push up the hem of her dress while he was at it.

"Do you remember the storm?" His voice was soft. "Remember how we attacked each other on the floor, in the dark?"

Rowan nodded. It wasn't like a girl could forget that sort of thing.

"I don't want that tonight."

"You don't?"

He shook his head, his smile becoming more sweet than seductive. "I want us to make love tonight. Just take our time to explore each other. I want . . ." Ash cut himself off, closed his eyes briefly, and reopened them. "Rowan, the last thing I want to do is freak you out, but I hope this is the start of something incredible for us. I want to take care of you tonight, show you how it feels when a man absolutely adores you, desires you so badly there aren't words for it. I want you to melt."

Since no man had ever said anything like that to her

before, she had no idea how to respond. Rowan tried to smile but felt hot tears begin to well in her eyes, which she struggled to keep at bay. In lieu of speaking, Rowan leaned down and kissed him, hoping she would be able to convey how his words touched her. She pressed her fingertips just under his chin as her lips roamed all over his. When she gently opened his mouth with her tongue and bit down on his bottom lip, he moaned with delight. Rowan's goal was to hear that sound from him many, many times tonight.

Her kiss went on. She tasted him and tested him, curious how he would react to every little thing she did. Would he let her decide the pace? Could he relax and receive? What seemed to send him over the edge? As Rowan toyed with him, she slid her fingers up into his loose curls, marveling at how intimate it felt to hold his head in her hands. There was no doubt about it—she was falling in love with Ash. With this kiss, she felt it pour out of her and into him. She couldn't help it. It was too late to change the course of her emotions. Even if she wanted to, it would be too late to talk herself out of loving him.

He slowly broke the kiss. With his gaze locked on hers, Ash reached up and untied the halter of her dress, holding the straps in his hands to control how much of her flesh was exposed and how quickly. Rowan saw how he looked at her. He had such reverence in his expression, and his intensity pierced her heart.

She knew he was falling, too.

Ash eased the straps down, over the tops of her breasts, over her aching nipples, finally allowing the halter to fall to her waist.

"Oh my God," he whispered. "So beautiful. You're the most beautiful thing I've ever seen."

Slowly and carefully, as if he wanted to savor the sensation, Ash dragged a single fingertip down the slope of her breast. He then cupped each one in a palm, a look of awe in his eyes. Ash lowered his head, kissing the tops of her breasts, the sides, then, one by one, her incredibly sensitive nipples. A shiver of pleasure coursed through her.

"You like that, don't you? I can tell."

She nodded, tipping her head back. It felt as if she were beginning to float, as if the bliss had set her free.

For many more minutes, Ash gave his complete attention to Rowan's breasts. She glanced down to observe how her flesh had become a playground for his fingers, hands, lips, tongue, and teeth. He hummed as he sucked her nipples, the vibration nearly causing Rowan to jump from the bed. The deep rumble of his chuckle only intensified the teasing.

"I want to play with you a lot, Rowan. Would that be all right?" Ash asked this as he drew closer, but he gave her no time to answer. He kissed her lips again as he unzipped the back of her dress. As if on cue, a warm breeze slipped through the bedroom window and skimmed along the length of her spine. Oh, it felt so decadent.

Slowly, painfully slowly, Ash pulled the dress down to her hips. His hands splayed out over Rowan's belly, and he held them there. Rowan was puzzled. He seemed frozen. Was he changing his mind?

Ash leaned into Rowan without warning, and she had to clasp her hands around his neck for balance. He gave her no time to recover, taking her mouth with his. Though Rowan knew from experience that he was still holding back, this kiss was far more intense than the last. It was deep and delicious, and the beauty of it left her too weak to hold on. Her fingers slipped. She fell back onto the bed, and Ash followed, continuing to slide his hot mouth all over hers, his hands all over her stomach.

"I want you so much, sweetheart. Rowan, I have to

have you." Ash left a string of kisses across her cheeks, chin, and forehead, then down her throat, between her breasts, down the center of her body. She felt her belly ripple with anticipation.

Eventually the kisses ceased, and Ash let his palms slide down inside the loosened dress. The instant she felt his fingers slip into her panties, Rowan arched her back from the shock of it, from the need that rocked her.

She knew how wet he would find her, and she knew the begging Ash had envisioned wasn't far off.

In a single motion, Ash rose to his feet and took the dress and panties with him, tossing her clothes aside. Rowan peeked under her lashes to see his beautifully masculine face shadowed by seriousness, that sensual mouth set in determination. She could only imagine how she appeared to him, stretched out on top of the comforter, bare, breathing hard. She probably looked like the desperate wanton she was.

"Please." Her voice came out as a raspy, impatient plea from a greedy woman. "Take off your clothes for me. I need to see you."

Ash seemed to enjoy her request and began to unbutton the front of his shirt. He took his sweet time, and Rowan felt he was teasing her. Eventually, he pulled the shirttail up and out of his leather belt, leaving the shirt hanging open, hands loose at his sides.

The vision left her breathless. His chest was hard and defined, with small pale nipples surrounded by blond down. Toward the top of his chest the hair was light in color, but it darkened and became streamlined as it continued into the waistband of his pants. Even with the movement caused by his breathing, the muscles of his abdomen rippled.

She couldn't help it. She licked her lips and made a helpless little mewling sound.

Ash seemed to like that, and he smiled as he brought his hands to the fly of his khakis. With a determined slowness that tortured her, Ash unbuckled the belt and let it hang open. He brought his fingers to the top button of his pants, twisted it free, then reached for his zipper.

That's when Rowan lost her patience. She started to sit up. She needed to touch his chest and stomach, needed that so much she was sure she'd die if he stopped her. She also wanted to do the honors with the zipper. Maybe she would use her teeth.

"No, baby." He grinned, gently pressing her shoulders to the bed. "What I need for you to do is stay on your back and let me open your legs. That's all I need you to do. Can you do that for me?"

She nodded.

"I promise it will be worth it, sweetheart."

Ash dropped to his knees once more. When Rowan felt his fingers on her legs, knees, and haunches, she shivered. When his hot breath hit the back of her knee, she gasped. When she felt his breath brush up the inside of one thigh, she groaned.

And when he delivered a long and languid lick along the seam of her sex, she cried out. *"Oh my God!"*

Rowan hadn't experienced anything like this in so very long. Too long. So long that she didn't remember what it felt like.

Ash put his entire mouth over her sex, cupped her bottom in his hands, and raised her up so he could feast on her. It went on and on, licking, sucking, nibbling . . . Rowan got so wet she feared Ash's mouth couldn't contain it, and she felt a warm rivulet of her passion slip through his lips and hands and run down her bottom.

"Oh my God. Please. Please. It's too much, too good . . . oh please."

Somewhere in the back of her mind she was aware

that the out-of-her-head crazy-woman voice she heard babbling in the background was her own. She planned to stop the nonsensical mumbling as soon as possible. "Oh God. Ash. Please. This is so good. Please. Please."

It was too intense, too wonderful. Her legs began to shake. Rowan let out a long and deep moan.

There was no turning back. The heat and pressure had built so furiously that it felt as if all the pleasure in the universe just converged like a laser beam, striking the most tender part of her being.

She was going to come. The night had hardly even started and she was about to explode.

"Not yet, sweetheart."

Ash took his mouth from her. He released her and lowered her bottom to the mattress. She would have complained but was unable to form words.

"Rowan."

She opened her eyes and saw Ash standing again, staring down at her with dark intensity. He unzipped his pants. She watched him hook his thumbs in his boxer briefs and yank everything down at once. Suddenly, the most beautiful man she'd ever seen stood completely naked before her. He was big and hard and he wanted her as much as she wanted him.

At that moment, there were only three words in the English language that would be of any use to her. So she said them.

"Take me. Please."

Ash bent over, carefully spread her legs wider as he pushed them back, and lowered his big body onto her. It was shocking how hot and hard he felt and how open and desperate she was for him.

He kissed her. Ash took her with his mouth, prying her open and letting her know how it was going to unfold. She was his. He was opening her, everywhere, and taking what was his.

He entered her body with precision. He moved slowly, unwavering in his goal of claiming what was his. Rowan reveled in the effortlessness of what was unfolding between them. It was a simple equation, the most loving and perfect moment Rowan had ever experienced. She threw her arms around him and held him tight as he unlocked her, body and soul.

The rest of the night was a timeless blur. They made love off and on until morning, stopping only for water, bathroom breaks, and at one point, they raided the freezer for butter pecan ice cream that they ate in bed, naked, with one spoon, straight from the carton.

She learned so much about Ash. She saw that he could be lighthearted even in the throes of passion. She figured out what made him lose control. She learned how much he liked her to grip him tight at the base of his cock while she gently sucked him. And she discovered that Ash had never preferred one sexual position over another, though he did reserve the right to change his mind in the future.

When the night was over and it was almost time for her to get to the Safe Haven kitchen, Rowan understood something about Ash that surprised her. He *needed* physical affection, and he wasn't afraid to let her know that. He responded so earnestly to her touch and was determined to give as much as he received.

Hands down, it had been the best night of her life. Ash had delivered on his promise—Rowan now knew how it felt to have a man absolutely adore her.

Ash turned off the shower and grabbed a towel from the rack, holding it open for Rowan. She turned away so that her back was to him, and he pulled her in tight, giving her skin a quick rubdown. "I wish you didn't have to go."

"Me too. But unless you want Mellie marching in here while you're naked, you'd better let me get to the kitchen."

Ash sighed, wrapping the towel tight, then hugging Rowan in his arms. "You're probably exhausted, sweetheart."

She leaned the back of her wet head onto his chest and giggled. "I'm exhausted—but happy."

"Happily exhausted."

"Exactly. How about you?" She peeked over her shoulder and smiled, pushing up the apples of her cute, freckled cheeks.

Ash wasn't lying when he told Rowan her smile made him forget his own name. But it was what it made him remember that was the real story. When Rowan smiled, Ash remembered that he was still alive, that happiness could survive sorrow, and that joy might be right in front of him.

"I'm doing pretty good for a man who got about ten minutes of sleep, but I don't have a bed-and-breakfast to run, either. I'm a man of leisure, you know."

"Must be nice." She tried to wriggle free of his grasp. "I really do need to get dressed."

"I can't convince you to come back to bed with me?"

Rowan laughed out loud. "Don't torture me like that. I'd love to spend the whole day in bed with you, but it's Tuesday, which means I've got to make a crap-ton of crepes before seven."

"Hmm." He kissed her wet hair. "Is that a Flynn family recipe?"

She laughed again and tried once more to escape his clutches, but he didn't want to let her go. One image after another flashed through his mind of the night they'd just spent together, followed by a rush of remembered sensation. Never in his life had he felt so much love in a woman's touch, so much welcome in her arms. She was a wonder, this Rowan Flynn, and he knew it couldn't be random luck that he'd found her. Ash chuckled into her wet hair, wondering if he had a magical fountain to thank for his incredible good fortune.

He hadn't meant to be pushy, but Ash found himself pressed up against Rowan's backside. He could tell by the way she stiffened that she felt his arousal.

"That's not helping at all, Mr. Wallace."

Ash lowered his lips to the nape of her neck and drew aside a clump of wet hair so he could kiss her there. She smelled like breezy body wash and warm Rowan. "You know, that's a great idea. I could help out in the dining room this morning. I've never worn an apron before, but I bet I'd look hot in one."

"I'm sure you would." Suddenly, Rowan escaped his embrace, and Ash was left holding the damp towel in his hands. She turned to face him, naked, her skin pink from the hot shower. One of the things he'd already come to love about Rowan's body was the pattern of freckles splashed across her chest and arms. He couldn't help but think of that cute and stubborn little girl in the photo on her fireplace mantel. She'd grown into a gorgeous and special woman.

Rowan took advantage of his preoccupation and swiped the towel from his grasp. "I know I have a lot of freckles. I hate them." She bent forward and wrapped the towel around her hair, twisted it into place the way women did, and straightened up.

Ash was puzzled. "You hate your freckles? Seriously? I love them!"

"Thank you, but I really have to go." She got on her

tiptoes to kiss him. While she was there, she smacked his butt, hard, then jumped out of the shower before he could retaliate.

Ash laughed. "So that's how you want to do this?" Still naked and wet, he followed at her heels, running across the hall into the bedroom. He grabbed her from behind, picked her up, and flipped her over his shoulder.

Rowan began pounding his back with her balled-up fists, laughing hard. "Put me down!"

"Whatever do you mean?" He pinched her cute little ass. "I'm simply taking you to find some clothes to wear to work. I am being nothing but a help to you. Should we check in here? See anything you like?" He swung around so fast that her feet pulled down several hangers from the closet rod.

"Ash! Please!"

"How about your dresser?" Ash riffled around in the top drawer and pulled out a lacy pink bra, then slipped his free arm through the strap. "Does this make me look flat-chested?"

"It makes you look like a six-foot-three dude with a bra hanging off his arm." She continued her drumming on his back. "I gotta get ready for work!"

Ash tried his best not to laugh, but Rowan was so much fun to play with! He couldn't remember the last time he'd allowed himself to prance around like a complete ass the way he was doing at that moment. Maybe that was because he never had. "Well, since you can't seem to choose what to wear today, how about we go into the kitchen so I can make you some coffee? Maybe that will help you think clearly."

He'd just made it through the bedroom door when he felt Rowan's hands go still. Before Ash could figure out what she was up to, the tickling started.

"Stop!"

"Are you ticklish?"

"No!"

"Oh, that is such a lie!"

She was right. Ash was exceptionally ticklish and knew he wouldn't be able to withstand much more of this torture, especially since she'd found his two weakest spots—under his arms and along his sides. He staggered into the living room and veered off balance toward the top of the stairs. "Come on now! Not fair!"

"Then put me down!"

"Never!"

"Rowan? Are you up there?"

Ash froze. Rowan's tickling stopped. Both didn't dare breathe. As if coming out of a daze, he realized he had a gorgeous naked woman slung over his shoulder, her ass about an inch from his face.

Rowan whispered harshly in his ear, "I told you! Oh my God—we're both naked. Hurry!"

Ash released Rowan and set her on her feet. She stood in front of him. In one smooth movement, Rowan turned to face the steps, whipped the towel from her head, and slapped Ash across the face with it in her rush. Maybe he deserved that. Just as Rowan opened the towel and pulled it taut in front of her, the carriage house door opened.

Imelda flipped on the stairwell light and narrowed her gaze at the two of them. But her eyes went huge when she realized the state of their undress.

"I'm on my way," Rowan said.

Mellie shook her head silently and left, gently closing the door behind her.

Rowan spun around to face Ash, and she was *pissed*.

Before a word could escape her mouth, he kissed her, then asked, "Has anyone ever told you that you're exceptionally beautiful when you're angry?"

She rolled her eyes. "Get dressed."

"Me?"

"Yes. You." Rowan snapped the bath towel against his bare butt as she walked by, and this time the attack was intentional. "You've got a crap-ton of crepes to make this morning, Mr. Wallace."

Clancy grabbed what appeared to be a banana-nut muffin straight off the baking sheet, headed toward the coffeepot, and decided to give himself a moment before he even greeted anyone.

It had been a long night. He'd had to drag four drunk, underage teenagers from the clambake, arrest a man for trespassing out at the marina, issue citations for a multitude of illegal beach bonfires, and deal with the usual marijuana possession, public intox, lewd behavior, and indecency complaints. Clancy took a sip of the good and strong coffee he knew he'd find here in his childhood kitchen and stared out the window. He decided that while he waited for the caffeine to kick in, he'd give himself a few minutes to do nothing but watch dawn break over the sea.

He sighed. Three days, three nights, and one morning was all that remained of this year's festival week. That meant there were only two major events to worry about from a public safety standpoint—today's reenactment at the museum and Thursday night's Mermaid Ball. He didn't count the annual Flynn family cookout tomorrow evening. There would be plenty of opportunity for conflict, of course—with his parents either ignoring each other or going nose-to-nose over the damn development project again—but it wouldn't be something that would require calling for backup. At least he hoped not.

Clancy knew the dynamic would be different at the cookout this year. For one thing, Annie would bring Nat along, and Rowan would probably have her pretty-boy prepster in tow. Clancy couldn't be too hard on the guy. He'd done some checking on Wallace and he seemed legit enough. He was chairman of a nonprofit just like he said and had earned his business degree from Harvard. He couldn't find much on the consulting business Wallace said he was closing, aside from his corporation filing with the state and a vague and brief Web site. Clancy figured he was some kind of mercenary, stepping in to help companies do their dirty work, like firing people for managers who didn't have the balls to do it themselves.

Once festival week was over, he'd make some calls to his buddies on the force in Boston. Maybe they could find out a little more on Wallace. But regardless of what the man used to do for a living, Clancy had watched how he'd patiently escorted the cantankerous Hubie Krank to the beach last night and had to admit Wallace had a decent streak in him.

Maybe his sister had finally found herself a good one.

And, of course, the other change to this year's cookout would be Duncan. His big brother might be a self-centered bastard, but at least when he graced them with his presence it provided an excuse to celebrate as a cohesive family unit.

But not this year. Clancy wondered where Duncan might be, and not knowing always left a vague sense of dread floating around in his brain. He might not be his big brother's biggest fan, but he loved him and wanted him to come home safe.

Clancy gulped down the rest of his first cup and set about getting another.

"Good morning, Chief."

Clancy paused, his hand on the coffee dispenser lever. The Safe Haven's kitchen had always been the domain of women. Mellie, Rowan, and the four foreign cuties were usually the only people in here at six thirty on a weekday morning. That said, he had a good idea whom he'd be eyeballing when he spun around. Yep. He'd been right. Kind of. Ash Wallace had just greeted him, but the dude was wearing an apron with cups and saucers and teapots and shit all over it.

"You must've pissed her off something fierce."

Wallace laughed. "I did."

Clancy shrugged and took another gulp of life-giving coffee. "Check in the walk-in freezer. There might be some butter pecan ice cream in the back."

"Might just do that."

Clancy let his gaze wander up and down Wallace's person. He looked ridiculous with his hairy legs sticking out of the bottom of the long apron, but he sure was happy. Why he looked that way wasn't anything Clancy cared to dwell on. "Saw you gettin' your dance on last night. Didn't think you had it in ya."

Wallace shook his head. "Are you always going to give me grief like this?"

Clancy shrugged. "How long you plan on sticking around Bayberry?"

"As long as she'll let me."

Okay. He'd given that answer without a second of hesitation and with complete certainty. Clancy had to hide his surprise. This guy really cared for his sister. Not that it wasn't warranted, because Rowan was a great girl. But, honestly, Wallace hadn't struck him as the type who wanted to settle down, especially on a lonely rock like this one. He wondered how long it would be before Wallace hatched a plan to whisk Rowan away to the city. He didn't even want to think of the fate of the B and B if that happened.

"Let's see." Clancy nodded to his sister's suitor. "I

suppose I'll be giving you a hard time as long as she lets you hang around. It's my job."

Wallace seemed to take it in stride. "Fair enough."

"So what's she got you doin' in here this morning?"

"Everything." He looked over his shoulder toward the stove, where Mellie and Rowan were running their usual crepe assembly line. "I've already made about ten pounds of bacon, and now she's got me cutting fruit. These guests are pigs."

Clancy chuckled. "Yeah, well, I've been in your shoes more mornings than I can count. When my dad closed the fishery and we turned this place into a B and B, we all had to work for our keep. Us kids did whatever had to be done—cleaned rooms, served food, kept up the landscaping. It wasn't until we all went to college that our parents hired seasonal help."

Wallace frowned, like that was something he couldn't comprehend. Clancy figured he hadn't had much personal experience with making ends meet.

"Ash? Would you grab the blueberries from the counter for me, please?" Rowan's voice was cheerful and sweet until she raised her head from the crepe pan and noticed her brother. "Oh. Hey, Clancy. I didn't see you there."

Wallace smiled at Clancy. "I'd better get back to work before she writes me up."

Without thinking, Clancy held out his hand. But he pulled it back a little, remembering that Ash had been on bacon duty that morning.

"Trust me, *Clayton*." Wallace grabbed Clancy's hand and gave it a forceful shake, grinning. "Trichinosis puts hair on your chest. I'm telling you straight up, man."

"Good morning, Karina. Ash Wallace calling."

"Mr. Wallace! I've been trying to reach you for days! Is everything all right?"

As James Martin's executive assistant at Oceanaire, Karina always struck Ash as the unflappable type. But this morning, she sounded pretty damn flapped. Ash knew he was partly to blame for her condition.

"I sincerely apologize for not responding to your voice mails, but I've been tied up with my last consulting assignment. It's become quite complicated, with some iffy ethical issues involved. I ended up resigning."

"But you're okay?" Ash heard the concern in Karina's voice.

"I'm fine, thank you. I still have details to sort out before I can get back to Boston, but I am happy to report that I am now officially Oceanaire's full-time chairman of the board. Is James around this morning?"

She remained silent for a moment, which caused Ash to sit up straighter in Rowan's dining room chair. "Karina?"

"Uh, before you talk to him, would you mind if I got you up to speed on what's been going on here? It's been an eventful few days."

"Of course."

"We had an unexpected boon last Thursday, Mr. Wallace. A generous donor has willed the foundation an extremely valuable stretch of oceanfront land on Long Island. We had no planned-giving contract with this man, no donor history at all, in fact, so the gift took us completely by surprise. That's why I've been trying to reach you. Mr. Martin wants you to join him for an analysis of the site as soon as possible. He believes it might very well be the perfect location for the institute."

Ash clamped his eyelids shut. "You're kidding," he muttered.

"Isn't it remarkable?"

"It certainly is. Thank you for letting me know. Is there any chance I can have a word with James?"

"Of course, Mr. Wallace. We hope to see you very soon. I'll put you right through."

While he waited for Brian's brother to pick up, Ash did his best to shove down his disappointment. Every moment that he hadn't been focused on Rowan—and granted, there weren't many—the idea Nat had pulled out of his ass at the clambake had consumed him. Ash really thought he felt the heavy hand of destiny in all this and had been anxious to get the ball rolling first thing this morning. It was only ten minutes past nine, and his bubble had already burst.

"Ash! What the hell have you been up to? Karina just told me you've officially resigned from your consulting work."

"Sorry for being out of touch, and, yes, I have. My attorneys will have to close out some outstanding retainer agreements, but I'm not taking on any new jobs."

"That's fabulous news. Listen, did Karina tell you about the property?"

"She did."

"You don't sound thrilled."

"I'll have to see it."

"I've already got our science division looking at what the site has to offer in term of density and variety of marine life, tidal pools, sediment, levels of thermal or chemical pollution, you name it. And I've already sent the topography and bathymetry to architects. Ash, the initial reaction from everyone is that this place has real potential. We're all pretty excited about it. I need you on board as soon as possible. When are you coming back to town?"

In all the years he'd known James Martin, he'd never heard him string so many words together so fast and without pausing to breathe.

"Ash? Did I lose you?"

"No." He drummed his fingers on the top of Rowan's dinette table. "Have you ever heard of a place called Bayberry Island?"

James laughed. "Sure. We've gone there with the kids a few times. The place is a trip. They've got this kooky obsession with mermaids."

"They do."

"The kids love it, though. They had a blast dressing up like pirates and eating their body weight in carnival food, but we ended up staying at this old bed-and-breakfast Maggie found online. Good grief! The place was a dump—the Safe Harbor or something like that."

"The Safe Haven."

"Yeah, that's it."

Ash pulled his lips tight and continued to drum his fingers on the table, deciding on how to present this.

"You there?"

"Yeah." Ash straightened. "Hey, James? I'm going to ask you to put the Long Island stuff on hold and bring a team to Bayberry—design, science, legal, and finance people, plus enough of the board to make a quorum—everybody. That's where I am right now. I think this is our place."

James laughed uproariously. "Are you fucking kidding me? Mermaid Island? You're there right now? I thought you were working!"

"I am. I was. Look, I was hired to acquire property here on the island, but it's not a good fit for the huge commercial project they have in mind. This is the ideal location for an educational and research facility, however. There's a rich and colorful history of human-marine cohabitation on Bayberry Island."

Ash heard himself and had to roll his eyes at his own shamelessness. In all his years of closing deals, he couldn't remember when he'd dished out such a load of bullshit. The truth was, he had absolutely no idea what he was talking about.

"Are you serious?"

"I am. The site boasts more than four hundred acres of oceanfront land, a beautiful beach, and existing improvements that could be easily adapted to the institute's needs."

"You're sure this land is for sale? I haven't seen it listed and I've been looking. Besides, even if it is, it's got to be outrageously expensive, and the New York property is already ours."

James had a point. "It would be unfair of me to compare the sites, since I haven't seen the other one, but I feel in my gut that this is the place."

James grunted. He wasn't falling for it.

"Have you heard of something called the Friendship Ledge? It's an underwater mountain range that's supposed to have—"

"Of course I know about it."

"Well, it's just northwest of the island."

"Sure. Okay. It is, isn't it?"

Ash could tell he had him hooked again. "Besides, if we own the Long Island property outright then we can sell it to pay for Bayberry. James, the idea here is to find the *right* place for the institute, not the most convenient. Plus our facility could help rejuvenate the island economy, which has really suffered recently. The institute would attract hundreds of visitors each year—students, their families, visiting academics. God knows, Long Island isn't similarly challenged in their efforts to bring in tourist income."

"How much do they want per acre?"

"I'm not sure on the numbers yet, but I'm making progress. There are thirty-seven individual property owners along the cove that have to set their price. When do you think you can be here?"

"Jesus, Ash!" James laughed. "I don't know. This is . . . this is a complete change in direction. My head is spinning. Maybe we can get there in a couple weeks."

"Look, here's the problem. We need to get in here before the resort developers send another closer to finalize the deal. I know they're going to be incredibly aggressive. Can you get everyone here tomorrow?"

James laughed again. "Are you smoking some of the island's best shit?" He groaned. "I'll do what I can. Today's Tuesday. There's no way we can get there by tomorrow, so it's going to be Thursday at the absolute earliest, but I'm not making any promises."

"Great." Ash started to breathe easier. "I'll arrange for a meeting with the landowners. We need to dazzle the locals, so bring the architectural models and anything else shiny and sparkly you got lying around. You'll have to fly into the Vineyard or Nantucket and charter a boat or helicopter."

"Uh, are you sure about this, Ash?"

Of course he wasn't sure about it. There was still an outside chance that the cove shoreline wouldn't be suited for the institute. Or that the locals would oppose the idea. Or that it was foolish to pass up the Long Island opportunity. There was only one thing he was certain of. Brian had always encouraged him to follow his gut feeling, and his gut was telling him to at least try.

"James, listen. This is going to sound really weird, so please bear with me."

"And the rest of this hasn't been weird?"

He chuckled. "I know in my heart that Brian would have loved this place. I think this is just the kind of setting he envisioned for his dream. The people here are adventurous and fun loving and they have a real connection to the sea. That sounds like Brian; don't you agree? And you said it yourself—kids love this island. Just think of how much they'd enjoy studying and living here during the summers. It's absolutely *perfect*."

James was silent at first, but eventually he surrendered to Ash's enthusiasm. "You might be right. We'll come look at it. I owe you that much. But there's one major concern I don't think you've taken into consideration."

"What's that?"

"Woods Hole. It's right there on the Cape. There's no way we could ever compete with them—they're the country's largest independent oceanographic facility. We would pale in comparison."

Ash felt himself smile. "But what if we didn't worry about competing and found a way to partner with them instead? That would make their proximity a huge plus instead of a minus. Think of the possibilities, James."

"I'm thinking. I am. All right, fine. I'll get the team together and tell them we're making a slight detour. Listen, if I call you, would you pick up your damn phone? I'll feel like I'm flying blind if I can't reach you."

"I'll keep my cell with me. See you Thursday. Thanks, James."

"Hey, wait! Should we plan on flying back on the same day or staying over? Where are you staying?"

Ash chuckled. "At the dump."

Chapter Fifteen

"You asked to see me, Jerrod?"

Kathryn took a tentative step inside her boss's office, uncertain what awaited her. A garden-variety bad mood? A grown man bouncing off the walls? Another obscene session of straw sucking?

Or was she about to get fired?

"Sit down."

Kathryn took a seat in one of the black leather chairs in front of his desk. She folded her hands and took a calming breath.

"You're on. The Mermaid Island is your baby. Make it happen."

Kathryn was stunned. For a moment, she could do nothing but stare, her mouth hanging open like a dolt's. *"Really?"*

Jerrod scowled at her. "You came in here all Zig Ziglar on me yesterday, and now you act like it's a miracle that I'd trust you with the assignment? Which one is it, sweetheart?"

She snapped out of her stupor. "Of course you can trust me. I'm on it." Kathryn jumped to her feet.

Jerrod laughed, shaking his head. "Hold up, honey. You're taking Brenda Paulson with you. I think the two of you could use some girl bonding. I've noticed you're not exactly BFFs, and you'll need to fix that."

He'd just lost her. "What? I'm sorry. Did you say something about Brenda?"

He chuckled again. "See, here's how I look at it. You close the Mermaid Island project and I promote you to vice president for acquisitions. Then I promote Brenda into your old job. But none of that's going to happen if the two of you continue with your catfight over Ash Wallace, although I must admit it's been entertaining."

Kathryn couldn't help it. Her eyes bugged out. This was the most ridiculous, sexist pile of garbage she'd ever heard come out of Jerrod Jessop's mouth, and that was really saying something. Fighting over Ash Wallace? How ludicrous could he get?

"I'm afraid you're mistaken, Jerrod. Brenda and I get along fine. She has a little bit of a crush on Ash Wallace, but I hardly think that's a factor now that he's out of the picture."

"Yeah, okay. Anyway, get to Bayberry as soon as you can. Meet with the landowners and get this fucking deal done. Everyone is going to lose a lot of money if we have to start over, looking for a new location."

"I understand. Absolutely." Kathryn headed for the door. "I'll keep you posted on all the developments."

"You do that."

"Gather 'round, ye 'maids." Mona heard the exhaustion in her voice and realized she was nothing but a hypocrite. She'd been berating nearly everyone for a lack of festival-week enthusiasm, and here she was, too tired to get up off her couch.

The group staggered in and took their seats. It was clear from the droopy eyelids and shuffling feet that the ladies had managed to consume their share of beer the night before even while carrying out their clambake duties.

Darinda sat next to Mona on the sofa sectional. In the last few days, Mona had noticed that she was one of the brighter and more observant Mermaid Society members, and her heart was in the right place. Darinda had become Mona's right-hand 'maid this week, and it was obvious there was real potential in her, possibly even the makings of the society's next president.

"Are you all right?" Darinda leaned in and patted Mona's knee. "You don't look so good. Is your arthritis bothering you today?"

"I have a lot on my mind this morning."

Darinda cleared her throat. "Sit down, everyone! We need to get started! Let's move it, people!"

Since those words hadn't been uttered by anyone but Mona for the last twenty years, the room went silent. Mouths hung open. Mona knew her friends well enough to be sure their response had nothing to do with jealousy. Not even a little. *No one* coveted the job of president of the Bayberry Island Mermaid Society. That's why Mona's unanimous reelection every two years was like that of a banana republic dictator—not exactly a shocker and greeted with a celebration that was mostly for show.

Mona glanced over her shoulder at Darinda and smiled. It felt good to know someone had her back for a change.

"Thank you, Darinda." Mona waited for the women to get settled. "As usual, if you take the last of the coffee, please put on a fresh pot. All right. Let's get started."

Polly opened one eye and raised her hand, rocking back and forth a little. "I'm not going to be able to work the crowd at the reenactment today. I'm not feeling all that great."

"I'm not either," Layla said.

"Me either," Abby said.

"That's not why I called this meeting. I don't give a rat's ass if anyone works the reenactment. You're grown women. You know your responsibilities as Mermaid Society members, and you can choose whether or not you feel like honoring them."

Someone's foot slipped off the coffee table and hit the floor with a thud.

"Uh, where's your binder, Mona?"

She shrugged at Izzy's question. "I don't know. In the kitchen, I guess."

"Want me to go get it?" Izzy began to get up from the sofa.

"No need. Let's just get on with the meeting, okay? I'm sure we all have better things to do."

Mona paid no attention to the exchange of glances, the head shakes, and the widening eyeballs. "This is only partly about society business, so let's get that issue out of the way first." Mona cupped each knee in a palm and straightened her spine. "This has to do with Rowan."

"No shit," Polly said. "She and the Man Grab were Velcroed to each other all night last night."

"I thought they looked incredible together," Izzy said.

"I don't think I've ever seen Rowan happier," Layla said.

"I know!" Abby did three quick fist pumps. "I think we've got our 'something big' to brag about. Just like Darinda predicted, our Man Grab was affected by the Great Mermaid, and she sent him to Rowan! How perfect is that?"

"Did you see how he looked at her?" Layla waved her arms around. "I can't remember the last time I've seen a man so smitten. It was like he—"

"Stop." Mona sighed. This was exactly what she had wanted to avoid. But of course the Mermaid Society members would focus on any possible connection between Rowan and Ash's new love and the Great Mermaid's magic—that was the whole point of the group. But Mona needed to nip this in the bud.

"I have a special request to make of all of you. I want us to step away from Rowan and Ash. No talk of the Man Grab or the Great Mermaid's powers, or Rowan falling in love. Please. I'm asking you for this not as your president but as Rowan's mother and your lifelong friend."

"Ooookay." Polly set down her coffee mug. "Did I miss something? Did something happen I don't know about? Why the sudden change of heart, Mona?"

Mona chuckled. "You're right. Something has happened to *me*. I realized last night that Rowan's happiness is more important to me than being right about the mermaid. I realized that Rowan and Ash have a right to their privacy. Even if their love is connected to the legend, we have no right to shove that concept down their throats. So I want us to back *waaay* the hell away from them. Give them their space."

A collective gasp went up through the room.

Abby looked as if she might cry. "But I thought we agreed we needed something to inspire the island, make people believe in love again."

"You know what I think?" Mona smiled sadly. "I think if people want to believe in love, they'll make that decision on their own. I'm sick of shoving love down people's throats, and I will certainly not allow my daughter to be bullied like that again."

"Holy shit."

That was the first time anyone had heard Darinda curse.

"But, Mona . . ." Darinda frowned. "Isn't that our charter? Isn't that the reason we're here, to help people remain open to the possibility that magic exists and that love is magic?"

"Absolutely." Mona nodded. "But not this time. Not with Rowan and Ash. Is everybody clear on this?"

Polly whistled. "I can't wait to hear the second reason this meeting was called."

"Well, then, I'll get right to it. I won't waste anyone's time." Mona looked into the faces of each of her friends so that they would know she meant business. "Ladies, I'm giving up my fight against the Mermaid Island Resort. I've decided we should all just sell."

The room erupted. A few women stood up and hooted with happiness, and others sat motionless and stupefied. Someone's coffee cup got knocked over in the fracas. Somebody whispered that they were going to be rich. Darinda grabbed Mona's forearm and squeezed so tight it was painful.

"Mona! No!" Her face was twisted with disbelief. "You can't do that!"

"I can and I will."

"Hold up. Hold up." Polly stood—a little wobbly—and sliced her flattened hands through the air like a referee. "Can we all just remain fucking ladylike here? There's got to be a good reason for this one-eighty turnaround, so let's give Mona an opportunity to explain. Thank you." Polly sat back down.

"'Fucking ladylike' is an oxymoron," Izzy said.

"Please just hear me out." Mona felt her chin quiver. She knew she'd have to be quick about this because her emotions were right at the surface. If she dwelled on it too long, she would surely burst into tears.

"As you all know, I've worked for more than a year to

stop the resort plans. It's no secret that it's taken a toll on my family, my marriage, and my relationship with my friends and neighbors."

No one moved.

"But yesterday I realized what my stubbornness was doing to Rowan. She's trapped here. She's miserable. It's like I'm holding her prisoner in the Safe Haven, and it breaks my heart to see how I've backed her into a corner. It wasn't all that long ago that I was a young woman in love, knowing . . . sure that . . . all I'm saying is that I had the right to make my own choices, even make my own mistakes. Because it was my life, no one else's."

Abby sniffed. She was crying. Mona pressed on.

"I've been fighting to save the house because I thought I was preserving our family heritage and way of life, but instead I've just hurt the people I love. The place is falling down, and there will never be enough money to restore it. I've put an impossible burden on my daughter and have only added to the burden of my friends and neighbors. It's time to let the whole ridiculous thing go."

"But what about the environment?" Darinda looked crushed.

Mona shrugged. "Maybe we can work with the developers to limit damage to the ecosystem. They might even be willing to do another environmental assessment."

"But the island will never be the same," Izzy whispered.

Mona smiled sadly at Izzy. "With or without the resort, the island is going to have to change. We can either work to maximize the positive impact of development, or we can sit back and watch the island slowly die."

Darinda shook her head. "This is terrible."

"I need a little time to arrange for a meeting with the developers to be sure the offer is still on the table, so I will ask for your discretion until then. Can I count on that?"

One by one, the members of the society stood and formed their sacred circle. Each woman placed her right hand above her heart and recited the pledge of secrecy, their lips moving in silent unison, their expressions solemn.

Ash headed toward the marine yard. When he rounded the corner and the *Provenance* came into view, his eyes scanned nervously over her clean lines, narrow beam, and elegant sloop rigging. Though an old crane had moored alongside his boat, its motor wasn't running and Sully was nowhere to be seen.

Ash's heart beat fast. He worried about whether Sully had been able to remove the old inboard engine without problems. And he worried if he'd know how to properly align and mount the new one, whether he did any maintenance to the bilge hoses while he was under there and if he knew enough to get the throttle linkages right. Now that he was no longer concerned about closing the Jessop-Riley deal, it made him cringe to think of the trauma he'd put the *Provenance* through. The next time he got behind the wheel, he'd make it up to her.

As soon as Ash reached the boat, he climbed aboard, poked his head down into the cabin, and sighed with relief. Sully had been smart enough to protect the floor around the engine compartment with a piece of plywood. It looked like the old motor had been removed without issue. Nothing in the cabin appeared to be damaged, and there was no sign of oil leaking.

"Mr. Wallace?"

Ash climbed up to see Sully standing on the dock. "Everything go okay taking it out?"

The mechanic shrugged. "Went fine. You got the boat from your grandfather, you say?"

"That's right."

Sully shook his head. "Well, he took mighty good care of her. She's beautiful. All new chrome fittings, pristine rigging, cabin restored to original specs. And I've never seen an engine compartment so clean in all my life. That engine was only about ten years old, by the way, with plenty of life left in it. Shame you ruined it."

He smiled. Grandfather Louis had been dead fifteen years. The meticulous care, cleaning, and restoration of the *Provenance* had been Ash's doing, but that would go unsaid.

"Is the engine here? Did you double-check all the measurements before you ordered it?"

"Should have it by lunchtime, and, yes, I did."

"Wonderful." Ash smiled at Sully but got no response. "And the chain plate?"

"Coming in today, too."

"Fabulous." Ash looked around the dock, acutely aware of how uncomfortable Sully was with conversation. "Do you feel good about dropping the engine into place and mounting it? Would you like me to come by to help?"

"Nope. I've done a hundred of these." Sully looked down at his feet. "So, are you planning on leaving tonight?"

"Uh, no, actually. There's been a change of plans."

He looked up. "Tomorrow, then?"

"No. I've decided to stay awhile."

"How long?"

"I'm not sure yet, but do you think she's going to be ready to take out for a sea trial by late Thursday morning, weather permitting?"

Sully frowned. He scrunched his lips together in

thought. "You can't keep her in this slip for the long term, you know."

"I understand, and I'll be happy to compensate you for your inconvenience, but would you mind if we discussed all this in a few days?" Ash stepped onto the dock, shaking Sully's oil-stained hand. "Thanks again for your excellent work."

As he walked away from the marine yard, Ash felt Sully's curious gaze on his back. He couldn't blame the guy for staring. When he'd arrived on the island five days before, Ash had been an incompetent boat owner with deep pockets. Three days later he'd morphed into a nervous sailor who couldn't leave fast enough. And today he was talking engine specs and his plans to stay indefinitely.

Though he had no personal experience with this sort of thing, he figured his behavior might be typical for a man who was falling in love.

Ash smiled, shoved his hands in his pockets, and headed into town. From the corner of his eye, he noticed a large crowd forming at the public dock, where it looked like yet another mermaid legend production was in progress. How many variations on the theme could there possibly be?

He slowed his pace enough to see that it was only a promotion for the adult theater troupe's reenactment, starting soon in the museum. A real-life historic fishing boat served as the stage for the promo, but he noticed the costumes were from the parade, the props were from the children's play, and some lines of dialogue were straight out of one of the brochures. The Bayberrian recycling ethic was exemplary.

He continued walking at a decent clip, aware that there was a lot on his agenda that day. He wanted to pay Hubie Krank a visit, but before that, he needed to pick up a couple bottles of wine from the liquor store—one for tomorrow night's cookout with Rowan's family and the other to share with Rowan during Thursday's sail.

Ash felt a grin spreading across his face. He'd never taken a woman aboard the *Provenance.* It had never occurred to him that he might want to reveal that side of himself to a woman.

Rowan was different. He wanted her to love his classic sloop. He wanted Rowan to experience her comfortable, sweet ride, feel how firm she was at the heel, and sense what a delightful companion she could be out in the open sea.

After all, Rowan had shared her home and family with him, so it was only fair to reciprocate. Ash was immensely proud of the *Provenance.* She was the only family he had left.

It occurred to Ash that he needed her support. Maybe if he told Rowan the truth while they were out at sea, on the deck of the *Provenance,* Rowan would be more open to what he had to say. At least she couldn't run away.

"I think he's really great. Nat feels the same."

Rowan sighed with relief into the cell phone, resuming her job buffing and sorting flatware in the dining room. "Thank you, Annie. I'm thrilled to hear you say that." It was important that they both liked Ash, since Rowan couldn't even imagine how awkward it would be if they didn't. Annie and Nat were getting married soon, and though Rowan tried not to worry too much about the future, she desperately hoped that Ash would remain in her life.

"But you're cool now with him being the Man Grab? I know it was shitty to find out the way you did. I felt bad that I didn't give you a heads-up."

Rowan opened the drawers to the old sideboard and put the flatware away. "I've gotten over my shock. I know I shouldn't have flipped out the way I did, but honestly, I just couldn't face the idea that Mona would come at me again the way she did with Frederick."

"I understand."

"Anyway, there's nothing for you to feel bad about, Annie. You had no way of knowing Ash was the stupid Man Grab, but my *mother* sure as hell did."

"I know you're pissed at her."

"Ugh." Rowan slammed the drawer shut. "Sometimes I feel like I'm being suffocated by Mona—by this whole place."

"I know, sweetie. But having Poseidon around has got to put a spring in your step on this fine summer morning. Am I right?"

Rowan laughed. "You're right—it's a lovely morning, but I'm not doing much springing, let me tell you. I'm so tired I can barely keep from falling over. Not that I'm complaining. *At all.*"

Annie giggled, then sighed. "Well, I have to say, you sound incredibly happy. I'm . . ." Annie paused. Rowan heard her sniff.

"Are you crying?"

"No," Annie snapped. "Well, maybe a little. But I'm just so happy to see *you* happy! It's been a really long time, and . . . Oh, Rowan! Nat has been such a blessing in my life, but all I've been able to think about the last eight months was that *you* should have the same sort of blessing. I've been praying for you to find happiness."

It was Rowan's turn to cry. She wiped her cheek with the back of her wrist. "I don't know what I would have done without you these last couple years, Annie. Well, the last thirty years, really."

"I feel the same."

"I think maybe Ash is the one." Rowan began to walk toward the kitchen, but lowered her voice so that Mellie and the maids wouldn't hear her. Her interest in Ash might be public knowledge at this point, but she could at least try to keep her most private thoughts between her and Annie. "The more time I spend with him, the more I let my guard down and just let it happen; you know what I mean?"

"I do."

"He's so attentive and loving. He makes me laugh. I miss him when we're not together. Oh—he wants to take me sailing Thursday if his boat is fixed."

"That sounds fun. Nat and I are going to the Mermaid Ball Thursday night. Would you two be back in time to join us?"

Rowan laughed. "Dear God, Annie. I haven't been to the ball in years!"

"But wouldn't it be fun? The four of us?"

Rowan wasn't sure how to answer Annie, since she suspected the ball wouldn't be Ash's idea of a good time. Costumes were required, and Ash had made it clear that he didn't do costumes. So she'd have to give the situation some thought. "Maybe we'll go. I have to talk to Ash first and see."

She headed through the swinging door to the kitchen, where she knew Imelda was busy doing prep work for tomorrow's breakfast. She looked up from the chopping block and smiled at Rowan.

"Tell Annie I miss her."

"Mellie says she misses you."

"I miss her, too! Find out if she's coming to the cookout tomorrow night."

Rowan relayed the inquiry, though she knew what the response would be—the same as it always was.

Mellie waved the knife around, shaking her head. "She knows I don't do those sorts of things. I have to get up early."

Rowan opened her mouth to answer.

"I heard her," Annie said. "She's so grumpy sometimes."

Rowan chuckled.

Mellie resumed her chopping. "Remind Annie that we need to have her final fitting next week."

Rowan spoke into the phone. "Did you hear that?"

"I know. I know. Mellie has saved my ass by making my dress. It's going to be gorgeous. But—" She sucked air through her teeth. "Why did Nat and I pick September to get married? I can't believe I suggested a date so soon after festival week! What was I thinking?"

Rowan smiled. "You were thinking it's the perfect time, and you were right. The weather is cooler, but still nice. The ferry is still running the summer schedule. And tourist season is officially over, so we'll have the Safe Haven and the beach completely to ourselves."

"Oh. Right. It's all coming back to me. I'm just dangerously close to freaking out over everything we've still got to do."

"Tell her not to worry. Everything will get done."

"Did you hear that?"

Annie laughed. "I did."

"We're here to help," Rowan said, trying to reassure her friend. "It'll all get done, and it will be beautiful. The reception food and the flowers will be finalized after festival week. The music is covered. Mellie's got the dress. It will all pull together. And you, my dear, are going to be the most smokin'-hot bride this island has ever seen."

"Yeah, okay." Annie didn't sound convinced. "I'd settle for looking calm and well rested."

Ash knocked on the weathered door of Hubie Krank's small cedar-shingled house. Then he knocked again, louder. After a few minutes, he realized the old man probably couldn't hear the beating on his door, so he slipped around the side of the house to the backyard.

"Mr. Krank?"

Nothing. A bolt of alarm went through him—he hoped nothing had happened to the old fellow. Ash stepped over the weeds and clutter until he reached what was probably the kitchen door. He pounded as hard as he could. "Mr. Krank!"

"What's all the fuss? Stop yelling! Stop banging!" The warped wooden door opened and Hubie's shriveled little face appeared. He frowned, scanning Ash up and down. Eventually, there was a spark of recognition in his watery eyes. "Oh. It's you. Has the Flynn girl got her claws in you yet?"

Ash had to smile. "As a matter of fact, she has."

"*What*?"

"Yes!"

"Well, what do you want? Hurry up!"

He yelled, "Could we talk for a moment, Mr. Krank?" Ash realized he would need a lot of lung power if he were to make any headway in this interview.

Hubie looked doubtful. "Talk about what?"

"Your land."

His eyes went wide and his crooked spine miraculously straightened. "Those damn Flynns! They sent you here to kill me off, didn't they?"

Ash let out a surprised laugh. "Of course not. I just came to talk about how much you want for your property."

Hubie wrapped his knotted fingers around the edge of the door and eased it open a bit more. "You say you want to buy my land?"

"Maybe."

"Are you rich?"

"Rich enough."

"Come on in. Watch your step."

Ash entered the old man's house and was immediately startled by the disorder and decay. Of course he'd assumed the house was as ancient as its owner, but he hadn't thought the appliances, electrical wiring, and furnishings would be of the Prohibition era as well. A quick sweep of the surroundings had Ash convinced that if he dug into the stacks of newspapers and magazines propped against the walls, he'd surely find headlines proclaiming the Apollo 11 moon landing, the bombing of Pearl Harbor, and the stock market crash of twenty-nine.

"Have a seat, young man."

It took Ash a moment to figure out how he'd be able to comply with that request. He opted to remove a stack of pots and pans from a kitchen chair and set them on the floor nearby.

"Tea?"

"No, thank you, Mr. Krank." He took his seat, not even wanting to imagine the state of perishable items in this house.

"Well, then? You want to buy my land? How much money do you have?"

Ash had reviewed his Jessop-Riley documents and found that Hubie owned about four and a half acres on the bluff. Initial contact was made with him thirteen months prior, and he'd accepted an offer of just over a half million, pending a zoning change. But that agreement, like all the others made with landowners along Haven Cove, had remained in limbo because the Flynns refused to sell. Ash's new challenge would be to get landowners to accept slightly less money from Ocean-aire, whose pockets weren't as deep.

He smiled at the old guy. Ash had been in this position many times before, meeting face-to-face with property owners on many projects, but this was the first time he could say he had honorable intentions. Before, it was all just about profit. This time, he wanted to do what was right.

"How much do you think your land is worth, Mr. Krank?"

He chuckled and shook his head. "Well, those Boston bloodsuckers offered me half what I want. So I'd say I need a cool mil or it's not even worth my time discussing it."

Ash nodded. "Hmm." He pulled out his smartphone and made a note to himself. "And what about the other landowners on the cove? Do you have any idea how much everyone else wants for their piece?"

Hubie frowned at him. "Well, of course I do. We have these landowner meetings, you know, and that's all we do is sit around and talk about how much money we want."

"I see."

"I got a piece of paper if you want to look at it."

"That would be helpful, thank you."

Ash waited for a few moments, trying his best not to stare at his surroundings. It was incredibly depressing. Nobody should live like this, and he realized that in addition to Hubie's obvious eccentric tendencies, a lack of money had to play a part in why this place hadn't been cleaned and fixed up. He'd seen it often enough—when someone was focused on surviving day to day, anything that could be delayed would be. Those delays could go on for years or even decades, until the task became insurmountable.

Like with the Safe Haven.

"Here you are, young man." Hubie set the single sheet of paper on the table, and Ash recognized all the names from the J-R documents. "Would you mind if I took a photograph?"

"Of what?"

"This piece of paper."

"With a camera?"

"With my phone."

"You have a camera in your phone?"

"I do. I can also access my e-mail from my phone."

Hubie shrugged. "I don't understand life anymore, but suit yourself."

Ash took a few shots, then returned his phone to his pants pocket.

"What do you want my house for?" Hubie asked. "You want to live here?"

Ash took a moment to think about his response. He wanted to be honest with Hubie, but he didn't want him to get his hopes up. At this juncture, his plan was still just wishful thinking. He had to convince James and the board before he could even begin negotiations on the land.

"Mr. Krank, if I had an idea for all the land on Haven Cove that would make everyone money, create a bit more tourist income, but not destroy the environment or the character of Bayberry Island, do you think the land-owners would sell to someone other than the resort de-veloper?"

Hubie's head reared back. He blinked a few times, and at first Ash thought maybe he hadn't heard him, de-spite his continued bellowing. "Did you hear what I said?"

"Of course I heard you! I'm not deaf!" He pushed himself up from the kitchen chair and slowly made his way to the sink. He filled up the teakettle, lit the gas burner, and got himself a tea bag and an old cup from the cabinet. Ash wasn't certain where this was headed or if Hubie had forgotten he was there, so he cleared his throat.

Hubie turned around. Ash was startled to see tears in his eyes.

"Young man, if you could do that, it would be a miracle, and all of us would be forever grateful. How can I help?"

Ash stood. "You can call an emergency meeting of the landowners association for late Thursday afternoon. I'm taking some people on a tour of the island, and they'd like to meet with everyone afterward, everyone at once. But there's one special request I have to make."

Hubie's doubtful scowl returned. "What?"

"You can't tell anyone the reason for the meeting. Please. It's important, because at this point I can't promise anything, and I would hate to cause anyone more disappointment than they've already experienced."

The old man nodded.

"So I can count on your discretion?"

The corner of Hubie's mouth curled up. "Of course you can. I'll call Sally, the head fairy. She's the president of the landowner's coalition. I'll tell her someone other than the developer offered me money for my land."

Ash had met Sally—it was her wing that had jabbed him in the eye during Island Day. "All right, but don't tell her anything more."

Hubie Krank smiled, revealing an off-kilter set of dentures. "If anyone asks me why there's a meeting, I'll pretend I can't hear a damn thing they're saying to me. Works like a charm."

Chapter Sixteen

Mona pulled out the business card she'd long ago tucked into the side pocket of her three-ring binder, picked up her cell phone, and dialed. Her heart was so loud that the pounding in her head dulled her hearing.

"Jessop-Riley Development Corporation. How may I direct your call?"

Mona asked to speak to the pushy woman named Kathryn Hilsom. She'd never liked her. Never trusted her. So the idea that she was voluntarily asking to speak with her made Mona feel sick to her stomach.

"May I ask what this is regarding?"

"Uh, a development. On Bayberry Island. For a casino and golf course."

The woman sounded positively giddy. "Oh! Of course! The Mermaid Island Resort. I'll put you through to Kathryn immediately. I'm sure she'd be happy to assist you. Just one moment, please."

Mona was put on hold. The thirty seconds she spent in the company of a horrid Neil Diamond song seemed like an eternity. She paced her small living room, feeling herself break out in a sweat. She decided if this woman didn't show herself in another ten seconds, it would be some kind of divine sign and she could just hang up.

"Hello. Kathryn Hilsom speaking."

Mona froze. She made a pitiful sighing sound.

"Hello? Mrs. Flynn?"

Mona couldn't find her voice.

"Is this regarding the Mermaid Island Resort? I assure you, I am here to do whatever I can to assist you."

Mona *hated* that name. Every time she heard it, she couldn't help but hear a hint of condescending humor in it, like they were poking fun at the island's Great Mermaid and the legend. But if Mona were going to go through with this phone call, then she damn well better get used to hearing it, hadn't she?

"Yes."

"Wonderful. How is the family? Is everyone well?"

She rolled her eyes. "Yes. Fine." Mona realized she must sound brusque, but really, did this Kathryn woman expect her to act like they were best friends? "I want to discuss money."

She heard Kathryn gasp. "All right. It would be my pleasure."

"I've decided that we will sell."

"Oh. Oh my God. That's fabulous! You want to sell?"

"Yes. God help me." Mona stared down at the twisted bones of her left hand. How she wished it hadn't come to this.

"All right, Mrs. Flynn. This is excellent news. May I ask what caused you to change your mind?"

"No. You may not ask. It's a private family matter. And you need to know this is the last chance for your company, lady. I've opened the door for you, and if you want to take advantage of this invitation, then do so. If not, don't ever bother contacting me again."

"Wait!"

Mona could hear this Kathryn woman's rapid and shallow breathing. "I will personally come tomorrow to ensure your family and all the Haven Cove landowners are generously compensated on the spot. I will collect everyone's signatures at that time."

"Tomorrow?" Mona was shocked that she wanted to move so fast, but supposed she wanted to make sure Mona had no time to change her mind. "Tomorrow won't work. I still have to speak to my family about this, and I won't have an opportunity until tomorrow evening."

"Thursday, then."

"Well, all right, but I'll need to call an emergency meeting of the Haven Cove Landowners Coalition, and we're still in the middle of festival week. I'll see if I can get a meeting room in the town hall, but I can't make any promises."

"Mrs. Flynn." The woman's voice sounded measured, almost as if she were about to explain a difficult concept to a simple-minded child. "I *can* make you a promise, and it is this: If you get them in the door, I promise that you and everyone else will walk out very, very rich people."

Mona sighed heavily. "Whatever." She rubbed her forehead, feeling on the verge of tears. What she was doing was unconscionable. She was selling out her beloved Bayberry Island to corporate scumbags. Mona forced herself to remember that she'd done it in exchange for her daughter's freedom and to put an end to the ill will that had ruined lifelong friendships—and her marriage.

But that did nothing to lessen the guilt she felt for doing business with Satan's handmaid.

"I will be there Thursday. Thank you, and have a wonderful day."

The line went dead.

Chapter Seventeen

Ash held the neck of a chilled bottle of pinot grigio in his left hand and Rowan's small, warm fingers in his right. They walked together at a comfortable clip up Shoreline Road toward Mona's house, the early-evening light of the Wednesday evening falling softly around them.

He knew there were countless details that had to settle into place in the days to come, but he wasn't worried. For the first time in his life, he had a sense that everything would be the way it was supposed to be, regardless of his efforts. He knew that his usual pushing and shoving and creative use of the truth wouldn't be necessary here.

The institute would be built on Bayberry Island. He could already see it.

The series of high-definition images in his mind revealed how it all would play out. If the Flynns were amenable, the Safe Haven could be restored to its original beauty and repurposed as staff housing and offices. There would be a residence hall for the hundreds of students who would rotate through the institute each summer, a low-impact research building, an education center with interactive exhibits open to the public, a conference site, plus a small marina for Oceanaire's fleet of science vessels. Maybe even a small outdoor amphitheater. Eventually, a luxury inn and restaurant might be added to the scope of development, since the island's additional visitors would need somewhere to stay.

Off in the distance, the early-evening ferry sounded its horn, announcing its arrival at the public dock. The familiar sound made Ash smile.

He'd been on Bayberry for only five days, yet his body's rhythm was already synced with the island. He knew how the rain smelled here and how the sun slanted through the trees during the day. He recognized the difference in the waves at low and high tides. At night, he waited to hear the low-pitched cry of the snowy owl that lived near the carriage house. His heart had altered its rhythm, as well, and was now aligned with the pretty woman at his side. He missed Rowan when she was working. He counted the hours until he could be with her again. And though the sensation was completely new for him, at some level it felt as if it had always been this way and always would be.

All that in five days. It was the damnedest thing.

Rowan shot him a sideways glance. "What?"

Ash looked innocent. "What, what?"

"What are you thinking over there? You're a little quiet."

"Just thinking about you."

Rowan laughed. "I think you're wondering what goes on at these annual family cookouts."

He squeezed her hand tighter. "It's probably a lot like the Martin family cookouts I used to go to."

She bumped her hip into the side of his leg. "Could the Martins drain a half barrel of beer in an evening? Were Brian's parents either not speaking to each other or exchanging nasty one-liners? Did Brian's mother dress up like a mermaid?"

Ash thought about that for a minute. "Uh, no. So . . . is everyone going to be in costume except you and me?"

Rowan laughed hard, draping her arm around his waist. "I was kidding about my mom. She won't be in her mermaid ensemble tonight, believe it or not. But what is it with you and costumes? Were you traumatized by a birthday clown or something?"

He chuckled. "Not that I recall. I really hate drawing attention to myself like that. The idea makes me cringe. Plus I'm a stuffy guy. Boring. Inflexible. You know how we Bostonians can be."

"Not hardly, Mr. Wallace." Rowan gave him a flirtatious smile. "But maybe one day I'll plan a special evening for us, you know, as a way to gently introduce you to the joys of costuming. We can read aloud from one of Annie's books and play a game of sea captain and mermaid."

That made Ash laugh in earnest, and one of his favorite lines of prose from the mermaid smut genre came to mind. With the breathiest voice he could muster, he said, "His sea-roughened hands clutched at her glistening mermaid flesh . . ."

Rowan stopped in midstride. "Wait. You've read her books?"

Oh shit. Ash couldn't lie—the idea of letting another falsehood escape his lips in Rowan's company made him nauseated. It would be inexcusable. He knew that once tomorrow had come and gone and his plan had unfolded, she would know everything. Rowan would know of his original intentions and how she had changed his mind. She would hear of his alternate plan for property along the cove. He could tell her the depth of his feelings and even admit that he'd read every one of Annie's mermaid erotica novels—for research purposes, of course.

"I confess." Ash shrugged. "I told you I went to her shop, right?"

"Oh." Rowan started walking again, her smile back in place. "For a minute there I thought you were holding out on me."

"Ha."

"So a costume night would not be out of the question, then?"

Ash looked at the playful expression in her eyes and knew that she truly enjoyed messing with him almost as much as he enjoyed messing with her. "Let's work up to it, all right? Maybe we can start small, like with you wearing your parade getup. That was hot."

"And you? What would you be wearing?"

"Not a fucking thing."

Rowan laughed, tugging him closer for a moment before she released him with a sigh. "Well, this is Mona's house. She's been living here by herself since she and Dad separated."

Rowan pointed toward a cute one-story cedar-shingle home surrounded by neatly trimmed boxwoods and an outrageous variety of roses. The front door was painted cherry red and featured an antique wrought-iron knocker. The effect was charming, and Ash bet that with a little elbow grease, Hubie Krank's place could look just as pretty.

"In all seriousness, there is one thing you need to know about tonight, okay?" Rowan looked up at him from under her lashes, sadness suddenly in her expression. "Duncan not being here is probably going to make everyone a little bummed out. He's missed only one cookout, and that was while he was in basic training. So I know we will all feel that something is missing. Ma's probably going to be extremely upset that he's not here, though she'll try to cover it up."

Ash had never heard Rowan use the word *Ma*. It had always been *my mother* or *Mona*. It revealed a tenderness he hadn't seen before, and it touched him. He knew the two of them had long-standing issues that had nothing to do with his arrival on the island, but he worried that he'd contributed to their distance. Maybe tomorrow's revelations would help mend the relationship.

Ash opened the wobbly front gate for Rowan and placed his free hand at the small of her back. It gave him a thrill he knew he'd never tire of.

Rowan looked over her shoulder and whispered, "Also, Dad won't show up until Clancy's here—they have an arrangement. My father can't handle a family thing without male backup."

"Gotcha."

"This way, around the side."

He followed Rowan, and up close like this he saw that the paint along the trim of the cottage was peeling, and storm shutter hinges were rusted through. Like most everything else on Bayberry Island, what appeared charming from a distance showed signs of neglect upon closer inspection. He hoped that within a couple years all that would be different.

They crossed beneath a weather-beaten wooden arbor heavy with roses and entered Mona's backyard. They were the first to arrive. Ash noticed that the grass was neatly trimmed, which was probably Clancy's doing, and under a large sycamore, Mona had set out a table fit for a *Martha Stewart Living* photo shoot. It was a long wooden table draped in a crisp white linen tablecloth and set with china and crystal. Ash counted seven places, and he made a quick calculation in his head—Mona, Frasier, Clancy, Annie, Nat, Rowan, and himself. In the middle of the table was a large centerpiece of wildflowers, cattails, and seashells. There wasn't a mermaid tail in sight.

On one side of the yard was a large charcoal grill already heating up. Off to the other side, an assortment of mismatched wooden and plastic lawn chairs and small tables were arranged around a fire pit already set for a bonfire.

"Oh! Hello!" Mona looked up, her eyes immediately filled with happiness. "So glad you're here!" She walked toward them, arms outstretched.

"Hi, Ma. It looks really pretty." Rowan met her mother and gave her a hug. It wasn't particularly warm, but at least she'd been willing to go there.

"You look lovely, honey." Mona's eyes scanned Rowan's blue polka-dot sundress and smiled. "You always look lovely."

She was right about that.

"Well, thanks." Rowan turned toward Ash, and he knew it was his turn to greet Mona.

"Thank you so much for the invitation," he said, giving her a hug as well. He embraced her an extra couple of seconds, so that she knew it was more than just for show. "Is there a cooler I can put this in? Or the refrigerator?"

"Oh, how thoughtful of you, Ashton!" She accepted the wine and smiled as she read the label. "This will go perfectly with the menu."

"I'm glad."

"I bet Boston Brahmins such as yourself know a thing or two about fine wine. Am I right?"

He realized Mona only wanted to make pleasant conversation, but he couldn't help but feel the sting of that barb. Mona's battle over the development had left her bitter about money, and Ash reminded himself that it had nothing to do with him. He prayed his news tomorrow would be a balm for all that bitterness.

Mona shook her head and closed her eyes for an instant. "I'm sorry. That was an awful thing to say. Please forgive me."

"It's okay." Ash gave her a genuine smile and wagged his eyebrows. "I do know a lot about fine wine, actually."

Mona laughed, then gave him another hug. "Well, you two make yourselves comfortable. Be right back." They watched Mona go into the back door.

"Sorry." Rowan crossed her arms under her breasts. "Sometimes it seems that it's always one step forward and three back with her."

"Sweetheart. It's not a big deal." He gathered her in his arms and counted in his head. One, two, three, four . . . until Rowan let her stiff arms relax and she leaned into him.

She lifted her eyes to his. "You have some kind of magical power over me, Ash."

"Then we're even." He kissed her. It was true. Even in that gentle kiss, there was magic.

"Break it up!"

Ash pulled away to see Nat and Annie stroll arm in arm into the backyard. Nat looked pleased with his sense of humor. Annie looked beautiful and happy. Mona came out of the back door, and there were more hugs all around, while Nat handed over a dish that Mona immediately set on the table. Soon, everyone was seated with a glass of wine or beer.

"Is Clancy going to be late?"

Mona shrugged at Rowan's question. "He hasn't called. I really don't know."

Ash was facing away from the backyard entrance, so when he noticed Rowan bristle, he had no idea what the problem was. He turned to see Frasier strolling their way, without Clancy serving as buffer. There was something more devilish than usual in his expression.

"Jeesh," Rowan whispered. "He's getting brazen."

Mona saw her husband and her spine went rigid.

Everyone stood up. Rowan decided to step in between her parents. "Is Clancy on his way, Dad?"

"Yep. Coming now."

Mona turned away from Frasier and began fiddling with the table. Just then Ash heard the sound of what was probably Clancy's police Jeep pull up to the front of the house. Within seconds, he'd popped around to the side yard.

"Hey, everybody." Clancy stopped under the arbor and shoved his hands into the pockets of his uniform trousers. "Ma, I decided to bring someone. Is that okay?"

Mona didn't bother turning around. "Of course, honey. Anyone is welcome."

"Well, if you say so." Clancy looked over his shoulder. "Come on! Hurry your ugly ass up!"

"Clancy!" Mona spun around. It was obvious she planned to chastise her son for his spectacularly bad manners. Instead, she let out a shriek of joy and slapped her hands over her face.

It was Duncan.

Rowan and Annie screamed, too. Mona began sobbing. Duncan made his way over to his mother and picked her up, hugging her tight. Then he draped his free arm around Rowan and kissed her cheek. Annie got the treatment next. Just then, Ash's eyes met Nat's, and Ravelle made his way over to stand next to Ash, giving everyone a chance to revel in their reunion.

"Damn," Nat mumbled to Ash. "I could've been a Navy SEAL, but getting into film school seemed like more of a challenge."

Ash laughed, noticing how Frasier hung back from everyone else, too, arms crossed over his chest as he smiled proudly. So that's how it happened—Frasier and Clancy had probably picked up Duncan at the ferry and come straight to the house. The only question was how long they'd known he was coming.

Duncan stared at Ash over the top of Rowan's head, his pale blue eyes flashing a warning. Obviously, Clancy and Frasier had filled him in about his budding relationship with Rowan on the ride over. *Great*, Ash thought. Another Flynn male to bash horns with. Duncan brought his overwhelmed mother with him, still tucked under his arm, as he moved toward Nat. He held out his hand.

"You must be Nathaniel Ravelle. I've heard all about you. Duncan Flynn."

"Call me Nat. Pleasure to finally meet you."

Duncan turned his attention to Ash. The eldest Flynn child was Ash's height, but had to outweigh him by a good thirty pounds of concrete, every pound of which had come courtesy of the US Navy SEAL program, no doubt. Ash braced himself for the intentional name-butchering.

"Ash." Duncan said this with a nod of his head and a faint smile. "How are you, man?"

"Hey, Duncan. I'm great, thanks. Very glad you could make it home." They shook hands amicably. And that was it. Not a single "Ashley" was hurled his way.

Annie and Rowan raced to set another place at the table, and the party began.

The food was outstanding. Mona had prepared a fish soup better than anything Ash had tasted outside of Barcelona—clams, mussels, prawns, and flaky hunks of cod, all floating in a perfectly seasoned fish stock. There was homemade bread, roasted potatoes, lamb, salmon, spinach salad, and a hot rice pudding with salted caramel sauce for dessert. The wine and beer flowed. Frasier and Mona got along fine, and Ash watched them exchange more than one glance of relief during the meal. Duncan coming home had changed everything.

After dinner the group moved to the fire pit, and Ash was given the honors to light the bonfire. For at least two more hours, they sat around talking and laughing under a canopy of stars. Duncan regaled everyone with stories of his latest adventures, taking care to gloss over most of the violence and details of geography and operations. And never once did the topic of the Mermaid Island Resort interfere with the family's time together. For that, Ash was grateful.

Many times that night, Rowan had offered her hand to him and he'd taken it, pleased that she was so comfortable. Once, she even gave him a kiss that pushed the limits of what might be considered an innocent peck. No one seemed to care.

At the end of the evening, they said their good nights and walked back to the Safe Haven, once again hand in hand. Without even discussing it, they ended up in the carriage house together, and after they made sweet and passionate love, Rowan began to fall asleep in his arms.

"Did you set your alarm?"

She grunted. "Ugh. Yes, unfortunately."

"I promise I'll make sure you get there on time."

"Thank you, Ash." She was asleep almost before the words left her lips.

He wished he could follow her, but his mind was too preoccupied for sleep.

Ash had felt his world expand tonight. He had been welcomed into a family circle, where hurt, love, and laughter coexisted. The Flynns were not a fairy-tale family. They were real. That meant that the warmth he'd felt from them could be trusted as real, too. He couldn't remember a night when he'd felt so filled up, so complete. And yet . . .

The hurdles he had to clear were huge, and there were no guarantees that everything would be settled by this time tomorrow night.

He'd arranged to take James and the Oceanaire team on a tour of the island immediately after tomorrow's sail. In his best-outcome fantasy, Rowan would come along, helping him convince the foundation that Bayberry was their new home. And after the tour, everyone would walk into the landowner's coalition meeting and begin negotiations.

More important, he hoped that by this time tomorrow he and Rowan would have started building something good and solid together, with no secrets between them.

But that was up to her. Rowan had to be willing to forgive him for how he'd misled her in the beginning. She had to be willing to trust him after he'd shown that he wasn't always trustworthy. And that was an awful lot to ask of anyone, especially a woman whose last encounter with a dishonest man had ended in disaster.

As Ash kissed her hair, inhaling her sweet and spicy scent, he felt his chest tighten with a sense of dread. Now that he'd found Rowan and had come to love her, he couldn't imagine how painful it would be if she were unable to give him another chance. Though he was old pals with loss, grief, and heartache, he wasn't sure he'd be able to survive losing Rowan. Because unlike every other loss in his life, he would have brought this one upon himself.

Ash put his lips against her temple. He whispered, "I love you, Miss Flynn," and prepared to settle in for a long, restless night.

Chapter Eighteen

Kathryn Hilsom hadn't planned on the ferry. She hadn't done a ferry since her family took one from the Cape to Martha's Vineyard when she was a child, and she'd spent the entire ride sharing her fast food lunch with the fish.

She wasn't faring much better now.

The J-R private jet had arrived on the Vineyard without incident, but the helicopter they'd reserved had inexplicably been rented out to another group, already en route to Bayberry. So here she was, on a smelly, loud, rumbling, nauseating old ferry, her head feeling as if it were a basketball being pummeled into a hard gymnasium floor.

Once again, she grabbed the safety rail and retched.

"Can I get you anything? A snack?"

She held her hand up and back as she dry-heaved, a warning to stay away. She planned to fire whichever idiotic team member had decided this would be the perfect time to review food and beverage options with her. She opened one eye. It was Brenda Paulson. Of course it was. Unbelievable.

"I'm sorry to disturb you." Brenda shrugged as she backed away, and through the narrow slit of one eye, Kathryn watched her join the rest of the J-R team seated inside the passenger cabin.

She managed to raise her head enough to search for the horizon line. Kathryn had read somewhere that if you could keep your focus there, your chances of getting ill were greatly reduced.

Or not.

She retched over the railing again, wondering how she was supposed to stand in front of thirty-seven property owners all rainbows and sunshine when she felt like a shit sandwich.

Rowan was a little late, but she knew Ash wouldn't leave without her. She approached the marine yard in time to see Deacon Sully leaving Ash's boat.

"Hey, Sully!"

His head snapped up, and he looked terrified to encounter her. Of course, Sully had never been all that comfortable with people, and women in particular, so his reaction wasn't surprising. How he'd ever been named a deacon in the First Presbyterian Church was something she'd never understood.

"Hello, Rowan." He looked down at his dirty boat shoes.

She stopped. "How've you been?"

"Fine."

"How's Ash's boat coming along?"

He glanced up again, a wary expression in his eyes. "Why do you ask? Do you think I took too long on purpose to fix it?"

Rowan tipped her head and studied him. On an island full of odd birds, Sully was one of the oddest birdbrains there was. "I don't think I understand. Why would I think you would do that?"

"No reason. Have a nice sail. I guess I'll be seeing you later this afternoon along with everyone else, right?"

"Uh. Sure." She watched him scamper away to the

safety of his office shack, giving herself an extra moment to shake off the crazy before she continued on to the boat slip. She had a feeling Sully didn't mean he'd see her when she returned from the sail, but Rowan didn't have time to try to decipher his ramblings.

When she didn't see Ash on deck, Rowan poked her head across the gangway. "Permission to come aboard?"

She heard Ash clamber up the companionway steps. He poked his head out and smiled. "Of course!"

Rowan stepped onto the deck of the *Provenance*. The last time she'd been here was Sunday, when she and Ash sat on the dock to eat ice cream. Though he'd told her all about his vintage sailboat, he hadn't invited her on board. He hadn't been comfortable enough with her at that point, she supposed. Sometimes it amazed her that less than a week had gone by since he'd shown up in her life.

He joined her on deck, grasping her upper arms as he smiled down at her. "Permission to kiss the first mate?"

Rowan giggled. "Of course. Always."

Oh, how she craved his kisses. It had been a whole three hours since she'd had one, and Rowan had to admit to herself that she'd gotten used to them. One of the things she planned on being brave enough to ask today was whether he still planned to leave now that his boat was repaired. She had a right to know, of course, but she still hadn't convinced herself she was strong enough to hear his answer.

"Come on. Make yourself comfortable. We'll be ready to go in just a few minutes." He scanned her clothes, and she looked down at herself. She'd worn pretty standard sailing attire—a pair of white cotton shorts, a navy blue polo shirt, and a pair of water sandals.

"What?"

He got a sly grin on his face. "Nothing. You're just so adorable."

"Oh." She felt herself blush.

Ash nodded at her duffel. "You brought a sweater though, right? It might get chilly in the wind. If not, I have lots of sweatshirts in the cabin."

"I think I've got it covered." She rose up to her toes to kiss him again. "You know, I've done this a few times."

"Kissed a captain?"

She laughed. "No. Well, a few, maybe. What I meant was I've done my share of day sails."

"Of course you have." Ash guided her toward a bench near the helm. "You're a daughter of the island. I bet you've sailed since you were knee-high to a pelican."

"Something like that." Rowan took a seat and watched Ash busy himself around the deck. His boat was gorgeous. She'd seen a few of these classic beauties come and go over the years, but this would be her first time aboard one. "Your grandfather had excellent taste in sailboats," she said.

Ash was bent over a line he'd just neatly coiled and set in place, and he looked over his shoulder and grinned. "He did."

"And what do you have excellent taste in, Ashton Louis Wallace the third?"

"Women."

"We have a winner!"

He laughed as he straightened. "Would you like to take the helm or get the fenders?"

She didn't miss what that question implied. Though she'd never been behind the wheel of this boat and had no idea how his new engine would handle leaving the slip, he still trusted her enough to give her the choice. "I'll get the fenders."

Rowan stood and passed through the causeway again, stepping onto the dock. She watched Ash turn the key and wait for the sound of the engine. It started like a dream, and he gave her the thumbs-up. Rowan untied the spring lines from the dock cleat, and with the last dock line in hand, she hopped aboard and shoved the bow away with her foot. Immediately, she retrieved the fenders from where they draped over the edge of the boat and stored them on deck. She went back to the bench.

"Once we get under way, I'd love it if you joined me here." Ash winked at her and concentrated on taking the boat out into open water. When he cut the engine not five minutes later, he asked if she'd like to help trim the sails. Of course she said yes, and for the next few minutes they worked together to get the sloop in position to take advantage of a pleasant, steady southwesterly wind.

"She's so smooth," Rowan said, leaning back on her hands and gazing up at the perfect tension in the main and jib sails. The boat had very clean lines, and she'd noticed right away that the fiberglass deck was in pristine condition, which was really saying a lot for a boat that he'd told her was nearly sixty years old.

"I'm glad you like her, Rowan."

She turned to respond and . . . *oh.* The vision took her breath away. This was an extremely happy man. He was set against the blue-green sea and baby blue sky. Ash's face was gentle and open as the breeze ruffled his hair, and though she couldn't see his eyes from behind his polarized Oakley sunglasses, she knew they were sparkling.

Rowan took a leisurely inventory of Ash. Every inch of his big body was relaxed. His feet were widely spaced and perfectly balanced. His hands caressed the wheel the way they caressed her body, the long muscles of his forearms rippling as he moved. This was a dance Ash enjoyed immensely and one he knew well. Which struck her as a little strange—how could a man so comfortable and at ease on his beloved sailboat let her run out of gas?

She supposed everyone was entitled to a bad day every now and again.

Ash wiggled his fingers for her to join him at the helm, and she squeezed her body behind the wheel, her bottom pressed into the tops of his thighs. Ash wrapped his arms around her while he steered, dropping his lips to the side of her neck.

"Thank you for coming out today."

Rowan sighed with pleasure. "Thank you for asking me. Do you bring a lot of people on board?"

"Nope."

He moved his lips up until she felt his breath on her ear. He nibbled on her earlobe, and Rowan squeezed her thighs together. Well, of *course* she did! It had been nothing but thigh-clenching every day this week! She giggled to herself.

"The only people who were ever on board with me were my Grandfather Louis and Brian. That's it."

Rowan leaned the back of her head against his chest and looked out to sea. There were a few sailboats dotting the horizon and the afternoon ferry was chugging its way to the public dock, but for the most part, it felt as if they were alone in the world. "Nanette never asked to come along with you on a sail?"

The rumble of Ash's laughter vibrated against Rowan's back. "She asked. I said no. She didn't know how to sail."

"And you didn't want to teach her?"

"Not particularly. Her idea of getting back to nature was driving her convertible Audi with the top down in the summer—"

"Which sounds perfectly lovely."

"—in heels, with the air-conditioning cranked and a cheetah-print scarf around her head."

"Ah."

"So you're it, sweetheart."

Rowan felt a tremble move through her body. It was the sound of those words—*you're it, sweetheart*. Of course she knew what he meant, that she was the only person to come aboard except for his grandfather and his best friend, but she wanted the words to have a deeper meaning. Right then, Rowan realized she wanted to be his woman. She wanted to be *it* for him, the woman he'd always wanted and the one he couldn't live without.

"Tell me, why did your grandfather decide to call his sloop the *Provenance*? There's always a story behind a boat's name."

"And this is no exception." Ash made a small adjustment to the wheel and leaned forward to adjust the jib sheet, all while maintaining contact with Rowan's body. "I told you that he owned an architectural preservation firm, right?"

She nodded, feeling her hair rub against his shirt.

"Well, the term *provenance* refers to a chain of ownership, or custody of a structure. Sometimes the history of a house adds to its value. For example, a house owned by Mark Twain would be more valuable than a house owned by Mabel Twain, his sister."

"He didn't have a sister named Mabel, and anyway, her name would have been Mabel Clemens, because Mark Twain's real name was—"

"I was just making sure you were paying attention."

Rowan laughed. "You like tweaking me, don't you?"

He chuckled. "I love tweaking you. I can't remember what my life was like before I had you to tweak."

She smiled, snuggling against him. "I'm sure tweaking yourself gets old after a while."

He laughed harder this time, then leaned down to kiss her cheek.

"So you were telling me about the name."

"Right." Ash straightened behind Rowan, pulling her

in tighter with one hand. "Grandfather Louis often had to do research to prove provenance on a building. So when he bought this boat in 1986 from an old buddy of his, he chose the name because it had special meaning. It was linked to his friend, his work . . . and to me."

"You?"

"Yes." Ash brushed a hand up and down her arm as he steered with the other. "I'd been living with him for only a couple years at that point, and he was my legal guardian. He told me the boat would be mine one day, and that its 'value' would be greater because of its provenance within the Wallace family."

Rowan froze. She had to blink back tears. At that moment she understood why he'd brought her aboard: This was all he had left of his own history. How strange it must be for him on the island. Ash couldn't swing a dead cat on Bayberry without smacking up against Flynn history. But all he had was a boat. By sharing the *Provenance*, he was sharing his world with her.

"Thank you for showing her to me," she said, her voice so low she wasn't sure he could hear. "Do you hope to have children one day? Someone to pass the *Provenance* on to?"

When a full ten seconds went by without an answer, Rowan assumed her voice had been too soft to have been heard above the sea and wind. It was probably for the best.

"I would love to have children someday. How about you?"

"I would."

They let the subject drop.

About an hour later, a decent gust of wind allowed them to take the boat to a good twenty-degree heel, both of them hooting at the joy of cutting fast through the water, Rowan's back against the lifeline as she skimmed just above the waves, sea misting her body from head to toe. There were few things more exciting in life, Rowan knew. A little later, on their way back to the island in calm wind, they shared a bottle of wine and a picnic basket Ash admitted Imelda had helped him prepare.

"There's something I'd like to talk to you about."

Rowan's hand froze, leaving a piece of crusty bread smeared with Brie hovering an inch from her mouth. The tone of his voice sent a chill through her. He suddenly sounded so . . . *businesslike*. "All right." She popped the bread into her mouth and chewed, telling herself she was being paranoid again. Ash was wonderful. He was sweet and loving and generous. She didn't know what she was so afraid of, since she'd be happy to talk about whatever he wished.

"Oceanaire, my foundation, has been looking for a home for its headquarters and a location for a new research and education center. When we get back, there will be some people waiting. They want to look around, and I was hoping you might come along, give them a local's perspective on what makes Bayberry Island so unique."

Rowan frowned, wiping bread crumbs off her hands. "Huh." She took a sip of wine, stalling, trying to identify why, exactly, this news bothered her the way it did. Then it occurred to her. "So you came to Bayberry looking for a site for your foundation? But you never mentioned anything about that to me. I thought you were towed in because your boat—"

"Rowan." Ash took one of her hands in both of his and leaned forward until she looked at him. "I really didn't come here with Oceanaire in mind. Nat put the bug in my ear at the clambake, and ever since, I've been trying to figure out a way to make it work. The thing is, I think our project might be perfect for the land along the cove, the land the developers wanted for the resort."

Rowan's eyes popped wide. "For real?"

He nodded.

"So . . . wait. You think your foundation might want to buy up all the property along Haven Cove? Including my family's land?"

"It is a possibility. That's what my friends are here to find out. I wasn't sure I should tell you this yet because I'd hate for you to be disappointed if things don't work out, but I decided you should know before we pulled in."

"But . . ." Rowan stood, staring down at Ash's up-turned face. "Have you talked to Mona about it?"

"Not yet."

"Because . . . wow. This might actually be something she'd agree to. I mean, it sounds like it would have much less effect on the environment and wouldn't cause the crowding problems the resort would. And if my mother ever did agree to sell—"

"We're just at the beginning stages."

Rowan couldn't help it. She squealed. She jumped up and down on the deck; then she threw herself into Ash's arms, nearly knocking him over. Rowan began kissing his face—his lips, chin, cheeks, brow, eyelids. She couldn't stop herself from thinking that if Mona agreed to sell, Rowan would be free.

It was well past one thirty when they returned to the marine yard. Rowan was floating in a sea of emotions, everything from languid happiness to excitement and anticipation. By then she'd learned much more about the institute and agreed that the pairing of Bayberry and Oceanaire felt almost like it was meant to be.

Just as they reached the boardwalk at Main Street, Ash stopped walking. "Hey, Rowan?" He placed a finger under her chin and tipped her face toward his. He kissed her sweetly.

"Thank you," she said. "You've completely spoiled me today."

Ash nodded, suddenly more serious. "Do you trust me?"

Very slowly, Rowan pulled away. She nodded, because she did. He'd never given her any reason *not* to trust him. But she had a feeling she wouldn't like what he said next.

"I . . ." Ash stopped, looked away, and rubbed his fingers along his brow. She'd never seen him like this. Suddenly, he looked down into her eyes with nothing less than certainty. "Do you know how much you mean to me?"

Rowan glanced around. Hundreds of tourists were wandering about. A reggae band was setting up on the public dock. A group of businesspeople had gathered outside the municipal building, and she had a feeling they were Ash's friends from Oceanaire. Why hadn't they had this conversation on the boat, where they had the luxury of privacy? "I . . . no. How do you feel about me?"

Ash cradled her face in his hands. "I am crazy in love with you, Rowan. That is the truth."

The world began to spin around her and her heart pounded. Had this funny, lonely, beautiful man just told her that he *loved* her? "I'm crazy in love with you, too."

"Keep that in mind and everything will be okay." He kissed her again, harder this time, then smiled. "All right. Let's do this." Ash took Rowan by the hand and they went to meet his friends. She was in a daze as she shook hands with everyone, and two minutes later she realized she remembered not one of their names.

Ashton Louis Wallace III loved her.

Chapter Nineteen

When Kathryn Hilsom staggered into the municipal building's public meeting room, Mona was startled by her appearance. She remembered the young woman as cool and smooth and impeccably groomed. But today the poor girl's blouse was stained and unevenly buttoned, her complexion was blotchy, and her hair was . . . well, Mona had no words for the state of her hair. Thank goodness Polly was at her side.

"Looks like the love child of Phyllis Diller and Don King," Polly whispered in Mona's ear.

She put an arm around her friend. "Have I ever told you how much I appreciate you, Polly?"

"Uh, is that a trick question?"

Following Kathryn was a cute, curvy girl in a pretty skirt and top and a half dozen nondescript corporate males in suits.

The cute woman made eye contact with Mona and came over to her. "Hello, Mrs. Flynn. My name is Brenda Paulson. It's a pleasure to meet you. Thank you for having us."

Mona nodded. "This is my friend Polly."

"Nice to meet you, too."

Mona glanced toward the faintly green Hilsom woman. "I take it you took the afternoon ferry?"

"I'm afraid so. It seems Kathryn is prone to seasickness." She smiled pleasantly. "So, is there somewhere we could sit and chat for a bit, before the rest of the landowners arrive?"

"Sure. Let's get this over with." Mona led the group to a small folding table in a front corner of the room, a heavy lump of defeat sitting in her belly. A few of the suits began to set up their to-scale model of the resort, even fancier than the one Mona had seen last year. And the company's lawyer, who'd arrived with a huge rolling briefcase, laid out contracts, all neatly indexed with color-coded tabs for signatures. The chat was a no-frills one, punctuated with Kathryn Hilsom's frequent dashes to the ladies' room. Mona had come prepared to accept Jessop-Riley's most recent offer, but the figure they presented had been jacked up by another one hundred thousand, and the company was offering increases of similar proportions to all Haven Cove property owners.

Frasier would be thrilled to sign on the dotted line.

Early birds began to straggle in, grabbing coffee from the back and taking a seat in the groupings of metal folding chairs set up around the room. Sally came in, taking her seat toward the front. Sally knew why the meeting had been called—Mona was surrendering and everyone was finally going to get rich. But Sally couldn't bring herself to acknowledge Mona. She suspected that once all this was over, the cash-strapped landowners who had spent the last year hating her would become rich ex-landowners who hated her. The old Beatles song had it right: Money can't buy you love.

The room began to fill up. Hubie Krank and his daughter sat together near an aisle. People Mona had known her entire life wandered in and got settled. She even recognized the annual nudist retirees from the B and B and gave them a friendly wave, wondering why they would show up. Then a few tourists popped in. The talking got louder. Clearly, even those who were actual coalition members had no idea why they were there, and half of them looked downright pissed off to be called away on the Thursday afternoon of festival week.

"This had better be good!" said Herman Suddith, who owned three forlorn and rocky acres abutting Adelena Silva's compound. As Mona had noticed over the years, Herman was one of those people who made a lot of noise but had nothing of substance to contribute.

Kathryn had managed to pull herself together by then. She'd smoothed her hair and fixed her blouse, though she still looked like a weary air traveler who'd been caught in turbulence. Everyone from Jessop-Riley sat behind tables at the front of the room. There was nothing to do now but wait.

Suddenly, Polly jabbed Mona in the side with her elbow. "Who's that? And what the hell are they bringing in here?"

Two young men in khaki slacks and matching black polo shirts angled a large display through the front door. At first Mona assumed it was another Jessop-Riley prop, but within seconds she knew that wasn't the case.

"Brenda!" Kathryn's voice was hoarse. "Tell those people we have the meeting room reserved. Go! Get them out of here! I want no delays."

Brenda reached the two young men and they chatted for a moment. Frowning, she returned to her seat while the men carried what looked like a second architectural model toward the front of the room. They set it down on a folding table against the wall.

Kathryn glared at Brenda. "Who are they? What are they doing crashing our meeting?"

Brenda shrugged. "I'm not entirely sure, Kathryn. They said they worked for an environmental foundation and they were here to give the people of Bayberry Island an alternative to the resort. They said they had the hall reserved."

"What? An alternative to Mermaid Island? There is no alternative to Mermaid Island! What the hell is this all about?" Kathryn shot to her feet. Her heels made sharp clicks on the linoleum floor as she marched toward the young men. She lectured them in harsh whispers, and stomped a spiked heel on the floor in aggravation.

"Ma'am, you'll have to take it up with our chairman," one of the men said. "We were told to bring this inside. We're just doing our jobs."

Polly leaned over and whispered in Mona's ear, "Do you know what's going on?"

Mona shook her head. "Not a clue."

Just then, Mona saw Frasier and Clancy enter the meeting hall, Duncan right behind. Both her boys waved at her, though they looked puzzled. Frasier shook his head in disgust, and Mona thought, *Isn't that just like you? You automatically think the worst. Well, you're in for the surprise of your life, you cranky old bastard.*

Kathryn continued, her voice becoming louder. "You cannot and *will* not put that there!" She motioned for her suits to back her up, and the men from Jessop-Riley rushed to her aid. "Stop them!"

Kathryn's underlings looked lost. Mona suspected they were more comfortable with tax codes than fistfights.

"Augh!" Kathryn's face flushed with anger. "Never mind!" She shooed her team away. "Who do you work for? I assure you, whatever underhanded, sleazy kind of stunt this is will not be tolerated. This is a private meeting of landowners and Jessop-Riley Development, not some kind of game show! I will not stand for—"

Just then, Ash and Rowan appeared, and he gestured for another group of suits to enter the meeting hall. The air in the room became charged. Mona began to get a very bad feeling about this.

Kathryn gasped, glaring at Ash as if she knew him. "What the hell are *you* doing here?"

Wait.

What?

Ash slammed his eyes shut and reopened them. Yes, Kathryn Hilsom from J-R was here. But that couldn't possibly be.

James leaned into him. "*What the fuck?* Who are those people?"

What the fuck, indeed.

Rowan gripped his arm. "I don't understand," she said. "Why are the resort people here? Do you *know* her? What's going on?"

Ash squeezed Rowan's hand and shook his head. "Not what I'd planned—that's for sure. I'm sorry, sweetheart. Why don't you take a seat for a minute while I figure this out? James?" The two men walked toward the front of the room.

Kathryn marched up to Ash. "Would you please tell me why you're here, Wallace?"

"Why are *you* here?"

"I was invited by Mrs. Flynn. We are about to finalize the land sale for Mermaid Island—a job that was apparently too much for you to handle." Kathryn gave him a satisfied smirk as a low rumbling went through the crowd and chairs scraped on the floor. Kathryn continued. "You resigned, Wallace! You're not even working the deal anymore. What are *you* doing here?"

Ash realized all his plans were about to disintegrate and he had to do something to stop it. He addressed the crowd. "Everyone, have a seat. Please. There seems to be some confusion here."

Sally the fairy stood up. "There should be no confusion. I called this meeting of the Haven Cove Landowner's Coalition because Mona Flynn asked me to."

"But this young man has a wonderful idea!" Hubie Krank pulled himself to a stand and began waving his fist around. "He's going to buy the land so some people can study the fish! He offered me money for my property and he'll do the same for all of you!"

"Daddy, sit down." Hubie's daughter cupped his elbow and tried to get him back in his chair. Hubie just swatted at her.

"And I told you that, Sally!" Hubie waved his arm around. "What's all this nonsense about? Didn't you hear me when I told you about somebody else wanting to buy the land?"

Kathryn gasped. Her head snapped around, and she narrowed her eyes at Ash. "*What?*"

Sally held up her hands. "I'm sorry. Honestly, Hubie, I thought you were confused. Mona called me right before you did, so I assumed you wanted a coalition meeting to meet with the developers."

"No! I don't like the developers anymore! I like the nice young man better!"

Ash appealed to the crowd. "Ladies and gentlemen, we have a complete breakdown in communication here. Please be patient while I try to unravel this mess."

"Pardon me." Kathryn's voice was hoarse, and she strained to talk over the crowd. "There is no breakdown in communication. Jessop-Riley is here by invitation. Mona Flynn called me two days ago to tell me she'd changed her mind and wanted to sell. She now welcomes the idea of the Mermaid Island Resort."

Loud shouts went up all over the room, and the loudest were from Mona's own family.

Mona stood up, looking panicked. "I was going to tell

everyone last night, but Duncan came home! I didn't want to ruin our celebration!"

"What the *hell*?" Frasier's huge voice vibrated off the walls. "You called the developer? After all the shit you've put us through?"

"Yes. I did!" Mona began to cry. "I did it for Rowan and Ash. Everyone can see they're in love, and I didn't want Rowan to be stuck with the Safe Haven anymore. I want her to be happy to live her life however she wants!"

"Oh, my flippin' God." One of the mermaid ladies, a large woman with a short haircut, had just moved out from where she'd been leaning against the wall. "I should have brought some wine."

Kathryn took advantage of the stunned silence in the room. "We are prepared to sign cashier's checks right now, on the spot." She motioned toward a neatly organized row of documents on a table behind her. "Everyone who owns land on the cove is officially rich as of right this moment. All we need are your signatures."

Ash stepped in front of her. "I am here to show you that there is another option! You don't have to destroy the island!"

With that, everyone seemed to speak at once, and the decibel level nearly blew a hole in the hundred-year-old ceiling.

"Cut it out!" Clancy wandered toward the front of the room, hand on his gun belt. "Sit down. Be quiet. Everyone calm down!" Clancy motioned for people to sit, and, eventually, everyone did. He had their full attention. "I think we're looking at a bidding war here, my friends. The tables have turned. So let's just sit back and listen to what each of them has to say."

"Well, there's something that needs to be cleared up here first, I believe." Kathryn crossed her arms over her chest and wobbled her head back and forth. "You're all acting like Ash Wallace is an old friend. I don't know what he's been up to this week, but—"

"Kathryn. Stop."

She laughed at Ash. "Oh? You don't want all your new friends to know the truth? How about your new girlfriend? Does she know who you are?"

"This is not how I planned to tell her."

"Tell me what?" That was Rowan.

Ash closed his eyes. This was a nightmare.

"Ash Wallace is nothing but a hired 'closer,' a mercenary sent to Bayberry Island to convince you to sell."

A collective gasp rose up from the room. One of them was Rowan's.

Ash lowered his chin and glared at Kathryn, coming even closer. "I said that's *enough.* I've resigned from the project. I sent Jerrod Jessop a resignation letter Sunday night. I am no longer involved in the Mermaid Island project in any capacity."

"Right." Kathryn smiled. "But after you called us with the inside scoop on how to get Mona Flynn to sell. Ring any bells?

Ash closed his eyes and sighed. *The environmental assessment.*

"Is what she said true?"

Ash spun around. Rowan stood near the back of the room, her hands clasped in front of her body, all the color drained from her face. She appeared smaller. Her eyes had lost their sparkle. And she'd asked that question in a tiny, flat voice.

"Don't give up on me, Rowan." He locked his gaze on hers. "She's right. I told them to soften the deal with a second environmental assessment. I apologize. But there is so much more to this story. Hang in there."

She didn't reply.

From the front of the room, Ash surveyed the faces of Bayberry Island. There was Sally the fairy, Sully the mechanic, and Darinda. He saw the girl from the tourist kiosk and Zophie and the other maids. He saw Hubie Krank, the DJ from the clambake, members of the marching band, and the chubby kid who'd dragged Ash to the mermaid fountain. He even saw the senior citizen nudists and the two party girls from the Safe Haven. It was as if this were just another official festival-week event they'd found listed in a brochure.

And every one of them shook their heads in disappointment—except for the dark-haired party girl. She'd just silently mouthed her room number and smiled at him.

Ash made the mistake of searching out all of the Flynns. He was greeted with every shade of confusion and anger possible. Mona looked stunned and baffled. Frasier looked like a kid at Christmas, since chances were good he'd finally be getting his money from someone. But when his eyes met Ash's, he glowered like a bull about to charge. Duncan had clearly decided to kill Ash but hadn't yet chosen a method, since he had so many options available to him. Nat just shook his head in disgust. And Annie's face was stained with tears, her fists balled up at her sides like she wanted to hit him.

Betrayal. That was the common emotion that radiated off these people, his friends. They felt betrayed. They believed Ash had betrayed Rowan.

Interestingly enough, Clancy hung back alone, away from his family, almost as if he wanted a better perspective on the cluster-fuck. His eyes flashed at Ash and he gave a lightning-quick toss of his chin. It was a sign that there was at least one person in the room who wasn't quite ready to convict him.

"May I have a word, Ash?"

Ash turned to his best friend's brother. He had never seen James Martin so furious. "I'm so sorry. I had no idea—" he began.

"This isn't our style, Ash. You know that. We're a small, nonprofit foundation, not contestants on a reality show."

"I know. Please bear with me. I didn't intend for this to happen."

Kathryn pointed at Ash. "This man is a professional liar. Do not believe anything he is about to tell you."

"She's right, to a point." The room went silent. Ash continued. "I was hired to close the Mermaid Island deal for Jessop-Riley, and I was working for them when I arrived on the island. I've done a lot of similar jobs in the last ten years, jobs where I'd do whatever I had to do to convince people to sell their land to developers, but I've had enough. My plan was to fulfill my obligation to Jessop-Riley and then quit. So, yes, I came to the island to buy land for the resort."

He heard a soft cry of anguish from Rowan. He couldn't look at her, but Annie ran to her side.

"So you staged your breakdown?" That was from the tugboat captain.

"I did."

"I knew it!" That outburst was from Sully.

Ash continued. "I had done a lot of research in preparation for this job. I knew all about the Flynns and their money troubles and what had happened with Rowan's fiancé. My plan was to get her to convince Mona to drop her opposition."

"*Oh my God, no.*" Rowan began crying, and Annie comforted her.

"Girl, that's what you get for thinking with your vajay-jay instead of your brain."

The room went silent. Everyone turned to stare at the

party girl. "What?" she asked, shrugging her shoulders. "It's the truth!"

Ash heard Rowan groan and he dared to look at her. She stood perfectly still, sadness and humiliation in her eyes. "Hang in there, sweetheart. Please." He addressed the crowd again. "As I was saying, I came here to convince the Flynns to sell, but soon after I arrived on Bayberry, I realized the island would be irrevocably damaged by the resort. I saw how the crowds and traffic and noise would destroy everything that makes this place unique. And" — Ash made eye contact with Rowan again — "I had already started falling in love with Rowan Flynn. So I put my obligation to Jessop aside, and I sent in my letter of resignation last Sunday."

"Ladies and gentlemen, you can't trust this man." Kathryn began to stroll around the room. "From what I can tell, he's been hanging around Bayberry Island all week, schmoozing every one of you. But did he ever once tell you who he really was? Why he came here in the first place? That he had faked his breakdown and had been doing background research on all of you so he would know how best to make the sale?"

"Kathryn, don't do this. This is none of your affair."

"Oh, but it is! I'm here to do real business, offer these people real money for their valuable land. You're a joke, Wallace." Kathryn smiled at the crowd. "All you have to do is sign. You're rich."

"Wait." Ash held up a hand. "We will match whatever Jessop-Riley offers."

"Wallace." James spoke firmly.

He turned to James. "Do you agree that this is the right place for Oceanaire?"

James nodded. "After seeing what we saw today, we all think it is."

"Fine. Then whatever this costs, I'll put up my own capital to make it happen. You know my grandfather made me a rich man, and this is how I'd like to spend the money. I will not bankrupt Oceanaire. Do you hear me?"

He saw James's eyes soften. "You love her that much?"

"I do."

"All right." James motioned for the young men to bring the architect's model forward, and Ash took a few minutes to describe to the landowners how they envisioned the small marine research facility, an educational building with exhibits open to the public, and a dormitory for the summer students. Everyone gathered around the model, and there were gasps of delight from the crowd.

"The design specifics might change because of the topography, but I wanted you to see that we are serious. Our mission is to preserve marine biodiversity and educate the next generation in conservation. Bayberry is the ideal place for this kind of learning and exploration to occur."

"They can't possibly be ready to offer you a deal today. This is ridiculous." Kathryn sniffed the air.

Just then Ash saw Annie escorting Rowan toward the front door.

"Please stay, Rowan," he said.

Annie glared at Ash. "Leave her alone."

He began to jog toward the women when he felt a hand on his shoulder.

"Don't." It was Duncan.

Ash faced him. "I never meant to hurt her. I'd rather die than hurt her."

The rest of the Flynns joined Duncan and Ash where they stood, right in the middle of the meeting room aisle.

Mona spoke first. "When did you know you loved her?"

"I don't believe in love at first sight—well, I didn't,

anyway. But by Sunday night, I knew there was something undeniably wonderful between us."

Frasier scowled. "Is that when you came up with the idea to bring Oceanaire's institute here?"

"No." Ash smiled at Nat. "Nat gave me the idea at the clambake. It was a stroke of genius. I started moving on it the next morning."

"This is true," Nat said, a hint of pride in his voice.

Duncan turned to James. "Is this a serious offer?"

James nodded thoughtfully. "I will admit it's sudden, but, yes. Ash is our chairman of the board. This is his choice of location. There is a lot of work to be done, but we are prepared to negotiate for the land along Haven Cove."

"It's going to be a hard sell, Ash." Frasier looked pensive.

"The institute?"

"No. That'll be a piece of cake. I'm talking about my daughter. She may never want to speak to you again. You lied to her. You lied to all of us."

"It's got to feel like déjà vu for her." Clancy shook his head. "You should probably just hit the road and save yourself the grief."

"It's likely you'll go to all the trouble of building your institute here and Rowan will never speak to you again," Frasier added.

Ash smiled at that. "I'm not giving up, Mayor."

Duncan laughed. "Why not?"

"Because she's worth fighting for."

Just then, Ash realized the entire assembly had gathered around them, straining to hear what was being said.

"Excuse me. Pardon me." A soft female voice made its way through the crowd. Brenda Paulson emerged, smiling at Ash.

"Brenda! How nice to see you." Ash gave her a hug.

"You too. Hi, everyone." Brenda glanced shyly at all the Flynns. "Um, I don't mean to intrude, but I wanted to say something to you all." She quickly glanced at Ash and looked away, embarrassed. "Despite what all this must look like, I know Mr. Wallace, and I can tell you he's always treated people with respect and decency. He has been very kind to me and my daughter over the years, even though we're just work colleagues. What's being said today makes him look bad, but I want you to think before you judge him. If you've spent time with him this week, you know the kind of man he is. I hope you rely on what you've personally observed about Mr. Wallace and not what Kathryn says."

Brenda lowered her voice to a whisper. "She hates Ash and has been out to get him. But that's because they're professional rivals and she's jealous of him. And just between us . . ." Brenda looked behind her to make sure Kathryn wasn't nearby. "I can't stand that woman. I've been offered a job at another company and I can't wait to get out of there." She broke out into a huge smile.

"Brenda!"

"That's her. I need to go back. Good luck with everything!" She popped up on her toes and kissed Ash's cheek.

The Flynns stayed quiet for a long moment. Finally, Mona spoke. "How do you plan to win her back, Ashton?"

"I'll have to figure that out. Any suggestions?"

"Whatever you do, don't let her stew," Mona said. "Do it now. And make sure she knows you're serious."

"Make it something big, something grand." That came from one of the mermaid ladies who had pushed her way into the circle.

"Oooh, that sounds wonderful!" That was one of the fairies.

Duncan laughed. He seemed to be enjoying this far too much. "Hey, you could always dress up as a sea captain and chase her around town. She'd love that shit."

A lot of people thought that was funny. Ash wasn't one of them. He looked at Rowan's mother. "Mona."

"Yes?"

"If I had a plan in mind to get Rowan to forgive me, would you be willing to help me pull it off, even if it were a little . . . *involved*?"

She nodded. "Brenda is right. I've come to like you, Ashton. I think that despite how this whole thing started out, you are a good man with a good heart, so, yes. I'll help you."

"Thank you. And, Nat, would you help me?"

"Whatever I can do, man, as long as Annie doesn't kill me."

"Clancy?"

He shrugged. "Sure, if you'll help me restore my boat."

"Done."

"Frasier?"

"Sure. I want Rowan to be happy, so sure. As long as we can wait until tomorrow."

"Tomorrow?" Mona looked horrified.

"We have the Mermaid Ball tonight. I'm master of ceremonies. We all have responsibilities."

Mona sighed and looked at Ash. "He's right."

"Where's the ball?"

"At the museum."

"I'll meet everyone there after it's over, all right?"

Ash expected the Flynns would agree, but instead nearly the whole room chimed in.

Sally's voice rang out through the hall. "This meeting of the Haven Cove Landowner's Coalition is now adjourned!"

Chapter Twenty

Rowan had decided the only good thing about being alive on that Friday morning was that, due to her intense public humiliation the day before, she had not been forced to make French toast before the crack of fucking dawn.

Other than that, she wished she were dead.

So the banging on her bedroom door was not welcome.

"Leave me alone."

"It's Annie."

"Go away."

"I'm not going anywhere."

"What time is it?"

"It's eleven a.m. on Friday. You can't stay in there any longer, Row."

"Oh, sure I can."

Rowan desired nothing but to continue doing exactly what she'd been doing since about five the evening before, which was hiding under the covers, curled in a fetal position while she cried on the narrow cot in the dusty old windowless storage room under the eaves of the Safe Haven. That was it. Nothing else about life — breathing, eating, seeing the sunshine or the ocean, nothing — interested her in the slightest.

"You've got to open this door. Seriously, girl. I *mean* it. If you don't open it, I'll kick it in. And I'm wearing my door-kicking-in shoes, so don't test me!"

"*Uuuggghhhh*!" Rowan threw off the blanket and lunged for the door, throwing it open.

Rowan froze. A whole crowd was out there in the third-floor hallway, waiting for her to make an appearance. Annie was joined by Mona, Mellie, and nearly every member of the mermaid mofos, plus, in a rare showing of solidarity, a few fairies.

"Hell, no." Rowan attempted to slam the door shut, but Annie shoved her foot into the crack.

"You need to get in the shower and get dressed," Annie said.

Rowan crossed her arms over her chest, suddenly aware that she was still in the shorts and shirt she'd worn to go sailing with . . . *whoever the hell that man really is.*

"I can't. I need to go back to bed." So that was what she did. She crawled in, yanked the blanket over her face, and curled up. Unfortunately, the all-female, body-snatching brigade would have none of it.

"Get up, Rowan Moira Flynn."

The blanket went flying across the room, but Rowan didn't have to open her eyes to know who'd just given that command. "I've had enough, Ma. I know you mean well and I love you for it, but please leave me alone."

"I will not. I wanted to stay out of your business, but, honey, I can't let you make this mistake."

Mellie patted her on the head. "Get up and wash your hair. We'll help you pick out something cute to wear."

Rowan sat up. The collective stares she was getting sent a chill up her spine. "What's going on?"

"Let's go." Annie pulled her from the bed, pushed her down the hall, and guided her into the maid's bathroom.

"Here you go. You've got a half hour at the most. Skirt or shorts or pants or what?"

Rowan spun around, baffled. "What are you talking about? I'm not going anywhere. What are you doing?"

"Pardon us." Annie looked over her shoulder at the group and inched Rowan into the bathroom, then shut the door behind her. "Sit down." Annie pointed to the toilet.

"You're going to order me to pee now?"

Annie laughed. "Rowan, do you trust me?"

Ash had asked her that very same question only yesterday, before everything—her hopes, her happiness—went to shit. Clearly, it would be wise to say, *No. I do not.* Unfortunately, with Annie, she couldn't bring herself to answer in that way. She closed the lid on the commode and sat down. "Of course I do."

"Good." Annie shoved the shower curtain aside and took a seat on the edge of the tub. "Here's what you're going to do: Take a shower, get dressed in something halfway decent, and walk with me to the public dock. We're going to the closing ceremony."

Rowan felt her mouth fall open. "Are you kidding? I don't want to go anywhere in public today. Maybe not ever again as long as I live."

"That's ridiculous."

"Oh yeah? Really?" Rowan blinked at Annie. "Have you ever been accused of thinking with your va-jay-jay during a town hall meeting, in front of your parents?"

Annie twisted her mouth into a knot. "No," she said.

"Of course you haven't. And that's why I don't want to go to the dock to listen to my dad suck up to the tourists, and why I *really* don't want to stand around looking happy while the giant-assed confetti canons go off all around me. Forgive me if I'm not in a confetti kind of mood."

"You don't have a choice." Annie leaned forward, balancing her elbows on her knees, and the look on her face became fiercely serious. "I am your best friend, and I am telling you that you must leave here with me in a half hour and go to the closing ceremony. It is the most important thing you will ever do in your life."

Ash. This is about Ash. "I don't want to see him. I don't want to talk to him. If I'd wanted to do either of those things, I would have last night, when he was sitting outside in the hallway for hours on end."

"He was here? After I left?"

"Oh, don't act so innocent."

Annie made a face.

"Seriously. It doesn't matter that everyone thinks he's some kind of hero for wanting to build his water-treatment plant here—I'll never be able to trust him."

Annie nodded her head, sadness shadowing her eyes. "Well, it's an educational institute."

"I know what it is, and I don't care!" Rowan dropped her head into her hands and began to rock back and forth. "My heart is a pile of frickin' dust right now. He lied to me. No matter what that man claims, the fact remains that he researched me like I was a school project and came here under false pretenses and seduced me so he could make money off my family!"

When Annie touched her knee, Rowan looked up. And though she didn't know how there could be a drop of moisture left in her body, tears spilled down her face again.

"Oh my God, Annie!" She grabbed her best friend's hand and squeezed. "I tried so hard to convince myself that Ash Wallace wasn't Frederick, and you know what? That's all he was—a better-looking version of Frederick."

Annie shook her head. "I'm not sure you have all the facts, Row. Before you act as judge and jury, you need to be sure you've seen all the evidence."

Rowan shrunk back. "You sound like you're on his side."

"I'm on your side. Always. Every damn time. That's why you *have to* come with me to the closing ceremony. *Please, Row.*"

"I don't want to talk to him."

"Fine. Nobody's going to make you do anything, except get a shower—"

"All right! I'll take a damn shower!" Rowan stood up. "Are you going to stay in here with me to make sure I wash behind my ears?"

Annie headed to the bathroom door again. "Skirt or pants?"

"Skirt."

"Short or long?"

"I don't give a barrel of crap monkeys, Annie."

"Short it is. Now, make it snappy."

"Lookin' real good, Ashley."

Ash ignored Clancy's latest jab. He stared at his reflection in the mirror that Mona had provided, propped against the museum warehouse wall. He took care to adjust his eye patch, pull his red bandanna down to mid-forehead, and tilt his pirate chapeau to the optimum angle. Then Ash fluffed the already fluffy sleeves of his shirt and checked the placement of his sword.

"I think your butt looks kinda fat in those britches."

Ash shook his head. "Clayton, mark my words. Once this is over and Rowan forgives me, I'm going to make your life a living hell. And that is a promise, man."

Clancy laughed loudly, and Ash couldn't help but chuckle along with him. He wished Brian were alive to see this spectacle. It probably would have been the best day of his life.

It had come to pass that Ash Wallace was about to get

on a parade float and roll down Main Street—in front of several hundred people—dressed as a fucking pirate. If baring his soul and chest was what it took to win Rowan back, then that's what he'd do. The truth was, he'd walk through a wall of fire for her, so he supposed putting on a one-man show complete with three costume and set changes, the canned movie sound track from *Titanic*, and a supporting cast of mermaids, fairies, and children was a relatively painless sacrifice.

"Ready, Blondbeard? It's time to make an Ash out of yourself." Clancy double-checked the tow hitch on the back of his police Jeep and got behind the wheel.

Ash climbed aboard his vessel. He took a deep breath, gave the thumbs-up to the chubby kid crouched behind the corrugated cardboard waves, and then they set sail.

The kid looked up at him with concern. "I think I have to pee, Mr. Wallace."

"You're going to have to hold it. I'm on a mission."

Her father tapped the microphone. "Is this thing on?" Ear-splitting feedback cut through the air at the public dock. "Sorry." He cleared his throat. "This has been an exceptional festival week here on Bayberry Island. In addition to our usual exciting events, last night we learned that a Boston-based foundation wants to build their marine conservation institute here on our island."

Enthusiastic applause rippled through the crowd.

"This is what you wanted me to see?" Rowan hissed at Annie. "I can listen to my Dad pontificate anytime. I'm going back to bed."

Annie put her hands on Rowan's arms and spun her around until she was facing the stage again.

"I am happy to announce that the Haven Cove Land-owner's Coalition has accepted an offer from Oceanaire. We have decided to sell our land so an institute can be built, and we look forward to the beneficial impact the new enterprise will have on our economy and our environment. We'll have more details to share in the coming months, but we hope to have an unveiling in two years. Be sure to check the island Web site for updates."

Rowan tried to leave again, but Annie blocked her. "Pay attention."

"As always, it has been a pleasure having everyone here for the Mermaid Festival. We hope to see you back next year. And now, without further delay, we have a special presentation for you—like nothing you've ever seen, I guarantee you—so sit back and enjoy! See you next year!"

Rowan felt Annie pushing her toward the front of the crowd. "No." She slapped away her friend's hands. "I don't want to be any closer. I'll watch from back here."

"Suit yourself."

Just then, music blared from the speakers on either side of the stage. Rowan cocked her head to listen to what she swore was a familiar children's song about the pillaging, looting life of a pirate.

She gave Annie a sideways glance. Her best friend looked straight ahead, no expression on her face, as if she didn't notice Rowan staring at her with giant bug eyes. She was about to pinch Annie's arm when Clancy's police Jeep came up the ramp to the dock, towing what looked like her father's parade float with no one . . . wait. A pirate jumped from behind the waves, slicing a sword through the air as he sang.

"Yo-ho, maties! Ahoy!"

The pirate was Ash. The sword was Hubie's. And her heart just fell to her feet. *He is in costume.*

"Oh my God!" she whispered.

Annie grabbed her hand.

She felt her body start to tremble. Why was Ash doing this? Did he really think that dancing around on a parade float in an eye patch would make up for how he'd lied to her?

Rowan tore her gaze away and stared at the sea, the silly kids' song now playing softly in the background. People all around her were chuckling, but she couldn't bring herself to look at Ash. Why was he doing this?

I will not cry. I will not cry.

More feedback, then Ash's voice rang out through the PA system. "I set my sights on Bayberry Island exactly one week ago today, a cutthroat by the name of Ashton Louis Wallace the third. I was a pirate of the business world, ready to pilfer the treasure of your land!"

Rowan made sure she didn't look at his face. She was still too angry to look at him. He'd tried to manipulate her. He'd lied to her. He'd hidden his true self from her.

"The skies went dark and the winds howled."

Silence.

Whoever was supposed to be manning the sound missed their cue. "Damn! Sorry!" That was definitely Polly Estherhausen. The howling wind sound effect blasted over the crowd, to a round of applause.

Rowan refused to meet Ash's gaze. She was afraid that if she saw his face, she would lose it.

"A nor'easter raced toward the shores of Bayberry Island, bringing me with it. And the thunder roared!"

Polly was on it this time. Thunder vibrated the dock. Rowan had to look.

Immediately, Ash's eyes locked on hers. He'd been waiting for her. Rowan froze. Though she was a good fifteen feet from the float and standing in a sea of people, she felt as if she and Ash were alone. In that moment, she saw a whole world in his intense blue eyes. She saw pain, regret, hope . . . love. But after the way they'd started, would she ever have faith in his love? Would she ever be able to trust it?

Without taking his eyes off hers, he continued with his corny lines. "Moments after I stepped on dry land, the children came for me."

A boy jumped up from behind the waves, grabbed his hand, and pulled him onto the dock. "You're coming with us!" Another half dozen kids popped out from behind the stage where Rowan's father had stood, and together, they dragged Ash down to the dock, in front of the float.

"By now, the rain poured!"

Someone waiting at the side of the float threw a bucket of water on Ash and the kids. Everyone laughed. Ash blinked water from his one exposed eye and continued.

"I was drenched to the skin by the time the children dragged me to town square. I was the Man Grab!"

Suddenly, Mona and a few of her cohorts appeared, carrying a cardboard display piece from the museum—of the Great Mermaid. Ash stared up at her likeness.

Mona addressed the crowd, squaring her shoulders. "Take the mermaid's hand in yours and kiss it. You will find your true love!"

Rowan winced, not only because of where this was headed but because of the way Mona had just waved her arm around dramatically—she prayed her mother's shells would stay in place.

Ash protested. "But I didn't come here for love!"

"Repeat after me: *I come to the mermaid in search of my heart-mate*!"

Ash shook his head. "I come to the mermaid because I was abducted by a bunch of unruly brats!" Ash gestured for the kids to leave, and they scattered like mice behind the stage.

"Say the words!" Mona commanded.

Ash turned toward the crowd, his eyes on Rowan's again. Annie began to lead her toward the front, and this time, Rowan found she couldn't resist. While they moved, Ash said his lines.

"I have come to understand that true love is like the sea. It is . . ." Ash paused. Mona whispered in his ear to help him out. "Beautiful, deep, and life-giving, yet it can be unpredictable, powerful, and even dangerous. I admit that I set out on my journey with a heart that was slightly less than pure and true, and I was wholly unprepared for how I would be tossed by waves of passion. But when I met the one intended for me, I found myself willing to drown in love's undertow."

Rowan felt her face go hot. She wanted to believe him. She wanted to love him.

"Are you now willing to go wherever love may lead?"

"I am!" Ash disappeared behind the stage. A few kids tossed a black drape over the side of the float while others carried in the cardboard Bayberry Island townscape used each year on the island council's parade entry. Rowan's father returned to his place center stage.

"The corporate pirate walked through town to the Safe Haven, where he knew he would find the lonely innkeeper's daughter."

Rowan rolled her eyes in embarrassment. "Awesome."

"He planned to seduce her to gain access to her family and convince them to sell the vast lands along the cove, provenance of the Flynns for more than one hundred and thirty years!" Her dad smiled at her. He was in on the private joke.

Ash returned, now dressed in his usual hiking shorts and polo shirt. "The innkeeper's daughter was beautiful, funny, and sweet. I was immediately smitten with her, and my mind became clouded—how could I pillage and plunder from this lovely woman?"

More thunder and howling wind.

"The storm raged on. She was kind enough to find me a place to stay, and in the darkness, she brought me light." From behind his back, Ash pulled out a little electric candle. He grinned at her, and Rowan couldn't hold it in anymore—tears dripped down her cheeks. She could taste them.

"Oh, sweetie." Annie's arm went around her. "This is the most romantic thing I've ever witnessed."

"But she did not trust me. She had been badly hurt before. And she did not believe in the mermaid's magic."

Rowan let herself cry. Ash saw her, and he paused for a moment to collect himself. A woman standing behind Rowan sniffed and sighed. Ash continued on.

"I learned she had a thing for butter pecan ice cream." One of the town fairies tiptoed across the dock holding the large ice-cream cone sign from Island Day, while everyone laughed. "I learned she loved to dance on the beach under the moon." Two fairies, one holding a moon and the other a star, performed a little dance in front of Ash, then flitted away. "I began to fall in love with this beautiful innkeeper's daughter and knew my pirate days were behind me forever."

Ash disappeared again, and Rowan's dad took up the microphone. "The days passed. The reformed corporate pirate spent more and more time with the lovely innkeeper's daughter. She fell in love with him, too—everyone could see it. But one day, an evil witch came to town and whispered to the innkeeper's daughter, 'Your lover is a scalawag.' It broke her heart, and she hid herself in the tower, where she wished to remain, wrapped in her sorrow, forever." Her father pointed to the cardboard cupola on the Safe Haven's roof, and Rowan had to laugh.

"But the town knew the witch could not be trusted, and the handsome pirate, who by this time . . ." Her father looked behind him to make sure Ash was ready, then nodded. "By this time, he wanted nothing more than to save his love, her island, and preserve its history!"

Ash reappeared dressed as a sea captain, his cap tilted jauntily on his head. Behind him, a bevy of mermaids pushed the architect's model of the marine institute, then made overly dramatic Vanna White motions with their arms, to the crowd's delight. The women scurried off.

"I love you, Rowan Flynn." Ash smiled directly at her. "I don't know what happened to me here on Bayberry Island, whether it was the mermaid, or fate, or just blind luck, but I do know this—it's magic. It's a magic powerful enough to rescue my heart and bring me back to life."

He held out his hand to her. "Forgive me. Give me another chance. Let me show you how it feels when a man adores you and wants nothing but your happiness. Help me make the institute a reality. Stand by me as I try to do the right thing for Bayberry Island—and for you."

Rowan found herself moving toward him, her head buzzing, whistling and applause exploding all around her. She went to him, and the instant her hand slipped inside his, she knew it was the right choice. At that moment, it became clear to her the difference between Frederick and Ash: Frederick was a taker. Ash was a giver.

I belong with him.

Her handsome sea captain took her into his arms, dipped her gallantly, and kissed her hard. Rowan heard the rest of the troupe gather around them to take their bows. Ash lifted his lips from hers and smiled softly.

"Thank you for saving me," he whispered.

Rowan nodded, cupping his face in her hands. "I think we saved each other, Captain."

He kissed her again, just as confetti rained down over the crowd.

Epilogue

Honey-sweet harmonies of flute and harp drifted across the Safe Haven lawn as Annie took measured steps on her way to the altar. The September sunset added glimmer to her golden hair and kissed the sheer skirt of her wedding dress. She held a bouquet of late-season wildflowers in her hands—daylilies, roses, daisies, seaside geraniums, and milkweed—all tied with a pale blue ribbon.

Annie smiled. Oh, how that woman smiled! Her face was alive with joy and happiness, and Rowan knew she was witnessing one of those rare, perfect moments in life. She would remember it forever, the hum of the ocean, the scent of waning summer, the beauty of her best friend, and the delight she held in her own heart.

From her vantage point as maid of honor, Rowan let her gaze drift away from the lovely bride to settle on the face of her impatient groom. Nat looked overwhelmed. He fidgeted, moving his hands to his back and to his front again, never once taking his eyes off Annie. It looked as if he wanted her to speed up the wedding march and get her ass to his side before she had a chance to change her mind. Seeing how much he adored Annie made Rowan's chest fill with emotion.

She looked past Nat to the best man who stood at his side, the strikingly handsome Ashton Louis Wallace III. Ash wore one of his custom-tailored dress shirts, this one a blue and white pinstripe, with a paisley tie and navy blue, pleated linen trousers. He looked every bit the wealthy, uptight Boston blue blood who'd decided to summer on a quaint New England island.

But Rowan knew better.

The man in those preppy clothes was her playful and passionate pirate, her lusty sea captain, a man who possessed a heart tough enough to rebound from loss and open to love. With his vision, Ash had made a commitment to make life better for the people of this island and the sea that sustained it.

He locked his eyes on hers, and Rowan felt the heat of his longing and the happiness that he carried in his own spirit. It was so simple—she loved him with everything in her, and she would do anything for him. Ash winked at her, then mouthed the words *I love you,* and Rowan was reminded that this wasn't a dream. This was her real life.

Annie reached the altar, and Nat gently took her hand in his. The music stopped. Deacon Sully welcomed the guests while struggling to keep his eyes to the front and not focused on his shoes. Rowan had to admit that the boat mechanic cleaned up well when duty called.

"We are gathered here today to witness the joining of Nathaniel Ravelle and Annabeth Parker, two young people who have pledged their devotion and faithfulness to each other and have expressed their wish to live in the partnership of marriage."

The ceremony unfolded seamlessly. Rowan glanced out at those gathered on the lawn. There was Mellie, looking proud of her dressmaking skills while dabbing her eyes with a hankie. Rowan saw Nat's family—his parents and his sister, her husband and their kids. Annie's parents had come up from their Tallahassee retirement condo to celebrate with their daughter. And Rowan's parents were there too, but they sat on opposite sides of the aisle, pleased for Annie but holding on tight to their bitterness. Now that the reason for their rift was over, Rowan wished they could find a way to forgive each other, but many hurtful things had been said over the last year. It would take a while to heal the wounds, if healing took place at all.

Clancy sat with his arms crossed over his chest and his long legs stretched out under the chair in front of him, a wistful expression on his face. Rowan knew that weddings weren't his favorite kind of party and that his own failed marriage had to be on his mind. Hubie Krank sat to the right of Clancy, a huge smile on his face as he fiddled with his new hearing aid.

The balance of the crowd was made up of Mermaid Society members, Nat's film school friends, and Annie's college friends—along with their spouses and kids—and many Bayberry neighbors.

"Annabeth, I take you to be my wife." Nat slipped the pretty white-gold band along the slim length of her ring finger. "I feel like the luckiest man on the earth to have fallen at your doorstep on that cold, icy December night of last year. You lit a fire in me, body and soul."

More than one sniffle emanated from the guests.

Nat continued. "I promise to honor you, respect you, and love you to the limits of my heart and beyond, in sickness and in health, in the off-season and the tourist season. Also, I promise to help you with any and all research for your books, baked goods, and chocolates."

Everyone laughed. Then it was Annie's turn.

"Nathaniel, I take you to be my husband." She slipped a matching band on his finger. "When you dropped into my life, my whole world changed. You are the first man I have ever loved, and you will be the only, the last, my beloved forever."

More sniffles.

"I promise to be yours without qualification. I promise to trust you, honor you, and love you every day I live. And I pledge to always give you the best of myself, in the off-season and in tourist season, in sickness and health, and even while I'm trying to finish writing a book."

A ripple of laughter moved through the guests.

Annie and Nat were pronounced husband and wife, and Nat placed his hand at the small of Annie's back, drew her to him, and kissed her. The kiss was so uninhibited that Nat's sister covered the eyes of her six-year-old. Most everyone else erupted in clapping and whistling. The newlyweds then linked arms and walked across the lawn. Rowan and Ash came together so they could fall into place behind the married couple.

"May I, Miss Flynn?" Ash offered his arm to Rowan, giving her that dimpled smile she'd come to treasure.

"Of course, Mr. Wallace."

They continued their promenade toward the side yard, where the large white reception tent had been set up for dining and dancing. But instead of steering Rowan under the tent, Ash tugged her away, ran toward the side porch and pulled her down with him on the love magnet. He arranged her on his lap and wrapped his arms around her waist.

Ash moved his hands over the fabric of her bridesmaid dress and traveled up her bare thigh. "I want you so bad, Rowan," he mumbled, kissing her. "I could barely keep my cool looking at you—so soft, so beautiful."

She snagged his wrist, glancing over her shoulder at the reception crowd milling around the lawn. She lowered her voice to a whisper. "Wait for me in the carriage house after the reception. Stand naked in the hallway and remember to cut all the lights. Act surprised when I get there. Can you hold on until then?"

Ash groaned in mock disappointment, cupping her face in his hands. "Yes, but on one condition."

"Name it."

"I get to ravish you." His smile spread to his deep blue eyes. "I get to see you naked and spread out on your bed, trembling because I'm about to bury myself deep inside you."

Rowan took a sharp breath.

"And, as much as I hate to tax the resources of your fine establishment, I believe I will need fresh bed linens in the morning."

She placed a demure kiss on his lips and smiled. "Whatever I can do to make your stay a pleasant one."

Dear Reader,

I hope you've enjoyed Ash and Rowan's story and your visit to Bayberry Island.

I came up with the idea for the Bayberry Island novels while on a writing retreat on the Outer Banks of North Carolina. While I took long solo walks on the beach, day after day, a kernel of a story began to form in my mind. I thought about how magical the ocean was, and how it was one of the few things in this overanalyzed world that could still elicit a sense of awe. I thought about how love had much in common with the sea—both were beautiful, deep, and life-giving, but sometimes dangerous and unpredictable. I saw a dolphin dance in the waves and smiled to myself, thinking that it was no wonder there have been folktales about mermaids for as long as humans have sailed the oceans.

Love, magic, and mermaids . . .

I hurried back to the beach house and got out my laptop, and for the next several days, I had the pleasure of letting a place, a family, and a story begin to reveal itself to me.

The Bayberry Island novels focus on the members of the Flynn family, descendants of the island's founder and benefactor, and ask a fundamental question: Can the bronze mermaid statue in town square really grant true love to those who kiss her hand and ask with an open heart? Come on, now. I don't write those kinds of books. My novels are based in the here-and-now, with characters who could be your neighbors or friends, people who face familiar challenges and long for real-life happiness and joy. I don't write supernatural stuff.

Still, even I have to shake my head at what happens to the Flynns in the course of these three novels. Mona and Frasier Flynn, the parents, have let their thirty-five-year marriage crumble. And their grown children—Duncan, Clancy, and Rowan—haven't exactly been lucky in love. Yet by the time their stories are told, some pretty incredible events have unfolded.

Some say you don't need magic to find love, that love is the magic. I'll let the reader decide. All I ask is that you keep an open mind, and come back to visit again soon.

Next up: Clancy and Evelyn's story. I hope to see you there.

Love,
Susan Donovan